FILTHY
Deal

NEW YORK TIMES BESTSELLING AUTHOR
LISA RENEE JONES

Part One: The Bastard

Chapter One

Eric

When the Kingston family decides to throw a party, it means no less than two hundred people at their twenty-thousand-square-foot Aspen estate, valets at the door, an abundance of Kingston Motors luxury cars in the drive, and money. Lots of money, because Jeff Kingston has nothing to do with anyone who doesn't have money, aside from me, his bastard son, otherwise known as the backup heir just in case my half-brother kicks the bucket.

I exit the guest house, where I'm staying until my meeting with my father tomorrow, which I shouldn't have accepted. I don't know why the fuck I'm even here, aside from the fact that these people are supposed to be my people, and leaving the SEALs was like leaving family. It's hard to let go of that need for a family unit. Family. Right. What the hell was I thinking? Like I could ever really be a Kingston.

I travel down a stone path shrouded in flowers and low hanging trees, twisting left and then right until I enter the courtyard filled with bodies in fancy dresses and tuxedos like the one I'm in now. A waiter walks by and I snag a glass of champagne when I'd rather have whiskey, but I'll settle for anything to get me through tonight's launch of a new model of car. I barely give a shit about the old model, which is exactly why my father shouldn't want me to work for him. I walk to one of the few dozen standing tables covered in white tablecloths, down my drink and accept another when my gaze catches on a woman, on *her* and *just her*.

She's standing on the other side of the pool, a princess in a strappy black dress, with flawless ivory skin and long brown hair, surrounded by her subjects. At least, that's how she reads to me, no doubt like every other socialite I've ever met in this godforsaken world, and yet I'm watching her when I never watch them. There's

3

something about this woman, a white swan among the black swans on a pond made of money and death, my mother's death more specifically, since that's how I got here.

My princess must feel my attention because she tunes out the conversation she's having with several other people, her chin lifting, her gaze sweeping wide and then catching mine. I don't even think about looking away. I don't care that she knows that I'm watching her. I don't care if she knows that I'm thinking about fucking her. I'm the bastard in these parts. From the time I was thrust into this place right before my senior year of high school, I do what I do and everyone whispers about it. I'm not going to change that now. Let them whisper about what I want, and this woman, whoever the fuck she is, is worth the whispers.

The man next to her touches her elbow, his gaze shooting my direction, his jaw setting hard with anger. Priceless and so typical of my father's class of people. He's pissed at me for getting his woman's attention. He should have fucked her better. My cellphone buzzes with a text message and I cut my stare, downing my champagne and then reaching for my phone to find a message from Grayson Bennett, a close friend from my first go at Harvard right before I left and went into the Navy. Unlike me, he's no bastard, but rather the true heir to the Bennett empire.

Call me, his message reads, which is typical Grayson. He wants something, he asks, and usually with actual words, not a text message. And since we have unfinished business, I don't want to be overheard, I walk toward the house where I know I can find both privacy and that whiskey I'm craving. Unfortunately, I might just find my way to the rightful heir to the throne, right along with our father as well, but at least I'll make my showing and get the hell out of here.

"There he is. My brother."

My jaw clenches at the sound of Isaac's voice even before he steps into my path. *Think of the devil and he shall appear*, I think, but this time, at least he's come bearing gifts. He offers me one of the two whiskey glasses he has in hand. "The good stuff. The kind we drink around these parts."

He doesn't mean "we" as in me and him. He means "we" as in the Kingston family, which excludes the likes of me. Our eyes lock and hold, the drama of the past, the hatred between us palpable, and I have no doubt the crackle of energy around us is the attention of the room. We are, after all, the much whispered about heir and the would-be heir who despise one another. Him the prince, with thick, dark hair and green eyes, while I'm simply the bastard, with wavy brown hair, blue eyes, and a good four inches on his short ass. He tells everyone he's five-eleven, but we all know he's five-nine. I don't look like I'm his blood. I damn sure don't feel like I'm his blood, but my mother made sure I can't be denied. She ordered the DNA test that changed my life and not for the better in my opinion.

I accept the glass and his gaze flicks over my Rolex peeking from beneath my white dress shirt and lingers on my tat before a smirk lifts on his face. "Looks like someone got all inked up."

"The bastard brother might as well look the role, right?"

"You're never going to let me live down calling you that, now are you?"

"We both know you don't want to live it down, but you will have to face me every day if I decide to join the company. It's my turn to smirk. "We both know that didn't go well for you at Harvard." It's a reminder of our shared college days, where everyone compared us, and he often came up short. "You must have been so damn relieved when I left school and entered the Navy, and frustrated as fuck that I'm back."

His eyes spark with a familiar anger I don't have to intentionally stir. He hates me for being the bastard child of his father's mistress, the brother thrust on him only months after his mother died. An ironic turn of events considering my mother's cancer. He steps closer, toe to toe with me, all up close and friendly. "If you think that because you're some sort of SEAL Team Six hero or something, that I won't buckle you right at the knees, you're wrong. You will *not* take what is mine."

"I see you two got right back into the brotherly love."

At the sound of my father's voice, Isaac grimaces and my lips quirk. "Seems we have," I say, as Isaac rotates and we both face my father, who looks fit and trim in his tuxedo, and far younger than his fifty-four years, a mere hint of gray in his thick dark hair. "I have someone I want you to meet," he says, and that's when my little princess steps to his side, her crystal blue eyes meeting mine as my father says, "Eric. Meet your stepsister, Harper."

Chapter Two

Eric

Now, isn't this interesting, I think, my eyes fixed on Harper, the stepsister I've never met, daughter to the woman my father married while I was in the Navy. I offer her my hand. "Nice to meet you, Harper," I say, and when our eyes meet at this close proximity, the spark between us is so damn combustible there's no way it goes unnoticed.

She presses her palm to mine, her gaze dropping to a portion of my inked arm, to the collection of colors and designs that make up my full sleeve and reflect everything and somehow nothing in my life. Her lips part, her expression that of intrigue and not the disgust I expect from a perfect princess. She tightens her grip on mine ever-so-slightly and looks up at me. "Nice to *finally* meet you," she says, and fuck, the raspy quality to her voice makes my cock twitch.

"Finally?" I ask, forcing myself to release her.

"Harper has become quite the protégé the past year," my father informs me. "Her father owned a competing business we've absorbed. The dogmatic way she fights for the company is impressive. You'd think she was blood, like you two."

"I was with my father night and day," Harper explains. "I learned a lot from him at a very young age."

This just gets more and more interesting. She's my father's protégé and if she didn't want to fuck me as badly as I want to fuck her, she'd probably want to fuck me right out of town. Yet another priceless moment. "I need to make a phone call," I say, and I don't wait for anyone's permission.

I down the whiskey Isaac handed me, set the glass down on a bench, and step around Harper, my destination once again the castle-like house that is the centerpiece of the property. No one stops me. Just as no one welcomed me when I arrived because despite living most of my childhood here, this was never "home" to me. It was just where I lived and thank fuck for it, or I might have turned out just like them. If this trip has done one thing for me, it's to contrast the Bennett family I now work for and the Kingstons. The Bennetts look out for their own. The Kingstons wait until you turn your back, and stab you in it. In other words, they're one step up from the devil's own family.

I reach my destination and enter the back door, directly into the kitchen which is the size of the mobile home I spent my early years in with my mother. That is, right up until the time she killed herself before the cancer took her. Of course, she didn't leave me in that trailer. She spent her dying days proving that I was the bastard child of Jeff Kingston and forcing him to claim me. I walk through the archway and down a hallway to the right toward my father's office, which is where I'll find whiskey a few grades higher than the bullshit Isaac gave me like I wouldn't know better.

Once I'm inside the man-cave of an office, with bookshelves lining the walls and a sunken seating area with couches and chairs, I walk to the bar in the corner, pour a thirty-year-old whiskey and sit down in a chair. After a damn good taste, I pull my phone from my pocket and dial Grayson, the billionaire who hired me, paid for my last two years of Harvard, and earned two things I don't give out freely—my loyalty and friendship.

"My man," he answers. "That stock you hooked me up with came through in a big way. You're a beast. That IQ of yours is financial genius."

That IQ I inherited from a mother who still ended up with nothing, and I don't know how that happened. "Glad it worked out, man. Are we even now?"

"You paid for the past two years at Harvard and then some. I took the extra money and invested it back into the stock market for you."

"Consider it yours. Interest for loaning me the money."

"I don't need the money. I'll reinvest it in you ten times over, but I know you have your own empire to run down there in Colorado."

I down the whiskey and decide that's it for me. I'm going to end up drunk if I don't slow the fuck down. "I'm the heir bastard, not the heir apparent. You know that."

"I know what you are," Grayson says, "and you're nobody's bastard. You have a place right here by my side, not in some office two buildings over—*if* you decide you want it. Otherwise, sign me up for a piece of Kingston Motors, but only if you're running it."

He's barking up the wrong tree. That's not going to happen. The question is, do I want any part of aiding in its success? I must. Why else would I be here? "Orian," I say of a stock I've been eyeing. "Buy big. Buy fast."

"You want in?"

"Yeah. Anything you made for me, put it in."

"You got it. When do you have that meeting with your father?"

"Tomorrow after this godforsaken launch party."

"Call me after it's over. But remember, you have a brilliant financial mind. You owe him nothing. Do what you do for you, not him. He needs you. He knows it. Don't let him convince you it's the opposite."

"Right. I'll call you tomorrow."

We disconnect and I stick my phone back inside my pocket before pulling a mini-Rubik's cube from my pocket, rotating the puzzle in my hand, and thinking back to the psychologist who'd placed the first one in my hand. My father had hired him to try to "normalize" my behavior. A savant, the physiologist had said, needs a focal point, a way to slow the data in my head, and he was right.

I scramble and solve the cube three times, settling my mind into a place of reckoning, and then shove the cube back in my pocket. The bottom line: I don't belong here. I never belonged here. I stand up and walk to my father's desk where I sit down and think about those words: *You owe him nothing.*

Not exactly true. My father took me in when my mother died. He petitioned to get me into Harvard based on my academic record, which had been dismissed because of my trailer trash background. I owe him, but I don't want to owe him anything more. I'm not going to work for my father. I'm leaving. I grab a pen and a piece of paper and write a note to my father:

Consider this payment for the whiskey I just drank and the roof over my head when I was growing up. Invest big in Orian and do it quickly. —Your Bastard Son.

I drop the pen and stand up, walking toward the door, my decision made. I'll stay for the meeting tomorrow, simply because he did give me a roof over my head, even if it was only a strategy to push Isaac to be better and do better, which meant shoving us into a perpetual dog fight. That's what he wants now, to use me to drive Isaac, but Isaac is vicious and not all that smart. I'll eat Isaac alive. The problem for my father is that I just don't care enough to want to anymore.

I exit to the hallway, and when I look left, Harper is exiting the bathroom. Fuck it. I'm out of here. Why hold back. I don't even hesitate. I walk toward her and when she rotates and finds me approaching, she freezes in place, and waits on me until I'm standing directly in front of her. She tilts her chin up, those brilliant blue eyes boldly meeting mine, the scent of roses and woman, lifting in the air, teasing my nostrils. Apparently, I like roses a whole hell of a lot more than I thought I did because her scent is driving me wild. I don't know what the hell happens, but my hand slides under her hair, and I lean in, my lips next to her lips.

Her hand settles on my chest and grips my lapel, that perfect mouth of hers tilting toward mine as if she's offering it to me. "What are you doing?" she demands, sounding breathless. I *want* her breathless *all night long.*

"What does it look like I'm doing? Kissing my *sister.*" My mouth slants over hers, my tongue sliding right past her perfectly puckered lips, and with one deep stroke, she moans for me, and I'm undone. I don't think I've ever wanted to kiss anyone more than I want to kiss this woman right here, right now. I deepen the kiss and press her against the wall, my free hand at her waist, her hand on my hand. Her tongue meets mine for every lick and stroke until I pull back and stare down at her.

Voices sound in the distance, but too close for comfort, and I seize what time we have left, and decide to do her a favor. I decide to be honest with her, like no one else in my father's world will. "He's using you to push Isaac, just like he's always used me. You'll never inherit. You'll never be anything but the princess standing next to the prince and his king. And just for the record. I'm not your fucking brother." I release her and walk away, making a fast path through the kitchen and out of the house.

Once I'm in the midst of the crowd, I cut through the mess of people and find my way back to the path to my cottage where I enter and have every intention of packing up and getting the hell out of here. I've barely shut the door when the bell rings. Who the hell followed me to the cottage, because someone sure as fuck did. I fling open the door to find Harper standing there.

"Because why would anyone think that I have anything real to bring to the table, right?" she challenges, as if we were still in the middle of our prior conversation, her beautiful blue eyes sparking with anger. "Because all my time with my father, learning his business, taught me nothing."

I grab her and pull her inside the cottage.

Chapter Three

Eric

In about thirty seconds, I have the door shut and locked, and Harper pressed against the wall, my thighs shackling hers. "You don't get to tell me what I can or cannot do," she hisses, as if she doesn't notice that I'm about double her size and presently the one in control.

"How old are you?" I demand.

"What does that have to do with anything?" she snaps back, not even close to backing down.

"How old?" I repeat.

"Twenty-three, but I still don't get why that has anything to do with this."

"How long have you been out of school?"

"Just because I'm not a thirty-year-old literal genius doesn't mean I have nothing to offer, and the suggestion that it does makes you an asshole."

"I'm not suggesting that you have nothing to offer. I'm telling you it doesn't matter to him. I thought it did, too, way back when. I thought if I was better than Isaac, I'd have a place. It didn't. I won't."

"Then why are you even here?"

"Apparently to kiss you." My fingers tangle in her hair and I lower my mouth to hers.

"This is a bad idea," she whispers, but her voice is raspy, affected. I can almost taste her hunger for me in the air.

I kiss her, a quick brush of lips, and a lick that has the heat between us damn near explosive. "Still think it's a bad idea?"

Her hands flatten on my chest but they flex rather than push. "We both know this is wrong."

"And yet you followed me here."

"You said that already."

"You knew what would happen if you came here," I accuse.

"I was impulsive, driven by anger."

I certainly know all too well how anger and family collide in ways I won't ever explain to anyone. My jaw sets hard and I release her, putting a wide step between us. "Stay or go, but if you stay, you're going to end up naked."

"I know your father's an asshole, but my mother loves him and my father's company is now a part of yours."

"His," I correct. "And the part where I said that if you stayed, you'd end up naked," I reach for her and pull her to me, "you did understand that, correct?"

"I don't scare off that easily. If I did, I wouldn't be working for your father and under your brother."

"It's me I want you under," I say, molding her close, my hands caressing down her back, and cupping her perky backside.

"I'm too young and stupid for business, but I'm just right to fuck?"

"I'm warning you, Harper, not talking down to you. And if you're young and stupid, so was I."

"You wanted to be here," she says, and it's not a question or the accusation I'd get from Isaac.

"Yes," I say, tangling my fingers into her hair. "I wanted to be here, just like I want to be right here, right now—*with you*." My mouth slants over hers, and I kiss her again, a deep thrust of tongue that's as unforgiving as my father would be if it came down to choosing her or Isaac. It's all about demand and I expect her to push back, to give me the rejection that sends her to the door and me to the fucking airport. That's not what I get.

Her hand on my chest doesn't push me away. She moans and her elbow softens, those perfect curves I'd admired from a distance now pressed nice and close, right up to the moment she jerks back. "My God. What are we doing? You're my s*tepbrother*."

I walk her back against the wall again, my hands caressing up her ribcage. "I told you," I say, unlace the strings binding the front of her bodice, and exposing her naked braless breasts; beautiful, full, perfect breasts, stroking my thumbs over her plump rosy nipples. "I'm not your fucking brother. Not now. Not ever." I cup her face, lean in and my mouth finds her mouth, and if she thought my tongue unforgiving before, it's downright brutal now. Because it's in my blood. It's who I am, who I was born to be. A bastard who wants her. A bastard who will demand everything she will give me and then leave when it's over.

A soft, sexy sound slides from her lips, so damn sexy, my cock twitches, expanding beneath my zipper. As if she knows, she presses her hand to my crotch and holy fuck, I need inside this woman. I push off the wall and shrug out of my jacket, my gaze raking over truly spectacular breasts. Her teeth scrape her bottom lip, and she moans softly at my inspection. I want her to moan again. And I want that mouth on my body. I want my mouth on *her* body.

I toss my jacket, and don't give two fucks where it lands, rip away my tie away, and she shows no signs of running away, as I half expect she will. She closes the small space between us, her delicate fingers fiddling with the buttons to my shirt, working them free, and when there's a deep enough gap, I reach behind me, and tug the damn thing over my head.

By the time it's on the ground, she's touching me all over, no inhibitions, which is fine as fuck by me, until one of her pretty little hands slides down to my crotch, and I react. I slow things down before I fuck her and this is over, and when it is, I'm gone. I'm not ready to be gone which is why I turn her to the wall, and force her hands to its surface, drag the top of her dress down to her waist, and only then do I nestle her sweet little ass to my rock-hard cock, and press my lips at her ear.

"You saw me watching you across the pool."

"*Of course* I saw you. You *wanted* me to see you."

"Yes. *I did.* And I wanted you to know I wanted to fuck you." I caress the top of her dress, and her bra straps, down her arms. "I wanted you to know I wanted you naked." I press my hands under her dress, and slide it over her hips and to her feet. I lift her and kick it away, taking a moment to appreciate just how perfect her heart-shaped ass is before I give it a smack.

She gasps, and I yank away the little string of silk between her cheeks, and then turn her to face me, my fingers tangle in her hair. "And since you're here," I add, "I will assume you got that message loud and clear."

"I'm still angry and you're still an arrogant asshole, but apparently it doesn't matter, but why don't you fuck me before I come to my senses."

I press my cheek to one side of her face, my hand to the other, my lips by her ear. "I promise to use my tongue in all the right places to make sure you have no regrets."

She pants out a breath that tells me my words affect her and I'm right there when she does, kissing her again, drinking her in, and damn she tastes good; one part innocence, one part wicked bad girl.

I could just fuck her right here against the wall, sate this damn craving for her I've had since the moment I saw her by that pool. And if she was anyone else I would. But not her, and not for any reason I can explain.

I scoop her up and carry her through the living area to the bedroom, because hell, I don't know, it just feels like I should fuck her on the bed. Once we're in the bedroom, I set her on her feet in front of the mattress and I fold her to me, my hand sliding under her hair and cupping her neck, controlling her. "This is where I lick and you come on my tongue."

Chapter Four

Eric

I'm about to go down on my knee and make good on that
promise to lick Harper to orgasm when she suddenly rejects that
idea and me. "No," she whispers, flattening her hands on my chest.
"No. This is a mistake. I need to leave."

She tries to pull away but I catch her waist. "What just
happened?"

"I don't do this kind of thing. Ever. I don't know why I'm half
naked with you right now."

"This is why," I say, cupping her head and kissing her, my tongue
stroking deep and long, the tension in her body easing almost
instantly, a tiny moan sliding from her mouth. "That's why," I
repeat, when she's all soft and yielding in my arms. "Because you
want me and I want you."

"You want *something*," she accuses as if she's decided I'm
motivated by some invisible agenda that doesn't exist.

"Sweetheart, you're the only reason I'm not driving away right
now."

"Because I fit your agenda?"

"My only agenda right now is you on my tongue." I kiss her again.
"And what does me between your legs do for me besides turn us
both on?"

"I don't want to be inside the family drama."

"Don't make this complicated. Don't make me complicated. I'm
here, I'm gone. I want to fuck you before I leave. You want to fuck
me, too, and right now, I'm going to kiss you again unless you—"

"Stop talking," she orders fiercely. "Stop and give me time to
think. I need—"

"I need," I say, and my mouth slants over hers, and the instant my
tongue touches hers, she moans and kisses me back, a wild hungry
kiss, my hand on her breast, her nipple.

She moans again, and God, I love this woman's moans. My cock throbs against my zipper and I need her on my tongue and everywhere I can get her. I lower to one knee, my hands on her hips, slipping her barely-there black panties down her legs. I wrap my arm around her and lift her, tossing them aside. When she's back on her feet, there's a hint of trepidation in her eyes that I don't want to exist, and I know is rooted in this screwed up family, and the war of brothers, my father eggs on every chance he finds.

"I'm going to make you forget everything about this night but me fucking you," I promise, my lips pressing to her belly, my tongue flicking against the soft skin there. She trembles in response, and holy hell, I'm so damn hard that it hurts.

Her hand presses to my shoulder and I caress her hip and cup her ass. My gaze lifts and her teeth scrape her bottom lip. *My teeth* go to her hip, where I nip, and then soothe the tiny bite with my tongue. I slide my fingers along her sex, as she's dripping for me. I slide two fingers inside her and her lips part in a silent gasp. I stroke her, pump my fingers into her, and she arches her hips and makes a barely there, but fucking sexy as hell, sound. I lick her clit and her fingers wrap around my hair, and not gently,

I'm also not about to let her cum this quickly.

But I liked it.

I rotate her and sit her down on the bed, and she's panting with my withdrawal, her lashes fluttering. My hands settling on her knees, my lips finding her inner thigh while my hand works a path up the opposite leg, just a little tease, for a short interlude. Impatience is not my friend and I slip my shoulders between her legs and my mouth closes down on her sex. When she moans, I pull her forward and force her to her back, lifting her legs to my shoulders, while I start licking and suckling, hungry for more of this woman, and yes, she's right. We're wrong. We're so fucking wrong that we are right in every possible way.

The very idea that they think they own her, and yet, she's chosen to be here with me, is *everything*. Every fucking thing, and I slide two fingers inside her again, reveling in the way she arches her hips, lifting into the thrust of my fingers. I lick her everywhere, the taste of her shifting from salty to sweet when she suddenly quakes into orgasm, her body spasming around my fingers.

I use my fingers and mouth to stroke her to completion, and when she's done, really done, I realize I don't have a condom and this night is going to be the death of me. Of course, it is. I'm on Kingston land.

I slide up her body to kiss her, and damn it, the taste of her on both our lips about undoes me. "I don't have a condom," I whisper.

"Oh god," she whispers. "Please tell me no."

"I wish I could," I say, kissing her and rolling us to our sides, facing each other. "No sex."

"Oh no," she whispers, sounding truly distressed. "How can you not have a condom?"

"I wasn't exactly expecting a hot stepsister I wanted to fuck."

Her teeth worry her bottom lip. "I owe you then," she says, her hand on my chest when I want it on my cock. I want it all over my body, but I don't move. I don't touch her, not when I'm dying here wanting inside her. "You owe me nothing."

"I do," she says, "because that was—I um, don't even have words for what that was you just did to me."

I laugh, and there is something as charming and vulnerable about her as there is sexy. "I'm glad you liked it, you don't owe me," I repeat. "I'm not *them*."

"Then consider what comes next, for me, not you."

"You don't fit them." Her hand slides down my tattoo sleeve. "But this fits you. I love this so very much." Her voice is low, and sultry, and I swear if she touches my cock, this is all over. I will forget why a condom matters. And I still want her to touch me.

Her hand settles on my stomach and holy hell, I don't know if I have enough willpower to not fuck her. She stokes down my zipper and traces the thick ridge of my erection, and I don't even stop her when she shoves me to my back and straddles me. Especially since she's naked and gorgeous, and I now have a perfect view of her breasts. And they are perfect. High and full, with these perfect little nipples.

"What are you doing, Harper?" I ask. "We *don't have* a condom."

"But we have each other. Isn't that what people say when times are tough? And no condom is pretty tough times, don't you think?"

I laugh again. "It is."

She moves to the side of me, her knees at my hip as she runs her hand over my zipper, stroking the hard length of my now throbbing cock. "We also have my mouth." She leans in and kisses my stomach the way I'd kissed hers.

I don't even consider resisting where this is going. Her mouth, my cock. Yes-*fucking-please*. Now. I want her too damn badly to say no and already my hand is on her head, her mouth kissing me through my pants, and there's no real preamble before she has my cock out and in her hand, but instead of sucking me, she shoves at my pants; as if they're a distraction we can't afford. I'm all about getting rid of the distractions. I sit up, kiss her, and then stand.

I'm fully undressed in thirty seconds, facing her with my cock thick and jutted out, the heat of her eyes on my body, on my erection, driving my urgency. I settle on a knee in front of her, at the same moment she rises to her knees to meet me there. Those beautiful full lips of hers part and lift, and I can't resist another taste. I kiss her, a deep slide of tongue, and she's so damn sweet, too sweet to be one of them and so fucking addictive, I am already lost in her. I take us down to the mattress, side by side and fuck, I know we don't have a condom, but I just want to feel the wet heat of her body pressed against me for a moment.

I press into the V of her body and deepen the kiss, my hands all over her body, her body molded close, both of us desperate in a way I don't ever remember being desperate. I reach between us and stroke my cock along her sex. "Eric," she whispers, her fingers curling on my chest. "We don't have a condom."

"I know that. I just want to feel you for one moment. Just one." I press inside her, sinking deep but I don't let myself move. "Holy fuck," I murmur, and I know I have to stop now but I slide back and thrust once more.

She gasps. "We have to stop," she whispers urgently but then we're kissing, and it's so damn good, too good. I'm going to fucking come if I don't stop now.

I pull out and we both pant with the impact. "Holy hell, woman," I say, flopping onto my back, and groaning with the effort it took to deny myself all that wet, tight heat enveloping me.

Harper scoots close to me, her soft, perfect curves pressed to my side, and she leans in and kisses me. "I really wish you were still inside me," she whispers against my lips, her voice so damn sweet and sexy, her hand sliding down my chest and over my stomach to grip my cock. "What do you need right now?" she asks.

"To be fucking you," I say. "In about ten different ways our lack of a condom says I can't."

"We can still do this," she says. "I can still do this." She doesn't use words to explain what "this" is. She slides down my body, her hand still wrapped around my shaft, as she settles on her knees beside me. Her eyes meeting mine, her tongue licking away the liquid pooling at the tip of my shaft, which I'm pretty sure is more than simple arousal. I don't even want to think about how close I was to coming inside her. She takes care of that mental rabbit hole though. She closes her mouth around me, sucking me long and deep, her tongue sliding around me as she does, and I tell myself to stop, I tell myself that I was so close to coming inside her, that it won't take much for me to come in her mouth. I try to stop. I try damn hard to pull her back. "Stop, Harper, or I'm going to—"

She sucks me deeper and it's all over. I can't hold back. I thrust into her mouth and I'm done. One more thrust and I'm shuddering with release and I can't pull back. She sucks me deeper, longer, and then slower until she's taken me all the fucking way. God, I think I'm in love with this woman, which of course, isn't possible. I don't do love, but if I did, I'd already be halfway there with all her vulnerable sexiness.

When she releases me and kisses my stomach, I drag her to me, kissing her and rolling her to her back. "I really hate that I don't have a condom."

"I don't," she says. "It means you're not a manwhore who's always prepared to fuck anyone, but it doesn't matter. You're leaving. They think you want to be here, but you don't want this place. Not anymore. I feel that."

"Why do *you* want this place?" I ask. "What makes you need this?"

"What made *you* need it?" she counters, avoiding a direct answer.

"Family. I thought I needed the connection."

"And now?"

"No," I say easily, the answer that wasn't clear when I arrived is clear now. "Not now."

"I wish I didn't." She rolls off of me and onto her back. "Why do you call me princess?"

I glance over at her. "You're the heir to a business that Kingston absorbed. You're royal blood in these parts, just not the right royal blood."

"I can't accept that. I can't just let my father's work be absorbed and forgotten. My mother—she made a mistake. My father worked too hard to have everything he created be forgotten with this merger."

I roll over and settle on top of her, my elbow by her head. "It's done. It's too late and Isaac will always be number one. You know that, right?"

"I don't accept that. Not at all. Isaac—*he's* the bastard. And worthless. He's about him, not about the company, not about the legacy or the future or—anything that matters."

"It's true, but it doesn't matter. He's the heir, the first blood, the golden child."

"I want you to be wrong."

I search her eyes and find the truth. "But you know I'm not," I say.

"Then why are you here? If you really believe that, if you believe we can't make a difference, why are you here?"

She hits a nerve and I shift off of her and onto my back again. "I needed to know I wasn't wrong."

"About your father?"

"About me," I say and I can feel her looking at me but I don't look at her.

"What does that mean?" she asks.

"I needed to find myself."

"And who are you?" she presses.

"The bastard." Now I look at her, now I let her see the real me in my eyes. I let her see who she just half fucked. "I'm him. I will always be him."

"I have much I could say about that," she comments, more thoughtful than anything.

"I'm listening," I say, certain this is going to be the moment she convinces me we're of two different worlds, when right here, in this bed, we feel like we're of one. I want her to convince me. I want her to give me every reason to get the hell out of this place, her included.

"You're different than anyone I've ever met," she says, running her hand down my ink and tracing one of the many rows of numbers on my forearm.

"How?"

Her eyes shift from my ink to my face. "It takes someone brave to be different and embrace it. I think you do."

"I didn't always."

"Because as you said, you found yourself. I like that you're the bastard but not for the reasons you might think."

I'm remarkably on edge waiting for her to continue but she doesn't make me wait long. She seems to know where she's going and gets there quickly. "You're cocky and arrogant, but you make me, and everyone else, believe it's because you're better than them. You do you, and most of us don't even know what that means."

"Meaning you?"

"Definitely me, but maybe I'll get there. I'm trying. And I don't know why I just told you that. I shouldn't have told you that."

I reach up and twine strands of her silky hair in my fingers. "Why?"

Her cellphone rings, a muffled sound in the distance that has her eyes going wide. "Oh God," she whispers, jerking away from my hand to sit up. "Oh God. I'm giving a speech. I'm late." She scrambles off the bed and rushes to locate her clothes, dashing for the living room.

I stand up and by the time I've pulled my pants on and located her by the door, she's fully dressed. "I have to go," she says, and I'm stunned at how much I don't want her to leave.

I catch her to me, kissing the hell out of her before I release her and open the door because if I don't let her go now, I won't. But she doesn't go. She seems to forget her speech, frozen in place, lost in a space that is me and her in a little cottage neither of us own. Those gorgeous blue eyes of hers study me, and I want to know what she's thinking, what she wants, because *I want her*. Time stretches for several more beats before she closes the space between us, pushes to her toes, and kisses me. "I've changed my mind," she confesses, her delicate, soft hands splayed on my naked chest. "I really do hate that we didn't have that condom." With that, she pushes away from me and rushes out of the door. I let her go, but fuck, I can't walk away. I can't *really* let her go. She's why I'm still here. She's why I'm still here. She's why I'm not leaving.

I finish dressing, the scent of her, all sweet and feminine, clinging to my skin, drugging me in the way only she seems to drug me. I need to see her again. I need to be inside that woman, and not just her body. I want to know why she feels insecure, and she does. I want to know why she's here when she could be so many other places. It's a crazy, out-of-character thought that I shove aside.

Nevertheless, I pursue her, walking down the path and find the party again. The crowd is still thick, the clusters of tuxedos and gowns gathered around a stage at the end of the pool, and there she is, Harper is on the stage. She's standing next to my father and my asshole of a brother, with her look-a-like mother, who's fifteen years my father's junior, standing next to her. She takes the microphone and starts speaking about the business and the family and damn it, my father kisses her cheek and I know I'm wrong about her. She's one of them. She's not a reason to stay. What the hell was I even thinking?

I turn away and walk down the path to the cottage, pack my bag, and with her still on my tongue, I leave.

Forever this time.

Chapter Five

Eric

I'm sitting at my desk, in my corner office of the Bennett Firm, our primary business in the legal field, with locations all over the country, but Grayson is all about diversifying his portfolio. That's where I come in and why I'm working on a buy-in on a sports team that's sure to add a few billion in sales on the books for the company and myself. Which is my job. Make money. Grow the business beyond worldwide legal services. Repeat, with Grayson's aggressive, but smart, stance on growth that works for us in ways it might not for other companies. I'm scanning the final contract when Grayson pokes his head in the door. "I have contract questions." He taps his Rolex. "It's seven o'clock. Let's talk somewhere that isn't here."

"Here-here to that," I say. "I could use a Macallan right about now." I stand up and roll my sleeves down before I shrug on my jacket, which never quite covers my tattoo sleeve, but I really don't give a shit. I'm long beyond giving a shit what anyone thinks of me. If they don't like my ink, they can move on and hope to make money elsewhere. Good riddance and good luck.

"Mia doesn't like clause eight," Grayson says, crossing his arms in front of his chest.

Mia being his fiancée and a criminal attorney with the firm, who's recently re-joined our inner circle and I'm damn glad she is back in his life after a year-long breakup. Whereas I'm a loner, a man without ties, Grayson needs Mia. I might not understand that kind of bond, but I understand him. "She's right. I already told the team owners to go fuck themselves over that clause."

He chuckles. "Of course you did, and probably not any nicer than you just told me."

"Probably not," I say. "I take it Mia has trial prep tonight?"

"She does," he says. "She's passionate about this woman she's defending. She's all in."

I shove my MacBook and a stack of papers in my briefcase and join him on the other side of the desk. "We're about to hit the holidays. When's the trial?"

"January."

"And the wedding is in March? Are you sure you don't need to push it back?"

"Hell no, we aren't pushing the wedding back. Mia's trying to shut down the prosecution before this even goes to trial. I hired help and we already planned this once. We're just duplicating those plans."

We head for my door and talk through a few pieces of the contract. We've just stepped into the lobby when the door opens and I'm suddenly standing face to face with a familiar brunette who's the last person I expect to see right now. "What are you doing here, princess?" I ask softly, reminding her of that night we spent together, reminding her that I know who and what she is, then and now.

"Obviously," she says, "I'm looking for you." Her eyes meet mine, blue eyes the color of a perfect sky, and I have no idea why I don't remember this about her. Because I remember far too much about this woman, both randomly and too often, just as I'm thinking about all the perfect curves beneath another black dress she's wearing today. This one is more demure than the sexy number she'd worn the night we'd met, but it doesn't matter. I know what's beneath. I know where my hands and mouth have been and so does she.

As if she's read my thoughts, she cuts her gaze abruptly and focuses on Grayson. "I'm Harper Evans," she says, offering him her hand. "I'm the—"

"I know who you are," Grayson says, shaking her hand, which I note is free of a wedding band. "And he told me quite a lot about you," he adds. "I must say that you're as beautiful as he claimed." Grayson does nothing without purpose. He wants her to know I spoke about her to take her off guard, to make her wonder what else I said about her. That's how he works. He discreetly takes control, and in this case, he's discreetly handed it to me.

"Thank you," she says, her attention returning to me, the awareness between us downright sizzling, as hot as it had been six years ago. "Can I please speak to you in private?"

Grayson's hand comes down on my shoulder. "Meet me at our usual spot."

I give him a small incline of my head and he departs. "Let's go to my office."

She swallows, her long, graceful neck bobbing with the action, drawing my gaze, and I wonder why I didn't kiss her there when I had the chance. I wonder what the hell it is about this woman, out of all of the women out there that refused to let go, that's still working a number on me, and it's a hell of a number at that. "This way," I say, motioning her forward, and at this late hour, there's no one in our path, my secretary included.

We walk side by side down the hallway, and I'm acutely aware of her, memories of pulling her into the cottage and pressing her against the wall in my mind. We reach my office and I open the door, motioning her forward. She glances at me and I sense that she wants to say something, but she seems to change her mind. She moves forward and I know what she'll see: an executive desk, a window with a view to kill for, and a seating area to the right, which I plan to avoid. I still want her beyond reason and the six years since we last saw each other, and that isn't to my advantage when she clearly wants something from me.

I don't even think about sitting, claiming a spot behind my desk, and leaning forward, my palms flat on my desk, as I say to her what she once said to me. "You want something from me." There's no accusation in my tone. It's just a fact, and we both know it.

She steps to the front of my desk and meets my stare and I find this confidence as alluring as I did six years ago. I see those years both in her blossomed beauty but also in the experience in her eyes, in the jaded history I don't pretend to know firsthand, but I understand in ways few others could. "I do," she says, "though I wish I could reply to that statement the way you did once and say I don't and mean it as you did." She hesitates and then adds, "You left."

That statement screams with personal accusation which is as surprising as her visit. "I told you I was leaving."

"I know." She doesn't add to that statement, but her cheeks flush a pretty pink before she admits. "I need help."

And there it is, the reason for her visit, which sadly is not to just go get naked and fuck again. "What kind of help?" I ask, caution in my tone.

"I know that you're a near billionaire now. Or maybe you are already. I know that you did all this yourself and you have no reason to look beyond here."

Tension zips down my spine and I push off the desk, intentionally towering over her petite height and frame. "What kind of help?" I repeat, because I don't jive well with anyone bringing up my money and the word "help."

She must read my reaction because she holds up her hand, a hint of panic darting through her eyes. "I don't want money, oh God, no. I'm handling this so very badly. I just need the kind of help someone as obviously financially savvy can offer."

I fold my arms in front of me. "I'm listening."

"We just had our second recall at Kingston Motors and this time after two people died in our cars."

"I read that."

"Something doesn't add up," she says, sounding earnest. "Nothing has changed in our process and on the books and inside our operations, everything looks right, but it's not."

They've grown too fast, I think, but I don't voice that opinion. "What does Isaac say?"

"For me to leave it alone. He has it handled, but our stock is down and I'm not you. I don't have the same head for numbers but I have a decent aptitude. There's money moving in unpredictable ways. I need your help, Eric. Please. It wasn't easy to come here. Not after you left, but I'm here."

After I left.

She keeps saying that like she expected me to stay and while I could find all kinds of pleasure in this woman wishing she'd had more time with me, I'm just too damn jaded myself to see this that simply.

"I really need your help," she repeats.

If this was that cut and dry, she'd have my attention, but it's not. There's more to her visit. There's more to this story. I sense it. I see it in her eyes. I lean forward again, and pin her with my full attention. "What aren't you telling me?" I narrow my eyes on hers and lean forward, my hands on the desk again, pinning her in a stare. "No," I amend. "Let me rephrase. What don't you want me to know?"

Chapter Six

Harper

I knew coming here was trouble but I didn't expect to stare into this man's blue eyes from across the desk and melt all over again. He is every fantasy I've ever owned—sexy, power, confidence. I'd been certain that I'd built the attraction up into more than it was over time, certain I'd turned it into more than it was, but I was wrong. He affects me and not just physically. I mean, yes, he's one hell of a good-looking man and he wears that expensive suit he's got on like he owns it and the world, but it's more with him. There is something raw and dark about him that reaches beyond his sharp cheekbones and jawline. Something in his eyes, something I feel in every part of me, that I hunger to understand. Which of course, I won't, considering why I'm here and who I am.

"What aren't you telling me, Harper?" he demands again.

Too much, I think. So much. I focus on the only part of any of this that might matter to him. "People died, Eric. I'm here to make sure no one else does."

"And whose idea was it for you to come here?"

"I wanted to come after the first recall," I say. "I did. I should have."

His eyes narrow. "Who sent you?"

And there it is. The question I hate with the answer that he'll hate. "Gigi, but—"

"Holy fuck," he growls, pushing off the desk at the mention of his grandmother's name. "You should have left that part out. *No* to anything and everything she wants, now or ever."

I lean on the desk. "Eric."

"Don't look at me with those big blue eyes and say my name and expect anything but another orgasm. And if you came here thinking the fact that I already gave you one influences me, you were wrong.

I can want, and do, when it comes to fucking you, and it changes nothing."

My body reacts, raging for this man, and just plain defies the level head I'm trying to have right now. It remembers that orgasm. Remembers his hands. It wants more, but he's trying to rattle me and I understand why. I know his past. I know why Gigi is the plague to him. I push off the desk. "I don't think an orgasm, or two—since you had one as well, in case you've forgotten—influences you. I'm just asking that you hear me out."

"For the record," he says. "I remember both orgasms with crystal clarity. I also remember everything about Gigi."

"I know, and I could have lied and told you I made this decision on my own, but I feel like I'm swimming in lies back at Kingston. I don't want them with you, too. I know Gigi was horrible to your mother. She told me that. She has regrets over trying to deny her, and you, your rightful place in the company."

"My place in the company? My mother was sick and we were living in a shithole of a trailer park we could barely afford. I'm pretty sure she didn't give a shit about my place in the company. I damn sure don't." He inhales, seeming to rein himself in before he folds his arms in front of his broad, perfect chest, his tattoo sleeve partially exposed. The tattoos that I know tell a story that I am certain has a lot to do with Gigi and his mother. "That woman doesn't have regrets," he adds. "Saying she does is a lie."

"She was horrible to me, too, but I was with her when she had a small heart attack a year ago. It changed her."

"Nothing changes who we are at the core and if you really believe that, then you're as naive as you were six years ago."

"Naive?" I repeat, my voice low and calm when I really want to punch him right now. "I guess if I was naive, we can blame my decision to get naked with my stepbrother on me being young and stupid." It's out before I can stop the words that place our intimate past right here in this room.

His eyes darken and heat. "Why would we do that? It wasn't a mistake."

"It was a mistake," I assure him, "for about ten different reasons I'm not going to list."

"The mistake was me thinking you weren't one of them," he says dryly.

I feel those words like a punch, with guilt I shove away before he reads it and me. "I'm not one of them," I say and I don't have to cut my gaze as I'm certain he expects. I've never meant those words like I do now. "I told you why I'm with them. The company is a piece of my father, all I have left of him."

"Six years is a long time to work with someone you're not devoted to," he muses. "And you're trusted enough to be their spokesperson to me."

"They don't know I'm here," I say, trying not to think of the hell that will follow if they find out or the many things about this past six years that he can never know.

"Gigi is them," he says. "If she knows, they know."

"She's been shut out."

"She's the primary stockholder."

"Who isn't exactly in great health. Your father threatened to go to the board to get her removed as CEO."

He rounds the desk and we turn to face each other and damn it, he smells just as earthy and perfect as I remember. And he's so big and overwhelmingly male. He's also had his tongue in all kinds of places and I need to not go there. "What are you thinking, Harper?"

"A lot of things," I say, and avoiding the past we share, I hold out my hands. "You've done so much. You're brilliant. They all know that. We need you."

"We or Gigi?"

"*We* need you, but Gigi said to tell you she's begging. This is her life's work. She's terrified of losing it."

His brutal perfect mouth quirks. "I'd almost be willing to go there just to watch her beg like my mother did for help."

His mother who killed herself. What was I thinking coming here? "This was a mistake. I should have just told her we'd find another way." I try to turn away but he catches my elbow, heat radiating up my arm. My gaze rockets to his and that connection I'd felt to him six years ago is present and accounted for, thickening the air between us.

"If there's another way," he says, "why come to me?"

"People died, and you're a genius, *literally*. You also have an understanding of the company, a connection, your family."

"Family? Like being the stepbrother who gave you an orgasm?"

"Now you're just being an asshole and you have a right. I get that, too, but I didn't do any of the things they did to you. Like I said. This was a mistake. Forget I was here." I jerk away from him and rush for the door, feeling as if my heart is going to explode in my chest on the way. I reach for the knob, escape only seconds away.

Eric is suddenly behind me, his hand on the door, his big body crowding mine, so close that I can almost feel his body heat. "Tell me why you're really here."

I rotate to face him and that's a mistake. He's overwhelmingly right here, in front of me. "Just let me leave."

He studies me for several intense beats, that piercing stare so damn probing and too intelligent. "You had to know that I wasn't going to help."

"I know that, but I had to try. *People have died.*"

"You came here because people have died."

"I keep saying that."

"But it's not everything. It's not the whole reason."

"It's the reason I was willing to come here and I know you might not believe me, but considering our past, this wasn't easy for me."

"Because I left or because you regret what happened between us?"

"Does it matter? I was one of them to you then and I'm one of them now."

He considers me for several long few beats. "I know that you have a trust fund from your father. Take it and run. Get the hell out now because you're right, even watching from a distance, and I am, there's a problem at Kingston."

I have a fleeting moment of fear that he knows because he's somehow involved, but I shove that idea away. He's not behind this. I know too much about what really is happening to believe he's behind this. "What do you know that I don't know?"

"To get out. I got out. You need to as well."

"I don't get my trust fund until I turn thirty-five and my mother loaned it to your father."

"You're fucking kidding me."

"No. No, I'm not."

"Then leave them and come here. I'll give you a job. You can make your way just like I did. Unless you don't trust your ability to make your own way?"

"Don't be an asshole, *again.* I was planning to leave. I told your grandmother right before her heart attack."

"And that made you feel guilty?"

"What part of *people have died* do you not understand? How many times can I say that before you take it in? I can't just walk away and your grandmother really has changed. She's old. She can't handle this alone."

He doesn't immediately reply. He just stands there, looking at me, seconds ticking by before his gaze sweeps my mouth, his body so close to my body, and Lord help me, I think he might kiss me. I think I want him to kiss me, but he doesn't. He pushes off the door. "The job offer stands. Safe travels, Harper, because we both know you won't stay."

My lashes lower with the rejection I've felt not once now but twice with this man. I open my eyes and force my gaze to his. "Thank you for seeing me." I open the door and exit, my knees weak as I rush through the offices and toward the elevator. I punch the button and the doors open, allowing me to rush inside, but once I'm there, alone in the car, reality hits hard.

I *am* alone. Eric isn't going to help me.

Chapter Seven

Eric

I stand there in my office, staring at the doorway, hot and hard, with the scent of Harper's perfume in the air, the memories of her naked and in my arms in my mind. I still crave her. I have always craved her, but we aren't even close to a possibility. She's on top of the Kingston throne. I will never kneel to that throne, and yet, she has stayed with me all these years. Maybe because *she's* on that throne. Maybe because she's untouchable. Maybe because she has those damn beautiful eyes. All I really know is that me wanting her this fucking badly makes her a weakness that every Kingston, perhaps her included, would happily use against me.

And while I want to believe her intentions are pure, six years in the folds of that family makes that a difficult sell. I'd also like to believe that I know more about what's happening at Kingston than her, which would make her visit authentic. I scrub my jaw and cross to my desk, where I grab my briefcase and head for the door. I have a deal to close and money to make for a man who deserves his success.

By the time I'm in a hired car on the way to the bar in Grayson's apartment building, I've replayed every word of that conversation with Harper ten times, but I keep going back to Gigi, that bitch of a woman who all but ensured my mother's miserable death. I hate her at least ten degrees deeper than I do my father, who at least saved his punishment for me, not my mother. The car drops me at my destination and I walk inside to find Grayson in his normal booth.

He lifts the bottle he's ordered, an expensive-ass whiskey I welcome right about now. "I thought you might need this."

"In duplicate," I say, settling into the booth as he fills my glass.

I down the contents and pull a contract from my briefcase to get to work. "Where were we?"

"Where were we? Talking about Harper."

"There's nothing to talk about."

"You damn near turned down this job to go back there again and we both know it was over her."

"That was when I thought she was too green to protect herself." I refill my glass. "She's been with them for six years. She doesn't need her hand held."

"She knows the company's in trouble," he assumes, downing his own drink.

"She knows."

"And?" he prods when I offer nothing more.

"You aren't going to let this go, are you?"

"No," he says. "Because friends don't let friends deal with shit alone, as you've proven over and over both professionally and personally. Talk to me."

"We have a contract to deal with."

"That we'll handle."

I inhale and let out a breath. "She wants me to go to Denver. She wants me to save them."

"Them or her?"

"Both. My grandmother sent her."

"Gigi?" he asks, incredulously. "Why would she think that you would ever help Gigi?"

"Obviously, that's why Gigi sent Harper. Or the whole clan of them sent her."

"You think they know you two hooked up?" he asks.

"When I look into her eyes, no, I don't believe she'd tell them or use me. When I'm with that woman, I'm one hundred percent into her. She seems honest, sweet, smart, too smart to be with those assholes. When I step back like now, I see six years of her with them. Something doesn't add up."

"You almost went back to them just to be a part of a family unit," he reminds me. "Maybe she needs that unit."

"It doesn't feel right."

"But she does, correct? She's not one of them."

His question comes from understanding. He's the only person I talk to, the only person in this world I really trust, outside of a few of my SEAL buddies, and we never speak. We'd die for each other, and be there for each other with one phone call, but they don't know me beyond blood and sacrifice. Grayson does. He knows about the moment I saw her on that stage. He knows how it affected me. He knows how I reasoned that away, as some Bastard/Princess head game I'd put on myself. "Six years, Grayson," I repeat. "That's loyalty, not obligation."

"But she doesn't feel like one of them," he presses. "You keep saying that for a reason, and you have the best instincts I've ever seen."

"I have a head for numbers. I have a head for statistics. That's not this. I can't trust my instincts when it comes to a woman I want to fuck. Maybe I just want what I didn't have or can't have."

He studies me for several long moments, not entertaining my musings. He gets right to the point. "You don't want to turn your back on her. What are you going to do?"

"I told her to get out of there and I offered her a job."

"Which you knew she'd decline," he comments, lifting his glass in my direction. "Where does that leave you and her?"

"I made sure she knows the door is open. She can leave."

"You mean she can come to you." He leans forward. "Do you really think she knows she can come to you?"

"I repeated the offer more than once."

"In a short meeting after a six-year wait for a reunion. How do you know anything about her and her motives at this point?" He taps the table. "Let's be honest. Let's get to the meat of this. We both know the state of that company for reasons you probably don't want to share with Harper. We both know there are things going on that spell trouble."

"Get to the meat, Grayson."

"How much trouble is that for her? Is she in danger? Maybe she can't get out without your help. Maybe she was afraid to tell you that, for reasons we can both surmise. You could turn on her."

"*Fuck.* Stop already."

"Do you care what happens to her?"

"I barely know her."

"And yet you never forgot her. That's how this works. It's how it worked for me with Mia. I met her and it was her. It was never going to be anyone else."

It's not her, I think. It won't ever be her. He just doesn't get the dynamic between me and this woman. He can't. He's never been the bastard. He's a better version of Isaac, the heir, and Grayson is the king now that his father is gone. I tap the contract. "Work. Money. *Your* money. *Now.*"

His lips quirk. "I hit about ten nerves, I see."

"Clause eight," I say, and once I start talking, I distract him with business, even if my mind is constantly going to Harper. Is she in danger? *I need help.* She said that several times.

I'm still thinking about those words when Mia appears by the table, looking gorgeous in a pink dress, her long dark hair loose around her shoulders. "Hello, you two handsome men." She slides into the booth and kisses Grayson, her hand settling on his jaw. "I missed you."

I have no idea what it is about this moment that gets to me. I see these two together all the damn time and I never think of me with someone else, but right now, I'm thinking about Harper. I'm thinking about me with Harper. "Fuck," I murmur, pushing out of the booth and grabbing my phone from my pocket.

I step outside, welcoming the cold October night, and I dial Blake Walker of Walker Security, a man who's not only a world class hacker and ex-ATF agent, he and his team, just helped us through another nightmare. I trust them. "Eric," he greets. "What's up?"

"Kingston Motors."

"I know the connection to you," he offers without prodding. "I make it a point of knowing the people I'm working with."

"Good. This will go faster then. Find out what's dirty there. If you can't get real answers, hack the financials with enough detail to allow me to dissect it all. Look at the officers, especially my half-brother and father."

"What else?"

"I'll email you a list of questions on my mind in a few minutes. I need this to be comprehensive. Take the time you need. What I need now: find out if my grandmother had a heart attack about a year ago. Text me the information."

"I can tell you that now." I can hear him banging on his keyboard and I wait, every nerve in my body on edge and I know why. I need one little piece of information proven to be honest, a pebble of truth that might indicate she isn't lying to me.

"Yes," Blake finally says. "She did, in fact, have a heart attack, but she's now recovered."

"Harper Evans," I say, relieved with his response but already wanting more. "I need to know everything there is to know about her and tonight."

"I can get you an overview tonight. The rest will have to be tomorrow."

"That works." I hang up and Grayson steps outside with me.

"You need to go deal with this."

"I need to be here closing this deal," I argue.

"You are more than capable of doing both. Close it from the road. She got to you, then and now, and this is your blood family."

"If I go there, I won't save them. I'll finish them off."

"Then maybe you need to go to her tonight and convince her to take the job. Or not. I just know that you don't have closure. I feel it. I see it. You need it. Go get it, and her, like you get everything else you decide you want." He doesn't wait for an answer. He walks back inside the bar.

I don't stand there and think about his words. He knows me and he's right. I need closure, not with my family, but with Harper. I pull my phone back out and dial Blake. "Give me an hour, man," he says when he answers. "I'm good, but I still require time."

"Harper's in town tonight. I need to know which hotel."

Chapter Eight

Harper

There's a quote I read once: "I'm just a good girl with bad habits."

That's me. I'm that good girl and making a fool of myself with my stepbrother is my bad habit.

After contemplating tucking tail and licking my wounds on an early return flight home, I decide against that cowardly action. I'm going to talk to Eric again tomorrow. Tonight, I'll wallow in self pity via room service and champagne, when I usually don't drink. Of course, champagne is the drink of celebration and I'm far from celebrating, but I'm improvising and turning it into a pity party drink.

Pity works well for me.

I'll wallow, work it out of my system, and wake up fighting again.

And it's a hell of a pity party, considering I've been dumped by the hottest man I've ever known not once, but twice. He's too good at goodbye. I'm too good at wanting him. I have let one night with that man affect me in lingering ways that make no sense.

I sit down on the love seat in the corner of the room and fill my glass, since I ordered a champagne dinner before I decided that was a bad idea, and right after pulling on sweats and a tee; because I'm feeling really, really sexy tonight after Eric barely gave me a blink. Once my bubbly is in my glass and I'm sipping, I think about how Eric affects me. That man makes me feel everything, and I don't even know what that means. I'm just aware in every physical and emotional way when he's in the room and no one else has done that to me. I've tried to make it happen. I've dated. I've dated attractive, powerful, sexy men who did absolutely nothing for me. It's ridiculous. I was with Eric one night and we didn't even have real sex.

The doorbell rings, and yes, there's a doorbell because that's just how they roll around here, I guess. I down my champagne and stand up, the buzz of two glasses hitting me rather suddenly. Clearly, I should have waited for my food before I indulged in the champagne. After all, what have I eaten today? Not much. Some cashews, I think. Does Starbucks count as a meal?

I cross the room and open the door, only to suck in a stunned breath to find Eric standing there. His jacket and tie gone, sleeves rolled up, his brightly colored ink that was once up and down one arm now on both. I stare at that ink, intrigued by the random designs—a timepiece, a skull, numbers—lots of numbers and the heat of his stare has me snapping my gaze back to his face, those blue eyes fixing me in a piercing stare.

I can't breathe. Why do I react like this to this man? "I thought you were room service."

Those gorgeous lips of his quirk. "I can be."

"Don't say things like that."

I don't even have time to process him moving, and he's right here in front of me, his hands on my waist, sending a rush of heat all over my body as he walks me inside the room. The door slams behind him, and suddenly we're so very alone. "Why wouldn't I say things like that, princess? We have unfinished business. I know you feel it, too."

My hand flattens on his chest and his heart thunders beneath my palms, and that tells a story. He's not as cold as I'd felt he was when I left his office. He's just as present as I am in this reunion, just as affected by us being together again, but I don't fool myself into thinking this means anything real, anything lasting. His desire where I'm concerned is all about anger and conquest of the enemy he believes me to be. I can feel it to my core and I don't like it. I don't want it. I twist away from him and with a rapid pace, place the coffee table between me and him.

"How did you find me?" I demand.

"I'm resourceful," he says, his voice pure silk. "If I wasn't, you wouldn't want me, now would you?" He glances at my champagne. "Celebrating?"

"Wallowing in failure," I say because it's true and I prefer every truth I can embrace, plus I'm buzzing. Buzzing makes the world sing with words, in my case, probably too many. "And I can't seem to drink anything else."

"I could help you expand your tastes."

There is innuendo in those words that has me snapping back at him. "But you won't be around to expand my tastes, now will you?"

"That depends on you."

"What does that mean? Because if sleeping with you is a negotiation strategy, I don't want to sleep with you."

He moves then, so quickly, he's around the table in front of me, and I have nowhere to go. He's close, but not touching me, so close I can smell that earthy scent of him again. He picks up the bottle, reads the label and fills my glass before drinking, his mouth now where my mouth was only minutes before. His eyes twinkle with mischief and suggestion as he says, "It's good," and then adds, "for champagne." He sets the glass down. "And yes, I want to fuck you. No, it's not a negotiation. Fucking you and getting fucked by the Kingston family are not synonymous, even if that's your intent."

"I didn't come here to fuck you, Eric," I snap, and now I'm angry. "I came for help. Just leave, okay? I told you, forget I was here."

"I can't do that."

"Not until you finish what you started?" I challenge.

"We aren't done with each other. I think we both know that."

"We've been done for six years."

"If we were done, I wouldn't be here right now. You're the only reason I'm here."

I cut my gaze, and I'm back living that night I met him, standing on that stage, staring out at the audience and looking for him. "Harper," he says softly, and when his voice was hard moments before, it's gentle now.

I force my gaze to his. "I went back to the cottage, hoping you hadn't really left."

His lashes lower and now he cuts his gaze, like the idea of me going there actually affects him, and when he looks at me, his blue eyes are laden with emotions I can't read. "I had to leave."

"I know," I say, because I do. He hates that place. He hates me as an extension. How can I want a man that hates me?

The doorbell rings again and it's sweet relief and my escape. "That's my food. You can go. I know you won't help. I knew almost the moment I walked into the lobby today."

He studies me a moment and turns to the door. My heart squeezes with how easily he's going to leave, how certain his steps, when I just told myself and him that's what I want. He opens the door and I hurry around the table to greet the delivery person. Eric steps back and allows the woman to enter, and I expect him to exit, but he doesn't. "Where would you like it?" the woman asks of the tray in her hand.

She asks this question of Eric, but he casts a querying look at me. "Right here," I say, indicating the coffee table.

The woman sets everything up for me and still, Eric doesn't move. I give him a "you can go" look and he replies with a short shake of his head, a silent no, and the look in his eyes is pure heat. I cut my gaze and sign the ticket with a generous tip. The woman hurries to the door and then I'm alone with Eric again. He saunters to the couch and sits down in front of my tray, and when he tries to lift it, I have no idea why, but it sets me off.

I rush forward, sit next to him and hold down the lid. "You don't get to know what I order or what I like. You left. You're going to leave again. Who I am and what I like is *not* your business." I stand up. "Leave now."

He pushes to his towering height and faces me, and I'm immediately aware that joining him on this side of the table was a mistake. He's close, big, and he smells all earthy and perfect. I have about ten seconds to have that thought before he drags me to him, and my God, he feels just as good as he did back then, and it's too much but not enough. "You keep talking about me leaving," he says. "Why? Because you can't believe that the bastard could walk away from the princess?"

Anger flares hard and fast. "I'm going to forgive you for saying that because I know how they treated you. I know where it comes from, but you told me not to make us about them, but you did, then and now."

"I was wrong when I said it wasn't about them. I saw you up on that stage, with them, a part of them."

"Really? Because I looked for you and saw you leaving."

"I was there just long enough to see who you are."

"You didn't see me at all. You saw what you wanted to see and for a really smart person, that was a shallow way of thinking. You barely knew me. I barely knew you."

"Do you *want* to know me, Harper?"

"It doesn't matter," I say. "You're leaving again. You won't help. You won't—"

"*Do you want to know me*, Harper?"

"I'm pretty sure you've already shown me the parts I need to see and they don't work for me."

"I was pissed when I saw you up there."

"I was pissed when you were gone."

His hand goes to my jaw and he tilts my face to his. "And yet here we are," he says, his mouth lowering, lips just above mine, his warm breath teasing me with the promise of a kiss that I shouldn't want. He's the bastard by his own admission and we both know he revels in living up to that title. He's trouble, but my God, I have long hungered for another taste of that trouble.

Chapter Nine

Harper

E ric's mouth closes down on mine and it's like I'm six years in the past. Just like then, I'm aware of the forbidden element of us like this, just as I'm aware of the divide, too, all too aware, and try to resist, I do. But I can't. The taste of him is like a drug on my tongue, addictive, sweet, and impossible not to crave. I know this whole "princess" label is all about conquest and division—his conquest, our division. I tell myself this isn't good. I *know* it's not good. I can't be with a man who ultimately hates me and that thought is a dash of cold water on the heat burning between me and this man.

I shove on his chest. "Stop."

"Are we doing this again?" he asks, his voice husky, rough. "Because I really don't think either of us wanted to stop then and I sure as fuck don't now."

"How many times did you stand on a stage or just by their side, Eric? How many times in the years you were part of that family?"

"*That* family?" he challenges. "You mean *your* family?"

"We both inherited them. I didn't ask for them, but you judged me for standing on that stage when we both know you did it, too."

"I'm not on that stage with them anymore."

"You were. For years, you were. We both know you were."

"And you still are."

"No," I say. "I'm not. Me being there isn't about them. I swear to you, Eric. It's not."

His fingers slide back under my hair, cupping my neck and dragging my mouth to his. "Tell me later." I barely have time to inhale the warm breath on my lips and he's kissing me again, a long stroke of his tongue against mine undoes me, weakens my knees.

"I need to tell you now," I whisper when his teeth scrape my lip. "I need you to hear me."

"Later," he repeats softly, stroking the dampness from my lips. "I'll listen."

"You will?" I pull back to look at him. "Promise me you will because—"

"I will," he says, his mouth closing down on mine and it's pure heat and fire. *He's* pure heat and fire and I feel the shift in us, the need that pushes us past family and divide. There is no divide right here, right now. There is just me and him and a night that was never finished but needs completion. Every part of me is alive in a way it hasn't been since I was last with this man. We are wild, hands touching and tongues tangling, but then suddenly there's a shift between us again and his hand settles between my shoulder blades, molding my chest to his chest.

His lips part from mine and our foreheads come together, both of us breathing heavily, the past between us again, so many questions and unspoken words between us with it, but neither of us wants those things to matter. The silent understanding that *later* is, in fact, better, is there, between us. That word "later" complicates our already complicated connection, but there is nothing complicated about the fire between us now or the sense of understanding. We're alike and yet we're different. Both pulled into a world we didn't ask to join, a world that is why we're here now.

"Eric," I whisper, and not because I want to break the silence, because I have this sense that he's waiting on me, needing something I don't understand.

His answer is instant, not in words, but actions. His mouth closes down on mine, and I feel the snap of tension in him; whatever hesitation was in him moments before is gone, and I welcome the deep thrust of his tongue, the press of his hand under my shirt, his touch caressing over my ribcage. My breasts are heavy, heat pooling low in my belly with anticipation of what comes next, and then his hand is on my naked breasts, fingers plucking my nipple.

He pulls back to look at me, the deep blue of his stare flecked with amber heat scorching me inside and out. He drags my tee over my head, tosses it away, and then that smoldering stare of his is raking over my breasts, devouring me in ways that inexplicably no other man ever has. Just him. My sex clenches and when I grab his sleeve, tugging him toward me, he doesn't make me wait.

His gaze collides with mine, and the punch of awareness and attraction between us steals my breath even as his hand returns to my neck as he drags my mouth to his. "God, woman," he says, his voice low, rough, almost guttural, "what the hell are you doing to me?" And this time when he kisses me, I sense the barely caged control, the edge of hunger clawing at him, and me with him.

I reach for the buttons of his shirt and he responds by backing me up until I'm against some wall. I don't even know what wall, and then he releases me just long enough to unbutton his shirt and toss it. I don't play shy. I've waited too long for this to hold back. My hands go to his hard, really perfect chest, my fingers twining in the light brown hair there. Especially that sexy line of it that runs from his belly button, beneath his waistband. I want to lick my way down that path, but there is so much with this man to explore, to experience, even as I contemplate that journey, I'm distracted by his tattoos and my hands move to his new ink, the right shoulder that is now a giant jaguar.

"I love your ink," I dare, and how can I not. I've thought of his ink so many times in the past, wondered what it all means, wondered so much about this gifted, enigmatic man.

Shadows flicker in his eyes, an edge to his mood now that isn't about sex, but that talk we haven't had. "Do you now?"

"Yes," I say, looking him in the eyes. "Why is that a problem? What just happened? Because I do love it. Very much, and I want to—"

I never finish that sentence, I never get to tell him how much I want my mouth on his ink and his body before his cheek is pressed to mine, his lips at my ear, breath warm on my neck as he declares, "I want you naked" his teeth scrape my earlobe, "in every way, Harper."

My lips part on those words that I don't fully understand and once again, just like six years before, he turns me to the wall and forces me to catch it with my hands. It's a power thing, I know, and it should perhaps bother me. He wants to control me, he *needs* control. It's about him ruling over the royalty, and to him, I'm that royalty and there's nothing I can do about it. He feels like I'm the girl on the throne who's fucking beneath herself.

He yanks my pants down and in seconds they're over my bare feet and I'm completely naked. His hands are all over me, and when he leans in, his lips at my ear, his hands on my breasts, my breath hitches in my throat. "You're mine now, princess. All mine. You get that, right? There's no turning back now."

"I don't want to turn back."

"But will you regret this and me?"

"I regret you leaving. That was a bastard move."

I feel him stiffen, and I don't care. It *was* a bastard move. "Is that right?" He pinches my nipples as if punishing me for the truth, and I try to move my hands, but I'm trapped between that wall and his big body, the thick ridge of his erection at my backside.

He folds himself around me, one hand on my hip, the other on my breast. "You have me now, but you might regret it, because this bastard is going to own you before tonight is over."

Chapter Ten

Harper

This bastard is going to own you before tonight is over, Harper.

Those words, Eric's words, are in the air between us, the implications of me against the wall and him at my back leaving no room to question his intent. He wants control. He has control. His hands go to my shoulders. "How do you feel about being owned?" he demands, and it's clear we're talking about a whole lot more than us, naked, tonight.

"They don't own me," I say. "They've never owned me."

"You seem pretty damn owned to me, princess," he says, squeezing my backside and then giving it a hard smack. I yelp at the unexpected sting that he squeezes away even as he steps to my side, caging my legs and cupping my sex. "But right now, you're mine."

"Because it turns you on to be the bastard that owns me?" I whisper, hating the way my hands are captive to this wall, wanting to touch him, wanting to hit him and kiss him and ten more things I haven't even considered yet.

"I do believe it does," he says. "Does it turn you on?" He slides fingers against the wet, slick heat of my body. "I do believe it does." His lips go to my ear. "I'll only punish you if you ignore my orders, but I promise to make it hurt so good."

"Punish me?" I demand. "What does that even mean?" His finger slides inside me and I bite back a moan as he pulls back that finger.

"I can give," he says, "and I can take away."

My gaze meets his. "Two can play at that game, you do know that, right?"

He laughs, this low, sexy laugh that I feel in the clenching of my sex and the empty ache he's created there. "We'll see." He rotates to stand behind me again. "Don't move," he orders, "or the next time I put my tongue on you, I won't finish you." With that threat, he steps away from me and I can feel the heat of his stare on my naked body, and the ache between my thighs has me clenching them together. There's a shuffle of clothing and the tear of the condom wrapper, and that's it. I can't take it. I'm all for playing a sexy game with this man, but his reasons for all of this get to me. They really do.

I turn around and my mouth goes dry as I find him naked, rippling, long, lean muscle from head to toe, his cock jutted forward, and the condom is in place. He drags me to him, his erection pressing to my hip. "I told you not to move."

"I've already had your mouth," I say, not even sure where this daring in me is coming from, but it's alive and well with this man.

His eyes spark with amber flecks but there is something more in his gaze, a knife of emotion that I feel like a cut. "Is that right?" he asks, his voice low, raspy, his mood as dark as a stormy night.

"Yes," I say, and I can feel his bottled-up torment in every part of me and it strips away my fear of being hurt by Eric. I dare to say exactly what I feel. "I hate that you left that night. I'm glad you're here now."

His lashes lower and I have this sense that he doesn't want me to read some emotion in his eyes before he looks at me again and says, "Me too, princess. Me too."

Those words, a few small words, hold so much implication and they expand between us, stealing my breath. We stare at each other and what passes between us is almost too much, it confuses me. It calls to me. He calls to me and I want to know him. I want to understand him. In some ways, I already do and I believe he knows this. Which is exactly why my hand settles on top of the stunningly created jaguar on his arm, and I don't miss the very Kingston-like blue eyes, or the fact that his animal is a symbol of the Competing car brand. "Is it a fuck you to Kingston Motors?"

"I'm pretty sure my father considers me a fuck you to the Kingston name." He leans in to kiss me, his mouth lingering just above mine. "I'd have already fucked them if Grayson hadn't held me back. You need to know that."

"Of course, you could have fucked them ten times over. Everyone knows it. And I know you don't believe me, but the idea that you could have and didn't, I like that about you."

He doesn't reply, but seconds tick by before his mouth is on my mouth, and this time, there's no holding back. He's not about control this time. He's about consuming me. He's about drinking me in and touching me and I don't hold back. I have wanted him for so very long. I've compared everyone to him for no justifiable reason except he was a fantasy bigger than life. A man with a common bond and more of an understanding of who and what I am than he ever knew. We are both wild, burning alive, touching each other, but suddenly, he pulls back, staring down at me, searching my face for something, I don't know what.

My fingers find his face, the rasp of stubble on my skin as I trace the strong line of his jaw. His hand covers mine and suddenly he kisses me again, a hard, punishing kiss, as if he's angry. I taste it. I feel it as he smacks my backside again. I yelp and I have no idea why I'm so incredibly aroused by him doing this, but everything with this man is well, everything. And that's it. That's why I'm so damn aroused. This is him. He's more exposed than not. His anger—and he *is* angry—is a piece of him.

"You want to punish me for who I am," I accuse, my fingers curling on his chest. "You want to own me because of who I am."

"I want a lot of things where you're concerned, Harper," he says, tangling rough fingers in my hair. "Too many fucking things."

"The bastard doesn't get to fuck me. Whatever you do, you own. Whatever I do, it's with you, Eric."

"Is that right?"

"Oh yes. That's right."

His jaw sets hard, his eyes burning a mix of hot fire and anger, I think. He turns me to the bed and before I know his intent, I'm on my knees in front of him. It's then that I realize just how determined he is to own me, how much he actually needs this from me. It's not about sex, either. It's about family, and the empire that has dominated his life.

It's about him owning me, and through me, them. It's about this moment. It's about now. No matter what I do, I can't change this need in him. I'm not sure I want to change it. Let him own me. In some ways, he has for six long years.

Chapter Eleven

Harper

His fingers slide into my sex and sensations rock my body. I arch into the touch, and his cock slides along the seam of my body, back and forth, back and forth, until—oh God—he's pressing inside me. He's stretching me, filling me in a long, slow slide until he's buried deep. And then he pulls back and thrusts hard.

I gasp and his hands shackle my hips, he's driving into me, pumping hard and fast, and I want more, so much more, that I forget what that even means—just more of this man, of this night, of everything where he's concerned. Yes, everything. I forget everything but the pleasure of him inside me until suddenly he stops and leans into me, his face buried against my back, his cock still throbbing inside me. "Eric," I breathe out, confused, and aching for more.

He shifts and pulls out of me, and before I can recover the shock to my body, we're on the bed, and he's pulling me to face him, lifting my leg and pressing back inside me; filling me again, and when he's buried deep once more, he strokes my hair from my face and tilts my gaze to his. "I decided I wanted you to know who's fucking you."

"Because you want me to know the bastard son fucked me?"

"No, Harper. Because I want you to know that I came here for *you*, not them. Just you."

My breath hitches in my throat at his words; words that don't divide us, but unite us. "I didn't come for them. I swear to you, this isn't for them. It's for me and—"

He brushes his lips over mine. "Just be here with me right now. This is just us. I'm leaving them out of it. I wasn't, but I am now. You leave them out of it, too." He strokes the dampness from my lips. "Just me and you and years of regret, because I *do* regret leaving."

"You do?"

"You, not them." His lips curve. "I should have picked up a box of condoms and then taken you someplace far away and used every damn one of them."

I laugh and smile, too. "Yes. Yes, you should have."

His mouth comes down on mine, and the energy shift between us is sharp and yet rich with passion and emotion. It's gentler. It's deeper. The press of tongue to tongue a caress, not a demand. The soft sway of his body against mine, seductive and slow. His kisses drink me in, seem to savor the taste of me as I do him, but at some point, I don't know when we snap. His hand cups my backside and he pulls me hard against him, his fingers stroking my sex from behind even as he pumps into me. We need now. We need so much and yet the feeling is there—the sense that we can't have more, yet we have to have it. We have to have each other. I have never felt anything like it. I have never wanted anything like this. I have never kissed anyone like I would die without the next lick of his tongue, but I do Eric.

We rock and grind and pump until that rise to pleasure is to the level of no return. I can't stop the tumble into release and my sex clenches around him, his low, guttural groan my reward, the shudder of his body following. We ride the rush of release together and when we collapse, we hold onto each other, but as seconds tick by, reality seeps into the room, and I can almost feel it trying to pull us apart. He hates the Kingstons and he won't help me. I know what's coming. We both know what's coming and that's another goodbye, but it won't come with any more closure than we had six years ago.

At least not for me.

He's right. He owned me tonight. In some ways, he's owned me for six years. I fear that he still will when I leave this city, no doubt now without him.

He strokes my hair, a gentle, regretful touch like he's thinking the same thing as me, but he doesn't speak.

He pulls out of me before rolling away and sitting up to toss the condom in a trashcan. I suddenly feel naked and exposed but it doesn't matter what I feel. It doesn't matter how much I don't want to push him to help me. Every reservation I just had about this being a bad idea matters. There are reasons it can't matter. I have to push him. I start to roll away to get dressed and ready for battle, but he's already back, catching my arm and now we're both naked on our knees on the bed, facing each other.

"Running away?" he challenges.

"I came here for you. Why would I run?"

"I won't help them."

"Help *me*."

"I'll give you a job at double the pay you make there and there are no conditions. If we never fuck again, we don't fuck again. I can place you in any state, or several countries, for that matter. I'll get you a new start."

"My mother—"

"Take her with you."

"She won't leave him," I say. "She married my father at a very young age. They were in love. Losing him left her devastated. Your father took over her life and her money when she was vulnerable and not in a good way. I can't leave her. Not in the way you suggest."

"You said you were going to leave."

"Before the recalls," I remind him. "Before she could end up in trouble with the rest of them. I *have* to go back. Go back with me."

"If I go back there, I'll finish them off. I won't save them. Still want me to go with you?"

"Yes. I do. Because I don't believe you're the bastard you want everyone to believe you are or you would have already done it."

"You're wrong." His jaw sets. "And there's nothing more to say, at least not by me." In other words, there's more to say, and I'm the one who has to say it. And there is, but I'm not sure any of it changes anything. It might even make it worse.

He releases me, leaving me cold and aching for his touch. I don't just want this man. Some part of me needs him beyond logic. Maybe it's the connection to something we both want to call home that can never really be that for either of us. Maybe it's more. I really don't know or want to understand. It doesn't matter. He's no longer touching me and maybe he never will again.

He's already dressing and somehow that feels like a slap. Me naked on the bed while he dresses certainly feels cold and done. He's done. He's made his decision to leave, probably before he ever arrived. He wanted to fuck me. He wanted to own me. It was all part of what he's just declared. He wants to ruin his father and brother. I'm nothing more than an extension of them. God, I'm a fool but what did I expect? The minute I allowed myself to be naked with him, it must have seemed like I was fucking him to get a favor.

Embarrassed, I scramble off the bed and find my sweats, pulling them on. Once we're both dressed, he walks to my room service tray and opens it. "Macaroni and cheese," he says.

"My favorite food," I reply and I have no idea why this feels almost as intimate of an admission as anything else between us tonight. I regret sharing this part of me with him, but then, why wouldn't I? I'm just a revenge fuck to him.

He closes the space between us and I tell myself to back away. I tell myself to end this now, but I can't stand the idea of never touching him again. I can't resist the need to feel his hands on my body just one more time. I suck in air, waiting for it, wanting it, and when he slides his hand under my hair to my neck, I feel this man, who would be my enemy by his own definition, everywhere, inside and out.

"Just one of the many things," he says, "that I would have liked to have known about you, Harper." He kisses me, a light brush of lips over lips, and then he pulls back. "But that can't happen. There's something you haven't told me. You haven't been honest with me and that makes you one of them." His hands fall away from me, rejection in the action, and then he's walking away, the door his destination.

I want to scream at him that I'm not one of them, but I don't, I can't. Because in ways I don't want to be, I am. I have to let him walk out the door and he does. He's gone. I'm alone, but no matter how I connect to his family, I'm still a fish in a sea of Kingston sharks, and I'm going to have to grow my own teeth.

Chapter Twelve

Harper

*There are people who float in and out of our lives, like ships
passing in the night never meant to stop or know one another,
but what happens when they do?*

The idea of leaving New York City and Eric behind is brutal, as if
I'm leaving a piece of myself, and that's just nuts. Last night was sex,
nothing more. Six years ago was also sex, nothing more. He came.
He made me come. He left. He didn't look back. And yet here I am,
fretting over leaving without seeing him again, to the point that I'm
pacing my hotel room and contemplating skipping my flight.

I tell myself it's because I need his help, but I know this runs
deeper for me. That man affects me and if I thought this trip would
provide closure that would allow me to move on from that party
six years ago, and him with it, I didn't get it. More of Eric fed my
need for even more of him.

The doorman knocks on my door, an alert that tells me, I'm out
of time. It's officially decision time and for me, that comes back to
one key thing: Eric was right. I haven't told him everything. I also
can't lie to him the way everyone else in this family has, but if I
turn the wrong pages, expose him to the deep, dark tales, his words
will prove true: he'll ruin the Kingston family and that means my
mother and my father's legacy along with it. I was playing with fire
coming here. It's time to go home before I do something I'll regret
the rest of my life. Decision solidified, I let the doorman in.

An hour and a half later, I'm on a plane, and when I should
be trying to decide how to move on without Eric, creating a plan
to save my family business, I'm thinking about him—and every
touch, every kiss, every word we've shared plays in my mind over
and over again and my regrets are many. I should have said more. I
should have stopped him from walking away, but I remind myself
I couldn't. He saw too much and it would be foolish to expect a

genius who sees too much to stop seeing too much. You don't ask a man like Eric to help you see what you can't and expect him not to see everything.

By the time I'm on the ground, it's early evening, and when I walk into my downtown home, I strip down to sweats and a T-shirt, order takeout, and sit down at my computer. It's time to focus on what's before me. My cellphone rings with Gigi's number and I let it go to voicemail. I need a plan before I talk to her. She's no spring chicken and the idea of Eric helping us seemed to have calmed her down. I need to give her another rope to hang onto. Heck, I need to give myself another rope to hang onto. Hiring help appears to be my next best move, and that help has to be someone that can't be bought off by Isaac. A difficult task when Isaac floats in a boatload of money while I have a canoe and possess limited resources.

An idea stirs, and I snatch my purse and pull out the business card I'd grabbed from Eric's desk. Confirming his cellphone and his email are on it, I pull up my own email and before I can talk myself out of it, I start to type:

Eric—

I grabbed your card from your desk. I wanted to call but it felt like you were pretty finished when you left. I wasn't, but that just seems to be how things work with us.

I stop myself. What am I doing? This isn't a personal email. I should delete that. I start again.

Eric—

I grabbed your card from your desk. I wanted to call, but I thought you might welcome an email more freely. I know that your history in Denver runs deep and dark. I shouldn't have asked you to come back here in the first place, but I need someone to help me figure this out. I need to hire someone and Isaac has money and resources that I don't. I need someone I can trust who can't be bought off. So, this is me asking for help one last time. Who would you hire to investigate Kingston Motors? Just a referral would be appreciated and I don't even have to mention your name.

Harper

I read the message and while there's more, so much more, that I want to say, I think better. I hit send and hope for a reply. In the meantime, I start researching and looking for someone I can hire on my own. I create a list of operations outside of Denver who will be less influenced by Isaac and my stepfather, who may or may not be a part of what's going on.

Hours later, I lay in bed, staring at the ceiling, my mind racing. I grab my phone from the nightstand, pull up my email, disappointment stabbing at me with the discovery that there's nothing from Eric. I'm such a fool. Obviously, I was nothing more than a conquest he needed to get out of his system. And he did. I *should have* known, and for reasons I can't explain, it felt like something more happened between us, like there was a real connection, something lasting, but clearly, I was wrong. It's time to move on. And yet, as I doze off, slipping into the haze of early slumber, I'm back in the past, living that moment by the pool when his eyes had found me, the tingling sensation running down my spine. The lift of my gaze and the force of that man's attention. I've clearly never recovered.

My memory floats forward to me standing on that stage, scanning the crowd for Eric and catching a glimpse of him disappearing down the path. I wanted to shout for him to come back.

"Good riddance," Isaac had murmured next to me. "I hope he's leaving."

And he had. He'd left. I'd felt that certainty like a sharp knife in my chest even before I knew. And yet still, the minute I was free of that stage, the minute the world of people I'd spoken in front of were focused solely on my stepfather, I'd hurried to confirm. I'd walked that path toward the cottage, my heart racing in my chest, and found the door unlocked. I'd also found the cottage empty. And I'd gone to bed that night, like I am this one, with the feel of his hands on my body, the scent of him in my nostrils. Those piercing eyes haunting me, and the two nicknames that define our separation in my mind: the princess and the bastard.

<hr />

I'm sitting on the slate gray couch of my living room with a whiskey in my hand and my MacBook on the coffee table in front of me, that damn email from Harper open and staring back at me as it has for a good two hours. I down the amber liquid in my glass, a smooth thirty-year, and much needed when stomaching anything Kingston. I snatch up the Rubik's cube sitting on the table beside me and start turning it, the numbers in my head telling stories that no one else would understand, and doing so every damn moment of my life. Right now, they're telling the story of the bastard and the princess.

I set the damn cube down and stand up, walking to the floor-to-ceiling window to the left of the main living area. I stop in front of the glass and nothing but inky night touches my eyes, a storm on the horizon. Out there beyond that darkness is a spectacular Manhattan skyline to kill for that I worked my ass off to earn. That no one named Kingston gave me. They don't get to give or take from me ever again. And they did take.

I press my hands to the glass, cold seeping through my palms and sliding up my arms, but there is fire in my blood, memories of the only person that could ever get me to give two fucks about anything Kingston in my mind: *Harper.*

My lashes lower, numbers exploding in my mind that become all about her again. And I end up replaying exactly ten different moments with Harper in my arms, with me inside her, the scent of her on my skin, the taste of her on my lips. What the hell is it about her that makes me need another taste? That makes me remember how she tastes? What is it about her that drives me fucking insane? It should be over. I finally had her. I fucked her, so what if I want to do it about another twenty times? It's over. That's how it has to be.

I need help, she'd said in her message.

My lashes lift and I shove off the window. I do not help the Kingston family.

The end.

The princess is part of their clan now, and six years deep, at that. Helping her is helping them, and she wasn't even honest with me. There was something she wasn't telling me. She didn't even deny that as truth. I sit back down on the couch and refill my glass. I don't like unknowns and where the Kingstons are concerned, that gets personal. Especially after they sought me out through Harper.

What don't I know and what consequences are there to not knowing?

Chapter Thirteen

Harper

*S*mart girls know their strengths and one of them is wearing high heels, my father once told me. They're weapons. You can seduce us men with them or you can beat our asses with the end of one of those heels. I'd laughed at the insanity of that idea, but now, I wish fighting was that simple.

It's my first day back in Denver after Eric's rejection, and while my body still hums with his touch, I've accepted I must find another way to save my father's legacy. I'm not someone to tuck tail and run. nor do I allow myself to wallow in failure for long. I take my blows, feel them hard and fast, and then dust myself off. I'm already there, already ready to fight again.

I waste no time dressing and hurrying to work, and by eight in the morning, I'm in my office at the Kingston corporate offices. Today my dark hair is tied neatly at my nape, rather than loose the way I like it, a style I see as no-nonsense and all business. I've dressed in a black suit, with a pale pink shell beneath it, because I like to remind the world that I'm not one of the guys any more than I'm one of the Kingstons. I need that distinction today, and I hate that part of it is to spite Eric.

No matter what he wants to believe of me, I'm *not* one of them. I am not a Kingston and will never be. I'm my father's daughter, and that means I fight for what I believe in and for others. Right now, I just have to protect our customers, my mother, and even Gigi, who hasn't always deserved being saved. Maybe she doesn't now. I understand why Eric despises her. When I entered this family, she was horrible to me, too, but seeing someone almost die and then beg for forgiveness has a way of getting to you.

I sit down at my desk and pull out my MacBook as well as the pad of paper where I wrote the different companies I want to call for aid, but I can't help myself. I power up my computer and I hate that I have enough hope left in me that I check one last time for a reply from Eric. I actually hold my breath waiting for my email to load, only to find nothing from him in my inbox. I said I was letting go and moving on, but the enemy of your enemy is your friend. And Isaac and my stepfather have always been enemies, even when I was too naive to heed the warning Eric had given me about being used with no endgame for me but defeat.

I stand up with the intent of shutting my door, only to have Isaac appear in the doorway, and in his ridiculously expensive suit, there's no way I can avoid a comparison between him and Eric. "I see you're back to work," he says, his voice rich with accusation. He's a good-looking man, his hair perfect, his jawline sharp, clean. He's refined, and some would say perfectly male, and yet unbidden, that memory of the rasp of Eric's whiskers on my belly reminds me that Eric is so much more than his brother. And I realize now that the two men do not resemble each other at all. Isaac's features are sharper, and his presence is all about demand and arrogance. Eric is more rugged male, a force of nature, effortless dominance in his very existence and Issac overcompensates in all the wrong ways to merely stand in his shadow.

"How was your trip?" he asks, hitching a broad shoulder on the doorframe, obviously planning to stay longer than I'd like. Well, unless he's going to give me the answers he's been avoiding about the recalls.

"It was a much needed long weekend," I say, hoping to avoid a topic laced with lies. My lies about why I took off of work.

"Who were you with again?"

"Don't play coy, Isaac," I say, fighting the urge to cross my arms in front of myself in a defensive move Isaac is too smart not to read. "We both know I didn't tell you who I was taking a trip with."

"And yet, I'm your brother," he reminds me, an undertone of accusation in his words. He's suspicious about the trip. I've questioned the recalls. I've tried to see paperwork he won't let me see.

"My *stepbrother*," I say, and then I dare to go to the place I don't want to go, but he's headed. "One who doesn't act like a brother and we both know it. Otherwise, you wouldn't have—"

"I get it," he snaps, straightening, clearly intending to shut me down before I can go down an awkward rabbit hole of unbrotherly love. "You don't want to tell me who you're fucking," he snaps. "I get it, but I need to know this isn't a distraction from your job."

"I live for this place."

"You haven't been here," he replies dryly. "And I have an issue that needed to be dealt with yesterday. You weren't here to handle it."

"I had my phone with me at all times. What issue and why didn't you call me?"

"I didn't call because this problem needs your full attention, and obviously, that wasn't here." He doesn't give me time to reply. "The union's bitching about the women's bathroom in the plant. I have no clue what the problem is, but it's a distraction I don't need right now. I need you to run front line on this issue—deal with them. Get them pink fucking toilet paper if you have to. They want to start negotiations tomorrow. I'll email you the details." And with that, he disappears into the hallway.

Pink toilet paper is what he wants me to handle? And he wants me to negotiate with the union, which isn't my job. We have an employee on staff who's an expert in this area. Angry now, I round my desk and head down the hallway, following him all the way toward the corner office that he calls his castle, quite literally. He disappears inside and I pass his secretary's desk, thankful she's not there right now. Not that it would matter. Belinda is in her fifties, quiet, reserved, and a mouse in a cat's cave who couldn't be more submissive to Isaac. That's how Isaac likes everyone.

Submissive.

He tries to shut his door and I catch it. "Why can't the union negotiator handle pink toilet paper, Isaac?" I ask, certain this is all about keeping me busy.

His green eyes are as cool as they are calculating. "You really aren't good at taking orders." He leaves me in the doorway and enters his fancy office, rounding his mahogany desk, a grand mountain view and expensive artwork on the walls on either side of us because he's showy. The entire Kingston family is showy, while my father instilled humility and graciousness in my mind. Though he spoiled my mother in ways that seem to have made a showy appeal to her or we wouldn't be here now.

Isaac presses his hands on the desk. "Just do your job," he snaps. "I have a meeting in fifteen minutes."

"Since when does a member of the family, a managing member of the executive team, just do their job without asking questions?" I ask, stepping into the room without closing the door. I don't do small spaces with Isaac. I learned that lesson the hard way years ago. I stop behind a leather chair and settle my hands on the back. "That's not what your father taught me. He said—"

"The union is breathing down our throats," he snaps. "Our product is good. If we have a flaw, it's human. They don't like my attitude on this."

Finally, he's actually talking about the problem. "How can you be sure our product is good? What have we done to ensure—"

"Everything," he says. "I have this under control. Just appease the union."

"Appease the union, or stay busy and out of your hair?"

"Both, Harper," he bites out. "I have this under control. I have everything under control."

"From where I'm standing, that's questionable."

Shock runs through me at the sound of Eric's voice. I rotate to face the door to find him standing there, looking like a rebel with a cause, his dark hair a rumpled sexy mess, his jaw shadowed, and apparently, he left his suits in his hotel room, at least today. He's dressed in faded jeans and a Bennett Enterprises T-shirt that hugs his hard body, his brightly inked arms in full, colorful display, his message clear: *The bastard is home. What are you going to do about it?* And when his blue eyes meet mine, they burn a path along my nerve endings, and deliver yet another message, one meant for me and me alone—I'm here for you.

Chapter Fourteen

Harper

I can't breathe with Eric's unexpected appearance, with the proof that he didn't ignore my email, that he didn't ignore my plea for help. He simply answered me in person, but when Isaac demands, "What the fuck are you doing here, Eric?" I'm suddenly trapped, a rat in a cage between two bigger beasts, and I don't know how to react. I don't know if this is what Eric wanted.

"Good to see you, too," Eric says dryly.

Isaac leans on the desk, perfectly manicured hands pressed to the hardwood surface. "Seriously, Eric," he says. "What *the fuck* are you doing here?"

Eric doesn't look at me. He focuses on his brother, his lips, those beautiful lips that I know to be oh-so-punishing when he wants them to be, lifting ever so slightly. "I'm family," he says, those words pure sarcasm. "Why the fuck haven't I been here sooner *should* be your question, but you know, you never call, you never write. It's really heartbreaking."

Isaac narrows his eyes on Eric and he pushes off the desk, unbuttoning his suit jacket and settling his hands on his hips, his gaze raking over his brother—no, his bastard brother. "You can't afford a suit with all those millions I hear you made?"

"A billion," I say before I can stop myself. "He's a billionaire now."

Isaac's attention rockets to me. "Bullshit."

"It's true," I assure him, because while yes, I've randomly read up on Eric's successes, Gigi told me before I ever left for Denver. "He just hit the billionaire mark." I can feel Eric's attention settle on me, heavy and sharp, and I suddenly regret those words. Now, it seems like I went to him, chasing his money.

My gaze snaps to his, the connection jolting me—my God, this man affects me. "You're very successful. That was my point."

"Was it now?" he says, shadows in his eyes that I do not wholly understand, but I am certain they relate to the bastard and the princess, and not in a good way. He thinks I'm one of them. He thinks I went to him with an agenda that wasn't what I claimed. He thinks I used him and now, he's here to make us all pay.

"I have work to do and so does Harper," Isaac snaps. "We'll have to have the happy reunion charade later."

Eric dismisses this idea in four words. "Later won't work for me." He advances into the room, all long-legged swagger, to stop in front of Isaac's desk. "I've been hired to do a full audit of the company's operations and paid well enough to ensure I'm willing to spend time here."

My cheeks heat with anger and embarrassment. I'm right. He's not here for me. Gigi paid him. Of course, she did. I told her not to. I told her that would change the dynamic of his presence here. Isaac laughs. "No one paid you to audit our operations. I'm the president and my father damn sure wouldn't have called you in."

I grip the back of a chair, my only shield in the war of brothers I've never quite experienced until now. I wonder if I knew how bad it was would I have gone to Eric, but who am I fooling? I would have seized any excuse to see Eric again. I all but craved another encounter with him. I still do, even knowing now that he most likely isn't here to help me.

Eric perches on the edge of Isaac's desk, power radiating off of him as if he's just taken ownership of the entire room. "You're scared shitless that Pops is up to his old games, aren't you?"

There's a flicker of something in Isaac's eyes that he quickly banks, but I saw it and if I saw it, Eric saw it. "I've earned my place here. He trusts me. So, no, asshole. I'm not afraid of anything that has your name attached to it."

"No?" Eric presses, his hand settling on his powerful thigh, muscle flexing beneath his ink, a portion of the jaguar exposed, lines of numbers beneath it. I wonder about those numbers. I wonder if he wanted that jaguar to be exposed to mock everyone in this building, including me.

"No. We both know you rode Grayson Bennett to the bank. Is there trouble in paradise? You need a new ride? It's too late for that."

"You're not afraid of anything with my name attached," Eric repeats. "Interesting and good to know. That'll make it easy for me to get everything I need from you."

"The only thing you need from me is a kick in the ass to get out of my office. I have work to do." He swats at Eric like he's a gnat, the bastard brother, only this bastard brother is a billionaire who is smarter than him. I fight my urge to protect Eric. He can protect himself and I'm terrified that Gigi has given him the opening to destroy us.

"You'll get him *whatever he wants.*"

At the sound of Gigi's voice, I turn to find her standing in the doorway, and at five-foot-one with flaming red hair and piercing blue eyes, she might be seventy-seven, but she's a force to be reckoned with. "You underestimate me, boy," she snaps, her voice louder than one would expect her capable of at her advanced age, but her hand trembles, and I swear Isaac does as well. "I told you I need to know what's going on," she adds, curling her fingers into her palms. "You told me to rock away in my rocking chair, which by the way, I don't own a rocking chair."

"Grandmother—"

"Gigi," she amends. "I'm Gigi around these parts, the woman who started this place, like Harper's father started her family's business. Now let's get real for once. Either there's something going on you don't want to tell me about or there's something you don't know. Your brother will figure it out."

"No," Isaac says in instant rejection. "No, he will not. There's nothing going on here but normal business. You will not disrupt our operation. You're getting old and paranoid."

She snorts. "Not old enough to suit you. Eric gets his brains from me." She looks at Eric. "Didn't know that, did you? I'm smarter than the average gal, despite the fact I let Grayson Bennett steal you away from us." She doesn't give him time to reply. She homes in on Isaac again and orders, "Get him what he asks for, son. Don't make this more difficult than it has to be."

"You don't have the power to make this call," Isaac argues. "I know you did this while Dad is in Europe for a reason, to sideswipe me and root Eric in my business before he could stop you, but he's one phone call away and our combined stock overrules yours."

"Actually," Eric says dryly. "My stock with Gigi's combined overrules any vote."

"You don't own stock," he snaps.

"I do now," Eric counters. "I bought out the bank this morning with a premium they couldn't resist."

Isaac goes completely, utterly still and I watch as hell swims in the depths of his stare. "You did *what?*" he bites out, while I reel at this unexpected turn of events that might just change this company forever, and I'm not sure it's for the better, not when I see the real anger between these brothers.

"Family needs to be protected by family," Eric says, his gaze shifting to Gigi. "Don't you think, Gigi?"

She swallows hard, a telltale sign that she had no idea he'd done such a thing. "Yes," she says. "And I haven't always remembered that, son. I do now."

"So, Harper tells me," he says dryly, eyeing Isaac, "I'll work in the conference room for now. Get me access to all databases and all facilities."

"That will take time," Isaac says.

"I'll get it done myself," Eric says. "I'm impatient like that." His attention shifts to me, his blue eyes sharp, but unreadable. "You'll work on the audit with me. Everything else will come second. It was one of my terms when I agreed to do the audit." Perhaps it's my imagination, but I swear that his voice lowers, the heat in his eyes smoldering with possession as he adds, "You're all mine."

Chapter Fifteen

Harper

I'm burning alive under Eric's scorching attention, melting right here in the center of Isaac's office with the message in his burning blue-eyed stare: he came here for me. He also promised to finish this family off if he returned. Maybe that means he intends to fuck me in every possible way this time. I don't know. I just know that as seconds tick by, our present company of Isaac and Gigi fades away and there is just the two of us and a challenge that I don't understand, but I'm certain I will soon.

"I'll leave you three to get this done," Gigi says, snapping me back to the room just in time to find her exiting the office.

"Go do your job, Harper," Isaac snaps at me. "Eric and I need to have a conversation alone."

Eric's lips twitch, his eyes never leaving mine, nor mine his. "I'll find you when we're done," he says, and there is this heady possessive undertone to those words that is anything but professional. This is a promise that we still have unfinished business, that we are far from done, and I have never felt so owned in my life. Considering this place, this family has made me feel pretty darn owned, that's saying a lot. It's different with Eric, though. *He's different* from Isaac and the rest of them in ways that connect with me on every level. I *crave* this man's confidence. I *need* this man's touch. I *understand* this man's hunger for revenge in ways that he can't know, and yet, I fear that very need in him is why he's here, is why he's now dangerous.

"You can leave the door open," he adds, his tone sharpening with a swift change in mood as he refocuses on his brother. "Isaac and I won't be long."

The air crackles and this time it's not about me and Eric. It's about him and Isaac and that snaps me out of my lusty haze and shoots me straight into fight mode. My gaze jerks to Isaac. "He's here because Gigi wants answers. I tried to tell you that. I asked and asked you to help me give them to her. You dismissed her as an old lady and forgot how much power she has. So, suck it up and just give Eric what he needs. Give Gigi what she wants." I look at Eric. "As for you. You aren't a bastard because he calls you one. You're a bastard if you choose to be one." I look between them. "We're family whether you two like it or not. You need to figure this out."

I march for the door and exit, Eric's voice following me as he says, "She has no idea what kind of bastard I really am, now does she, Isaac?"

That statement, layered with history, halts my steps and I lean on the wall waiting for more. What does that even mean? I need to know what that means and I wait for an explanation, but the door shuts. I'm shut out. Damn it. I push off the wall and hurry down the hallway, reaching the elevator just as it closes, no doubt missing Gigi by seconds. I cut right and take the stairs, rushing down the winding path until I reach the bottom level just as the elevator doors open.

Gigi steps out and pauses to smooth the red dress she's wearing, oblivious to how the color clashes with her hair, which is more orange than red. "I expected you before I made it to the elevator," she says, cutting me a look, her blue eyes so like Eric's in this moment that I shiver. "You're late," she adds and starts walking toward her office, which is the only office down here by her design.

"That wasn't exactly neutral territory you left me in," I say, easily catching up to her despite the fact that she's remarkably spry for her age. "And you know I don't like you down here. You don't even keep a secretary. What if something happened to you?"

She waves me off the way Isaac tried to wave off Eric and with the same failed results. "I'm fine down here. This is the she cave, no men allowed." She pauses at her doorway. "Eric's quite the looker these days, isn't he?"

My cheeks heat and she laughs. "You noticed." She disappears through the doorway. "And I noticed the spark between you two," she calls over her shoulder.

Of course, she did. "And you," I say, swiftly changing the subject and following her inside what is more a small executive apartment than an office, "should have warned me about what just happened."

"And you," she counters, "should have told me when you left New York City. He called me."

"And you offered him how much money?"

"Enough to get him here."

"He's a billionaire now," I say. "He doesn't need your money."

"He damn sure took it," she says, pointing at the chair next to her. "Sit."

I ignore the order, stopping in front of her, my hands on my hips. "He didn't need that money," I repeat. "He took it because he could make you pay him. Because he hates you that much. He's now got stock. He came here to destroy us."

"And you really think that if he would have come without the payday, he would have had another motive?"

"He's here to take over," I say because it sounds better than his promise that his return would be to "finish us off."

"Better him than someone else," she shocks me by saying. "At least then I'll die with this place in the hands of someone who's blood, someone who will make it thrive. We don't know what is going on, but we know it's bad. This is my legacy. I don't want it to end in jail."

"Gigi—"

She holds up a hand. "He's brilliant. He'll save your father's legacy along with mine. Go. Work. Get him what he needs. This is what we both wanted. Eric here, finding out what's wrong. We got it. Now he's here."

"For the wrong reasons," I say.

She purses her lips. "We'll see. He wanted to be a part of this family from the day he met his father. We didn't make him feel like he belonged. And understandably after that, he needed a reason other than that need to be here now. Money, and even revenge, serve that purpose. Now go. Keep an ear to what's happening."

I could fight with her, but that achieves nothing obviously and I really do feel a need to be back upstairs, but she's dismissed my stepfather in all of this. "Your son—"

"Jeff will suck it up and deal with it, just like you. Go."

I give up, at least for now. I turn and head for the door. "Harper?"

I turn to face her. "Yes?"

"I love you, honey, and you've been there for me this past year, but when I tell you to do something, you do it. This is still your job. We both know I gave you instructions where Eric was concerned and you ignored me.""

She's right. I did. I didn't want him back here this way for reasons I'd point out, but she won't listen. I nod and exit the office, a million emotions clawing at me, but I show none. Emotions are used against you in this place. My need to protect my mother and even my father's legacy is why I'm still here. That need is an emotion. It's trouble, like Eric, and I can't seem to walk away from that combination.

Eager to be in my own space, where I can privately melt down and then stand back up and fight, I hurry up the stairs. The doorway to my office is like sweet relief. I enter my office and I've made it all of two steps when I hear. "Hello, princess."

I whirl around to find Eric in the doorway and he doesn't stay there. He shuts the door and strides toward me, the look in his eyes as predatory as the jaguar on his arm, and like all prey, I'm thrust into a moment where I must make a decision to stand and fight or run. And I am prey. His prey, and before I can make a move, he's standing in front of me, that earthy male scent of him seducing me.

"We're not done yet," he says. "Just in case you hadn't figured that out by now."

Chapter Sixteen

Harper

I have about thirty seconds to process Eric's declaration that we're not done before he pulls me close, all that sinewy muscle absorbing my body, that powerful edge that is this man, owning me, and he owns me all too easily. I try to resist. I know I'm the enemy to him. My hand settles on his chest but I'm not sure if it's to touch him or push him away.

"Eric," I whisper, and I feel the charge radiating between us, the heat, the ten shades of lust that come from deep, dark places for him and for me; they just exist, because he exists.

He tangles his fingers in my hair, and lowers his mouth to mine. "We are definitely not done yet," he repeats, the words almost guttural and then his lips are on my lips, his tongue stroking long and deep, stealing my breath and driving away everything but how he tastes, how he feels; that's how easily I'm lost and found in this man. It doesn't matter that he could very well be the one to destroy us. Not in this moment, not when he's kissing me, not when I get that one last taste of him I've wished for these past hours, but it's not a kiss that he allows me to drown in, it's not even a kiss that lets me swim in the moment.

He tears his mouth from mine, his lips a warm breath from another kiss that I hunger for in ways I didn't know any man could make me hunger. "I'm here now," he declares. "Just like you wanted."

His touch, his taste, his very existence in this room is burning me alive, but so is the hate between him and this family, *his* family. "This isn't how I wanted you."

One of his hands slides up between my shoulder blades, molding me close. The other caresses up my waist, cupping my breast, sending a wave of sensations through my body. "How did you want me, Harper?"

My lashes lower and I pant out a breath. How did I want him? Too many ways. So many ways. "Impossible ways," I say, trying to tear away from his grip, but he pulls me back to him, that damn earthy scent of him driving me insane, consuming me the way he's threatening to consume me. The way he already has in some ways for six long years.

"Let go," I growl. "Let go *now*."

"What impossible ways?"

"Without the hate. You can't be here and not hate."

"Is that what you think? That I hate you?"

"The bastard and the princess. You say it over and over. I felt it in that hotel room. You wanted to punish me."

"I wanted a lot of things in that hotel room. I still do."

"You don't even deny it."

"Did I want to spank you? Yes. Did I want to fuck you hard and fast and do it all over again? Yes. Did I want to fuck you out of my system once and for fucking all? Yes, I did. But I failed. I failed and now I'm here." He maneuvers me to the desk and presses me against it, his big body caging mine.

"Stop. I'm not fucking a man who hates me again, but apparently, I am going to get fucked by him in all kinds of ways. I should've never asked you for help. And yes, you *are* a bastard, and not by name. I told you. You claim that with actions."

"What haven't you told me, Harper?" he demands, wanting information with me as a side order.

I ignore the question that bites in more ways than he will ever know. "We're not finished, you said?" I dare, hating that I melt for him when he has an agenda, hating even more that I opened the door to that agenda. "You mean you're not done using me?"

"Who's using who, princess? You came to me."

"I didn't use you. I'm *not* using you, unless a request for honest help is now considered using."

"No?"

"No. And who is really using who? You just kissed me to get information."

"I kissed you because I couldn't fucking help myself, and for the record, I don't like what I can't control."

"You hate me. Stop kissing me."

"I don't hate you, Harper. I hate secrets and lies. What aren't you telling me?"

"Like Gigi didn't tell you?" I scoff. "I know she told you." I shove at his chest, a sudden need to have the clear head his body touching my body won't give me.

His hands shackle my hips, the touch scorching, possessive. Controlling. "Tell me yourself."

"I was supposed to offer you money. I didn't. I refused."

His eyes narrow, lips thin. "And why exactly didn't you offer me money?"

"You don't need it."

"Is that right?" he asks, sounding amused.

"Yes, it is. You don't need it, but that wasn't the point. The point was that the man who came here for money, came here for financial gain, not to help his family."

"These people are not my family. *You* are not my family."

I recoil as if slapped. "I know how you feel about me. I get it. I just told you that. That princess thing is all about reminding me that we're divided."

"We're only divided if you're with them."

"I'm trying to make my way, just like you did, Eric, but my mom is here and she's made foolish decisions. That doesn't make me love her less, though. If it were your mother—"

"I'd have gotten her out."

"You think I haven't tried? She's a fool for your father and for the record, I fucked you. I kissed you. That doesn't mean I can't think beyond an orgasm. I won't be a fool for you like she was for your father." I shove on his chest. "Get off of me. Get back."

"Is that what you really want? For me to back away? For me to get back on a plane and go away?"

"Like you'd do that now? You bought stock. You decided to take over."

"You don't take on a Kingston without leverage. I made sure I had leverage. To help you. You asked for help. I'm here. So, let me repeat this," His hands settle on my face, his voice softening, "I came *for you.*"

Heat sears the air between us, a hot flash of desire fueled by how good we are naked together, by how much we really aren't done with each other. "I'm afraid to trust you."

"Good," he says, pulling back to look at me, wicked heat in his eyes. "I haven't earned that trust."

"I haven't earned yours either," I say, and it's not a question. "And I never will."

"If I wasn't willing to see beyond this family, I wouldn't be here."

"You're here to ruin them, and me with them."

"From what I've seen, and I've seen far more than Isaac thinks I've seen, you didn't need me for that. I could have sat back with a bag of popcorn and watched the fun."

Realization hits me. "You came because you knew you could take over. It wasn't about saving us. It's about getting what you always wanted."

"Princess, I haven't wanted or needed this place in a long time. I got out and got right like you should have."

"I couldn't. I told you that. I told you why. I would have left the legacy behind, if not for my mom. Seriously, what if it was your mother? Would you just leave? I don't know why I'm telling you this."

"Because you want me to be human enough to care."

"Are you?"

He cups my face. "Enough to bow to a princess, it seems." His voice is low and raspy as he leans in and brushes his lips over mine and then suddenly, he's kissing me, drugging me with his tongue, before he says, "Decide what you're going to do with that power, Harper. Then I'll decide what I'm going to do with mine." He strokes his thumb over my cheek. "I'll see you soon." He releases me and in a few, graceful strides, he's out of the office, and I'm alone. Only, I'm not sure I am alone anymore.

I'm with him, I'm with Eric, but I'm not sure if he's my friend or my enemy. I just know that if that man touches me, I'll melt, and I won't care if that means pain or pleasure.

Chapter Seventeen

Eric

Harper's like the apple in the Garden of Eden, tempting me in ways that I simply can't resist. I know she could be poisonous. I know she could be playing with my head, but I still want her and in a wicked, fierce way. I want her so fucking badly that I'm here at Kingston Motors in a building I swore I'd never step foot in. The taste of her. The feel of her against me. The sweet floral scent of hers that clings to me as I exit her office, a distinctively *her* scent that's a giveaway to how that conversation behind closed doors went just now: up close and personal, the only way I want things with Harper.

I won't hide that fact from her or anyone. That's not my style. I want. I need. I take and I never shy away from announcing that intent, nor would that benefit Harper, considering her present position. With the way my appearance went down, she's officially placed herself inside a war zone. More so, she's declared herself standing on my side of the battlefield, and for that, she'll pay without my protection. Isaac will come at her with that desperate viciousness I know all too well, just as he knows where that leaves him with me. He needs to know what that means with Harper.

In fact, there's no reason to play this on the lowdown with Isaac. I'm halfway to the lobby when I turn around and walk my ass back to Isaac's office. His door is shut but I don't care. I open it and step inside. He's standing at his window, his phone in his hand, with his back to me. He whirls around and his expression reddens the way it had every time our law profession pitted us against each other in mock trials.

"I need to call you back," he says to whoever he's talking to before he disconnects the line. "Knock, you little bastard," he snaps. "You might be performing an audit, but I run this place."

"Last I heard, your father still ran this place. Good to know who's responsible for its current state of destruction. I won't keep you. I have data to dissect. I just want to be clear. Harper's a pawn Gigi used to get to me. If you use her or lash out at her, you'll suffer, and as in the past, when I make a promise, I keep it."

"No matter what you have to do to make me pay, right?" he challenges. "I thought Grayson Bennett and his ever talked about moral compass would have changed that in you."

"I operate based on who I'm dealing with and we both know you don't even understand the words moral compass. Leave Harper out of this."

"Harper put herself in this. She wants the company." He leans on the desk. "Smarten up, brother. She's brought us together for a reason. We just don't know what it is yet, but I promise you, at its root, it's about power. It's about how damn much she thinks her father contributed to this company."

"Last I heard, she's the one who contributed and with no stock to show for it. You have her trust fund."

He gives an amused snort. "I didn't know you were so fucking naive," he says. "She has no trust fund. Her father left it fluid and under her mother's control. She wants you to take me down so she can take over. She wants what's mine and assumes as the bastard, it will never be yours. Believe me, man, she'll fuck you up and down and sideways to get what she wants."

He hits a nerve I didn't realize still existed about this company, this life, and even the woman I came here to help, but I beat it down. "What you fail to understand, dear half-brother, is that I don't want or need this place. If she takes it from you, I'll be amused. This isn't my life."

"Then why come here at all?"

"We're family," I say dryly. "Harper said so."

"That's why you wear the jaguar, a competing emblem, inked on your arm? Because we're family?"

"That's exactly why. It's all about family to me."

"If that's family to you, you're ten more shades of fucked up than I even realized."

"I have a feeling we'll be reinventing how we define family and fucked up many times over before I leave." My lips quirk. "Harper works for me. Remember that. You need her, you come through me." I turn and exit the office, cutting left and down the hallway.

I've just cut right when I end up toe to toe with Harper, who all but runs into me.

I catch her shoulders, and holy fuck, touching this woman sets me on fire, muddying the water in ways that I allowed to pull me into this hell. "Hi," she says softly.

I narrow my eyes on her, thinking about her six years with this family, thinking about what it takes to live like one of them that long. "You wanted me here. You got me. You work for me now. You report to me now. Put together any data you think I need to see and don't make any move related to that data, and I mean *any* move, without talking to me first." I release her. "I'll be in the conference room." I turn away and head for the front office, but I don't make it far.

"Eric," she calls out, and my name on this woman's lips easily halts my steps, but I don't immediately face her. For a moment I'm back in that hotel room with her naked, in my arms, me buried inside her when she used my name and told me that she saw me, not the bastard. I wonder who she sees now. I wonder who she really saw then. My jaw clenches with that thought and I turn around to find her stepping in front of me, the small space of the narrow walkway shrinking and wrapping us in intimacy.

"I don't know what I sense in you right now," she says. "But remember this: Isaac has trashed you every day of your life you've been connected to this family. You think we're different, but he sees me just like he sees you, and he is not kind to me. I deal with it. I handle it, but to you, we're different. To him we're alike."

"And to you? Are we alike, Harper?"

"In some ways we are. We both got forced into this family and we both wanted it to be a real family. I, however, wasn't smart enough to get out of here like you did when I could have, but I was smart enough to ask for your help. Because the way I see it, doing nothing wasn't an option. If you take everything, then at least I'm finally free." She turns and walks away and I watch her disappear into her office, the damn floral scent of her every-fucking-where, the way I want her naked in every fucking thought. Which would be fine if that nerve Isaac hit wasn't jumping again.

I came here for her.

He knows it.

She knows it, too.

That's only a problem if there's something going on here, and my gut says that it's designed to fuck me over. I don't know why I'm a target, but I am, and if Harper knows the truth, she's going to tell me, even if I have to strip her naked and cuff her to my bed to get it out of her.

But I'm still not sure she does. I'm not sure that she's not being used or even targeted herself.

A thought that I can't quite materialize claws at my mind, the way so many do until I realize them, until I turn them into numbers that no one but me can understand. I need to be alone and think. I also need Harper naked and cuffed to the bed, but that comes later. Not much later. *Tonight.* It happens tonight when I decide if I trust her or I just want to fuck her.

Chapter Eighteen

Eric

With a vow to have Harper naked and in my bed tonight, I turn on my heel and walk into the lobby where I stop in front of the receptionist, a pretty blonde I'd guess to be in her twenties—and knowing Isaac, his fuck buddy. That's what he does. He surrounds himself with pretty women who place him on a throne and kneel in front of him. A thought that has me remembering Isaac's comment inferring Harper would fuck me to get what she wants, though her fucking me for any reason suits me just fine. Now, if she fucked him, that would be another story, and a really fucking bad one I'd have a hard time believing.

The receptionist eyes the back office where I just exited and then me again, obviously trying to figure out how I got back there without her knowing. "Can I help you?"

"I'm Eric Mitchell, the other brother."

Her eyes go wide and then as often is the case, they rake over my tats, and then sharply lift. "You're—as in—"

"The bastard?" I ask, but I don't have to wait for her reply. I get right to the confirmation. "Yes. I'm him and I'm a stockholder called in on behalf of Gigi to audit the operation. I'll be working in the conference room, if I have calls or deliveries or if anyone simply wants to share operational concerns."

The phone rings and she looks awkward, like she's not sure if she should do her job and answer the phone. "Answer it," I order. "I'll wait."

She smartly picks up the phone. "Kingston Motors, can I help you?" Her lips part as if she's heard something shocking. "Mr. Kingston. Yes." Her gaze darts to me as she says, "He's standing right here. Yes. Of course." She punches the hold button. "He wants to talk to you."

"Conference room," I say, heading to the left of the desk toward a set of stairs that will lead to a lower level opposite Gigi's private domain. Gigi, who might have convinced Harper that she's a new woman, but I know better. She has an agenda, something she's after, something I can give her, and she's smart enough to know I'll find out what that is and she's willing to take that risk.

I take my time going down the stairs, aware that my father could have called my cellphone. He called the office phone to record my reply, or allow Isaac to listen in, or both. Once I'm at the double glass doors of the lower level, I open them to enter the massive conference room, where I head to the end of the mahogany table and grab the phone, punching the line. "Father," I say, though that word is acid on my tongue.

"I understand you're now a stockholder." His tone is dry, unaffected, but then he enjoys games, and while I don't, we're smack in the middle of one.

"I never pass on a steal of a deal. I got it cheap. Those recalls haven't been kind to your stock or apparently your cash flow."

"Our cash flow is just fine."

"Considering you had to sweep Harper's trust fund out from underneath her," I say, "I imagine it is."

"Sweep her trust fund?" He laughs. "That's a joke. You don't know half the story, boy, but you will. I'm on a private jet about to head home. We'll talk and I promise you that even that genius brain of yours will feel enlightened." He disconnects and I lean back in my seat. *I don't know half the story*. He's right for once where I'm concerned. I don't know half the story, but I'll know it all soon.

My cellphone rings and I snake it out of my pocket to find Blake's number on the caller ID. "Talk to me," I say, answering the line.

"There are cameras and recording devices in the room you're in, which from what I can tell has been the case for years."

"Of course," I say dryly, finding the idea of my brother recording people and using those recordings against them—me included if I give him the chance, which I won't—highly probable. "What else?"

"About fifteen minutes after you left your brother's office, the tech team for Kingston Motors suddenly began deleting chunks of data; which even dumb shits like me that don't have your genius IQ can assume is to hide damning information before you gain access."

"Only it's too late to matter."

"Exactly," Blake confirms. "I have everything downloaded as planned for comparison. I'll send you a secure data file that homes in on exactly what was deleted. It'll take a few hours once they finish what they're doing to finish the analysis on our side, but it'll allow you to see what matters, which is what's now missing."

"That's going to be an interesting study."

"Even more interesting, we've hacked all cellphones, emails, and external communications. Isaac somehow called his tech team and your father without me knowing when he did it, which tells me that he has a phone line or device that we don't know about."

In other words, he was operating off the grid before I walked in the door. "There's a person I wanted you to focus on," I say, redirecting the conversation to where I want it: Harper.

"You wanted to know where Harper fits into the family hierarchy. She doesn't. She's not close to any of them. She isn't even close to her mother anymore. Word on that is there's tension between them, perhaps over the trust, though Harper still sees her twice a week. Outside of that, she doesn't socialize with your brother or father."

"Not now," I say. "What about in the past?"

"We've gone back two years. She's been removed from the family for at least that long."

"And yet she's still here," I comment, half to myself. "What about Gigi?"

"She has more contact with her than the others, but I'd still call it limited."

"Then there has to be someone else. Who?"

"If you mean love interests, we're already working that angle, but on first glance, there are only two men she's dated over the years. They're both rich, powerful and involved with your father and brother. However, that doesn't raise a red flag to me, necessarily. They were in and out of her life and inside her normal social circle. That's who she'd be exposed to, and gravitated to, naturally."

Rich, powerful, men. The kind I wasn't when she met me. The kind I am now. I could let my head go all kinds of places, but I don't. My mind jumps from there to my father's comment about Harper's trust fund.

"I'm texting you a question when we hang up," I say, focused on discretion. "I'm also about to grab my computer and set-up here in the office. I'll be waiting on that data."

"Don't do that," he says. "The cameras are too wide-sweeping. Take your ass out of that place. I'll find you a sweet spot in the building by tomorrow."

"Find it right here in this room."

"They'll know you had it swept."

"Works for me."

We disconnect after a few more words that amount to not much and I send the promised text: *There could be more to the trust fund than meets the eyes. Look deeper.*

Once Blake confirms receipt of the message, I reach in my pocket and start turning the mini-Rubik's cube inside, processing all that I've just learned, playing with the numbers in my head. I abandon the cube and stand up, ready to ask questions around the facility. Ready to see Harper. I'm almost to the doors when they open and she enters. We now stand a few steps apart, the charge between us combustible. The two of us in the same room is like a match to a flame.

We stand there, staring at each other, the air thick, that charge all but lighting us up and I, for one, say fuck it to the family drama. I'm thinking about her naked on this conference table, and if we wouldn't become Isaac's nightly porn viewing, that's exactly what I'd make happen.

Her lips part as if she knows where my head is and she cuts her gaze. "Do you need something from me, Harper?" I prod.

She swallows hard, that long, elegant, regal throat of hers that needs my mouth, bobbing before she looks at me, her stare unwavering. "Need? Yes. I need. *To talk.* And to give you this." She holds up a file in her hand. "This is—"

I shake my head to silence her. Her brows knit and she tilts her head, realization seeping into her intelligent stare. She knows we're being watched and I close the space between us. "I'll take that," I say, that sweet scent of her teasing my nostrils again, my cock twitching, blood heating.

She offers me the file. "You wanted my schedule," she improvises. "I didn't have your email, so I brought you a hard copy."

"Good," I say. "Because you're all mine now until I leave."

"And when exactly will that be?" she asks.

"When I get what I came for," I say.

"And what's that?"

I lean in close and lower my voice. "More. I came here for more."

Her eyes jerk to mine and her reply is rapid fire. "Define more, because, under the present circumstances, I'm not sure how I feel about that word."

"I plan to and in great detail," I assure her. "I'll look at your schedule. We'll discuss where that leads us."

Her lips press together, and I can tell she's biting back words before she settles on, "I have questions."

"As do I, but now isn't the time for the answers we both want, and in fact, demand."

"When?"

"Tonight," I say.

"I'm not sure that works for me," she says.

"I'm certain you can make it work. If you can't, I promise you, I will. I think I've proven that."

"No, you haven't," she says, anger radiating in her voice. She grabs my arm and leans in close, her voice low, a whisper for my ears only. "I didn't get naked with you to get you to come here, and I won't do it again to keep you here. I didn't pay for your services, nor is any version of the word 'more' a given." She leans back and looks at me. "That you think it is, is arrogant, and frankly, a bastard-like assumption that I don't like."

That comment smacks like a palm. "It's what you expect, right? Why would I disappoint?"

"It's not actually what I expect. Not from you. Not at all." With that, she turns and leaves me standing there, staring after her, hot and hard, and ready for more, however we define that word.

Chapter Nineteen

Harper

I don't know what just happened, is all I can think as I enter my office and shut the door, letting my mind chase answers now that I'm alone. The first thing that comes to my mind is: *That man.* My God, that man. Eric is making me crazy. I want him. I'm angry with him. And we're really being watched? Am I being watched now? That idea jolts me and I push off the door and walk calmly to my desk. If Isaac had turned into a peeping tom, I'm not giving him an emotional show for him to use against me or Eric for that matter, despite the way he just treated me.

Yes, Eric just acted like that bastard label he too readily owns, but considering the power play at hand, I can't say I blame him. I don't have his trust. He doesn't quite have mine, but after talking to Gigi, I don't know if it matters. She's right. We're better off in Eric's hands than Isaac's. Even if I lose my trust, which at this point feels pretty gone anyway, at least I leave this place without liability, and so does my mother.

I hope.

I don't know.

Eric could burn us, but I just don't feel like he will. Not unless he feels that we're trying to burn him. I think that's exactly what he thinks. He thinks I fucked him to fuck him. I want to scream with this idea. I want to go right back down those stairs and shake him and quite possibly get naked with him. How can I want to be naked with a man who basically accused me of being a whore? Okay, that's extreme. He didn't exactly say that. I'm exaggerating and I don't usually exaggerate, but he's making me crazy. And confused. I've always been confused about that man, or at least, emotionally. My body feels no confusion. It just wants to feel him close.

The intercom on my desk buzzes and the receptionist announces, "Jim Sims from the union is on the line for Isaac, but he told me to give the call to you."

Jim Sims, who would do about anything for me if I got naked with him, which is exactly why I don't deal with him. Isaac knows this. He doesn't care, and this isn't even about Eric, considering this was my assignment before he knew Eric was here. It's about me asking too many questions and making too many demands for answers. Which wouldn't be a problem if Isaac wasn't hiding something.

I pick-up the line. "Jim."

"I hear you're lead on the upcoming labor relations topics."

"I hear that as well. I was just about to catch up on the file before tomorrow's meeting."

"Yes, well, we both know bathroom preferences are below your pay grade. I suspect your brother hoped you'd distract me and calm me the fuck down on some of the bigger financial issues."

"What issues?"

"A topic better discussed in person. Let's meet."

Of course he wants to meet, and to be all touchy-feely while he's at it. I glance at my clock. It's eleven. "How about three o'clock at your office? That gives me time to get up to speed."

"How about happy hour, at the wine bar up your direction in Cherry Creek? You still live in Cherry Creek, right?"

How does this man know where I live? "Yes," I say. "I'm still up that direction."

"Good. These matters are easier to stomach when diluted by wine and you won't have far to travel after we indulge."

"I'm not good with wine," I say. "I need a clear head today and tomorrow. Let's stick with the coffee."

He's silent a few beats and then says, "Then we'll do coffee at five. I have meetings this afternoon."

We disconnect and I pull up my email to find an email from Isaac titled "Union" that I skip right on past when I see one from EricB@kingstonmotors.com. My heart thunders in my chest and I click on the message to read: *My new address, just to make my presence official.*

My forehead knits at the "B" that most certainly stands for "Bastard" and I type: *Did you choose that email address?* And then hit send.

His reply is instant: *I never let anyone else make my decisions. You shouldn't either.*

I ignore his obvious reference to my reasons for staying with Kingston for six years and type: *Did you really make it Eric B, for bastard?*

He replies with: *There's another Eric in accounting. I didn't want anyone to get confused. Here's my phone number. Use it. Often. 212-415-2333.*

I grab my phone and compare the number to the one I got from his business card, and it matches. I send him a text: *Now you have my number.*

He replies with: *I already had it, princess.*

I stare at that message, not sure if we're talking about phone numbers or that conversation downstairs about me fucking him to get him here. I suddenly don't know if I should be angry or not, thus I have no idea how to reply. Yes, I do. I type: *And I already had your number as well, BASTARD.* I stare at the message and erase the *BASTARD*. I replace it with *ERIC*. He doesn't get to hide behind the bastard persona with me. He gets to own every asshole moment.

I pull up my email and click on the entry from Isaac to read: *Make the union happy. The last thing we need in the press right now is a union scandal.*

He says nothing more. He doesn't even sign the damn thing. I grimace and download the union files. The list of issues they want to negotiate stretches well beyond a bathroom and I have a gut feeling this is about keeping me busy. That was his plan before Eric got here. Get me so entrenched in union hell that I didn't have time to look at him and his handling of the company. He played that card too late. Eric's here and one thing I'm certain of, he's not leaving until "this" whatever this is, is over.

I move to my conference table and set-up my MacBook, and settle into reading the union data. Two hours later, I have pages of notes on a legal pad, with nothing in here that our labor relations manager couldn't handle. There is nothing that would become a problem for the company and yet me blowing it would certainly be a reason to dispose of me from the company. Is that what this is? A set-up to get me out? It's such a paranoid, insane idea that I toss my pen down and stand up. I need food and out of this office.

I head to the break room for a cup of coffee. That and a power bar will have to be my lunch. I've just finished doctoring my cup to perfection when Isaac appears in the doorway, hitching a shoulder on the doorframe. "He's not family."

"He's more family than I am. He's blood, whether you like it or not." I march toward him, trying to force him to move. He doesn't. "I need to get back to work."

"You brought him here to take what you want. He's going to take what he wants. Those two things won't connect."

"You assume you know what I want," I say. "Because you assume everyone wants in the same ways you do."

"You assume you know what Eric wants."

"No, I don't," I say. "I asked him." I leave out the part where what he wants is to destroy this place.

"And he said what?"

"I'm not going to pretend to have any right to speak for Eric. Ask him yourself. Now. I have a meeting with Jim to prepare for, and for the record, I know you know that man is all hands and this is torture for me. Now you have the satisfaction of confirmation, but if you think I'm going to screw this up because Jim is pawing at me and give you a chance to push me out, you're wrong."

He studies me for several beats. "Perhaps you should treat me the way you treat our bastard brother, and ask me what I want, rather than assuming."

"What do you want, Isaac?"

"Just what's mine and now you've made me have to fight for it, and if it gets bloody, that's on you. It didn't have to be that way. It wasn't that way."

The words cut and accuse and I don't know what to do with them or what to feel. He steps out of the break room and pauses a moment, glaring to his right before he turns and disappears left. I know even before I enter the hallway that Eric's standing there.

I suck in a breath, preparing for the impact of his presence, and then he's replaced Isaac in the doorway, big and broad, with all that ink and muscle everywhere but next to me. I want him next to me again, and it doesn't seem to matter what he might think of me if that happens. His eyes, those crystal perfect eyes, meet mine—no they crash into mine, and seem to grab hold of me, deep inside and hold on.

"This isn't on you," he says, stepping closer, lowering his head near mine. "He's responsible for every decision that drove you to me." He pulls back to look at me. "And later tonight, ask me what I want again." With that, he turns away and exits the kitchen.

Chapter Twenty

Harper

A t four-thirty, I pack up my briefcase and contemplate calling
Eric, or at least texting him, to tell him I'm leaving. He
declared himself my new boss and on that, there is no argument
to be had. The silence since that claim, however, is disconcerting,
and I'm feeling generally confused about what he and I are doing. I
head for the lobby, let the receptionist know that I'm leaving, and
exit the building into the chill of a November day. Quick stepping
as I dig my keys from my purse, and click the lock on my Kingston
vehicle and wonder what it would be like to have the freedom to
drive something else. I try to remember my early years here when I
was all about the brand.

I'm about to cut between cars to my door when a car pulls up
next to me, and I hear, "Get in."

At the sound of Eric's voice, I turn to find the passenger window
down on a black F-TYPE Jaguar and him inside it, causing my heart
to flutter. When has any man but this one ever made me react in
such a way? I force a tiny breath, which is remarkably hard to draw
in, and walk to the open window where I lean in and find those
blue, blue eyes of his fixed on me.

"Get in," he repeats.

"I have a meeting," I say. "That union thing I was talking to Isaac
about. I'm on my way there now."

"I know. I'm going with you."

He's going with me? Do I want him to go with me? Yes. No. "The
thing is," I say, "you can't go with me. The union contact wants a
one on one with me."

"To grope you and make you miserable. I get that, which is why
I'm going with you. Now, get in."

He wants to protect me from being groped? I *want* to be
protected from being groped. "If you come, he'll be difficult."

"I'm good with difficult people," he assures me. "I had a year of practice with this family which for all their faults, have served me well."

"You're in a Jaguar."

"Quite the statement car, don't you think?"

"Like your ink?"

"Like sending the princess to bring the bastard home."

"That's not how that played out," I say.

"No?"

"No," I say.

"Get in the car and tell me."

"We make Kingstons," I counter. "Let's take my car."

"For the love of God, woman. Would you just get in?"

"Fine," I breathe out. "I give up. I'll get in." I open the door and he grabs my briefcase and sets it in what little backseat there is in this version of Jag. "A hundred-thousand-dollar F-TYPE," I say, claiming the seat next to him, the earthy, clean scent of him teasing my nostrils. "Impressive ride considering you just got into town." I reach for my seatbelt which doesn't want to move. "Well, except for the seatbelt." I yank hard and Eric catches the belt halfway across my body and the two of us end up holding it, a warm blanket of intimacy surrounding us.

"The dealer warned me that the belt can snap back," he explains softly. "I wouldn't want you to get hurt."

But I will, I think, and not by a belt or this family. By him. He will steal my breath and own my body, and then leave. I can't stop it. I don't think I even want to try. He slides the clip into place, his hand intimately brushing my hip as the belt snaps together, but he doesn't move away. His eyes sharpen. "You have to be careful with shiny, new things. They look pretty but sometimes they bite."

He's not talking about the belt or the car. He's talking about me. He's telling me he doesn't trust me and yet he's here.

He settles back in his seat and places the car in drive while I decide that I'm back to generally confused with this man. "Starbucks, right?" he asks.

"How do you know where my meeting is being held?"

"Anything you say in that building is being monitored."

"By you?"

"As of today, yes, but that place has been wired to the hilt for years from what my people can tell."

My heart lurches and I rotate to face him. "My office?" I ask urgently. "Are there cameras in my office?"

He pulls us to a halt at the exit to the parking lot and glances over at me. "Yes. Your office."

I hug myself and face forward. "I change for the gym in there a few times a week. I don't even want to think about what that means." He pulls us onto the highway and starts the short, two-block drive to the coffee shop. "I don't know if the idea of Isaac or your father watching me freaks me out more."

"I wish I could comfort you, but I'm the bastard child of a father who was having an affair."

I press my hands to my face and then drop them to my legs, thinking back over the years. "Isaac is the one recording me," I assert. "Your father doesn't see those recordings. I'm certain of it. Isaac uses them and me. He's always a step ahead of me. He knows what I'm going to do before I get to do it. He claims every big moment I attempt. Your father always ends up impressed with him and disappointed in me. He steals my ideas."

"Once a cheat, always a cheat," he says, pulling us into Starbucks. "That's his way. That's how he beats you."

He's right, I think as he parks the F-TYPE. That is Isaac's way, and yet I've foolishly played this game his way all this time. Eric kills the engine and I turn to him. "He didn't beat you. Everyone knows he didn't beat you. You came out on top, better off than him. I know that doesn't come without personal consequence for you, Eric. I know asking you to come here was selfish, but I need you. We need you."

"Because he didn't beat me," he repeats.

"Exactly. He didn't beat you. He *can't* beat you."

His jaw sets hard. "Right," he says flatly, that word, his only reply, holding about ten thousand meanings I want to understand. There is so much about this man I want to understand. I wonder if anyone really knows him. I wonder so many things.

"Eric," I say, a million possible words playing on my tongue when my cellphone starts ringing in my purse. I ignore it and focus on him, taking a chance, and assuming I might read him right. "I hate that you might think me needing your help translates to me using you like they would. I'm not them. I wanted—more than that between us." My cellphone finally stops ringing.

He shifts to face me, the full force of his piercing blue eyes on me now. "More," he repeats.

"Yes," I whisper. "More."

My cellphone starts ringing again.

"Take the call," he orders softly.

"I don't want to take the call," I say. "I want you to talk to me."

He surprises me then and reaches up, his fingers brushing my cheek, a light touch I feel everywhere, and I want everywhere, sending a shiver down my spine. My phone stops ringing and starts all over again. His hand falls away. "Take the call, Harper. It could be your union groper."

"He is a groper and yes," I reluctantly agree, "it could be him." I grab my phone to find my mother calling, no doubt about Eric. "It's my mother," I say, sticking my phone back in my purse. "I'll call her back."

"You sure?"

"Positive." My phone starts ringing again. "She goes for three," I explain. "After that, she leaves a voicemail."

He studies me a few beats, something dark and unreadable in his stare, but I don't need to read his expression to read his thoughts. He knows I don't want him to listen in on this call. "Look," I say. "She probably found out that you're here. She's going to be a freaked-out mess, afraid of you, and pissed at me. I really don't care if you hear that call, but it's going to be painful and long." It rings again. I grab it from my purse and hit decline before sending it to voicemail. "Eric—"

"Don't let me find out you're lying to me, Harper." His voice is low but hard. "That's a broad statement so let me repeat and expand on it. Don't let me find out that you lied to me about anything."

"I'm not," I say, looking him in the eyes, letting him see the truth. "I swear to you, Eric. I'm not lying to you about anything. There are things I haven't told you, but not because I don't want to tell you. I just haven't had the time or privacy."

"I seem to remember things differently."

"You mean the night you told me the only way you'd come back was to finish off the family?" I challenge.

"I didn't come back to ruin them," he says, his blue eyes watching me closely as he adds, "I came back for you."

He's here for me.

Those were the words I'd wanted to hear from this man, but now that he's said them, they're layered with complexity, the meaning holding a world of possibilities, some good and some not good. "That could mean a lot of things," I say.

He leans in closer, his hand on the back of my seat. "What do you want them to mean?"

Chapter Twenty-One

Harper

*H*e came for me.

I want to know what that means to him.
He wants to know what that means to me.

Eric lets those questions linger in the air between us and he's so close, so very close to me, his hand on the back of my seat, his face so near my face that I could reach up and trace every handsome line. "I wanted you to come here, and yes, I wanted you to come for me. But I also never wanted you to leave, not from the cottage or the hotel room, but you did. Easily. You walked away without looking back, so it's hard for me to believe that you came for me without another agenda."

"I left and you stayed. For six long fucking years, you stayed with them. And Gigi sent you to me. I could easily believe that you have an agenda."

"I told you my agenda. I need your help. I don't want to be your enemy, Eric."

"I'm only your enemy if you make me your enemy."

"You made me your enemy the day you met me, before you ever spoke to me. I was the princess, and you were the bastard. That was based on your baggage, not my actions. My allegiance is to my father, and he was a good man. A man you would have respected. A man who would have respected you for all you've done on your own.

"I can make that your nickname, princess." He reaches up to touch my face.

I catch his hand. "And you like being the bastard?"

His gaze lowers to my mouth and lifts. "I am who I am, Harper."

"Well, I'm *not her*," I say. "I'm not on a throne. I'm not above you because I inherited money I don't even have, or because I'm my father's daughter, or whatever the case."

"I'm here. Stop obsessing over a name."

"How can I not obsess over that name? I was in that hotel room with you when you were calling me that name. I felt the anger in you when you used it."

"Not at you, Harper."

"Now who's lying to who? I was there. Let me repeat myself. *I felt* your anger. You hated me for being a part of this family."

"And yet you fucked me?"

"Right. I did." My throat constricts, hurt and anger colliding, and yet my voice is remarkably calm. "I must have wanted something. I get it. That's what you think of me." I turn away from him to face forward.

Eric doesn't move away. He stays right there, leaning over me, watching me. "Harper," he says, his voice low, rough. "That's not what I meant."

"It doesn't matter," I say, my skin tingling with the need for him to touch me. How can I need a man to touch me? How can I need *this* man, who hates me, to touch me?

"It *does* matter," he says. "*You* matter or I wouldn't be here."

I want to believe him. I want to touch him. I want him to touch me. I want him to kiss me and I know he will if I turn to him. I know I'm setting myself up for heartache with this man. I know he could use me, but I'm so damn drawn to him.

"Look at me, Harper," he orders softly.

"I can't," I whisper, emotion welling in my throat. "I really can't right now."

It's at that moment Jim exits Starbucks, his long legs eating up the parking lot in a near run as he charges toward his car. "That tall, dark-haired man is Jim," I say, reaching for my seatbelt. "He's the union guy. He's leaving." I let my belt fall away. "Why is he leaving?" I open my door and climb outside, the cold contrasting all the heat Eric and I were just generating and I shiver as I call out, "Jim!"

His gaze lifts my direction and I swear it's like he's seen a ghost. He doesn't stop, quickening his pace toward his car, a Mercedes that says he's paid well for his negotiation skills he isn't using right now. I chase after him, certain now that somehow this meeting was

Isaac setting me up for a fall. "Jim, wait," I say, catching him at his door. "I thought we were meeting?"

"I have a situation," he says, scrubbing his jaw. "I can't meet with you tonight."

Eric steps to my side. "Hi, Jim," he greets, and it feels familiar, like they know each other.

"Eric," he bites out. "I just heard you were back in town."

"I noticed," Eric says dryly.

Jim's lips thin and he looks at me. "I'll see you at the meeting tomorrow." He opens his door.

"I thought we were talking through the hot points?" I press.

"I told you," he says, pausing with his hand on his door, "I *can't* meet."

He *can't*. What is going on? "What about in the morning?" I press, confused by this change of attitude.

"I'll see you at the meeting," he replies, cutting his eyes and disappearing inside his car. His engine revs and he's backing up in sixty seconds flat.

I rotate toward Eric, holding out my hands in utter frustration. "What was that?"

"The Bennett Corporation operates one of the largest law firms in the world. We've had a few thousand dealings with the union."

I shake my head in instant rejection. "No. No, he was afraid of you. He knew *you*. He feared you."

"He fears the beast that is the Bennett name and I'm a large part of Grayson Bennett's brand."

"There's more to what just happened," I say, a cold gust of wind biting through me, while Eric seems immune to anything as real as the weather. He's colder than I thought. He's harder. Why didn't I know this? He's a self-made billionaire and he didn't get there by being a bleeding heart and gentle soul. "You said you want more from me," I say. "You demanded more of me, and yet all you're giving me is accusations and a blow-off answer to something that directly affects me." A few people walk out of the coffee shop and I lower my voice. "You want more. Well, I want more, too. I *demand* more." I start walking to the car, my steps thundering on the pavement, my heart all but bursting from my chest. I need in the car. I need away from him before I lose my shit, and I'm so close. With shaky hands, I open the door. And then he's there.

Eric shackles my arm and drags me around to face him, sinewy muscle and warmth touching me everywhere, and Lord help me, that's where I want him. Everywhere. I want him so badly it hurts, even though I know that he's going to hurt me, maybe even destroy me. "You want more?" he hisses, his voice sandpaper rough.

"Yes," I hiss back, and do so without hesitation, some part of me aware that this moment defines us, it defines me in a way I do not yet understand, and yet, my answer is unchanged. "Yes," I repeat, barely able to breathe for the combustible heat between us. It's suffocating me. He's suffocating me. And God, I think I might want to die just like this, next to him, craving him.

"Say it," he orders as if he thinks I can't or won't. As if he needs to know I know what I'm agreeing to, and I do. "Say the words. I want more."

"I want more." My voice trembles with the declaration.

His eyes glint fire and ice in the same moment, still managing to burn me alive. "You sure about that? You might not like where this leads you, Harper."

Somehow my hand has settled on the hard wall of his perfect chest, and his heart thunders under my palm. We're not talking about the Kingstons anymore. We're talking about me and him and I'm already all in, already drowning in this man. There's no reason to hold back. My fingers ball around his shirt. "But you *cannot* walk away this time."

"You should. You don't know who I am or what I am capable of."

His mouth closes down on mine, his tongue licking into my mouth, a deep, drugging stroke followed by another before he rips his mouth from mine, my breath heaving from my chest as he orders, "Get in the car, Harper."

Chapter Twenty-Two

Harper

I climb into the car, letting the soft leather absorb my body. He shuts me inside, and in a few moments, he's here with me, the implication of what just happened between us, and where it leads, crackling in the air, sexual tension off the charts to the point my body trembles. The tug of war between us all lust and hate, and I tell myself that is dangerous. *He* is dangerous. And yet, I sit here, alive in a way I have never been alive before with this man.

He doesn't immediately turn on the car. He just sits there next to me, seconds ticking by until a long exhale escapes his lips and he tilts his gaze in my direction. "Are you hungry?"

A bubble of strained laughter escapes my lips. "Am I hungry? Not, are you lying to me?"

There's a punch of something in his expression there and gone before I can even try to understand it. "We need to exist outside of that family, so yes, Harper. *Are you hungry?*"

Now I breathe out, his reasoning warming, calming me, giving me hope we can exist outside that realm where there is only lust and hate. Seconds tick by and the simple question settles easily between us, the tension of moments before uncurling just that easily. This is new territory for us. We have never shared a meal or a real conversation and I am quick to welcome such a thing. "Yes, actually, I am. I had a power bar today. That's all."

"I had a bag of peanut M & M's which I promise you were better than the power bar. Let's go to Cherry Creek and eat. I know you live there and it's also where I booked my hotel and not because I'm stalking you. It's my old stomping grounds and I wanted to revisit some of my favorite spots while I'm here."

"I didn't know you lived in Cherry Creek. How long?"

"Four years. I went to undergrad school around there. My favorite Italian restaurant is there, which is on my list of places to hit while I'm here."

I perk up. "North?"

"North," he confirms. "You like it?"

"Love it. My favorite, too."

"Is it?"

"It is."

We have this moment of connection then, that isn't really over North or Cherry Creek, but rather us. Just us and the pull between us that refuses to be ignored. "Then North it is," he says finally, revving the engine and backing us up. "How'd you end up in Cherry Creek?" he asks once he's driving us through the parking lot.

"I went to a lunch there with my mother when I first moved here and fell in love. It reminds me of home. Well one the quaint little areas, at least."

"New York City?" he asks, pulling onto the highway.

"You've read up on me," I say to the reference of my home state.

"Of course, I did," he says, offering no apologies or explanation.

"Is there a file I can get on you?"

He casts me a sideways look. "I'm right here. Just ask me."

"As if you're that approachable."

"I am," he says, glancing over at me again. "Tonight, I am."

"Why tonight?"

"It's time." He doesn't give me a chance to press again. "Why does Cherry Creek remind you of New York City?"

"We lived in a tiny pocket of the city there. Everything we wanted was in a small space. Cherry Creek is like that in that everything is right there, within reach, minus the smog, rats, and crush of people. It's quaint and safe, hidden from the rest of the city in so many ways."

"It's the hidden part I liked," he says. "It's like a small city boxed off from the rest of the city."

"Yes," I say. "One hundred percent yes." Then I dare to test his open book. "So, after your undergrad, you went off to Harvard?"

"Yes. And then I went off to Harvard before joining the Navy. And yes, that's a complicated story." He turns us into the Cherry Creek neighborhood. "And yes, you can ask me about it while we eat."

"I will," I say, "and actually, I live two blocks from the restaurant. You can park there if you like. Though, I guess if you're at the Marriott, North is practically next door."

"I'm at the Marriott, but I'll park at your place." He doesn't ask me where I live. He just cuts right and then left and pulls into the driveway of my gray-finished house, then around to the back. "The address was in your file and I have a photographic memory."

I look at him. "As in literally?"

"Yes. Literally." He opens his door. "I'll come around to get you." He exits the car and I hear the trunk pop. I open my door and by the time I've settled my legs on the ground, he's in a sleek black leather jacket, and pulling me to my feet and to him.

He shuts the door, and I end up against the car with his hand on the side of my face, this warm, intimate blanket surrounding us, consuming us. There are no lies, no doubts, no divide. There is just this crazy, hot connection we've always shared. "I'm going to have to kiss you now, Harper." His mouth comes down on mine, his tongue pressing past my teeth in a slow, deep stroke that has me gripping his jacket and leaning into him.

He eases back, his mouth just a breath from mine, lingering there before a band seems to snap between us and we're kissing again, and this time he doesn't hold back. He kisses me deeply, completely and when I whimper with just how much I need more, he pulls back. "Let's go eat, sweetheart. We need to talk and we won't talk if we walk in your door."

"Sweetheart? Not princess?"

His hands go to the lapels on my trench coat. "You were right. I use it to divide us. No more princess."

"Why? What changed?"

"You hit a few hotspots back there in the car. This place makes me become way too much like my father and my brother for my own liking, and I'm certain, yours. They taught me to distrust and attack. The SEALs and the Bennett family taught me to reserve judgment and give people the benefit of the doubt. I prefer that version of me."

"Meaning me? You're going to give me the benefit of the doubt?"

"Yes." He strokes my hair behind my ear, and despite the chill of the night, his touch is fire. "You. Definitely you, but I don't trust my judgment with you, Harper. I'm way too invested."

"Invested?"

"You know I am or I wouldn't be here."

"You have a lot to be invested in here that isn't me."

"Nothing I want to be invested in *but you.*"

"But you—"

"Left. I know. And as I said, I'm here now. This time is different."

"Despite all of your anger, I do believe it is."

"We'll talk about my anger. We'll talk about a lot of things." And with that coded promise, he wraps his arm around my shoulders and turns me toward the front of the house. "Let's go get that pasta."

He sets us in motion and for a short bit, we stroll the path to the restaurant in what is surprisingly comfortable silence. "Tell me about Harvard."

"I got into some trouble when my mother was sick. We had money issues and I shoplifted. It fucked up my academic history."

I'm stunned at this confession and I want to ask about it, but we've reached the door of the restaurant. He opens the door for me and we're greeted by a hostess that takes our coats and promptly escorts us to a half-moon-shaped booth. I slide in one side as Eric goes to the other and when I think we'll sit across from each other, he scoots all the way around and pulls me close, his hand on my leg.

I am thrilled by the way he touches me, and seems to want me close, butterflies in my belly, fluttering about.

"This okay?" he asks.

"Yes," I say, sounding a bit breathless, but how can I not? He's touching me. "It is," I add and my voice is not one bit stronger.

"*Good.*" His voice is a low rasp, his eyes warm and reluctant as they leave my face and focus on the waitress who's just appeared. "Let's start with drinks." He looks at me again. "You do like wine, right?"

"I like the idea of wine. I love trying it."

He laughs, a low, sexy laugh. "You sure you like trying it?"

"I do," I promise. "I really do."

"Then I'll order my favorite here and you can tell me what you think." He works out the details with the waitress and when she departs, his elbow settles on the back of the booth as he rotates to face me and I do the same of him. We were close moments before, but somehow closer now that we're facing each other, the air crackling between us. "You still feel like I'm your enemy?" he asks softly.

"I should ask *you* that. I've never seen you as the enemy. And if you think taking over the company makes me see you as that, it doesn't. The only thing that makes you my enemy is if you turn on me or my mother."

"Your mother is aligned with my father."

"I know," I regretfully admit. "I've tried to get her to see that we have real problems, but she's blinded by love. I feel like there's something illicit going on. She's not involved, she's just not helping to solve the problem. So, I'm asking you to please keep her out of this. I'm begging you."

His eyes narrow in a barely perceptible way. "There are very few things I would even ask you to beg for, all of them involve pleasure."

Heat rushes to my cheeks, and mischief burns in his eyes. "You have my word."

I have his word, but I'm not sure if he just told me he's going to make me beg for pleasure, or he's going to protect my mother. And I need to know. For my mother, I need to know. "Eric—"

"Your wine has arrived," the waitress announces, but his eyes, those gorgeous, intelligent eyes hold mine, seconds passing before he says, "I'll protect her Harper, as long as she deserves it." With this, he turns his attention to the waitress who hands Eric a sample of the wine and waits for his approval before filling our glasses.

As long as she deserves it.

His words echo in my mind. She deserves it. Of course, she deserves it, but what's his definition of her crossing a line? And why am I even worried there might be a line she crosses?

Eric approves of the taste of wine he's been offered and our glasses are filled. Once we're alone, I sip the beverage, a sweet yet oaky flavor touching my tongue. "It's excellent," I say.

"Glad you like it."

I burn to ask him about my mother again, but the moment feels lost and a new one resists introduction. His arm is back on the seat, his body angled to mine, and there's an easiness in him I do not want to lose. This man interests me, and it has nothing to do with this family, or business, though certainly his ability to manage all of the above is sexy as hell. I might not be a Cinderella waiting to be rescued, but there is a strength and confidence about Eric I find beyond appealing. I envy this quality, but I am also drawn to it in him. I set my glass down and rotate toward him, eager to test his claim to being an open book tonight. "About that anger."

He reaches up and strokes my hair behind my ear, an unexpectedly tender touch that shivers through me. "I'm angry at you for making me want you so fucking badly that I had to come here."

Those words are raw and real, vibrating along my nerve endings. "Are you going to make me regret it?"

"There are many things I want to make you feel, Harper, but regret is not one of them."

Chapter Twenty-Three

Harper

Eric presses his cheek to my cheek and whispers, "Do you know how badly I want to take you to the bathroom and fuck you right now?" Heat pools low in my belly as he pulls back to look at me and adds, "Or anywhere, for that matter?"

My body melts while my mind fights for reason. I can't end up naked and confused again with this man and in no different a place than we are now. "Which would be fine if you could do it without hating me along with the rest of the family," I say, and somehow my hand is on his tattooed arm and I should move it, I know, but I don't want to stop touching him.

"Do it the Bennett way, not the Kingston way, and judge me for me."

The waitress chooses that moment to reappear and say, "Are you two ready to order?"

I curse the interruption and Eric grits his teeth as if echoing my sentiment. "Do you know what you want?"

"Yes. Spaghetti and meatballs."

He glances at the waitress. "The same for me."

The waitress asks a few questions and then she's gone. For several beats, he faces forward and then shifts back to me, his stare warm enough to sizzle. "I *want* to know your story. I want to know *you*."

I'm pleased with this admission and yet, I remain, I believe, rightfully skeptical. "I know you told me why the change, I do, but it's hard to digest that right now. You've tried so very hard to hate me."

"Fair enough," he says. "Let's be frank."

"Please," I encourage. "Please do."

"You were the only one in this family that had a chance to get me here, and you knew that."

"Because I'm not them. Not because we slept together, and I hate so much you might think that and it makes me feel like the last place I should be is right here, right now."

"But you want to be here. Don't you, Harper?"

"Would you believe me if I said yes? You have a file on me, but files don't tell you the real story. Not about people."

"Then you tell me."

"Are you going to really listen?"

"I assure you, sweetheart, no one has ever had my full attention more than you do now, for about ten different reasons. *You* tell me *your* story." "And you'll tell me yours?"

"I already started telling you my story. You know far more about me and my life choices than I do yours."

A story of lies, secrets, and pain that I push aside. I hunger for a deeper look into this man, but I push that burn aside. He doesn't want to talk about him. He wants to talk about me and my willingness to open up helps erase the divide between us. Or I hope it will. "I was close to my father and his heart attack pretty much destroyed me, but my mother was such a mess that I somehow found a way to step up and be strong. I was close to my mother, too, until we joined this family."

"Why until?"

"I don't know. She was a young mother, seventeen when she had me, and instead of dividing us, it brought us closer together. But since she married your father, there's been a slow divide."

"But you don't know why?" he presses.

I hesitate. "I don't want to say this and have you judge her harshly. I'm terrified you'll act against her."

"I don't want to hurt you, Harper. And the best way to keep me from acting against her is honesty."

"I'm trying. It's just hard not to be protective."

"And I respect that in you. Family is supposed to protect family."

"But yours never protected you."

"I don't need protection. Tell me about your mother. Why the divide?"

"I think it's because I push back and fight for what I think is right in the company, more so this past year when I felt that there were things that didn't add up. I felt it even before the recalls. That pushback has not been well received. My mother just wants me to appease your father and brother."

He leans in closer. "What don't I know?" he asks, those blue eyes glinting with intelligence. "You said you needed time and privacy, but that there were things you hadn't told me."

"You already know I'm aligned with Gigi. That was the thing I dreaded telling you the most, but I did tell you. I knew I needed to tell you."

"*Aligned*?" he asks, his mood darkening with whiplash speed. "You didn't use that word and I do not like it. How fucking aligned?"

"Not against you. I swear to you, not against you. And between you and I, I don't believe Gigi is fully repenting for her sins. I believe she's worried about losing the company. She doesn't want her legacy to go down in flames."

"You do know that I hate that woman enough to want to burn it to the ground, right?"

"You said you came for me, not her."

"I *did* come for you, Harper."

"Then please, I beg of you, don't burn it to the ground. My father's world was half that company."

"Your father is gone. His legacy is *you*. You don't need that place."

"So that's it then. You're going to ruin Kingston," It's not a question and I try to turn away. He catches my arm, turning me back around.

"Nothing about those people affected my life. I don't need to do that. I don't need them at all."

My fingers catch his lapel. "But you thought you did. You told me that in the past."

He draws in a breath and turns away from me, facing forward, his fingers laced in front of him on the table, seconds ticking by, while I hold my breath, not sure what comes next. Are we leaving? Is he leaving? Finally, he rotates back to me, more thoughtful than angry at this point. "I had a need for family after I lost my mother and the Navy filled that void. I came here to Denver the night I met you because I'd lost that connection. I thought I needed family but these people were never family."

My gaze goes to one of the tattoos on his right arm, a black and gray skull with an anchor that I assume represents his years as a SEAL. "Harvard graduate. Genius IQ. Navy SEAL. Self-made billionaire. You are so many things that this family is not."

"My fellow SEALs, and anyone with the Bennett name, that's real family to me, the kind that would bleed to protect you. This family will kill you to get ahead. You'd be smart to remember that."

"If I didn't know, Eric, I wouldn't have come to you. After that night," my hand falls away, "it was embarrassing. I thought you'd think I used sex to get to you. And you did. It was one of the first things out of your mouth."

He catches my hand and lays it on his powerful thigh, a silent message in the action. He doesn't regret the physical connection, but that doesn't mean he doesn't hold it against me. "Money is power, sweetheart, but once you have it, you swim in an ocean of sharks and snakes." When I try to recoil and remove my hand, he closes his around it. "I'm not talking about you. I'm simply telling you where I come from."

"I don't have money, Eric. That will always be between us."

"It's not between us."

"It is. You don't trust me and I don't know how to make you trust me."

"Just be you. Let me understand you."

"You already do. You protected your mother. You have to understand why I stayed for mine. I know you do. You say you don't, but you're not seeing me and the real picture. The company is all I have left of my father and my mother—I *love* her. She might not be perfect, but she's all I have."

He inhales and cuts his stare before he looks at me again, his eyes turbulent, a story in their depths that I hope I will one day understand, but I'm not sure he'll stay that long. "I understand why you were here," he says. "I don't understand why you're *still* here, though."

"My mother—"

"Is my father abusing her? Is she in danger?"

"Maybe. Maybe I am, too. If there was negligence that was intentional, there's criminal liability that she could get wrapped up inside. I could end up with that liability, too. You know Isaac will look for a fall guy. I'm terrified. I can't leave now. *I* could end up the fall guy."

His gaze sharpens. "Have you done something to create an exposure?"

"No." I pick up my wine and sip, my trepidation as bitter as it is sweet.

"Harper?" he prods.

I set the glass down and meet his probing stare. "Not that I know of, but I'm scared, Eric. Who knows what fingerprint I could have on something I don't understand. I don't know what's happening. I just know something is. The recalls. Weird money movement."

"You need to be honest with me."

"I *am*. I am being honest with you."

"What don't I know?" he presses, and I want to scream with the impossibility of this situation.

"Stop repeating that question. I already answered. I can show you everything I have collected, the paperwork, the notes I've taken. The information Gigi gave me. I have it at my house."

His eyes glint steel, his mood tangibly darker. "If you burn me, Harper, you won't like the results."

Frustration bites at me at this back and forth that always leads to the same distrustful place. "I have. What can I do to make you trust me?"

"Tell me *everything*."

"I am," I whisper, frustration bubbling beneath my surface. "Stop already."

"Clearly the only way I'm getting everything from you is with your clothes off. I need you to talk and I need to fuck you. I can't do either of those things here. We're leaving."

Heat and confusion collide, rushing over me with wicked fierceness. "You don't have to get me naked to get me to talk. I'm talking."

"Let's do it anyway. Any objection to that plan?"

"No," I whisper, because this is all too emotional and public for me. "No objection."

Chapter Twenty-Four

Harper

After announcing that he's basically taking me home to fuck me, Eric kisses me, a deep slide of his tongue that is over too soon, but he doesn't pull back. His lips are a breath from mine, lingering there, taunting me with another kiss that doesn't come, and the sound of the restaurant buzzes around us, fading away. The intensity of the pull between us stealing my breath. "Holy hell, woman," Eric murmurs, stroking my hair and then lifts his hand to flag the waitress.

That stroke of my hair undoes me. It's possessive and tender, a command and a question. No man has ever made a simple act so very provocative. No man has ever affected me like this one. He's ruined me for anyone else and that's a little bit terrifying.

The waitress joins us and Eric is quick to get us out of here. "We need boxes," he says. "We'll take it all with us."

The woman looks confused. "Oh. Yes. Of course."

"Quickly," Eric adds, impatience to his tone that he makes up for by adding, "There's a big tip in it for you."

Her eyes go wide and she rushes away. Eric immediately leans over and brushes his lips over mine again. "You taste like trouble."

"I wish I weren't," I say, my eyes meeting his, "but you're right. I am."

"Yes, but trouble suits me, sweetheart. Wait and see." He winks and my stomach flutters. God, how he affects me with the smallest of acts.

The waitress re-appears and in a few quick minutes, our food is boxed up, wine corked, and the bill paid, all the while I'm thinking about his comment about trouble suiting him. He's not wrong. It does suit him, but I hope he remembers how tricky it can be. Trouble has a way of growing roots, and doing damage. I don't want to be the end of him and I plan to tell him that when we're alone.

Once we're ready to go, we both stand and Eric laces his fingers with mine and leads me through the restaurant. With each step, I can feel the swell of need between us, the connection that is as combustible as it is dangerous. Because of that trouble. Because of all the trouble.

We pause to grab our coats and Eric helps me with mine. That simple act is intimate, the air around us charged.

We exit to the street and he folds his arm around my shoulders, and aligns our hips. We start walking, neither of us speaking for a full block, a mix of sexual tension and unspoken words between us. A push and pull of lust and need with questions that need answers. It's then that this connection I have to Eric, *with* Eric, drives home another feeling. Guilt dives about inside me and burrows deep.

I stop walking and turn to face him, the dim lighting of the cozy little neighborhood now mixed with the beam of a bright full moon. "I don't want to be trouble for you, Eric."

"I told you. Trouble suits me."

"I was selfish asking you to come here. I know what Gigi did to you and your mother. All I could see was my own problems, my fear for my mother. I was selfish and wrong. *I'm sorry.*"

"I'm a grown ass man, sweetheart. I make my own decisions and you have nothing to be sorry for. As for Gigi fucking me over, she's doing it to you, too," he says. "You just don't see it."

"At least she wants what I want. That's where my head is. I can't do this alone. I've tried. I can't get answers from Isaac or your father. I got shut out."

"You have me now."

"Because I pulled you in. Because I didn't let you just do what you wanted and stay away."

"I did what I wanted," he says. "I came here for you. I wanted you. I *want* you. I need to trust you, though, Harper. I don't like your connection to Gigi."

"Trust is two ways, I need to trust you, too. And to be clear, I'm done trying to save the company. I don't care what your plan is if it saves my mother. Take the damn company. You're right. I'm my father's legacy. I don't recognize Kingston as anything he was anymore." My eyes burn and I glance skyward, a silent plea in my mind to my father, to forgive me for allowing his company to be destroyed.

Eric's hands settle on my shoulders, his touch snapping my gaze to his, and then, and only then, he says, "Deep breath, sweetheart. Better things are coming. I promise you. You know what we both need right now?"

I laugh, knowing where this is headed. "To be naked?"

"Good answer. Yes. We need to go fuck and get lost in each other, and drive this damn family out of our heads, just like we did the night we met."

"Is that what I did for you that night? Helped you drive them out of your head?"

"And a lot more, sweetheart, or I wouldn't be here now. Come on," he says, twining the fingers of his hand with mine and leading me down the sidewalk.

The remainder of the walk is a short one block, and everything but me and him, and all that is happening between us fades away. Already we're driving away the Kingston family, lost in anticipation, in each other. And there *is* something happening between me and Eric, and it's not just sex, and it simmers with intimacy between us. My skin is flushed. My sex has clenched just thinking about being naked and in his arms again. We turn down my drive. "Back door," I say. "I always go in there."

We close the space between it and us, that combustible need between us, just that, combustible. I'm burning alive, anxiously enough that my hand trembles as I unlock my door. So much so that Eric takes my key from me and finishes the job. We enter the house directly into the kitchen, white stone beneath our feet. I flip on the light, illuminating an island in more white stone, and cabinets a slate gray wood wrapping a half-moon-shaped room. I slip off my coat and set it on a barstool, turning to face Eric as he shuts the door and locks it.

We don't speak. We don't really have words on our mind.

He shrugs out of his coat, his T-shirt stretching over his broad chest, before he drops it on a stool next to mine, his eyes never leaving me. He steps close, aligning our bodies, and I feel the heat of him, the change in us. This isn't a power play. This isn't hate anymore.

His hands frame my face. "I nicknamed you princess because you were so fucking beautiful and regal standing there by the pool that night."

The compliment sizzles through me, but I reject the comparison, and the idea it suggests that I am somehow above him. That we are not the same. "I wasn't regal," I say. "I don't want you to think of me that way."

"In a good way, sweetheart. This is me telling you that you had me before hello."

It's everything I want to hear from this man, perhaps too much, because I'm not sure how long he'll be in my life. I just know it won't be long enough. "Did you know it was me? Did you know who I was?"

"No, I didn't."

"I knew it was you. I'd seen pictures."

"And?"

"And I knew I should stay away," I admit.

"Why?"

"That whole forbidden, taboo stepsibling thing."

"And yet you still came to the cottage?"

I laugh. "You made me mad."

"Let me make it up to you," he says, claiming my mouth, the first lick of his tongue driving me wild. I moan and that's all it takes. We're crazy, wild, kissing, his hands sliding over my waist, over my hips, cupping my backside. I tug at his shirt, desperate to feel warm skin over taut muscle. Desperate to feel him. He presses his hand under my skirt and that's when my doorbell rings.

We stiffen, eyes colliding in surprise. "Expecting company?" he asks.

"No. No one visits me."

He pulls my skirt down and strokes my hair again. "Get rid of whoever it is."

I nod and hurry down a hallway that leads to the front door. I peek through the curtain to find my mother standing there. "Oh God." I rotate to find Eric in the hallway.

I hurry toward him, eager to prepare him for the storm soon upon us and already, my doorbell rings yet again. "It's my mother," I say softly. "She's going to go off on me about you."

"Are you saying you want me to leave?"

"No, I want you to stay, but I don't trust her not to repeat everything to your father."

"You want to save her but you don't trust her?"

"She's not logical with him."

"I'll choose my words with that in mind."

"Okay." I give him an apologetic look. "I'm sorry about this."

He cups my head and kisses me. "Make it up to me."

He's teasing but I don't smile. "I will," I promise, and I love that he's being so easygoing about this.

I hurry back to the door and open it. My mother is standing there, looking stunning and far younger than her forty-six years, her ivory skin pale perfection, her black pantsuit sleek and elegant, her dark hair in waves around her shoulders. "Why haven't you called me back?" she demands.

"Come in, mom," I say, backing up to allow her entry.

She steps into the foyer and her eyes lock on Eric. "What the hell is he doing in your house?" she demands and then pins me in a stare. "Don't you even know why he came here?" Her scathing attention lands on Eric. "I know why you're here."

Chapter Twenty-Five

Harper

"I know what you're doing," my mother snaps at Eric again, and my God, she charges at him so quickly that I barely have time to put myself between them.

"Mom!" I shout urgently, my hands catching her arms. "Stop. Stop it right now."

"What are you thinking?"

"I'm thinking we need him. And as for why he's here, he's here because I went to New York. I found him. I asked him to come here."

"Then you're a fool. We have something to lose, and he has everything to gain."

Frustration and anger shorten my patience. "He's a billionaire, mother. He doesn't need anything from this family."

"He's not a billionaire."

"Yes," I say. "*He is.*"

"It doesn't matter what he is or isn't. *We* are your family. He is not."

That pisses me off. Now, she's doing what the rest of this family has done to Eric and that's not the person I know. She doesn't hurt people. "*He's* family. He's a Kingston. He's blood. We aren't. Don't act like them. You're not one of them."

"We *are* them," she says, driving home every accusation Eric has ever made toward me.

"We are *not them.*" And because I don't want her to say anything else to hurt him when this family has done nothing but that, I turn to face Eric. My hand settles on his chest, my need to touch him, to let him know that I'm with him, not them, absolutely. "I'm sorry," I say, my eyes meeting his, my hope that he sees the truth in my words, in all that I have told him, in them.

"There's nothing to be sorry for," he promises softly.

"Yes, there is," I say, wishing he'd touch me. I really want him to touch me, especially since I know I have to speak to my mother alone to get her to see reason. "Can you give us just a minute?"

"Of course," he says, his tone and stare unreadable, that hardness that is so a part of this man, back and etched in his handsome face. His blue eyes cold, ice I know is meant for the Kingstons, and now I'm a Kingston to him again. I hate that ice. "I'll be in the kitchen," he adds.

"Don't leave," I whisper urgently, my fingers closing around his shirt and I don't care if my mother hears. I add, "Please. Her words are not mine."

The ice in those eyes of his, warms, the hard edge of his mood softening as he covers my hand with his. "I'm not going anywhere." He tightens his grip. "Let me know if you need me." He releases me and turns to walk down the hallway.

"Are you sleeping with him?" my mother snaps at my back with Eric still within hearing distance. Honestly, I'm fairly certain he will hear everything from the kitchen anyway.

"That has nothing to do with this," I say, whirling on her.

"That's not a no. You are."

"He's helping us. How about being glad that he's that kind of man? That he actually came here to help."

"He didn't come to help. Your father says—"

"My father is *dead*. Gone. And your husband is letting everything he worked for, including your future, get wiped away. You could go to jail."

"We are not going to jail. No one did anything wrong."

"You could actually," I say. "People died, mother. If there were choices made that ignored risk to human life—"

"Stop," my mother says now. "Stop right now. That didn't happen."

"And you know this how? Because even Gigi is scared. She wanted Eric here."

"Gigi hates him."

"Gigi was afraid of him when she should have embraced the one person in this family that has his shit together."

She steps closer and actually grabs my arm, lowering her voice. "Gigi treated him horribly," she whispers. "I didn't know he was a billionaire, but I knew he was powerful. He'll try to take everything. Don't let him use you to do it."

"Don't turn him into the monster. People didn't die on his watch."

"You don't know what you're diving into here," she warns. "You have no idea."

Those words come with such conviction that I narrow my eyes on her. "What aren't you telling me?"

"There's nothing to tell," she says. "You're creating problems that don't have to exist. My God, Harper, fuck him out of your system and send him home. Please. I beg of you."

I feel those words like a slap. My mother doesn't say things like that. Ever. "What aren't you telling me?" I repeat.

"I have done nothing but love you and take care of you and so has this family. Treat us like it."

"This family has done nothing for me. You are another story. *You* are my family. I'm trying to protect you."

"You're trying to ruin my life. Your father—"

"Stop calling him that. Please."

"Jeff," she bites out. "He's not pleased that it's my daughter that brought this problem to his door."

"He's a solution, not a problem, and one day you'll thank me for this. And I hope you'll thank Eric as well."

"Get rid of him. I beg of you. No. I order you. End this tonight." She turns and opens the door and exits, slamming the door behind her.

I stand there and the room seems to weave around me. I'm trembling, I think. I don't tremble, but my mother is my world. She's all I have and she's never talked to me like this, but Eric—he's the one helping her and me. It's then that I dare to admit that he matters; he's the guy that could hurt me. He's the one that I could trust and be burned alive because I did so. He's that guy for me. He always has been.

His footsteps sound behind me and I turn to find him standing in the archway. We stare at each other, the air thick with an uneasy feeling between us that I don't want to exist.

"Could you hear it all?" I ask.

"Yes," he says, his expression impenetrable but he closes the space between us, stopping a reach from touching me but he doesn't. He *doesn't* touch me. "I could hear everything," he says. "What do you want right now?"

My hand presses to his chest. "You. I want you."

"You want to fuck me out of your system?"

"I tried that. It didn't work."

"Do you think I'm here to hurt you?" he asks.

Tension crackles between us. My body aches everywhere he's not touching me. "No, I don't. And I hate that she acted that way. I hate the things she said to you. I know they hurt you. I know you could choose to hurt me because they hurt you but I can't seem to care. I know we're just fucking, but—"

He drags me to him, his fingers tangling in my hair. "Sweetheart, if we were just fucking, I wouldn't be here." His mouth closes down on mine, and then he's tasting me, claiming me, his tongue licking deep, and I feel it everywhere. I feel *him* everywhere. But we can't ignore what just happened. We can't just kiss it away.

I press my hand to his chest. "Eric—"

"Forget what just happened. We're here. We're now. Be in the moment with me."

We're here. We're now. Something about those words both pleases and taunts me in a strange combination that I never get the chance to understand. He's kissing me again, drugging me with the taste of him, spicy, male, demanding, and suddenly he's scooping me up and walking under the archway toward the living room.

The next thing I know, I'm on the couch on my back and he's coming down on top of me, his legs aligned with mine, his hands at my face. "Ask me what I want, Harper." His voice is this low, raspy seduction that is both silk and satin on my nerve endings.

"What do you want, Eric?"

"You," he says, "from the day I met you. You. I've fucking wanted you, but you were the enemy."

"And now?"

"And now this," he says, and then his mouth is back on mine, warmth spreading through my body, consuming me the way only he can. He does. He consumes me. It's terrifying. It's addicting. He's addicting.

What do I want?

More.

Him.

More of him.

And despite it perhaps being the definition of insanity, I know there will be a price to pay, but I don't care what he costs me.

Chapter Twenty-Six

Eric

There is something about this woman that burns through me like sunshine on a winter's day, warming even the cold of this city, this family. She is *why* I'm here. Hell, she's always been in my fucking head, burning me with memories of touching her, with wanting her. I mold her close, my lips brushing her mouth, the scent of her—a sweet, floral spice—wrapping me in the spell that is this woman. She cast a damn spell on me at the pool the night we met, a spell that time and space didn't erase.

"Not a princess," I murmur against her mouth. "A witch."

Her fingers curl on my jaw. "*Not a princess. A witch.* What does that even mean?"

"It means," I go to my knees and pull her upright with me, yanking her jacket down her shoulders to hold her arms captive, "you cast a damn spell on me or I wouldn't be here."

"No, I—"

I kiss her, my tongue stroking away her objection before I say, "You did or I wouldn't have thought about you for six long years."

"You thought of me?"

"Yes, Harper, I did and I resented you for it. For that power over me."

"I thought of you, too. Let go of my arms. Please, I want to touch you."

There's a part of me that doesn't want to let that happen. That doesn't want the crazy way she affects me to steal my damn control, because she does. No one else can, but she absolutely does. There is something in her voice, in her eyes, a vulnerability, a need I haven't sensed until tonight. A vulnerability I know comes not just from my ability to affect her situation. It's about her mother. It's about how painful I know that conversation she just had with her was, and I get it. My mother and I had so many fights driven by the family. I lost her and though Harper's mother doesn't have cancer to drive a suicide like mine did, Harper is still worried about her safety.

I kiss her again, the taste of her, the feel of her, is sweet honey on my tongue that I've craved every day since I left it behind. "You, woman," I say when I tear my mouth from hers, and just barely touching my lips to her lips.

"You," she whispers. "You. *Eric.*"

Eric.

She's telling me she sees me, not the bastard. "Harper," I whisper, making sure she knows I see her, not them. I stand up and she follows me, this tiny, feisty, beautiful woman. She tosses her jacket and kicks off her shoes. I turn her and unzip her skirt before sliding it and her panties down her hips and lifting her to kick them away. I drag her blouse over her head and toss it. My hand goes to her belly, pulling her to me, while I unhook her bra and then cup her breasts, holding them in my hands. She leans into me, her backside pressed to my cock, my fingers tugging at her nipples. She moans and I bury my head in her neck, inhaling that sweet scent of her, just breathing her in. I've never done that with any woman but this one. I never wanted to savor a woman instead of fuck her. I want both with Harper and I don't even know what to do with that.

Fuck. She's dangerous and I can't seem to walk away.

She's in only thigh highs now, and I press her to her knees on the couch, placing her backside in the air, and I stroke my hand over her hips, my cock throbbing, but it's so fucking much more with this woman. My gaze rakes over her body and I lean over her. "Don't move," I order, scraping my teeth over her shoulder, cupping her breasts and then dragging my hands down her ribcage, before I straighten and pull my shirt off. I stand there then, watching her, making her wait and I tell myself it's to drive the tension, to drive her to the edge, but another emotion claws at me, a need to control her, to control what she's become to me. What she can do to hurt me, like the rest of this fucking family, but she's not them.

Damn it.

I want to hate her.

I don't.

Not even close.

I undress, pull on a condom, and sit down on the couch and take her with me, pulling her onto my lap. Her hands come down on my shoulders. Our eyes lock, and holy hell, I feel this woman in ways I can't even describe. I lift her and press inside her. She takes me in a slow slide, and then she presses down, taking me all, straddling me.

Her teeth scrape her bottom lip and she moves back and forth, as if she just needs to feel me there, everywhere. I tangle my fingers into her hair and drag her mouth to mine. "Do you know what I want?" I demand.

"To hate me?"

"It would be easier that way."

"What would be?" she asks, breathlessly. "Fucking me?"

"Everything," I say. "Everything would be easier if I hated you like I do them, but no, I don't want to hate you. I don't want to forget you. Not anymore."

"Then what do you want?"

"Everything," I say, admitting out loud everything I feel with that one word. "Everything, Harper." I drag her mouth to mine and kiss her. She sinks into it, our mouths, our tongues, colliding with hunger, that's all I can call it—hunger. So damn much hunger, that we're touching each other, kissing each other, moving together, a sway of her hips, a pump of mine, repeat. There is nothing but us, here, now, and this. Whatever the hell this is, but I can't feel anything but her.

I pinch her nipple and she covers my hand on her breasts, kissing me even as we move. Everything. I want everything and more, I roll with her, pressing her back to the couch again and then I'm driving into her, pumping with a need that comes from somewhere deep, to the point that it's clawing. "Eric," she pants, and I kiss her, rolling to my side, and pulling her leg to my hip, thrusting as I do.

Her fingers dig into my shoulders and she pants my name again, and I thrust again. She buries her face in my chest and I can feel her quake before her body is spasming around me. God. I feel every moment of her orgasm, and it pulls me in, drags my release from me the way she pulls me to her and doesn't let go. My balls tighten, a knot of tension low in my groin, and then I'm shuddering into release with such intensity that I damn near black out.

When I come back to the world, I'm holding Harper, and she's holding me, our bodies molded intimately together, and I don't want to get up. I want to hold her, but there's a condom to consider. I ease back to look at her, and the minute our eyes connect, the pull between us is just as strong as before we fucked, and I know I'm here to stay. This isn't going to end like the other two times we were together. Because I'm not leaving. Not tonight. Not without her.

She's mine now. She's been mine since that night six years ago. It just wasn't our time yet, but now, now is our time and I'm not walking away. Not from the mess, the family dragged her into and not without her.

Chapter Twenty-Seven

Eric

Still lying on the couch, still inside her, and still wearing the condom, I stroke a lock of hair from Harper's face. "I should get up."

"I know," she whispers and there's regret in her voice that stretches beyond this moment.

I catch her chin and tilt her stare to mine. "I don't want to get up. I'm not leaving, Harper."

Her eyes soften, warm. "Good," she says. "I don't want you to leave."

"Good," I echo and kiss her. "But," I say really quite seriously, "if I'm staying, you have to feed me. I'm wasting away here."

She laughs and it's a sexy, sweet laugh that I could easily find addictive. "We can't have that, now can we?" She shoves on my chest. "Get up and I'll order food. I have an idea."

"Which is what?" I ask.

"I'll surprise you. And as a bonus, this place I have in mind is one block down. Delivery is fast."

I pull out of her and we both groan, with more laughter following. I help her to sit up and pull her to her feet. "I could hunt for the bathroom, naked but for a condom, or you could direct me to the right spot."

"I would enjoy the naked and wandering around my house option but since you're starving, there's one by the front door." She pushes to her toes and kisses me, the spontaneous act somehow as sexy as everything she just did when she was fucking me.

I wrap my arm around her waist, folding her close, and I kiss her this time. "I'll be right back. Consider the food on the way."

I scoop up my pants from the slate gray wood flooring, a color that matches the L-shaped couches that frame a stone fireplace. There are two high-back chairs by the window, both a lighter gray.

The décor is almost masculine, a bit like my own. That is until you add in the fluffy cream-colored throws and flower-shaped light bulbs dangling from above. This space is Harper, a little piece of her, and somehow a little is not enough. I really don't know what to do with that information but I have to figure this shit out.

I cross the room and the foyer to enter the bathroom. Once I toss the condom into the trashcan, I pull my pants on commando style and lean on the sink, staring at myself in the mirror, and when I see my father in the image I look away, I grimace; it's a comparison I haven't made in years and I don't like that I do so now. A symptom of being here, I decide, in this city, in the midst of this screwed up family.

And yet, I'm going nowhere, I already know that, not without Harper, which is not good news for the Kingston family.

In fact, I think it's safe to say, they're fucked.

I exit the bathroom just as the doorbell rings. I grab the takeout order that turns out to be Chinese food, my stomach downright bitching me out at this point, I'm so fucking hungry. With the food in hand, I walk to the end of the stairs and glance up to the second floor, where I assume Harper's bedroom must be located, therefore where I plan to spend the night. "Harper?!"

"I'm right here," she calls out, hurrying down the steps I was just eyeing, and doing so in a pair of black sweats and a pink T-shirt, her nipples puckering against the thin cloth. "I just couldn't put those work clothes back on."

I'm waiting on her when she reaches the last step. "Oh good," she says, "the food came. And I just realized that we forgot our pasta back at the restaurant."

I wiggle my brows at her. "We had other things on our minds."

"*You* had other things on *your* mind," she laughs and her hand settles easily, comfortably on my waist.

"I like you like this," I say, only partially talking about her nipples, under the T-shirt.

She smiles, and she has a smile that can light its way through a thunderstorm. The smile of a princess. She motions up and down her body. "This is what I call grunge princess," she jokes. "I'm so glad you approve."

"I like you natural. Casual. Relaxed for once."

A hint of pink colors her cheeks. "Yeah, well you make that easy," she says softly, a bit shyly. "It means a lot to me that you're here." She follows that with a grin. "And as for casual," she pokes my chest playfully, "I love the jeans and T-shirt you had going on at the office. And aside from you looking just as good in denim as you do a suit, you know why I liked it?"

I have no idea where she's going with this, but I'm all in for finding out. "Why did you like it, Harper?"

"That was clearly a 'fuck you' to your father and brother." She pinches her lips. "No. Just your father. I don't think you give one second of thought to Isaac."

She's perceptive. I like that. "I have no need to impress either of them," I say, "but *you* are another story."

"You impress me most naked," she assures me, but somehow, she manages to remain so very wholesome. The girl next door every guy fantasizes about, most certainly me.

I laugh. "Is that right?"

"Yes. Definitely right." She snags one of the two bags from my hand. "I'm going to feed you now, but I have a condition."

"Another orgasm?"

"Orgasms are always good," she says, "but I want you to tell me what all of your ink means."

"My ink," I repeat, when I'd expected her to want to know about my money, my success. Or even how I'm going to deal with Kingston. "That's what you want to know about me?"

"Yes," she says motioning me toward the kitchen. I follow her that direction and when we're behind her kitchen island I say, "*That's* what you want to know?"

She laughs. "Yes. Why is that so hard to believe? That ink clearly tells a story. I want to hear that story."

It's an astute assumption and right on target. My ink is my life history in ways she seems to intuitively understand which is surprising but also interesting. *Harper* is interesting, complicated, smart, thoughtful—kind in ways I will never be or become. She needs to understand that, but then I think she's trying to do just that, to understand me. She begins removing the containers from the bags.

"How old were you when you got your first tattoo?" she asks. "And before you answer, you're okay with me sticking these in the microwave, right? It feels a little cold."

"Of course," I answer, perching on a leather barstool while she pops the food in to warm. "And to answer your question, I was eighteen when I got my first tattoo and it was a stopwatch that's still on my right forearm in the middle of more ink." I turn my arm and show her. "Pissed off my father which only made me like it more."

"And what does the stopwatch mean to you?"

"All things come in their own time. And that statement has meant many things to me in my life." My eyes meet Harper's. "Like us, sweetheart. It wasn't our time six years ago. It is now."

"All things come in their own time," she repeats softly, her gaze sliding over both of my arms. "You only had one sleeve when I met you six years ago."

"A lot has happened in six years."

"For you," she says. "I know it has."

"Not for you?"

"I feel like I've done nothing but fight the same battle." She gives a choked laugh. "You know that saying. The definition of stupid or insanity or whatever it is, is to keep doing the same thing and expecting a different result. You're right. Six years was too long." Pain stabs through her eyes but the microwave beeps and gives her an excuse to cut her stare. She looks away and pulls the first tray out, checking it and then replacing it with the second.

"This one is ready," she says, closing the space between us to set it in front of me.

I drag her to me, between my legs, not about to let her comments go unanswered. "You didn't make a mistake. There have been times when I thought I left too soon and too easily."

"You didn't. You would never have been accepted."

"I know that now," I say. "I knew that at the party. I didn't know it during some of those years in the SEALs."

"Yes, well as you said, six years makes me a damn slow learner."

"I never said that and it's clear that you stayed for your mother." The microwave goes off again and I motion to an unopened bottle of wine on the counter. "How about some of that wine?" I ask. "It'll take the edge off."

"That was a gift from my mother, who has expensive tastes these days, that she never had before. I couldn't drink it. It felt like accepting who she's become."

"She loves you, sweetheart. Don't overthink her gifts. Drink the wine and do it because you're with me. Forget about everything else. Yes?"

She gives a little nod. "Yes."

"You're sure?"

"Yes. I'm sure."

"Perfect. Where are the glasses?"

"Cabinet by the sink to the left."

I cup her head and kiss her before I open the wine and fill two glasses. We sip the red blend with approval and Harper shivers.

"It's chilly in here," she says. "I can turn on the fireplace in the living room and we can eat in there."

A few minutes later we're settled on the floor in front of her coffee table eating. "Holy hell, this is good."

"It's my favorite," she says. "I have a lot of favorite places around the area. North is one of the few places that has been here since you were here. This place is new."

We sit and chat about the neighborhood and all the places we both know and love, until we're both done with our food. As we sit back and turn toward each other, the air is thick, the pull between us palpable. She reaches out and catches my arm, tracing the rows of numbers randomly placed between a clock and a skull with an anchor.

"What do the numbers mean?"

"Numbers are how I process everything. If I'm thinking about anything, anything at all, there are numbers in my head."

"Even me?"

"Yes. Even you. It's a part of my life in all ways. It's how I make money. It's how I negotiate. It's how I brush my damn teeth. It's how I saw mission paths in the SEALs that no one else saw."

"SEAL Team Six," she says, running her finger over the skull and anchor before looking up at me again. "That's intense. You saw blood and death. I'm sure you had to take lives."

I cover her hand where it rests on my tattoo, and I don't even think about denying who I am. I've been done with that kind of self-doubt a good decade ago. "Is that a problem for you?"

"Of course not. You're a hero. I just hate that your family drove you to that life. You could have died. You have to have nightmares and just stuff—baggage."

"Less than you might think," I say. "I compartmentalize extremely well."

"I don't," she says. "I'm pretty all-in emotionally when I'm in. You should know that about me."

All in.

I *want* her all in.

I lean in closer, my hand on her cheek. "I want you all in."

Her hand covers mine on her face. "Until you leave again."

"Let me clarify what I just said. Yes, I compartmentalize easily, and yes that means I shut people and things off easily. But not you. Never you."

"I didn't see you for six years, Eric."

"I told you. I thought of you often."

"As one of them."

"As the woman who wouldn't just fucking get out my head."

She pulls back sharply, bristling a bit, as she says, "Well, you wouldn't fucking get out of my head either."

"But you didn't come to me, did you?"

"You left in a way that made it clear you were done with me."

I lean back and hold out my right forearm, running a finger along a line of numbers with a crown at the end of it. "Do you know what that is?"

She sucks in a breath at the crown and covers it with her hand. "Is it bad? Is it something bad about me?"

"It says *Princess* in the numbers that correlate to the alphabet. I added it two full years after our night together."

"You tattooed the nickname you gave me on your body?"

"Yes, princess, *I did*. Now do you believe that I didn't forget about you?" I cup her face and her hand settles on my chest. "Now isn't then, it's not the past. You know that, right? I didn't come here to walk away. Not from you."

"Eric," she whispers, her voice trembling with emotion and I want those emotions, I want to know how they taste on my tongue. How she tastes right now, this night, in this room.

I lean in to kiss her, right as the doorbell rings, followed by pounding on the door. "Open up, Harper!"

At the sound of Isaac's voice, my jaw sets hard and Harper launches herself to her feet. This can't be good."

I'm standing with her by the time she's fully straightened. "Relax, sweetheart," I say, my hands settling on her arm, "He's a gnat that needs to be swiped. Nothing more. I'll handle my brother." I start to turn away and Harper grabs my arm.

"Wait," she says, pulling me around to face her. "Let me talk to him. Obviously, my mother told him you're here. He's going to make a big deal out of this. I can shut it down."

I drag her to me. "You mean deny we're together?"

"No. That's not what I meant. Of course, that's not what I mean."

"Good. Because we're together now. That means we don't hide. And if that makes the Kingstons uncomfortable, fuck them. Do you have a problem with that?"

"No," she whispers. "You're right. Fuck them."

"Then I'll handle Isaac, sweetheart. No one has my brother's number like I do."

Chapter Twenty-Eight

Eric

"O h no," Harper says, catching my arm as I try to leave her to answer the door again. "I'm fine with Isaac knowing about us, but you're shirtless and commando with your pants unzipped. That screams 'we're fucking' not 'we're together.' I draw the line there."

"Anyone in the same room with us for sixty seconds knows we're fucking, sweetheart."

"Don't taunt him with me. I don't like that. I don't want to feel like a weapon between two brothers, not even in a war I invited you into."

I catch her hips and walk her to me. "What the hell does that mean?"

"Not now. Later. Right now, we have to deal with him so please, zip your pants and put on a shirt before you walk to the door."

I reach down and zip my pants before scooping up my shirt, my eyes never leaving her face. "You're going to explain that little weapon between two brothers comment."

"I will," she promises. "I'll tell you."

"Yes, you will, *princess*," I reply and make sure it bites.

Her eyes flare with anger that I don't stay to answer. Not when Isaac is shouting at the door again and pounding while holding a finger on the bell. "Jesus," I murmur, running a hand through my hair. "His degree of ridiculousness obviously hasn't changed." I take off for the door and this time Harper lets me go.

The ring and knock cycle has started again by the time I get there, along with another shout of, "I know you're in there, Harper! Damn it, open up."

I unlock the door, open it, and greet my dear brother. He's wearing a scowl and a trenchcoat over the same expensive ass three-piece suit he had on at work today. It also, from what I can tell, must have come with a stick up his ass. "You're here for me, right?" I ask. "Here I am." I step forward, crowding him and forcing him onto the porch.

"I'm here for Harper," he says, unbuttoning his jacket and settling his hands on his hips.

After the exchange I just had with her, those words punch me in all the wrong ways. "To warn her away from me," I state, disliking the obvious history I don't know about and irritated as fuck Walker Security didn't tell me about in advance.

"Her mother's worried about her."

My lips quirk. "And you're the superhero here to pretend to save her while saving yourself? How'd that superhero routine work for you in the past?"

"There's nothing here for you."

"We both know that's not true. We both know that's never been true."

"You don't need the money. You want what no bastard deserves and you're using her and her ridiculous paranoia. She's your damn stepsister and you're fucking her, you sick fuck."

I smirk, unaffected by the ridiculous remark meant to get under my skin. He stopped getting under my skin about a year into this family. The problem for him is that's when I started getting under his skin. "Harper and I aren't blood," I say, "but we are, and we both know that's why she doesn't scare you, but I do." I step closer to him, damn near bringing us toe to toe. "And you *should* be afraid because we also both know you're hiding something. One last thing we both know—I'm good at finding out your secrets." It's a reference to a shared past that he can't run from, a past I don't want to run from. But then why would I? I'd fast-tracked to law school and joined him there. He hated my success. He'd wanted an edge. He even fucked our law professor to try to win her over and destroy me. He almost succeeded.

"I could have ended you."

"You should have done it while you could because that ship has sailed. Walk away, Eric. You don't know what pot you're stirring."

"But I will."

"I don't care about your fortune or the Bennett Empire behind you. Walk deeper into this and you might not walk away in one piece."

"Are you seriously threatening me?"

"I don't need to threaten you. I'm stating a fact. Consider this a brotherly warning. The only one you'll receive. Get away from her before you take her down with you and all of us for that matter." He pokes a finger at my chest and that's one thing Isaac doesn't do. He doesn't get physical. It's uncharacteristic and I read palpable panic in him. "Go home now," he bites out but he doesn't move. He stands there, glares at me, but in the depth of his eyes, I see fear, the kind of fear I've seen in men's eyes seconds before they ended up dead. He turns and walks down the stairs, leaving every instinct I own saying this is bigger than I thought it was. Isaac is into something he can't get out of and it's time I meet with my father and find out if he's in it, too.

I walk to the railing to ensure Isaac leaves, a muscle in my jaw ticking as I watch him shut himself inside his silver BMW. My grip tightens on the wood beneath my palms with a mental replay of his words: *I'm here for Harper. Get away from her before you take her down with you and all of us for that matter.* Isaac backs out of the driveway and I don't move until he's out of sight, my certainty absolute that Harper is now ten feet deep in something that smells dirty and dangerous.

I turn back toward the house, an icy gust of wind rushing over me. It's nothing compared to the cold I've experienced in the past, during those years in the SEALs, and in too many ways, the year of my mother's death, ending in her suicide. Gigi had been the last one to see her, the last Kingston to taunt her. Nothing about that has ever felt right to me, which is exactly why Harper's alignment with Gigi will never be a comfortable one. I've accepted her reasoning, but her fucking Isaac and then me in whatever order that I might have occurred, would not be.

I'm about to open the door, but at the same moment it flies open and Harper is standing there. "What happened?" she asks.

I advance on her, shut the door and lock it and then turn her to press her against it. "Did you fuck him?"

"No," she says. "I didn't fuck him. He tried. I turned him down. He's treated me like shit ever since."

"Then why protect him?"

"*Protect him?*" she asks, her tone incredulous. "I didn't protect him. I protected me and you. He's vicious. He lashes out. He competes with you and I'm not interested in being a pawn. And come on, Eric, you didn't want me to be a pawn to Gigi. But you're okay with using us to taunt him?"

"If he's uneasy, he makes mistakes. I'll catch him making those mistakes. I'll get you out of this."

"It's more than that and you know it. You want to hurt this family."

"Yes. I do. And I could have a thousand times over. Wanting and doing are two different things."

"Why didn't you?"

I look skyward, that question one I've asked myself over and over and come back to one place. I look at her and go there now. "Because my mother didn't want that. She protected them when they destroyed her. It was all in the letter she left me when she died. Which is exactly why I eventually left for the SEALs. I could have ruined Isaac. I wanted to. The temptation was too great. I had to leave. Every time I'm here, I have to leave. That's why I don't come here, but I came for you." My eyes meet hers, burn into hers. "The idea of you fucking him and fucking me kills me."

"I told you—no, I was never with Isaac." Her hand settles on my chest, that small touch burning through my body, *she* burns through me. "I didn't fuck him. I never wanted to fuck him and he hates me for it. Like you hate me. *Princess.* Already I'm her again and I can't be her." She shoves on my chest and tries to move away. I catch her to me, and she pushes harder. "Let go."

Let go.

I should. I could. I'd be smart to do just that, but that's not going to happen. I'm not letting her go. I'm not going to walk away, and that might end up being the worst thing that ever happened to this family.

I tangle fingers into her hair and stare down at her. "I don't hate you. I'm obsessed with you."

"You can still hate me and be obsessed with me."

I kiss her, my tongue licking and exploring, looking for lies that I don't find. There's just a moment of resistance, then her sweet, soft submission, her soft curves melting against mine, her desire moaning from her lips. I want her submission. I want her desire. I want more than I should when I know I'm headed down a deep, dark rabbit hole, but Isaac was wrong. I won't be the death of her, but she might be the death of him because she's why I'm staying. She's why my mother's letter can't save him this time.

Chapter Twenty-Nine

Eric

*D*irty. Filthy. Fucking.

That's how I tried to frame this thing between me and my little princess, but now, here, in her foyer kissing her, I admit that it was never that. She slid right under my skin and stayed there from the moment I first laid eyes on her. I don't want to let her go, but she, apparently, doesn't have the same sentiments.

She shoves against my chest, tearing her mouth from mine. "No. No. My version of together isn't hatred and obsession. It's not me being a princess to you."

"Sweetheart, I tattooed *Princess* on my body. I tattooed *you* on my body."

"You also tattooed a jaguar on your shoulder in spite of your father."

"That jaguar isn't about revenge. It's about the world being bigger than the Kingston name. It's about not putting limits on myself. Everything inked on my body is a piece of me, Harper. You became that. You affected me."

"*You walked away.*"

"Be glad I did. I might have wanted you then, Harper, but I wasn't the same man I am now. It wasn't our time. *Now* is our time."

"And yet you came at me like I'm fucking your brother."

"I had no right to tell you that you couldn't, but had you fucked us both—"

"Oh God," she says, trying to pull away, but my leg slides against her knee, my hand going to the wall by her head.

"What just happened?" I demand.

"You implied that I'm some sort of whore who wants to do two brothers."

"I did no such thing. I told you how I feel."

"I slept with you. You affected me. You have always affected me, Eric, even when I wanted you out of my head."

"What does *that* mean?"

"It doesn't matter," she says, her eyes blazing with anger. "Let me off the wall."

"Not until you tell me what that means."

"You made me feel dirty, and like a weapon."

"I need a weapon. I *am* a weapon. That's why you brought me here."

"That's not how I see it. I don't like being put in the middle of Kingston drama. It's consumed my entire life."

"I'm not a Kingston if that's what you're implying."

"Yes, you are. You *are* a Kingston," she says. "You are your father's son just as much as I am my father's daughter."

"I was born a Mitchell and I will die a Mitchell."

"What are we doing right now, Eric?"

"You tell me. You're the one who pulled me into this and now you're telling me to let go."

Her expression softens. "I don't want you to let go."

"That's what you said. Let go. Your words, not mine."

"Those comments about me and Isaac turned me back into the enemy. Maybe not in context, but I felt the distrust in you. I heard it in the nickname, and don't tell me it's inked on your skin and that makes it okay. We both know it represents a divide."

"A divide that's now what brought us together."

"Don't let him divide us."

"He's not dividing us," I say. "I'm not walking away this time. This time is different. You have to know that. You have to feel that. We're together now."

"I don't know what that means."

"You do know. I know you know."

My cellphone rings, and I glance down at the number to find Grayson calling. I hit decline and curse under my breath. "Look, sweetheart, we need to talk but I'm negotiating the purchase of an NFL team and I have a small stake in the deal. Grayson is calling me and he knows I came here for you. He wouldn't be calling if there wasn't a problem."

"You're—wait—you're buying an NFL team?"

"Packaging the project, but yeah. It's a big deal for the Bennett Corporation and for me."

"Take the call. That's incredible. I want to know what happened with Isaac, but I can wait."

"I'm going to call Grayson while I go to the hotel and grab my bag to move over here with you, unless you have a problem with that."

"I'd have a problem if you were staying at the hotel. That is unless I was with you."

"Good," I say, walking into the living room to finish dressing. "I want you to lock up," I add, when she joins me. "If Isaac comes back, call me and don't open the door." I pull on my leather jacket and walk to the front of the house where I check the locks. Harper is in the foyer when I turn around.

"Do you think he plans to come back?" she worries. "What haven't you told me?"

"He's running scared," I say, taking her hand, "and when he's scared, he acts erratically." I lead her into the kitchen and to the back door. "I'll explain my brother's version of crazy when I get back." I kiss her. "Flip the locks behind me."

"Okay, but now you've made me nervous, so hurry back, please."

"I will. I'll be fast." I exit the house and wait for her to shut the door, then listen for the lock to flip into place.

I'm already dialing Grayson as I settle into my leather seat. "What's happening?"

"Julius Monroe is trying to back out," he says, of a major player in the NFL deal. "He won't talk to anyone but you."

"Fuck. What's his problem?"

"A competing bidder made a sweeter deal for him," Grayson says.

"Who the fuck is the competing bidder?"

"You tell me," Grayson says. "I didn't know we'd opened up a bidding process."

I scrub my jaw. "I'll call him and call you back." I start to hang up and he stops me.

"What's happening there?"

"I'm pretty sure my brother just threatened to kill me and Harper," I say. "If that doesn't tell you how well this is going, I don't know what will."

"Isaac talks a lot of big words," he says, knowing him well from Harvard where he and I met. "Same ol' Isaac, or something more this time?"

"He's scared. *Really* scared. Harper was right. She's over her head because he's over his head, and about to take her down with him."

"Then bring her here," he says. "Get her out of there."

Harper, in New York, in my bed. That works for me. Me leaving and not knowing this is over, doesn't work for me or her either though. "I might send her to you and then join her later."

"Send her. Sooner than later if she's in danger."

"I'll let you know and I'm calling Julius now." I disconnect and leave Julius a message.

I back out of the driveway and I'm about to pull away when I catch sight of a car parked to the far right, next to the curb with a light flickering behind the shaded window. Unease radiates through me, the kind that used to set me off while in the deep, dark bowels of enemy territory. That threat, the idea that Harper might know more than she thinks she knows, that someone might think she'll lead me there, hits ten wrong places in my gut. I back up, place the car in park and walk back to the door where I knock.

"Harper, it's Eric."

She opens the door. "What are you doing?"

I pull her to me. "Come with me. I want you with me."

"Yes," she says softly. "I want me with you, too."

"Good," I say. "I want you to want to be with me." I lead her to the car, and that feeling of uneasiness I'd felt with the idea of leaving her behind is not gone. In fact, it's stronger. Someone is watching us.

Chapter Thirty

Eric

Halfway to the car, Harper shivers, and I pull her close, under my arm and against my body. "I should grab a coat," she murmurs.

"I'll get it for you and lock up," I say, wanting her inside the car where I can get her the hell out of here. I click the locks and open the passenger door. Obviously eager to escape the cold, she slides into the seat. I kneel beside her, my hand settling on her leg, and when she looks at me, when this woman looks at me—and I mean every damn time—I feel a punch in my gut. She's no longer just sex and revenge to me, and I'm not even resisting.

I hand her my key. "Turn on the engine and the heat. There's a seat warmer, too."

She laughs. "I know. Because I'm a Jaguar expert."

Amusement lifts the corners of my mouth. "Are you now?"

"Of course I am. They're the enemy and the competition."

"But I'm not, sweetheart. Remember that. Where's your coat?"

"Pretty sure it never made it out of the kitchen."

"Got it. Lock the car door."

"What? Why?"

"Lock it, sweetheart." I don't give her time to ask questions I'm not going to answer until I get some precautions in place. I stand up and shut her inside, waiting until she clicks the locks. Then and only then do I head toward the house, walk inside and retrieve my phone from my pocket to dial Blake. "I have thirty seconds," I say when he answers. "I don't want Harper to hear this conversation until I have time to explain myself."

"I'm listening."

I grab Harper's coat and her keys from the counter and then step back into the doorway to keep an eye on the car. "There's someone

145

staking out Harper's house in a black sedan. This, after my brother threatened me and Harper."

"Gut feeling about who's watching her?"

I step outside and pull the door shut. "If I had a damn gun, I'd yank the asshole out of his car and make him tell me. Hell, I might do it anyway."

"You think it's your brother's hired hands?"

"Maybe," I say, securing the lock, "but the look in Isaac's eyes tonight tells me that he's running scared. Really fucking scared. He's in trouble, which means Harper is in the line of fire."

"I'll get you a weapon. Where are you headed and what's your plan?"

"We're about to leave for my hotel to grab my things, which is only three blocks away," I say, walking toward the car with a slow pace meant to buy time to end this call.

"You're staying with her then?" he asks.

"Damn straight I am. I came here for her. I'm keeping her safe and close."

"I'll leave a weapon outside her place and text you the location. And that data you needed is in the electronic folder I set-up for you along with my analysis. Text or call me when you look at it." He disconnects.

I stop at the car door and unlock it before climbing inside the now-toasty interior. "You're all set now," I say, offering her the coat.

"Thank you," she says. "I guess I really didn't need this. The car is warm and we're stopping right at the hotel door."

"The wind is still cold, really fucking cold actually. Is there a storm blowing in?"

"There's a winter storm warning," she says. "I saw it on my phone earlier. And normally my mother would be the weather woman warning me. She's not this time."

"She sent Isaac to warn you instead," I assume, shifting the car into reverse.

"You're the bastard storm?"

"That's not always a bad thing to be," I say, backing us up and then placing us in drive, easing us down the path and eyeing the car that's still parked in the same spot.

My cellphone rings and I grab it to find Julius returning my call. "I have to take this. There are problems with the NFL closing."

"Of course," she says. "Take it. Then you can tell me what you haven't told me. No secrets, right?"

No secrets.

I can't agree to that statement. I do have secrets. Secrets she won't like. Secrets I don't intend for her to find out. "We'll talk," I say instead and answer my call.

Harper

We'll talk.

The man who demands no secrets, doesn't claim he's not keeping them from me, but at least he didn't offer complete denial either. Still, I don't like it. But do I really want to go down this "no secrets" path?

"No," he says, joining me, still talking on the phone. "That's not the deal." He's calm but hard, a sharp-edged quality to his seemingly nonchalant tone that I'm not sure is about me or his caller. "I don't like being played with," he adds. "We'll replace you." He disconnects the call and we pull up to the hotel and the valets are immediately upon us.

My door opens and I slip on my coat even as I step outside, and watch Eric palm the driver a large bill, a hundred, I think, which drives home just how successful and rich he's become, but more so, it shows a generous side of this self-made man. And while this might appear like flashing his money, I don't believe that. I don't sense that in him, at all. He's hard on the outside, steel forged out of pain, but how he's survived and thrived is part of what makes him incredible.

Somehow this only serves to drive home the fact that I've already made mistakes with him. And I know those mistakes could hurt him, at least, if he ever found out. I don't want to hurt this man. I'm falling in love with him, and that very idea has me walking toward the hotel rather than waiting on him, afraid of what he might read if he looks at me right this moment.

I push through the automatic revolving doors and suddenly Eric is behind me, navigating the small moving space with me, his body pressed to mine, his hands on my waist. "You don't mind if I join you, do you?"

"Depends," I say and then I have no idea what the heck I'm thinking with what comes out of my mouth next. "Are you going to tell me your secrets?" We clear the doors at that moment and he doesn't reply.

He cozies up to me, wraps his arm around me, and sets us in motion, greeting staff on our path to the elevator. I don't push him, already living the regret of driving so hard on a topic sure to burn me and him.

Halting at the elevator bank, he punches the call button and one of the doors immediately opens, his fingers lacing with mine as he guides me inside and uses his card to confirm his floor. The minute the doors shut, he pulls me to him, his fingers tangling in my hair, his thick erection throbbing against my belly. "My secrets would hurt you more than they'd help us." And then he's kissing me, and we taste like pain and heartache. He will hurt me. He will leave me. And this time he'll take everything I am when he does, and I can't even seem to care.

Chapter Thirty-One

Harper

"D amn coats," Eric murmurs, trying to pull me closer, and there's a frenzied energy between us, so raw and uncontrollable, it feels dangerous. He takes all of me and I can't stop it from happening. I can't protect myself with Eric.

He's danger.

He's safety.

The elevator dings and he reluctantly parts our lips, his hand stroking my hair in an act that is somehow tender and erotic at the same time. "Let's go to the room," he says, his voice low, gravelly. Affected. I affect this gorgeous, intense, brilliant man, and even now, I have moments like this one where that doesn't feel possible. I'm the enemy. I'm the princess. I'm hated and I've even felt that in his touch, in his kiss, only I don't feel that hate anymore.

"Yes," I whisper. "Let's go to the room."

His eyes smolder with amber heat that's melted the icy condemnation of the past. I hated the ice. I love the fire. I love *him*. He catches my hand, leads me out of the elevator, and I'm relieved to find his room a short walk to our immediate left. We stop at his door and nerves flutter in my belly as if I haven't spent hours with him this very night, as if what happens next will be our first time together. He doesn't give me time to live inside those nerves though. He pulls me in front of him, his big body behind mine, and even with my coat on I am aware of every inch of hard muscle pressing against me, promising wicked dirty deeds to follow.

He opens the door, and when I would dart into the room, he holds onto me, keeps me with him, and walks me forward while he stays at my back. It's a power play, one he does well, one that is remarkably arousing, considering how valuable control is to me.

The door slams shut, and I think he locks it, but I can't be sure. I don't even try to turn around. There's too much for me to see, and

I wonder if he thinks the same of me. We're swimming in an ocean, but we're trying to hide in the sunshine of our passion.

We both know it. Oh, we know it so very well.

He eases us forward into the room and then shifts behind me. His jacket lands on a desk in the living room to my right. Already he's dragging mine off my shoulders, holding onto me as he drops my coat on top of his.

He catches the hem of my T-shirt, dragging it over my head. It's barely hit the floor when his hands are on my breasts and he's leaning forward, his lips at my ear. "Do you feel me the way I feel you, Harper?" he asks, his breath a warm fan on my neck that still manages to shiver down my spine. His lips are a whisper of a touch like his words at my ear.

The words, the feelings he describes, would read undefinable to most, but not to me. We're in the moment, we're lost and found together. We're enemies, lovers, friends. We're hello and goodbye. We are so many things we may never fully understand. And that's what he means. *That's* what he feels

"You know I do," I say, my voice raspy, affected, my hands covering his hands.

"Are you sure about that?"

I'm not afraid anymore, no longer hiding from what lurks in the shadows of my mind. "Let me turn around and ask me again when you're looking at me."

"I'm not ready for you to turn around," he says, tilting my head back and bringing our lips together. "I was never ready for you." I'd insist the opposite was true, but he doesn't give me the chance. "What am I feeling, Harper?"

I say what comes to me, and I don't think before I say it out loud. "Resistant."

He goes still, utterly still, and then he's turning me to face him, his hands shackling my waist. "Resistant to what?"

"Me. Us. This."

Seconds tick by, heavy beats, his handsome face all shadows and stone, unreadable, seemingly impenetrable but I don't need to see what I already feel. What I know is happening between us. And that's resistance.

Abruptly he moves, his fingers sliding into the long strands of my hair and twining, almost roughly, as if he's angry with me or maybe with himself. His mouth slams down on mine, a wicked claiming, all consuming, and just that easily, he owns me, I can't stop it from happening. I don't know if I really even try. "Does that taste like resistance?"

"It tastes like you claiming control, like you need it."

His hand slides under my sweats and he squeezes my bare backside. "I seem to remember you liking me in control."

"I do," I dare. "I like it a lot when I shouldn't."

"Why shouldn't you, Harper?"

"It's not what I do. I don't let other people take control of me or my life, not even my pleasure. That's not what my father taught me, but it is what this family, the Kingston family, taught me. Because they take and take and take some more."

"I'm not a Kingston."

He's right. For the first time since he's denied that birthright, I let him. I understand now that it's not about what he deserves. It's about who he is, who he's become. Where he came from. "Exactly. You're a Mitchell and I like that about you."

Shadows play in his eyes, a storm in their depths before he's kissing me again and it's wild, taut with emotion, demanding. He's demanding, and when I've just lost myself to the passion, his mouth is gone, and he's tugging his shirt over his head. He tosses it and his hands slip under my sweats at my hips and in a blink I'm naked, so very naked with this man, on every level.

"You do have control, Harper. And I don't think I like it."

I laugh, a raspy, choked sound, that sounds as affected as I truly am by this man. "I'm fairly certain that's the first lie you've ever told me."

"You don't think you have control?"

"I'm talking about your claim that you don't like it. I think you do."

I'm teasing but he doesn't laugh. "I like *you*, Harper. I like you more than I ever meant to."

The air crackles and I'm hot all over and there's a little somersault in my belly. "Me too," I whisper.

His gaze lowers, and does a hot inspection of my breasts, and I ache to have him in the most intimate part of me, buried deep and fucking me. I'll settle for his mouth. I push to my toes, and press my lips to his, boldly sliding my tongue past his lips. He groans low, and rough, and cups my head, devouring me, and I like it. As he says, he *likes me*. And like is such a small, inadequate word for what is going on between us.

And we both know it.

My palms absorb the warmth of taut skin over rippled, perfect muscle. The man is hard all over and I need that hardness next to me, inside me. "Eric," I whisper, sliding my hands under his waistband. "I need—"

"Me too, sweetheart," he says, kissing me again, and then he's releasing me long enough to grab his wallet and hand me a condom. "I'll put you in charge of this," he says, heat radiating between us, but the condom hits a hotspot in my chest that I don't like.

He undresses, and I'm aware of every perfect inch of him, his cock jutting forward, his ink on display in all its glorious, colored perfection, but still the condom and the past it represents torments me. I'm frozen. I can't move. Eric's hands come down on my shoulders and he drags me to him. "What just happened?"

What just happened?

There's the question.

The one I now have to answer.

Chapter Thirty-Two

Harper

"What just happened?" he repeats and the words jolt me back to the moment.

"Can you just kiss me again already?" I ask, his heart thundering beneath my palm, or maybe it's mine radiating down my arm. I don't know.

"Not until you talk to me," he counters, and I can feel his stubbornness punching through me. He's not going to let this go. I want him to let this go. And what I need, is out of my own head right now.

"This is what happened," I say, holding the condom between us. Even as I push to my toes and press my lips to his mouth.

One of his hands cups my head, the other squeezing my backside as he gives me what I want. He kisses the hell out of me, drugging me with the taste of him, and driving away anything but him and now. He maneuvers us and sits down on the couch, pulling me onto his lap, his thick erection pulsing between us and the condom might as well be burning a hole in my palm.

I *will not* think about the past, I chant in my head. I will not.

"Harper," he says roughly against my lips and then he's tangling his fingers in my hair, using an erotic tug to force my gaze to his. "I'm no angel and I've had my share of fucks, but the condoms are all about you and me and us. I bought them for us."

Understanding hits me hard, slugs me with guilt. He believes the condom made me feel like one of many, and maybe it should, maybe it would have if I didn't have other things on my mind. "I know," I whisper, a tremble to my voice.

"I saw the look on your face," he says, "you *don't* know. I told you. We're together now."

Until he knows, I think, but my hand frames his face and I say, "Show me. I need you to show me. Please."

His eyes flicker with something I cannot name, an understanding in him, that is all about me, even if I don't truly understand it. He drags my mouth to his and then he's kissing me again, but this kiss is not like the others. It's different, greedy and wicked, seductive and possessive. Addictive. So very addictive. I'm lost, so very lost in the feel of it, the lust of it. The taste of it, and him. I'm not just kissing him back, I'm consuming him, I'm breathing him in. And his hands are all over me, mine all over him, sinewy muscle flexing beneath my touch.

I'm so into the moment, so lost in Eric, that I don't even know when he takes the condom from me, until he's tearing it open. I catch his hand. "I'll do it."

His eyes darken, the lust in their depths, trembling through me. He releases the condom, and I toss the wrapper, gripping his erection, and reveling in the low groan that escapes his lips. There is power in pleasure, *his pleasure*, and I like it. I like it more than I ever imagined possible. I slide the condom down his cock, and then wrap my fingers around him.

His hand closes over mine. "You have no idea how fucking hot you are and that's part of what makes you that hot." He folds me close, wraps his arm around my waist, and lifts me, and I guide him inside me. He's ridiculously hard, and it's one of those pain is pleasure kind of moments, sliding down him, taking him deep, settling against him.

Finally, I think.

Finally.

I lean forward into him, my fingers lacing around his neck. His hand settles between my shoulder blades, fingers splayed wide and he molds me close. "God, I could live inside you, woman," he murmurs. "What the hell are you doing to me?"

"Nothing you aren't doing to me," I whisper, "and as for living inside me —yes. Please," but we still don't move, we don't kiss. We just breathe each other in, savor this one moment that can never be repeated, that can never be this exact instant ever again.

I ease back just enough to press my hands to his shoulders, and with that one act, sparks fire between us. His hand cups my head and our lips collide, in a ravenous kiss, my fingers diving into his hair, tangling roughly, desperately, in the silky strands.

Eric growls low in his throat and thrusts into me, pulling me hard against him. I breathe out against his mouth, gasp with the sensations he rockets through my entire body. And then we're swaying together, slow and sexy, sensual kisses, and caresses, guiding us to what feels like the next impossibly wickedly extreme.

I don't want this to end, but my body is on edge, the tension building, and I can feel myself growing frenzied. As if feeding off my urgency, his thrusts become deeper and harder, and I cannot hold back. I'm rocking against him, grinding my hips, seeking that sweet spot, and hiding from it at the same time.

But there is no hiding.

His cock is too hard, too deep, too absolutely perfect.

Suddenly I'm there, in that place of no return, my body squeezing him, spasming, rocking me to the point that I literally quake, and burying my face in his shoulder. His arm wraps my waist, and he lifts his hips, pumping into me, a guttural, almost animalistic sound sliding from him, his body shuddering with his release.

We collapse into each other, our breaths labored, our bodies sated and heavy, and for long seconds, we just lay there, as if we are both afraid or unwilling to move. The first sign of life is his fingers flexing where they rest on my head. "I want things from you that I shouldn't want," he murmurs softly.

I suck in a soft breath, surprised and pleased by this announcement, but also aware of just how complicated it is as well.

I lift myself up and meet his tormented stare. Oh yes. We are so very complicated, two damaged people, who've come together, who are found in each other. But that doesn't mean we won't destroy each other in the process. And maybe that's what he's trying to tell me. "Is this your way of telling you're going to make me hate you?"

He catches a strand of my hair and drags it through his fingers. "I hope like fuck not."

His cellphone rings and I'm aware of what I wasn't aware of while we were in the throes of passion. "It's been ringing. You have to get it. Your deal and Grayson—"

He rotates me and lays me down on my back on the couch. "Grayson will understand. Get dressed. I want out of this hotel room and in your bed, at least until I can get you in mine, where you belong." He pulls out of me and sits up, leaving me a bit stunned.

His bed?

I'm not sure what to do with that, considering his bed is in New York City, and yes, I can visit him, but then what?

I sit up, and grab a blanket, wrapping it around me. "I won't leave my mom behind. You need to know that."

He walks to a trashcan, sheds the condom and then reaches for his pants, pulling his phone from inside, reading a message before he pulls on his pants. "We'll talk about it."

"No," I say standing up, that comment reading like another play for control. "We won't." I grab my tee and tug it over my head, but when I would reach for my pants, he pulls me around to face him.

"We'll make sure your mother's safe," he says. "We'll protect her. I promise you."

My eyes go wide. "Safe? What does that mean? Are you talking about protecting her from a lawsuit? Or is this more than that? Is she in danger?"

"Let's get dressed and talk."

My heart races and then dodges and weaves. "Eric, damn it, is she in danger?"

"Put on your clothes, Harper."

He releases me, snatches up my pants and hands them to me. "Get dressed."

He grabs his T-shirt, and puts it on, but not before I note the tensions knotted in his broad shoulders. I decide I need to be dressed, too, just like he said. Dressed equals control and right now, I feel like I have none. Trying to gather my emotion, I give him my back and pull on my pants but somehow, we manage to sit on the couch at the same time, side by side, to lace our shoes. We don't look at each other, we don't touch, but I'm so aware of him, it's unnerving. His energy, his smell, his dark mood.

His phone buzzes with another message that he replies to this time, his jaw setting hard before he sticks his cell in his pocket. I stand up and face him, my arms folding in front of me.

"Talk."

He unfolds his big body, and faces me, no, towers over me, his tone obviously measured as he says, "I need you to know that I hired a top-notch security company to find answers. Walker Security's staff includes ex-special forces, CIA, and FBI, and the list of credentials goes on. With their skills and mine we'll uncover what's happening with Kingston Motors."

"Which is great but that's not what you want to say to me right now, is it?" I ask, all too aware that he hasn't told me everything. I sense it. I can almost taste it in the air.

"I had Blake, my contact at Walker, get someone from his team in place at your house."

His push for locked doors comes back to me hard and fast. "Why? Just say it."

"Someone's watching your house, which most likely is nothing more than my brother's paranoia over my presence. He most likely hired someone to keep an eye on me or us."

"Most likely? What are the other options?"

"I'm working on that answer. Whoever this guy is, he either wanted me to see him, or he's really bad at his job. Either way, I'm going to talk to him."

"Talk to him?" I ask incredulously. "Are you crazy? What if he has a gun?"

"I'm not without skills. That's the part of my life you missed, and I'm glad you did." There's a knock on the door and my heart is racing all over again. "Easy, sweetheart," Eric murmurs, catching my shoulders and walking me to him. "Blake, one of the owners of Walker Security, sent a man over. I need to go talk to that asshole watching us and nip it in the bud. Blake's man will stay with you until I get back."

"Stay with me? I'm not staying here with some stranger. This is crazy, no you're crazy, and if you're going to be crazy, I'm going with you."

"I swear to God, Harper, I will tie you to the bed and keep you here. Stay here. It will take half an hour at most."

"Do not go caveman on me," I warn. "You will not like the results."

"You wanted my help. You wanted *me*. You got me now, and I'm telling you to listen to me and stay here."

"I do want you, alive and well."

"There's no such thing as an ex-Navy SEAL. I'm still that guy. If someone gets hurt, it won't be me. Don't fight me on this. I protect what matters to me and that means you. I need to talk to this guy before he's gone."

I matter to him. That brings me down about ten notches. I inhale and let my breath out. "Yes. Okay."

"Blake's man is going to stay at the door to be sure you're safe. Come lock up."

He catches my hand and leads me to the door and when he would leave, I grab his arm. "Please don't get hurt."

He cups my head and kisses me. "I'll be *right back*." And that's it. There's no holding him back any longer. He exits the room. I lock the door and lean against it, all too aware of the obvious. If

Eric didn't think there was a real threat, there wouldn't be a guard at my door. He also didn't promise not to get hurt.

Chapter Thirty-Three

Eric

I exit the hotel room to be greeted by a burly guy with a beard wearing a blue suit and an earpiece. He gives me a nod. "I'm Jensen."

I don't introduce myself. He's been briefed and while I trust Blake's judgment, Jensen is still staying in the hallway. I'm not letting any guy I don't know into a room alone with my woman, even Blake's guy. If this turns out to be trouble, I'm getting her the hell out of here. "Don't let anyone in or out of that room."

"Understood. Adam's in town. He's at her house."

Adam being one of Blake's men and a fellow SEAL. I'll take a SEAL at my back any day of any week. I give a nod and add, "I'll be back in half an hour."

I don't say more. He understands. If I'm a minute longer, there's a problem. I head down the hallway with the scent of Harper on my skin and the taste of her on my lips. She's under my skin, in my head, and the idea that I almost left her to deal with this alone, is not a good one. She needed me. I needed to be here. I needed to be here a long damn time ago and maybe she wouldn't still be here in this mess. She's not staying and I'm not leaving without her.

Eager to deal with this problem and get back to her, I don't bother with the elevator. I take the stairs and I'm at the front of the hotel in a blink, but I don't stop for my car. I walk toward Harper's house and dial Blake. "Talk to me."

"He's still there," he says. "And the plates are registered to one of the neighbors."

"He pulled them off another car."

"That's my bet," he agrees.

"That's not a stupid, half-assed PI move," I say.

"Not all PIs are stupid," he reminds me. "Quite the contrary. There's a Glock at the back door in the bush to the right of the entrance. I only had two men available outside of Adam and one is tracking down Isaac. Adam's with you. He'll find you when you need him."

"Got it." I disconnect and jog the rest of the way, coming up a street that will bring me to the rear of the vehicle. I slow as I turn a corner, my target in view, parked in the same spot, but I don't give the driver time to see me.

I cut left down the side of one of the neighbor's houses without any resistance. I enter the unfenced backyard and cross two more open rear yards before I'm moving through the shadows of Harper's property and arrive at her back door. I grab the Glock and holding a weapon, any weapon, is like holding an old friend in my hand. I check the ammunition, and shove the weapon into my waistband, under my jacket before I head to the side of the house.

Once I'm there, I find the car still boldly parked across the street, almost daring me to confront him. I rest my back against the wall and Adam, dressed in all black, down to the beanie on his otherwise curly black hair, appears by my side. "He's alone," he says. "He wants to talk. You don't announce yourself to a SEAL and expect to be ignored."

Spoken like one of us.

A SEAL.

Not ex-SEAL.

Because as I told Harper, a SEAL is always a SEAL.

"Agreed," I say, "and while I could assume it's a trap, I don't really give two fucks. If he wants to talk, I'm not going to disappoint him."

"I do like how you think." He pulls his weapon. "I'll cover you."

I push off the wall and start walking toward the front of the house. The minute I clear the wall and the bushes, and I'm in the open, the driver revs the engine of his car, rolls down the window and holds up a lit cigarette. He starts rolling forward and tosses it, along with something else. He floors his accelerator and drives away. I walk toward the cigarette, more interested in the rolled-up piece of paper next to it. Adam joins me, and offers me a pair of rubber gloves from his pocket and hands them to me. He's prepared, but that doesn't surprise me. He's Adam. He's Walker. He's a SEAL.

I pull the gloves on and squat down to grab the little gift I've been given and find a line of numbers with random letters. My brain plays with them—translating letters to numbers and the reverse—memorizing the fourteen digits before I toss the paper and the cigarette into the baggy Adam is holding open for me. "What was it?" he asks, eyeing the items in the bag. "A code? Aren't you a numbers guru?"

"It's not a cipher, code, or a translatable message. It's not even a point in history. It's an identifying number, like a name, but it's not a VIN number or a parts number."

He gives me a deadpan look. "You know all of that in the sixty seconds you were looking at that number?"

"Yes," I say. "And as you said, he wanted to talk and that's what he did." I motion to the bag. "If we find out what the identifier's attached to, we'll understand that message."

"Or it's a distraction to focus you in the wrong direction," Adam suggests as we walk to the front of the house.

His pocket vibrates and he pulls his phone out and glances at a message while I consider his thoughts. It could be a distraction, but if it is, it's someone who's studied me. Someone who knows how damn obsessed I can get about a series of numbers. Isaac isn't that detailed or focused. My father is another story. He knows things about me, like how I used to get hung up on equations and struggled to spread my focus. But that was then and this is now, and thanks to special training in the Navy, I'm beyond that.

"Isaac's at home," Adam says, sliding his phone back into place. "He went straight there from here. He didn't meet with anyone."

"Anyone but you watching his house?"

"No one. You think he's being targeted, too? I thought you believed he was behind your watcher?"

"I'm not ruling out anything just yet. Isaac's running from more than me and Harper. Was tonight related to his fear? Yes, but I'm not sure how. As for tonight's visitor, was he a tipster trying to help me? A hired goon trying to fuck with my head? Someone trying to mock me with the message in numbers? The options are many."

"Agreed. We're in this all the way with you. I damn sure am. I'm not going back to New York until you go back. You staying here or at the hotel?" he asks.

"Here," I say, disliking hotels where strangers come and go too easily.

"Then so am I." He motions toward the side of the house and then heads that direction and I don't even care that anyone watching knows he's here. In fact, I hope they do and then stay the fuck away.

I scan the area, but I see no one and sense no danger. I start walking, reaching in my pocket, and removing a mini-Rubik's cube, and close it in my palm. There were years that I had to work the puzzle to focus my mind, but now if I'm holding it, it streamlines my thoughts, clears my mind. Just that easily I'm chasing those numbers on my little gift, searching for their meaning: an employee badge number, a reference number to a medical claim. The list becomes a dozen long, with no end in sight.

By the time I reach the hotel, Blake is calling me.

"The numbers mean nothing to you, genius?" he asks, as I enter the lobby and head toward the stairs. "What the fuck?"

"They're an identifier," I say, moving my weapon to the rear of my pants. "In other words, Mr. Hacker Genius, find out what they identify."

"Already working on it. It's not a VIN number or car part."

"I already told Adam that. Think outside of the box. I'll send you a list of prospects if you need them, but of course, you're a genius hacker, right?"

"You just can't stand the idea of someone else being the genius, now can you?"

"I'll believe you're a genius when you find out what that identifier means."

"Rolling my sleeves up now, asshole. Get ready to feel stupid for once. Our lab will run prints of the stuff you and Adam bagged tonight. How present do you want my men in Denver?"

"Present, but out of sight until we know what the hell really happened tonight."

"What's your gut say?"

"I still think this is a symptom of a bigger problem and we don't know the real problem or who is behind that problem."

"Agreed," Blake says.

We talk another minute, and disconnect right as I exit the stairwell to my floor, the Rubik's cube all but imprinted on my left hand. By the time I reach my door and relieve Jensen of his duties, I've decided to look to the obvious place for an answer to what that identifier represents—Harper. That man was at her house. It hits me then; I've been assuming the message is for me because of the number format, but the truth is, it could be for her. Certainty fills me; the message is for Harper and for reasons that are pure instinct, that feels like a problem. That feels dangerous. It feels like something else Harper still hasn't told me and if she was anyone else, I'd be bordering on pissed.

But I'm not sure I trust my instincts with Harper. I'm too fucking into her. And the very idea that at this point, Harper could be holding information back, does not sit well. I want answers or I'm out.

I slide my keycard and open the door. I've made it all of four steps when Harper charges at me, flings herself into my arms, and breathes out, "Thank God."

Thank God, spoken with relief.

"I was so worried." She pulls back to look at me. "I'm glad you're back."

She has a million questions, I'm certain, but she's not asking them. She's focused on me and I don't remember the last time anyone worried about me or focused on me for any reason that wasn't to hurt me or compete with me. I don't remember a time when anyone defended me as she did with her mother. Her mother, who is all she has, the only one she calls family. No one understands what that means to her, more than me. My mother was all I had, too.

I stroke her hair from her face and tilt her gaze to mine and in that moment, I decide right now that if she's hiding something, she's afraid. Words Grayson has said to me over and over come back to me: *You get what you give.* If I don't give Harper my trust, she'll never give me hers. She doesn't trust me with her secret because she doesn't trust me not to leave. I've done so two times before. I've earned her distrust, not her trust.

"Why are you staring at me?" she whispers.

"I'm not going anywhere. I know you don't know that yet, but you will. I promise."

Her eyes cloud and darken. "Promise?"

"*I promise.* Now, take me home to your bed."

"Is it safe?"

"Yes. I'll tell you everything on the way. Just like I hope you will tell me everything there is to tell, Harper. When you're *ready.*"

I don't give her time to deny or reply. I don't place that pressure on her. I kiss her again, grab my bag, and lead her to the door. I'm giving her my trust. I'll earn hers. And I won't allow either of us to regret those decisions.

Chapter Thirty-Four

Eric

I manage to usher Harper to the elevator without much explanation, but once the car doors shut and I've punched in the lobby level, she's ready for answers. "What happened when you went to my house and why do you want to get back there now with such urgency?"

Because I want her home where I know we're secure, where I can control our environment, and where I know Walker Security is guarding the exterior or the property. "That was the whole idea," I say instead. "Get my bag. Go back to your place."

"We're in this together, remember? No secrets. I deserve to know what just happened at my own home. Tell me what happened when you went after the driver of the car."

"The minute I walked in his direction, he rolled down the window and tossed a cigarette and note out."

"A note? What kind of note?"

"A piece of paper with a fourteen-digit sequence of numbers and letters."

She frowns. "Nothing but the sequence? That's—*odd.*"

"Correct," I say.

"Then it has to be a message for you, right? Do you know what it means?"

"I don't. I ruled out a lot of options but nothing more so far."

"Maybe they're saying, your genius doesn't scare them? Or they know you. They know how you operate."

"Or it's meant for you," I say.

"Me? I mean, *maybe.* It was my house he was watching, but the numbers feel related to you, not me." The elevator dings and the doors open.

We step into the lobby and start walking toward the door. "You don't have any idea at all what it means, Eric? Are you sure?"

"It's a name that isn't a name," I say, and when most people would just stare at me after a statement like that, she goes with the flow.

"Like a VIN or part number?" she asks.

"It's neither of those things. I'm hoping once you look at it it'll mean something to you." We exit the front of the hotel and I snake my phone from my pocket and key in a message. "I just sent you a text with the sequence," I say, following her to the car door that the doorman is holding open for her. "See what it means to you, if anything."

"I left my phone at home."

I hand her mine with the message pulled up, and palm the doorman a large bill. Once Harper's in the vehicle, and safely shut inside, I round the hood and enter on the driver's side. Once I'm settled in, I find Harper staring at my cell screen. "Any idea what it means?"

"I wish I did," she says, sighing and glancing my direction, "But I don't." She shifts my direction. "You're sure it's not a parts number?"

"Not one in any recognized database."

"But there's so many parts and manufacturers and—"

"It's not a parts number," I repeat, exiting the driveway and heading toward her house.

"What about a VIN number for a competitor?"

"No."

"How do you know?" she presses. "I mean, I get that you're a numbers guy, but VIN numbers could be data added and deleted from databases that you might not have access to."

"It wouldn't be sequenced in that manner," I insist, pulling us into her driveway. "But we're not without resources. Blake Walker is considered one of the best hackers in the world. He'll look for a connection that isn't obvious."

"The part where he's a hacker. Is that a good or bad thing?"

"He's one of the good guys. The kind our own military contacts for help. He's going to run the sequence and see what technology reveals." I park and kill the engine.

"Okay, then another question: is this a warning or a clue?"

"If it were a warning, it would be something more obvious."

"Right," I say. "I mean, people have died. It makes sense someone would want to help us. Someone perhaps closer to this than I am in some way. It also makes sense that someone like that would know your family, and maybe even know you'd be the one that would stand up against the Kingstons." Her gaze shifts to the front door of her house. "I bought this place a year after meeting you, my escape from Kingston hell." She glances over at me. "I didn't know you'd lived in this area and yet I gravitated here. That's odd, right?"

"Kismet, sweetheart," I say softly.

"Yes," she says, the air thickening between us. "Kismet."

I stroke her cheek. "Let's go inside." I reach for the door.

She grabs my arm and her attention is riveted on the house. "Are you really sure this is a good idea? Is it safe?"

"You have me, sweetheart," I say, giving her a wink. "You're safe."

"From everyone *but* you?"

"If you had protection from me, how would I ravish you night and day?"

She laughs and strokes her fingers over my jaw. "And I do want to be ravished by you."

"That's what I want to hear." I kiss her and straighten. "I'll grab my bag and then come around and get you. Wait on me."

I exit the car, waste no time grabbing my bag, and right as I reach the passenger door, Harper pops it open. I offer her my hand and help her to her feet, walking her up close and personal. Her arms wrap my waist, and I know the moment her hand manages to hit the gun she's miraculously missed until now. Her eyes rocket to mine. "Walker armed me," I explain before she can even ask.

"If you expect me to complain, I won't. I approve and so would my father. He made me learn to shoot, and I carry."

"Do you now?"

"Yes. I do. I should never have left without my purse or my Baby Glock."

It's not the weapon I'd choose for her, but we'll deal with that another time. She's carrying, and that could be a good thing or a bad thing. Weapons can be used against you if you don't handle them correctly. "How often do you practice using it?"

"Not as often as I should." She shivers. "My coat is in the car. We need to go inside."

I catch her hand in mine and start walking toward the house, and then dig her keys from my pocket to quickly turn the locks and shove open the door. "Your castle awaits."

She shivers again, but holds her position, nervous to enter her own safe place. I pull her in front of me, my body cradling hers. "You have me, remember? You're safe, and as a bonus, Walker has a man watching the house." I nuzzle her ear. "I got you, Harper, and one day you'll know that."

She darts away with those words, grabs her phone from the island, and then turns to face me. "Don't make promises you can't keep."

I shut the door and lock it before giving her my full attention. "I never make a promise I can't keep."

"Actually, I said don't make promises, but I don't think you've really made any. And forget any of that just came out of my mouth. I'm rattled and I'm not proud of it, either. My room is upstairs." She turns away and starts walking down the hallway.

I don't stop her. I follow. Her room and her bed seem like the perfect place to finish this conversation.

Chapter Thirty-Five

Eric

My first look at Harper's bedroom comes as I pause in the doorway and scan the room as gray and curiously masculine as her living room, but for the slice of femininity represented by the red pillows and red lampshades offer. I have a strong opinion on why, too. I spent years of my life being molded to a specific way the Kingstons live, dress—hell even eat and even breathe. She's living in a Kingston, male-dominated world, barely holding onto herself. If I hadn't shed their hold on me when I did and entered the Navy, I don't know what I'd have become. She needs the same kind of cleansing, but it won't take a trip around the world with the Navy. She has me.

She steps to the side of the bed and sets her phone on the nightstand as if she just needs something to do with herself. I toss my bag on a chair, remove my gun and stick it inside the bag, and then shrug out of my coat, dropping it on top of the rest of my things. When I turn to face Harper, she's still standing by the bed, staring at me, and her energy vibes like downstairs. She's still in whatever mindset drove her to blurt out that comment about promises never being made. Which is obviously about this tug of war of hate and lust, and everything else we aren't ready to talk about.

I amble her direction, and stop just in front of her, but I don't touch her, not yet. I give her room to set the tone, to show me what she wants. "I am glad you're here," she says. "That's all. I just want you to know that whatever else happens, I'm glad you're here. I'm going to use the bathroom to change now." She cuts her gaze and tries to move away.

I catch her arm and walk her in closer. "Me, too, Harper. Me fucking, too. Why don't you understand that? I didn't come to help you. I came because I couldn't leave you alone. I didn't have it in me. If I had my way, I'd take you and your mother the hell out of here, and we'd leave Isaac to burn in hell on his own."

"She won't leave. She won't, Eric."

"Get her to," I say. "Convince her that staying is dangerous."

"Is it?"

"Dangerous enough for me to urge you toward an exit strategy and I'm that strategy. I'm your ticket out of here."

"I don't want you to be my ticket anywhere. Just like you didn't want your father to be your ticket. That's not what you are to me."

"I'm not offering. I'm *insisting* you use me." My eyes twinkle. "Any way you see fit."

"Eric," she breathes out, her serious mood not yet dissuaded. "I can't leave. I could have access to information we need."

"Blake has everything you could have and more at his fingertips."

"There's value to in-person, physical presence to investigate, especially when my mom's name is on the line."

"She's not a strong person," I say. "You are. Get her out," I repeat.

"How? How do I do that? I have nothing but my suspicions to support an argument for her to leave, and that's not enough. She's afraid to be without your father."

"But does she love him?"

"No. I don't think so. No. I know she doesn't. She doesn't act at all with him like she did with my father."

"Then she'll leave him. Let's find the motivation for her to get out." I walk to my bag and retrieve my MacBook, holding it up. "Let's dig in."

"My briefcase is still in the car," she says. "I need to grab it." She glances at the door and I don't miss her unease. I'm driving home the theme of danger. It's messing with her head.

"I'll get it. You get comfortable." I head for the door and on my way down, my phone buzzes with a text from Blake: *I hacked the HR files and looked at employee numbers and even union membership numbers for Kingston. No go. No matches. Still working. More when I know something.*

I shove my phone back into my pocket and make quick work of running out to the car for Harper's briefcase. Once I'm back upstairs in the bedroom, I find Harper comfortable all right. She's perched against the headboard, her bare feet crossed at the ankle, and it doesn't matter that she's in sweats and a tee. My cock throbs. I want to strip her naked. I want to fuck her. I want to make love to her. But I also need her out of this Godforsaken city.

I cross to the bed and set her briefcase down. "Thank you," she says, giving me this sweet, sexy look that almost changes my priorities to dirty play instead of my dirty brother.

I sit down next to Harper and we both unpack our computers. For me, that means my MacBook and a full-sized Rubik's cube. Harper picks it up. "A Rubik's cube?"

I study it in her hand, the woman that is now holding a piece of me, the way I control my mind, an explanation of which exposes weakness. I could say what I say to everyone and I do just that. "It helps me focus," but unlike the rest of the world, she doesn't stop there.

"You're a savant," she says. "I read up on it. Most savants have time when the data in their heads takes over, when it overwhelms them and comes too fast. I even read about a man that has seizures when that happens."

She tried to pull back downstairs, to place a wall between us. I fight the urge to do the same now. I don't want to pull back with Harper and so I tell her what only Grayson and a few doctors know. "I collapsed in a swell of numbers when my mother died. My father paid for expensive doctors and one of them actually helped me, but when I got pulled up to law school three years early, and with Isaac, he was angry. He tried to trigger my episodes, as someone started calling them, but it's like the harder he tried, the stronger I got and the more desperate he became."

"And when you could have ruined him, you didn't," she says, repeating what I'd told her earlier.

"Yeah well, he's lucky I dropped out of Harvard. Joining the SEALs was good for me. They changed me, tamped down on my anger and resentment. They helped me hone my skills and turn them into assets, not detriments."

Her cellphone buzzes with a message on my side of the bed and she climbs over the top of me and ends up straddling my lap. I arch a brow. She laughs. "I need my phone. You were in the way."

"Do you see me complaining?"

She laughs again and rolls off of me, propping herself against the headboard again. "The message was spam which I hate almost as much as your father. Change of topic." She glances over at me. "Do you tell people you're a savant?"

"No. Never."

"Does it bother you that I know?"

"No, it doesn't. I don't announce what I am, but I own it."

"When was the last time you had an episode?"

I cover her hand with mine, tension sliding down my spine. "Why, Harper?"

"You don't have to tell me. Sorry." She tries to get off of me and I hold onto her.

"Why, Harper?" I ask again, intent on getting an answer from her.

She rotates and settles on her knees to face me. "I just—if something happened, if you had one, if being here triggers one, I want to know how to help. I should know what to do and what not to do."

I'm aware on every level that this is information she could use to hurt me. But I can't seem to focus on that part of the equation. No one has ever asked me what to do or not do to help me besides my mother. I sit up and slide my hand under her hair, cupping her neck. "This," I say, dragging her mouth a breath from mine. "Kiss me. Wildly, passionate, with all you are."

She presses her lips to mine and her cellphone starts to ring. She groans and settles her forehead to mine, her hand on my jaw. "Twenty dollars of your billion says that will be my mother."

I'm struck by her ability to talk about my money and have it not feel like a play to get my money. That's the thing about having money, I've learned. It comes with agendas, other people's agendas.

"Talk to her," I say, stroking her hair. "I'll be here when you're done."

"Let me just make sure it's her." She leans to the nightstand and grabs her phone and almost falls. She yelps and I catch her, helping her settle back on the bed.

"Yep," she says. "It's her. I think I need that wine we didn't finish to survive her tonight."

"I'll get it," I say, standing and walking toward the door. Her phone stops ringing without her answering it.

Puzzled, I turn to find her staring at me, giving her a curious look. "What is it?"

"Sorry."

"Don't apologize. Talk to your mom."

"Not just about the interruption again. About how she acted earlier, Eric. You're being really great about her and she doesn't deserve it."

"You already said all this."

"I know. I just needed to say it again."

I soften with her concern, and I wonder how anyone that thinks about everyone else the way she does, me especially, has made it this long in this family. "Talk to your mom," I order again and head down the stairs.

Once I'm at the bottom of the stairs, I punch in a text to Adam, who I've had in my phonebook since a job Walker did for Bennett Enterprises a few months back: *How do we look out there?*

Like we're both in Denver instead of New York City, he replies. In other words, he's a smart ass and everything is clear. I walk into the living room, snag our wine glasses and the bottle and head back upstairs, ready to dig into the data Blake sent me before grabbing a few hours of sleep.

I re-enter the bedroom to find Harper missing and the bathroom door shut. I set our glasses on the nightstand, fill them, and then settle on the bed to wait on Harper. I key my MacBook to life and it's just about ready for use when Harper's phone buzzes on the bed next to me. My gaze lifts instinctively and lands on a flashing text message from Gigi that says: *Do not tell him.*

Chapter Thirty-Six

Eric

I'm standing at the bathroom door, my arm resting on the jamb when Harper opens it. "Eric," she proclaims with a physical jolt.

"Start talking, Harper. No more fucking lies."

"You read my text messages," she says, and it's not a question. She knows I did, but I go ahead and drive that point all the fucking way home.

"Damn straight I did," I say. "You left your phone on the bed to flash right at me."

"If I wasn't going to tell you, do you think I'd leave my phone on the bed?" she challenges and yanks her phone from my hand and starts reading. "*He has to know everything. You wanted him here. I'm telling him.*" She looks at me. "Does that sound like I had something to keep from you?"

"Looks to me like you ran to the bathroom to pull yourself together."

"I had to pee, Eric." Her tone bristles with defensiveness. "I'm human like that. Do you want to listen to me or are you just going to attack?"

"Talk."

"I sent Gigi the message and she freaked out. She thinks it's a wire transfer number that points to her. She said she had wires into her account that were large and random. Isaac said they were bonuses, but then he asked for the money back as loans. And for the record, she just told me this. I didn't have a secret to keep. I just found out." She tries to duck around me.

I catch both of her wrists and pull her to me. "Why the fuck are you telling Gigi anything?"

"I thought she might know what the sequence was. I thought she could help."

"Don't tell Gigi anything you don't talk to me about first. Do you understand?"

She sucks in a breath and nods. "Yes," she whispers. "I get it. You hate her. You have reason to hate her. I just—"

"Don't say another word," I order, tenson rippling down my spine. "I don't want to hear anything but your promise that it won't happen again because I want to trust you, Harper, but I can't if you're with her."

"I'm not. I'm not with her. You *know* that. We've talked about this."

"And yet you were texting with her about the note."

"I was trying to help," she argues. "I thought—I thought she could help."

I search her eyes for the truth that is hers, but all I find is the one that's mine. I release her and leave her there, exiting the bedroom to the hallway and my hands come down on the railing, the past playing in my mind. Gigi. That fucking bitch Gigi. I squeeze my eyes shut with a flashback, me at sixteen, my mother barely forty and sick, but all she thought of was me. I'd gotten a ride home from a buddy. I'm back there now and I never go there:

Kevin pulls his Jeep into the drive, in front of our trailer that seems more broken down these days since my mother got sick. "Who's the old lady with your mom?" Kevin asks of the woman standing with my mom on the wooden porch a neighbor built us a few years back.

The answer to that question punches me in the chest and I stare, squeezing the stress ball in my hand that the special teacher I'm seeing swears will calm my mind. "No idea," I say, squeezing harder now, fighting the assault of numbers threatening my mind, "but the church has been coming around a lot lately."

"They helping you guys?"

I shrug and crush the ball, holding onto it. "I guess. See you tomorrow." I open the door and get out, slamming the door behind me, and worried my mother needs my support, I head up the stairs.

A wrinkled woman with orange-ish hair is standing in profile to me, facing my mother, and God, my mother looks so thin. She hugs herself and speaks to the woman. "You need to leave."

"Mom?" I say, uncertain about this reaction. My mother is a kind person. She doesn't speak to people like that.

The old lady turns her attention to me. "Is this the little bastard you want to call a Kingston?" She looks me up and down before eyeing my mother. "He's no Kingston. He will never be a Kingston. Stay away, you little con artist." She charges down the steps, passing me, and when my eyes meet my mother's, I see the pain slicing through her stare.

I rotate and charge after the old lady. "My mom is no con artist. She's dying, you bitch! You're horrible. Who are you?"

"No one you will ever know. No one to you ever. Remember that in case she doesn't. You are nothing. You will never be anything to me or us." She climbs in the car and I rotate again and run toward my mother who is now inside the trailer.

I enter to find her waiting for me, her arms folded in front of her chest again. "We need to talk," she says.

I shut the door. "Who was that woman?"

"I have lied to you your entire life."

I clutch the ball in my hand. "What?"

"Your father wasn't a Navy SEAL. He didn't die serving his country. That was your uncle, my youngest brother."

"I don't understand."

She grabs another stress ball from the bar behind her and walks to me, pressing it into my free hand. "I had an affair. I slept with a married man, but I swear I didn't know he was married until I was pregnant. He called me a slut and liar and—" She sobs and covers her face with her hands.

I know on some level I should comfort her, but I can't do it. Numbers begin to stream and speak to me, they speak in ways I can't explain, in ways I can't calm. They tell me what to ask, what to think. "Who was that woman?"

"Your grandmother. You're a Kingston, son, and before I die, you will be claimed. That will be my gift to you. A ticket out of this hellhole."

My temples start to throb and data punches at my mind like fists on a bag. I start to lose reality and I can't hold onto the balls anymore. I try. I try to squeeze them, but they tumble to the ground. I can't think. I can't see beyond what the numbers want to say to me. I sink to my knees and in the depths of thousands of numbers, I see only one thing. That old lady with the red hair's disdainful look as she'd looked at my mother and called her a con artist right before she turned her attention to me, "The little bastard?"

I blink back to the present, my knuckles white where I hold the banister. I'm not a little bastard now. I'm a big fucking bastard that could hurt that woman. Harper slides under my arms in front of me, her hands pressed to my ribcage, heat radiating from her palm and down my arms. "I'm sorry," she says. "She just—"

"Choose now. Her or me."

"You," she says immediately. "There's no question there. *You, Eric.* If you would have given me the chance, I would have shown you that a long time ago."

"You were always one of them."

Pain darts through her eyes. "I was never one of them, but clearly, I'm a fool. You'll never believe that." She tries to duck under my arms again and my leg captures hers, blocking her way.

"Actions speak louder than words."

"Exactly," she says. "I made a mistake tonight. I know that, but you give me no room to be human. I'm perfect or I'm a Kingston. I can't do this. I can't feel what I feel for you and have you destroy me the way you want to destroy them." She tries to move away again but I don't even think about letting her free.

"Let me go," she demands, her voice trembling. "Let me go and maybe this time I'll have the reality check to finally let you go."

"What do you feel, Harper?"

"Anger."

I cage her against the railing, my legs shackling hers. "You said you can't feel what you feel if I'm going to destroy you. What do *you feel?*"

"Too damn much for a man who knows nothing but his own hatred. For a man who wants to destroy everyone attached to this family, and that means me."

"If anyone can destroy anyone, it's you. You could, if I gave you the opportunity, if I trusted you enough, you could destroy me like no one else ever dreamt of destroying me."

"*If* you trust me? Because you don't?"

"Why should I give you that power? *Why,* Harper?"

"You shouldn't," she whispers, her voice a rasp of emotion. "It's too much. Just like I shouldn't with you. I can't do this."

She means it. She's done, and the very idea shreds me. Her words radiate through me and shift something inside me. I need this woman and damn it, I'm about to lose her. I know she could destroy me, but the bottom line is I don't fucking care. I cup her face, and tilt her gaze to mine. "It's not much with you, Harper. It's never enough. And I'm not used to feeling like this. I don't know if I'm coming or going. I don't know what I'm doing."

Her fingers curl on my chest, and she whispers, "Try not pushing me away."

"Does this feel like I'm pushing you away?" I cover her mouth with mine, and I don't just kiss her. I devour her, and I demand more than ever before, because I finally understand the way Grayson craves his woman, the way he will do anything for her, risk anything for her. There is no such thing as too much with this woman; even if she becomes the end of me.

Chapter Thirty-Seven

Harper

With the banister at my back and Eric in front of me, kissing me, his hands all over my body, it's like something has snapped between us. It's a matter of seconds, it seems, before my pants are off and his are open, a condom in his hand. It's the condom that gets to me again, driving home how much I need to talk to him about certain things I haven't yet, but now doesn't feel like the time. Now *really* isn't the time because he's already kissing me again, lifting my knee to his hip and pressing inside me.

Another few seconds and my legs are wrapped around his waist, and our version of makeup sex is wild, fast, and hard. We're both shuddering to release far too quickly, and yet it's somehow perfect. I come back to reality with my face in his neck and him carrying me to the bathroom. He sits me on the sink, pulls out of me, and presses his hands on either side of me, anger burning in his eyes that sex clearly did nothing to tame. In fact, if anything, the opposite. He's angrier now, like he's pissed that he couldn't help but fuck me. "What is happening right now?"

"Me or Gigi," he says roughly, his face all hard lines and shadows.

"How are we having the same conversation *again*? I answered this in the hallway. You. *You*, Eric. You can read the messages. All of them."

"I will. Don't tell her anything without talking to me first."

"I already told you what happened and that it won't happen again."

He tosses the condom in a trashcan, zips his pants up, and then settles his hands on his hips. "You do know she could be setting you up, right?"

"I know what she's capable of," I say. "I was going to tell you what she said." I'd scoot off the counter, but I'm half naked and he's now fully dressed. It just feels weird. I grab a towel and pull it over me before I jump down. "Can you hand me my robe behind the door?"

He stares at me a moment but does what I ask. Once it's in hand and then on my body I push to my feet and face him. "This is not right what you're doing right now. You need to read the messages." I start walking and he shackles my wrist and pulls me back to him.

"I need to be able to trust you, Harper. There is no in between for us."

There are so many ways I could come back at him for that statement, that's getting really old. We're on repeat but I force myself to breathe and remember it's obviously for a reason. He needs to hear my answers again, and I get it. He's wildly successful, incredibly intelligent, and some might say irreparably broken. I'm not one of those people but he has plenty of reasons to be guarded. "You can trust me," I say, my tone no longer combative. "I swear to you, Eric, on my father's life, on all that I am, that you can trust me. I'm sorry. You went downstairs and she texted me to see if we had any news and I just—I asked her about the number."

"How long have you known about the wire transfers?"

"Just read the messages, Eric. I'll get my phone for you."

He reaches into his pocket and produces my phone. "I have it, remember?"

"Right. Good. Read the messages. Read *any* of my messages."

He stares at me, ignoring the messages, searching my face, and I don't look away. I want him to see the truth in my eyes. I'm with him, all in, and loyal but time ticks and we're still standing there and it feels like he's waiting on me to say or do something. "I *will not ever* go to Gigi or anyone without talking to you first. I know what she did to you and your mom. I should have thought—"

"Yes. You should have." He steps around me and walks into the bedroom. I quickly follow entering the bedroom as he sits on one of the chairs and starts reading through my messages.

I cross to sit in the chair angled his direction, right next to him, holding my breath as seconds tick by. Abruptly he angles my direction and hands me my phone before he reaches for his own. Without a word, he punches an auto-dial number, and it takes only a moment for me to realize we're on speakerphone.

"Morning, sunshine," a man answers.

"Blake," Eric greets. "You're on speaker. Meet Harper."

"How the fuck are you, Harper?"

I laugh. "Well, you made me laugh, but otherwise"—my eyes meet Eric's—"I'm not very fucking good, actually."

"Talk to me," he says. "I'm everyone's therapist. Well, I'm not actually anyone's therapist, but I am their kick in the ass, and problem solver. Hit me with it, all of it."

Eric sets the phone on the table between us. "Gigi freaked out when Harper told her about the message we got tonight. She thought it was a wire transfer number. Seems she's been getting some large wires and then pulling the cash for Isaac."

"Indeed, she has," he says. "I sent you proof of those transactions. As for her pulling the cash and giving it to Isaac, I reserve judgment on that idea. If I can't prove it, I don't believe it."

"Agreed," Eric says. "What do you know about the wires she's been getting?"

"The identifier as you called it, is not a bank transaction, a foreign exchange number, or anything that pulls up electronically with any ease at all. I'll dig into personal emails and documents over the next few days. I'll let you know what I find."

Eric's eyes are on me as he asks, "Questions for Blake?"

"A very broad one. Do you have any idea what's going on?"

"A cover-up for sure," he says. "My concern is that it could be a set-up with Eric as the target."

My eyes go wide and I straighten, "I'm not setting him up. Eric, I'm not setting you up. I'm not part of this."

"We'll talk later, Blake," Eric says, disconnecting the line. "I know you're not setting me up, but *they* may be setting me up through you and I can't allow that to touch Grayson Bennett. He's been too damn good to me."

Panic rushes over me and I pop to my feet. Eric is there with me, his hands settling on my arms. "I'm not going to let them hurt me or you. I'm here. I have a world of resources, which means you have a world of resources."

"There's something weird about Isaac having me take over this union negotiation."

"Meaning what?"

"Involving me came out of nowhere. It's not what I do and it could have been to keep me busy, but it feels like more. My instinct, the first thing that came to my mind, was that he was setting me up in some way."

"Never disregard your instincts," he says. "And I'd already planned on going to the union meeting with you."

"Maybe that's the idea. Connect you and me to something unsavory. Don't go with me."

"I'm going with you, Harper. End of subject."

"Eric—"

He drags me closer and kisses me. "It'll be fine."

"We don't even know what's going on. We don't know where the bullets are coming from. Blake's assumption feels right. This is a set-up. I brought you into a set-up. You have to leave."

"I'll leave if you'll come with me."

"You know I can't do that."

"Then I'm staying."

"I'm a bad person. I need to tell you that I'm a bad person."

His eyes narrow, and I feel the slight stiffening in his body next to mine. "What does that mean, Harper?"

"The honorable thing to do right now is to make you leave."

His expression softens. "You can't make me leave."

I wish that was true, I think. I wish so much that I didn't have a secret that would make him hate me. I tell myself to tell him now, but it's embarrassing and I'm ashamed that I didn't handle a piece of my life, of *his* life, in a better way. He'll leave when he finds out. He'll go home and that means he'll be out of this. He'll be protected and I care about this man. I need to suck it up and take the hate. I need to force him to leave. I need to just tell him. I need to do it now.

But then he strokes my hair in that way he does that is both tender and sensual, and it undoes me. "We're in this together, Harper," he says with that warm, gravelly tone of his that is sex and sin and friendship all in one. "Which is why," he adds, "we're going to get comfortable, drink wine, and dig through the data Blake gave us. Together. We're going to do this together. Say it."

"Together," I repeat, and I like this word for us. I like it so much that I'm selfish. I can't tell him right this minute. I'll tell him tomorrow. I'll tell him everything in the morning.

Chapter Thirty-Eight

Eric

With the word "together" between us, I reach up and untie the sash of Harper's pink silk robe and then turn her to face the door, dragging it down her shoulders, letting the silk pool at our feet. "Let's get comfortable and get to work," I say, my lips by her ear, my fingers catching on her shirt, and pulling it over her head.

"And that requires I be naked?" she asks.

I remove my shirt and slip it over her head, the material falling past her knees as I turn her to face me and she slips her arms into the sleeves. "My way of reminding you that we're together as we dig into the investigation. Together, Harper."

"Together doesn't mean jumping to conclusions like you did over Gigi without talking to me first."

"I'll concede that to be true," I say. "And I'm *sorry*."

She blanches. "You're sorry?"

"Yes. I'm sorry, and in case you didn't know, savants are good at apologizing, in my case, if it mathematically makes sense."

It's a joke, but she doesn't laugh.

"You're not going to say anything more about the Gigi incident?"

"I believe you had good intentions," I say, and I do. "I believe you'll talk to me next time first."

"I will. I promise."

"Then let's put it behind us. That's mathematically logical as well."

She smiles. "I like this mathematically logical stuff you do."

"Good, because it's who I am, sweetheart." I glance at my black and silver TAG Heuer watch, one of the first expensive things I bought myself, and then back to her. "It's ten. I want to analyze the data Blake sent me and have you show me the data you collected before we catch a few hours of sleep."

"Of course," she says. "I have a paper file I put together. I was paranoid about the electronic data getting wiped out or it being discovered by the wrong people." She moves to the side of the bed where she's taken up residence for the night, and I claim my spot as she pulls a folder from her briefcase.

"This is what I've pulled together, but honestly, I'm not sure it helps much. It tells us there's funny stuff going on but we know that already and it's nothing." Her cellphone rings again and she glances at the caller ID. "My mother," she confirms. "I'm taking it on speaker. My reminder to you that I'm with you." She doesn't give me time to approve or object. She sits back down in her chair and answers the line.

"Hi, mom."

"He's still there with you, isn't he?"

I sigh and sit down, removing my cube from my pocket. This is not going to be a short conversation nor a gentle one.

"Yes," Harper confirms, glancing at me as she adds, "He is. We're together. We're seeing each other."

"He's your stepbrother. That's embarrassing."

Harper reacts about the same way I did to Isaac issuing that same jab. Irritation flits across her face and she snaps back. "We're adults that never even lived together and I can't even believe you went there. You're married to a man who out ages you by a huge number. I know how sensitive you are to that, but when it's me you're going to attack?"

"Your father—"

"Okay, mom. This is more of the same conversation we had when you were here tonight. He's not my father, and frankly, I'm tired of you dishonoring my real father, the man that was supposed to be your soul mate, by calling Jeff my father. I'm not going to say more. Right now, you're not in a state of mind to listen."

She's silent for several beats. "There are things about Eric you don't know. I need you to hear those things before you continue down this destructive path."

"I'm going to let Eric tell me about Eric. Just like I want him to let me be the one to tell him about me."

"When your fath—Jeff, gets here tomorrow, you're going to have to talk to him about Eric."

"Jeff needs to talk to Eric," Harper says, "*his son*, which is what I will tell him."

His son.

Fuck, I hate the way that reference cuts. I didn't think it could cut anymore, but it does.

Harper's mother is silent for several beats. "I beg of you, daughter, please don't do this."

"I'm protecting you," Harper says. "One day you'll thank me." Her mother sobs and hangs up.

Harper sets the phone on the table. "I'm all for digging into the data." She grabs my cube and stares at it. "I can never work these things. Can you?"

I take it from her, use a few rotations of my hand and solve the puzzle before setting it down. "Talk to me."

For several beats she just searches my face, just looks at me. "What if I don't know her anymore, Eric? What if she's one of them now? What if she knows what's going on and has willingly stayed involved?"

I lean forward and stroke a strand of hair from her eyes. "Then you save her anyway. She's your mother."

"That's not what you said when I told you I had to save her."

"I changed my mind."

"Why?" she asks, covering my hand with hers.

"Because, sweetheart, I wanted to save my mother from this family and I couldn't." It's a confession I've made to no one, ever. "Just like your mother, she didn't want to be saved."

"Your mother was trying to save you, not herself. That's different. She did what she did out of love for you. Mine. Mine doesn't seem to care about me at all."

"Or she's desperate to protect you," I suggest. "She wants you to back off before someone hurts you. Give her the benefit of the doubt."

She breathes out, her teeth worrying her bottom lip before she says, "Thank you, Eric. I know that you're seeing her in a different light to help me. It really matters."

"Yeah, well, sweetheart, I wouldn't have gotten so damn pissed at you over Gigi if you didn't matter to me. Trust is everything to me."

She sucks in a breath and glances away before looking at me. "Because this family hurt you so badly."

"They cut me, but I don't bleed easily, not anymore." Her phone buzzes with a text and she glances down at it and then shows it to me. It's from Gigi and it reads: *Answer me, Harper. Do not tell Eric.*

I study it a few beats and look at Harper. "I'm not objective about Gigi. I hate her and I don't hate easily. Tell her okay, you won't tell me. Give her space to feel safe and we'll sit back and see what she does next." I wait for Harper to reject this directive, but she doesn't.

She snatches up her phone, types a message and shows it to me. It reads almost identical to what I suggested she say, but she hasn't pressed send yet. "Good?" she asks.

"Good," I approve.

She hits send and sets her phone aside again. "We have to find the answer in that message we were sent. I know I don't have the capacity to wade through information with the same results you can, but let me help. What can I do?"

"Show me the file you've put together and explain what concerns you, what looks shady."

From there, we dig in. After reviewing her data with me, she starts reading through the files Blake sent me. In the midst of it all, I tease another investor on the NFL deal, refuse calls from Julius, the asshole trying to set-up the deal, and ensure Grayson knows what card I'm playing. It's one in the morning when Harper is snuggled next to me, sound asleep, and I move her MacBook to the nightstand. With her pressed to my side, I continue to work, and I decide that I could damn sure get used to this woman by my side, in a bed, any bed, with me, for a really long time.

Maybe even a lifetime.

Holy fuck, what is happening to me?

She's a damn witch, but she's the sweetest, sexiest witch I've ever known.

I flip through her data again, my Rubik's cube in my hand, and I compare it to the files that were deleted from Kingston's systems. I end up focusing on Isaac's email records to the point that I set the cube down. He deleted every email to a man named Tim Carlson, who just so happens to be a high-ranking officer of the automobile union. And Harper is not only meeting with the union tomorrow, she feels like it's a set-up. I don't like how that looks, feels, or sounds, especially when Gigi, who I don't trust, befriended Harper and now she doesn't want me to know about cash deposits. But she wanted me here. She sent Harper to get me. Blake's right. Harper and I are being set-up.

Chapter Thirty-Nine

Eric

I wake at sunrise with Harper pressed to my side, the heat of her body next to mine warming me in places I thought to be unbreakable ice, but I was wrong. She's changing me. She doesn't know it, but I do. With every moment that I'm with her, she seeps deeper inside me, and she was already there to begin with. She's been there for six illogical years. Proven by the fact that for a solid fifteen minutes, I lay there, just listening to her breathe. When I finally force myself out of the bed to get ready for a phone conference I've set-up on the NFL deal, I stand above her and watch as she snuggles into the covers, and to me—this represents trust. With all she has going on, with all the fears she's nursing, she feels safe with me here. And she is.

No one is ever going to hurt her again.

I pull on my boots I took off hours ago, drag my jacket on without a shirt, stick the gun in the back of my jeans, and then head downstairs, exiting the house into a cold Denver morning to grab my garment bag from the trunk of my rental. I check in with Blake by text, despite texting with him a few hours ago. When I re-enter the bedroom, Harper hasn't moved. I finish showering and she's still in a deep slumber. I shave and dress in an expensive as fuck suit, worthy of the Bennett brand, and then accessorize with the gun at the back of my pants, under my jacket. I make coffee and predict how Harper takes hers based on the supplies she has in the house and then head upstairs.

I set the cup on the nightstand, sitting next to Harper, my hand settling on her arm. She blinks and brings me into focus. "Eric? God, is that really you?"

My lips curve at her sleepy, dreamy reaction. "Yes, sweetheart. It's really me. I brought you coffee."

She rockets to a sitting position. "Eric?"

I laugh. "Yes. It's still me."

"I was—I think I was—"

"Dreaming?"

"Yes. I was really asleep and I think you were—It was just a dream."

Dreaming of me. Fuck. She's undoing me here. I should have come back for her. I never should have left her.

"Oh God," she says, grabbing my arm. "What time is it? I have that union meeting."

"It's only six-thirty." I offer her the coffee. "You have time."

"You really made me coffee?"

"I really made you coffee," I confirm as she accepts the cup and sips.

"And you made it how I like it. Was there some statistical reason you chose my perfect mixture?"

"I guessed based on how you stock your supplies."

"You did good," she approves, "and how very un-bastard-like of you." She eyes my suit. "You look really, really good in that suit. Actually, you look really, really good in a T-shirt. And apparently, I have no filter this early in the morning."

"No filter equals honesty. Keep it coming. And for the record, you look damn good in my shirt. You'd look better in my bed. I may have to go back to New York for a meeting on this NFL deal. Come with me."

She sets the coffee down. "I can't leave in the middle of this, but you need to leave before this all blows up on you. I fell asleep thinking about that. You need to go."

"I'm not going anywhere without you. Come into my world, into my life, and be a part of it."

"Would that include you telling me what all your tattoos mean?"

"Yes, Harper. I'll tell you what my tattoos mean."

"That's tempting, really tempting and I wish I could, Eric, but I can't leave. You know I can't leave."

"You can," I say, and when she opens her mouth to object, I hold up a finger. "Hear me out, sweetheart."

She hesitates but nods before I continue, "We'll convince them that I gave you a reason to leave and backed you the hell out of this mess. In theory, they then let down their guards while the Walker team is hacking and watching."

"You really think that will work?"

"I know this family far better than I wish I did, Isaac especially. He is never smart about how he covers his tracks."

"He covered them well enough to keep us from uncovering them now."

"You've been in his face, you've been pushing him. Come to New York with me." My hand comes down on her leg. "Sleep in my bed with me. Live in my world with me. See what life outside the Kingston world is like. They've consumed you. And if you see it, if you love it, you'll sell it to your mom."

Her eyes soften. "I want to. God, I really want to."

"Then do it. Remove yourself from the target zone, too."

Worry pinches her brow. "Does that put my mother there instead?"

"We'll watch for trouble, but I don't see her as a target."

"How would that look? What would we do to set this up?"

"I'll go at them hard for a few days and you stay your course. Don't change how you've been acting at all. Don't say a word to Gigi about backing down. Then I'll pull back and tell my father that I'll bow out in exchange for your protection. I've walked away before. He'll believe me."

"You think it will work?"

"Yes, and I read my father well. I'll know when to play the cards if it's working."

She considers me several beats. "Me going to your home is our play?"

"Yes."

"Me in your bed?"

"The best fucking play ever," I assure her.

Her lips curve, her mood shifting to yes before she ever speaks it. "I have a condition," she says, her eyes lighting with mischief.

"What condition?"

"Every tattoo I lick, you explain."

I laugh and kiss her hand. "Condition accepted and feel free to start that process before we get to New York and my bed."

"A suggestion worthy of consideration."

I lean in and cup her head, dragging her lips to mine. "How about I lick *you* all over instead?"

"Can we take turns?"

I kiss her, and the throb of my cock is instant, while my conference call is imminent, and it's all I can do to leave her in her bed, all but naked in my shirt. But I do, and only because soon she'll be in *my bed* where she'll s*tay* naked.

Harper

I have to tell him my secret before I can go to New York with him. I have to. I will. It's the right thing to do. It's the only thing to do. These are the thoughts in my head as I dress in a black dress and lace topped thigh-high but it doesn't stop there. My mind is racing the entire time I go through my morning routine. I'm falling hard for this man. I have been from the day I met him and now, we're here, we're together, we're doing this, and the past hangs over our heads. The consequences of our first night together reach far beyond what Eric believes to be the reality.

I grab my purse and briefcase and head downstairs, following the echo of Eric's deep, sexy voice to the kitchen. I find him at the island, coffee cup in hand, his MacBook open on the counter, while the phone is at his ear. His tattoos peek from beneath his sleeve, a canvas of all the lives he's lived and I want to know them all. I can't bear the idea of my secret destroying us, but not telling him isn't an option. We said no secrets and this one isn't one I could dare keep from him.

I approach the island, his gaze warming with the sight of me in that way every girl wants a man of her heart to look at her. And he *is* the man of my heart. I'm falling in love with him. I have always been standing on a ledge above a sea of wild blue love with this man, ready to jump. But I can't jump and have that water become ice.

"Let me call you back, Blake," Eric says, disconnecting and shutting his computer, his eyes doing a wicked glide up and down my body. "You look beautiful, Harper."

"Thank you," I say, stopping at the island across from him and it's the wrong time. I know it's the wrong time, but when I look into his eyes, when the warmth of his stare radiates through me, I can barely contain this explosion inside me. "Eric, I need—"

Both of our cellphones ring at the same time. Eric winks and my moment of poorly timed confession is gone. Eric declines his call. I eye my caller ID, find an unknown number, and decide I have to answer, only to have it turn out to be my union contact. "Jim," I greet. "We're still on for our meeting this morning, right? At the union office?"

"No meeting."

"Why?"

"Isaac and I talked last night. We agreed on terms."

"Just like that?"

"It's done. No meeting." He hangs up without another word.

I frown and slide my phone into my purse, glancing up to find Eric watching me intently. "What just happened?"

"The union meeting is cancelled. They agreed to our terms. So actually, I'm turning your question on you. What just happened?"

"Isaac deleted the union messages when I walked in the door. Now the meeting between you and the union is cancelled. Kingston's obviously in bed with at least a portion of the union. My presence and history with the union has everyone spooked. Add to that the fact that my father just called and demanded to see me at the office right now and I'd say our plan is working. The one where we leave and you end up in my bed."

Unless I don't, I think. Unless he decides he doesn't want me there, because I can't go to New York City without telling him what I don't want to tell him. What I have to tell him.

Chapter Forty

Harper

Eric and I decide to ride to work together which is all good and fine. What is not, is his choice of car. Eric pulls us into the Kingston parking lot while driving his Jaguar rental. "I can't believe we're in a Jaguar," I say. "I work for Kingston. You're a stockholder."

"You're making a statement," he says yet again, since we had this debate at my house. "The Kingstons don't own us. They don't own you. And that's an important message. It's the one that puts pressure on them. It's the one that makes them feel relief when I convince you to leave."

"Right," I say. "I know you're right." But the idea that his father will be here today, and most certainly get all in my face over this, is not a good one. Isaac I can deal with. He's an ass that makes you hate him. Jeff is another story. My stepfather has a way of crawling under your skin and cutting you from the inside out.

Eric parks us right up front, kills the engine, and turns me to face him. "You've been their 'yes' girl for six years."

I scowl at him. "I'm the one who's been pushing them about the recalls and funny money. I'm the reason you're here."

"But for six years, you played a role in the company, you played the good little employee. And you did it so well that no one thought twice about using your trust fund."

"My mother allowed that," I say. "I still can't believe she allowed that to happen."

"Here's what you need to remember, sweetheart. Your father didn't believe she'd let it happen. He believed he took care of you. Your mother has changed, she's inside the Kingston web."

"Yes, but—"

"I know you want to save her, but you don't save someone by ignoring what you're saving them from. She's brainwashed and that means she will act to protect them and convince herself that's in your best interest even if it's not. She burned you. She will burn you again if you let her. Understand?"

I flash back to the night I found out she gave my stepfather my trust fund. We were at one of our mother-daughter Sunday brunches we do once a month, sipping coffee and eating waffles:

"I need to share something exciting," my mother says, setting her coffee aside.

I sip from my cup and do the same. "Exciting is good. I'm all ears."

"Jeff is going to invest your trust fund and he's assured me you'll get a twenty-percent return."

I blanch. "What? What does that mean?"

"He says that seven million dollars shouldn't just sit when it could be earning money for the company your father helped build and for you. I gave him the money a month ago, and he says it's already earning you ten percent more than the way it was banked."

"You did what?"

"This is great news, honey."

"How did you do this? That money is in my name."

"I'm the executor and—"

"I'll never see that money back again." I lean forward and all but growl. "What have you done? How could you do this to me?"

"Harper?"

I blinked back to the present and into Eric's blue eyes. "Where were you just now?"

"Remembering the day my mother told me she gave my trust fund to Jeff and how great it was going to be for me."

"What did you say?"

"I was angry. I knew I'd never see the money again. I started looking for a job. I wanted out, but unlike her with me, I put her first. I stayed when the fatalities happened to protect her. But you're right. She's brainwashed. I think she really believes I don't appreciate what Jeff does for me."

"My father is a master manipulator and she's a willing victim."

I tilt my head, curious about the words that just came out of his mouth. "I'm surprised you call him your father."

"My mother told me that I had to own what I wanted."

"And you wanted him to be your father?"

"I wanted what my mother wanted. For him to claim me as his son, but that was a long time ago and he told me to call him father.

Of course, he was trying to push Isaac to step up. He was using me."

"And you still address him as father?"

"Every time I call him father, I remind him that my mother was never a person to be ignored." Shadows flit through his stare before he refocuses on me and his cellphone buzzes with a text. He snakes it from his pocket and reads the message before replying and updating me. "Blake hacked all the recording devices in the building but didn't install his own. He said after careful consideration and review of the camera placement with more detail, he has full access, which means whatever is said in this building he'll hear."

I know the answer already, but I just need to confirm. I need to hope. "My office was for sure recorded, right?"

"Yes," he says, stroking my cheek. "I know you hate that they saw you change clothes."

"Yes, well, just another reason to kick your brother and father in the balls, even if it's a proverbial kick."

"That's my girl," he says, the endearment doing funny things to my belly. "Lead the conversations you have where you want them to go. Everything you get the family to say while we have access to the recordings could be useful if we need to protect your interests."

"And innocence?"

"They won't frame you or me for their crimes. That's not going to happen. Let them move things around while we watch. Then when we leave, they'll make bigger moves."

"We hope."

"We expect," he says. "My father flew back because I'm here. They feel the pressure. I'm going to ensure they feel it ten times over. And when he comes at you, you do the same. That's our plan. Stick with it."

"I know. I will."

He leans over and kisses me. "Stick with it."

"I said I will."

"Just making sure," he says, giving me a wink. "I'll come around and get you." He exits and I gather my briefcase. By the time I have my petite purse stuffed inside it, Eric is opening my door and offering me his hand.

I slide my palm to his, and I swear every time this man touches me, I light up. I'm alive in ways I didn't realize I could be alive, in ways I want to be for the rest of my life, and that's a scary thought. This man could hurt me, and that has nothing to do with the company or the family. It's all about us and what I feel for him that I'm afraid to name. I need to just enjoy him, and love the time with him. I need to live in the now.

"Whatever you're feeling," he says softly, walking me to him, "I am, too."

My gaze rockets to his and he brushes his knuckles over my cheek. "I'd tell you what I feel if we weren't here in this Godforsaken place." He settles my hand on his elbow, and unlike me, he's not wearing a coat. "There's much to talk about, Harper. Alone. In New York City. Away from this place. Today helps us get there. Let's go do this."

"Yes. Let's go do this."

He turns us toward the building, and arm in arm we walk to the main entrance, our relationship on full display. Eric opens the door for me and nerves assail me. His father is here. He's going to confront me. My mother is going to confront me. Isaac and Gigi, too. But they'll go at Eric as well, and that's what we want.

I enter the lobby first but Eric is by my side in an instant. The receptionist stares at us a minute before she says, "Gigi wants to see you."

I'd expected as much, but it's then that I realize Eric and I haven't talked about what I'm going to say to Gigi. "Tell her I'll find her when I get settled."

The receptionist clears her throat. "Sorry. I meant Eric. She wants to see you, Eric."

"I'm sure she does," he says, glancing first at a text message, and then at me, before motioning for me to step back outside.

I nod and follow him to the right and down the stairs. As soon as we're behind closed doors, he turns and faces me, drags me to him and whispers in my ear. "Treat Gigi like she's setting you up. Get her to talk."

"Yes. Yes, okay."

The doors behind us open and Eric rotates us to face the door, where his father has just entered the room, no doubt having witnessed our embrace.

Chapter Forty-One

Eric

I stand toe to toe with my father, a man who we all know looks more like me than Isaac, and that hasn't changed. He's tall, athletic, his eyes the same blue as mine, his hair now streaked with gray, but still the same wavy brown. All little details that feed Isaac's insecurity and bitterness. As for my genius, per Gigi, that's her doing, a detail I just don't care enough about to research.

"Father," I say, tightly.

"Leave us, Harper," he orders without looking at her.

I catch her arm and meet her stare. "I'm here if you need me."

"I'm here if you need me," she replies.

Holy hell, this woman charms the fuck out of me. I barely contain a smile at her reply, but I manage to give her a nod and release her. She walks around my father and exits the conference room. "Are you going to tell me how you're killing people with your cars, or give me a few more days that might only take hours to figure it out myself?"

"You don't belong here."

"I'm family, blood, *your son*. If any of that mattered to me, I'd be offended. What matters is money. Gigi paid me to find out what you won't tell her."

"Gigi is old and senile, and we both know you have more money than God. You don't need her pathetic money."

"Any man that makes money and keeps that money values it. She's concerned enough to make it worth my while, but let's get real here. Harper is why I'm here. You hurt her, I hurt you. That's the bottom line."

"Your stepsister."

"Who I'm fucking, yes. Now that we're past the taboo part of that equation, you're in trouble. We both know you're in trouble. Trust your son to help."

"We aren't in trouble, *son*. Harper's pissed off about us using her trust fund and you're letting her grab your balls and pull you around."

"Harper doesn't need that trust fund. She has me and you of all people know that I know how to turn money into more money."

"We'll pay you off," he says. "Go back to New York City."

"I'm a stockholder now. I'm not going anywhere, and with Gigi's stock offered up for my purchase, if you push me too hard, I'll take the majority, and you might be the one who's gone."

His lips quirk. "You had your chance. You walked away."

"As if you ever wanted me to run this place."

"I wanted the best man to win and the one that ran away wasn't the best man."

"I didn't run," I say. "I stepped outside your limitations. Now you're confined to your mistakes and we both know you've made them. Suck up the pride and let me help while it's still possible to save this place."

"Just like your mother. You think you can arm yourself with some small weapon and control me. I don't do anything I don't want to do, including claiming you as my son."

"You claimed me to fuck with Isaac. I wonder now if it's him that got you in trouble or vice versa. Did your crown prince endanger your empire? Or maybe you two dared down this path on your own."

"You're playing with matches, Eric. Don't light the match because you'll be the one who burns. I brought you into this world, I quite literally can take you out."

"Who will end who?" I say. "Is that the new game you're playing and are you really sure it's one you want to play with me?"

"I might not be able to beat you, son, but I don't have to beat you. There are others that will do it for me."

He turns and leaves. I stare at the door as it closes. I stare after the man who's supposed to be my only living parent, yet he just threatened to end me. And unlike my pussy brother, I believe he'd act on that threat, but there's a theme here between the two of them. Someone else is involved. Someone who will kill me. Someone who thinks they have the skills to do it despite my skills. They don't, but I want Harper the fuck out of here and then I need to end this family before they have the chance to come after her.

My cellphone buzzes with a text and Blake taps me into Harper's office and I know why. Gigi is on the attack and Harper's become her target.

Harper

I've barely sat down at my desk when Gigi walks into my office and shuts the door, her red hair a mess she never allows it to be. "You told him?" she demands. "Did you tell him?"

I stand up and lean on my desk. "Why didn't you tell me? Wires into your account that you pulled out and gave Isaac. It looks like you're helping them and setting him up. You made it look like I was setting him up."

"I did what I had to do!" she shouts, shocking me with her outburst. "He wouldn't have come here to help if I told you because you wouldn't have helped me and gone to him."

"Why would you pull cash and give Isaac that money? What is really going on here?"

She charges toward me, but I don't miss how unsteady she is as she does. She presses her hands on the opposite side of the desk. "I thought I was helping my grandson."

"Like you tried to get rid of your other grandson? You hurt Eric. Now you want him to help you without knowing the facts?"

"I can't undo the past. I can't. I told you. I regret what a bitch I was to him and his mother. I have nightmares about her suicide. I know what I did to her." She starts crying, deep sobs. "I don't know how to fix any of this."

"Start by walking up to him and telling him you're sorry."

"That won't matter to him."

"That doesn't mean he doesn't deserve it. He deserves it."

"And when looking at me disgusts him so much he leaves?" she demands. "Then what? He's going to take me down with them, isn't he?"

I could tell her no, I could tell her how honorable he is, and how much his mother inspired his actions. How much the

Bennett family grounds him, but I don't. She doesn't deserve that security and I don't trust her not to repeat it anyway. "Holding back information from him certainly isn't the way to inspire his kindness."

"You're the only one who can inspire his kindness. I know you're seeing him. I know you were with him years ago at the party. I saw you go to his cottage. Protect me. Please."

I feel manipulated. I feel used. "Tell him everything. That's how you protect yourself. I can't. I won't. He deserves more than me using our relationship as a tool or a weapon."

She stares at me for several long beats and then walks toward the door. She pauses there and then exits without another word. The door shuts and I pray I've done my job right. My cellphone buzzes with a message from Eric: *I was watching and A) you scared her. That's good. What she does next could tell a story, but most importantly B) I really want to come in there and fuck you right there on your desk but there would be too many perverts watching. That doesn't work for me. I don't share. Not now. Not ever.*

I smile and reply with: *Then I guess we'll have to use your desk in New York City when I go there with you.*

His response is instant: *Yes, fucking yes, and if you keep talking like that I'll fire up a private jet and take you there now, tonight.*

Warmth fills me and for the first time, I really let myself believe that maybe, just maybe, we have a future and I'm willing to walk away from my past to make it happen. I'm willing to walk away for him. And *I want* to walk away before this family does something to ruin us.

Chapter Forty-Two

Harper

It's nearly lunchtime and I've avoided any further encounters with the Kingston family. I spend the quiet time digging through every record I can find that might lead me to that fourteen-digit identifier we were given last night. It's noon, and I'm utterly frustrated when Eric appears in my doorway. "Want to grab lunch?"

"Yes, please. I'm suffocating in this place." I grab my purse and cross the office to greet him. He grabs my coat from the coat rack right inside my doorway, helps me into it, and then uses the lapels to pull me to him, kissing me soundly on the lips.

"How the hell does it feel like a year since I did that?" he murmurs against my mouth, his hand a warm branding on my lower back under my coat.

"Because it has been, right?" I ask, sounding and feeling breathless. I live breathlessly with this man.

He laughs a low, sexy laugh that I feel from head to toe before he takes my hand and leads me toward the front desk. We enter the lobby at the same moment that Isaac walks in the front door. "Aren't they cute," he says dryly. "Fuck break or lunch break?" he asks in front of the receptionist.

He then shifts his attention to me. "Lunch, right?"

His nonchalant, unruffled reply guides my equally unruffled reply. "Can we decide in the car?"

"Whatever you want, sweetheart," he says, leaning in to kiss me before he lifts a chin at Isaac. "Later, brother," he says, and we step outside into a gust of wind.

Eric pulls me under his arm. "Sorry about that in there," he says, glancing down at me. "He was looking for a reaction I didn't want to give."

"Me either," I say. "I'm glad you handled it like you did."

His eyes meet mine, and there is this swell of intimacy between us. There is no divide between us anymore. There is just us against them. The past is history. The future before us.

A few minutes later, we sit inside an Italian restaurant that specializes in pizzas, and once we place our orders, Eric updates me on the recent developments. "Gigi left the office with my father right after he and Isaac had this exchange." He offers me his phone and headset and I watch a short video that shows his father storming into Isaac's office, slamming the door shut and then going off on Isaac.

"Clean up your mess and do it now," he bites out. "Your brother is not an idiot, nor is he without resources."

"Our mess," Isaac snaps. "You sent me down this path."

"I sent you down a dirt road. You turned it into a fucking highway."

"Eric owns stock now. Gigi—"

"I'll deal with my mother. You clean it all up. Now."

The video ends and I slide the phone back to Eric. "I was right. It's something illegal."

"Yes," Eric confirms. "You were right."

"Any luck finding out what this is all about?" I ask.

"Not yet, but I have a contact at the union in New York City. He owes me in a big way and he wanted inside the NFL deal. I called him. I told him he might have an in. We're meeting Monday."

"It's Wednesday," I remind him. "That's a long way off."

"I have to clear a path to get him into the NFL deal plus I need time to find out what the hell that message was about last night."

"I tried all morning with no luck. I think I need to go see my mother. I can search the house."

"Don't do that," he says. "Not while my father's in town. It's too dangerous. Promise me."

"But it could—"

"Blake can get a man in there. You don't go. I'm right about this. Don't do it. *Promise me.*"

I sigh. "Fine. I promise."

"Good. Let's go to New York tomorrow."

"So soon?"

"I need you out of here." He catches my hand and presses it to his leg, covering it with his own. "I *cannot want you* this damn badly, Harper, and have something happen to you."

Want me this damn badly.

Those words expand between us, wrap us in a warm awareness that says everything, even if it says nothing at all. There is so much more than its obvious meaning in that statement. He's afraid of wanting me and losing me like he did his mother, like he did this family when they were supposed to be his future. I understand him, and in this moment, I feel him in every part of me. Something is happening between me and this man. He needs me and I need him and I don't know if that's a forever thing but it's good, it's really good and right.

"I'm not going anywhere but with you to New York."

He kisses me, and it's a long, seductive, inappropriately public kiss that ends when our pizza arrives, and we eagerly dig into our food. That's when we leave the Kingstons out of the rest of the meal. We talk about New York City and all the places he wants me to see and experience with him. It's perfect. It's just me and him, and it feels like coming home in a way I have never been home before.

Eric

I spend the afternoon in the conference room with the taste of Harper on my lips, the smell of her perfume on my clothes, and a mission on my mind: Get her the fuck out of here. I spend the bulk of the time that consumes our hours apart with the Rubik's cube in my hand, and the bank accounts for the company on my computer screen. Patterns emerge that I track back two years, movement of money that exposes wires to a bank account that I don't have a name to identify, but right now I focus on the numbers, just the numbers. Once I come out of my zone, I have a list of ten wires that I suspect were sent to Gigi, as the wires match those to the account I know to be hers. It's nearly six when I text Blake the number and ask for the owner of the account. His reply is instant: *Give me five minutes.*

I start reviewing more data and five minutes later exactly, Blake sends me a message: *Go outside and call me.*

I don't like the way that sounds and unease rolls through me, the idea that this could be related to Harper grinding a hole in my heart. This isn't about Harper. I need to fucking know what the hell is going on and I'm up the stairs in about thirty seconds, exiting the lobby in another thirty to step outside into what is becoming a bitter cold.

I dial Blake. He answers on the first ring. "The account is closed."

"Who owned it and please don't say Harper."

"The account had Harper and her mother on it."

Those words punch me in the fucking chest. "Who closed the account?"

"Harper."

"She knew about the wires then?"

"I don't know the answer to that question, but yes, I would assume she did."

My jaw tics. "I'll call you back."

I disconnect the line, walk back inside and head to the conference room where I pick up my Rubik's cube and I try like hell to calm my mind. I start turning it and turning it, casing every moment with Harper in numbers, in a way no one but me would understand. The numbers just keep fucking coming. Exactly an hour and thirty seconds have passed when I come back to reality and to three text messages from Harper that I don't answer. I need out of this office. I grab my things and head upstairs where the offices are closed up.

I exit to the parking lot into the darkness when it hits me that I rode with Harper. I'm about to turn back to the building and do what I should have already done; talk to her. I need to talk to her. Why the hell am I leaving? I'm two steps from the front door of the offices when Isaac joins me outside. "There he is, my brother." Isaac greets with a sneer that tells me he's up for games and nastiness and I'm not in the mood. "Coming back to get your woman?"

I ignore him and reach for the door when he says, "She needs you until she doesn't. She helps you until it doesn't work for her anymore. That's how she works."

The way he says that, like he knows her intimately, claws at me, and I take the bait I would never take if it wasn't Harper. I stop and turn around, numbers exploding in my mind in random bursts. "She won't help you now," I say. "No one will."

"She needed me once. Gigi told me you fucked her not long before that. She saw her go to your cottage. Then she came to me. Harper had a miscarriage, and fuck, it was a disaster. She's a disaster that started rumors. She bled out right here in the office. I took care of her the way you want to take care of her now. I wonder if the brother thing gets her off." He smirks. "But I'm sure you don't care. You're just fucking her to fuck me, right?" He turns and starts walking toward his car.

Numbers pound at my mind again. I want them to replace the emotions that threaten to consume me. I try to open the lobby door, but I don't have an after-hours card. I dial Harper. "Come outside," I order when she answers. I disconnect before she can reply.

I lean on the wall, watching as Isaac drives away in his two-hundred-thousand-dollar special edition Kingston convertible. Harper exits, pulling her coat on as she does. "What's wrong?"

I grab her and pull her in front of me. "Did you fuck Isaac?"

"God, no. No. No. We had this conversation. Where is this even coming from?"

"Did you have a miscarriage?"

She pales, her hand settling on her belly and I know even before she whispers. "I was going to tell you. I was—"

"What happened to no, you didn't fuck Isaac?" I challenge, those fucking numbers beating at my mind.

"It wasn't Isaac's. It was—I was going to call you, but I—"

"Call me? We didn't even finish fucking, sweetheart. Why would you call me?" I don't give her time to reply. "Don't answer. I don't care. I'm gone. I'm done. Save yourself." I start walking and she screams after me. "Eric! Eric, wait."

I don't wait. I climb into my car, and she pounds on the window but I don't care. I meant what I said. I'm gone. I dial the airport, book a private jet, and head that direction. I can't get out of this city fast enough. I can't get away from *Harper* fast enough.

Chapter Forty-Three

Harper

I stop outside the lobby door and try to pull myself together. There are cameras inside. There are people watching me but I can't stay outside in the cold and I don't have a car. I swipe my card and enter the lobby, my knees wobbling as I walk. It's a herculean effort to reach my office and the minute I'm inside, I shut the door, as if that offers privacy in this place, but it's something. It's all I have. I lean on the door, and the tears explode from me the second I draw another breath. The tears that I cried six years ago. The tears that I have cried randomly since my miscarriage, and I wanted to call Eric every one of those teary nights. I don't know how long I cry now, but I just can't seem to stop. It guts me, it cuts me, it tears me into pieces. He's gone. Isaac told him and he's gone. My phone rings and I reach into my pocket, praying it's Eric but it's my mother. I disconnect the line and try to call Eric. He doesn't answer. I try again. And again. I cry some more.

Somehow, I'm on the floor, lying on my back, staring at the ceiling when I return to reality, tears sticky on my cheeks. Every part of me hurts. I should have told him last night. I should have told him six years ago. I roll to my side and hoist myself to my feet and I do what I have done every time I've tried to survive this. I go to my desk and try to work. I'll find out what that damn sequence is. I'll find answers and somehow that will make this better, somehow that will make Eric forgive me. No, he won't forgive me. He believes Isaac. He thinks I fucked his brother.

I dial him again and when he doesn't answer, I burst into my confession on his voicemail. "I wanted to tell you. I just didn't want you to think I was playing you and then you got all that money and I was afraid you'd think it was about money. I can't make you believe me, but you know—I'm pretty sure I'm in love with you so

I just have to tell you." The phone beeps and disconnects. I let out a sound of utter frustration. God. No. I need to say this.

I dial the phone again and when the machine answers I pick up where I left off. "I got pregnant the night we were together six years ago. I know you pulled out, but you were inside me and it happened. I wasn't with anyone else. I didn't think you'd believe me and what would forcing you to believe me, achieve? It was too late to change what happened. I lost the baby." The machine beeps again and I redial, my hand shaking as I do. The machine beeps again and I launch into the rest of the story. "When I missed my period, I thought it was stress, but then one night I was working late and suddenly I was bleeding. Lots of blood and Isaac was here and I was bad. I was hemorrhaging and—I had to let him help me. I didn't even know what was happening. I was scared and when I found out there was a baby—" The machine beeps.

I sob with the pain of doing it like this, with reliving this but I dial again. "Bottom line," I say when I can speak again. "I hated so much that Isaac was the one who helped me. And I really wanted that baby, our baby, but now I'm damaged goods anyway. I don't even know if I can have kids. They said—"

The machine beeps and tears stream down my cheeks. I can barely take this but I started down this path. I have to finish. I dial again and this time the call goes straight to voicemail. Eric turned off his phone. Obviously, he's tired of me calling. I force the words out. I start talking again. "Eric," I whisper. "I didn't betray you like everyone else in this family. Have Blake hack my medical records. If I was with Isaac and he was the father, why would I fight the ER staff and insist that I couldn't be pregnant? Why wouldn't I put him down on the medical records? I just—I need you to know that I didn't betray you. You matter to me. You've always mattered to me and I regret that I didn't call you. I regret—"

The line beeps and I add, "So much," even though he can't hear me. My emotions overflow and I throw my phone, pain behind the force that smashes it against my door. My emotions are suffocating me. I can't take it.

I stand up, not sure where I'm going, but I need to occupy my mind. I need to escape this feeling. I need to escape the pain. The sequence, I tell myself. Think about it. Think about the message. Figure out what it means. I start walking, exiting my office and walking toward the human resources office. I enter the dark office and search through files, looking for a clue. An hour later, I have nothing. I stand up again and walk toward the warehouse. That sequence has to relate to production in some way. I enter the warehouse that is now empty, as we don't run winter night shifts.

I start walking the assembly lines, looking for that fourteen-digit sequence, checking every possible place: on the parts, on the vehicles, in the paperwork at each station. I'm at this for a good half hour when I decide the foreman's office is where I need to be. I hurry that direction and I'm about to enter his office when the lights go out. I freeze in the utter, complete darkness, sucking in a breath, and willing myself to remain calm. It's a power outage. Nothing more. I reach for my purse that's not with me, but in my office, right along with my destroyed phone.

A sound, a tiny sound, jolts me. Someone is here. There is a whisper in the air. Someone is right beside me. I launch myself forward into a run, but it's too late. Someone grabs me from behind.

Part Two: The Princess

Chapter Forty-Four

Harper

Darkness engulfs me inside the Kingston warehouse as I try to escape the hand on my mouth and the big body at my back, but then I hear a whispered, "Easy, sweetheart," at my ear and everything familiar about this man washes over me with relief. It's Eric. Oh God, it's Eric. He came back. He's here. He's with me and I have never been so happy to feel someone this close as I am now.

"Shhhh," he murmurs softly and then releases my mouth.

I rotate in his arms and hug him so tightly that it hurts, but somehow, it's not tight enough.

He holds onto me, his hand flattening between my shoulder blades, but this is not just about affection. This is him holding me, keeping me still. This is him listening for movement and the necessity of my silence replaces my relief.

We aren't alone.

This wasn't a random power outage.

I stiffen and softly inhale a calming breath. Eric strokes my hair as if in approval and then kisses my temple before pulling me around and then in front of him. His hands go to my shoulders, and he starts walking us forward, and I have no sense of where we are in the Kingston warehouse, but somehow, he does. I sense this. I know this. I remind myself he's not only a genius but an ex-Navy SEAL. About that moment is when he abruptly stops walking and we just stand there, and stand there, and I swear there is a whisper of movement somewhere nearby.

I don't know where.

I just know it's here. It's close. Someone is definitely in here with us.

Just when I feel as if we will be frozen in place for eternity, Eric suddenly moves me forward but we only manage five fast steps before he stops us again. He reaches around me and my hands plant on what I think is a door. He walks me inside, the blue light of an aquarium telling me this is the foreman's office. Eric shuts us inside and leads me into a corner. For the first time since he arrived, I can see him, and even in the shadows, he's beautiful and intense.

"You came back."

"I should never have left," he says, cupping my face. "And we have a lot to talk about when this is over." He kisses me and then takes my hand and presses a gun into it. "Shoot first. Ask questions later." He shrugs out of his jacket and tosses it. "Call 911, but don't move. You could run right into a problem. I'll be right back." He starts to move away.

I catch his arm, my heart lurching as I plead, "Wait. Don't go. Wait on the police. You could get hurt."

"I won't get hurt." His hands settle on my shoulders and as if he knows I need to hear more, he repeats, "I'll be back. Don't move." He starts to step away again, but suddenly halts, holding a finger to his lips to silence me. I nod and he turns toward the door, silently stepping into a spot that places him behind it as it opens. The next thing I know, Eric and some man in all black are exchanging punches. Eric throws him across the desk and I don't even consider running. I hold the gun ready to shoot the minute I know Eric is safe, but he's across the desk and on the guy so quickly I can't fire. I also can't call 911 because I don't have my phone, and the only phone in the office is now on the floor somewhere, out of sight.

I hunt desperately for it, but what I find is Eric flying across the desk this time, landing at my feet. The man he's fighting charges at him and I manage to retain a level head. I fire the gun, but I'm clearly out of practice. It pulls left and misses the man and before I can recover, he's on top of Eric, both of them rolling as I hit the wall. I run for the desk, searching for the phone, but as sure as I'm hunting, suddenly the man Eric is fighting runs out the door.

"Harper!" Eric shouts, motioning me forward. "We need to get out of this office now!"

I run toward him and he grabs my hand and then I'm running again as he pulls me forward into the darkness. I have no idea how he sees where we're going and my stomach is all over the place in anticipation of the phantom object we're about to run into, but never do. Abruptly we halt and he presses me against a wall, his big body against mine and it's sweet relief, like everything wrong is now right. I've found my shelter and that shelter is him.

"Don't move, sweetheart," he whispers and then that shelter, his body, is gone. "We're getting out of here."

A moment later, he opens a door, and I mentally scramble to place us at the exit by the parking lot. Eric leans out of the door and then grabs my hand. The next thing I know, we're outside in the cold and a black SUV halts in front of us. Eric opens the back door to the vehicle and ushers me inside before following. "Airport," he orders the driver. "Now." The vehicle starts to move.

My heart races. "Airport?" I ask urgently, grabbing Eric's arm. "Are you leaving again?"

"*We're* leaving," he says, turning to me and cupping my face. "We need out of here. We *are* getting out of here. Are you okay? I need to know that you're okay." His voice is low, urgent, and rough with emotion.

"Yes. Are you?" I touch the cut down his cheek. "That man—"

"Was a professional. The kind you pay to do a job." He eyes the driver. "What do we know?"

"There were three men in the warehouse with you," the man behind the wheel answers, placing us in drive. "They left in a car with no plates." He turns us onto the main road. "Police or no police?"

"Now that I know we're dealing with professionals, no police. They limit our response." He reaches for his phone and punches in a number. Seconds pass and I can hear the line ring and ring before a muffled voicemail picks up. "Brother," Eric bites out at the beep, "when you get this message, replay it and think about the implications of what I'm about to say. And when I say think, I mean think hard, because we know you're not the sharpest tool in the shed. Three men attacked Harper in the warehouse tonight. You better hope I don't find out that you sent them." He disconnects.

My stomach rolls with the sickening implications of that message. "You think Isaac sent those men to attack me?"

"Yes," Eric says, without even a second of hesitation. "I do."

"As do I," the man driving states, glancing over his shoulder at me. "And I'm Adam, Harper. At your service."

"He's with Walker Security and he's a SEAL like me. He's exactly who we need with us right now."

There's a sharp sensation in my chest that I'm pretty sure is panic bubbling to the surface, and a choked laugh escapes my throat. "He's a SEAL," I say, "as in a Navy SEAL, who is driving us to the airport to escape after three men attacked me in a warehouse. Three men who probably wanted to kill me."

"Easy, sweetheart," Eric says, stroking my hair. "You're safe and you're going to stay that way, but we do need to be careful. We need to get distance between you and whatever this is while we sort through what's really going on."

Dangerous. That word rockets through my mind with fear and realization. "My mother. What about my mother?"

"Walker has men watching her."

Adam chimes in. "Some of our best men. She's safe."

"For now," I amend, focusing on Eric. "I can't leave her."

His jaw sets hard, stubborn. "Whether you like it or not, Harper, she's one of them. That means she's safe. You're not and I'm not leaving you here."

"I'm not leaving her here," I insist, my jaw setting just as stubbornly as his has.

But he's ready for me, pushing back, fast and hard. "We're leaving, and I promise you, Harper, if you try to fight me on this, I'll throw you over my shoulder and carry you onto the private jet waiting on us."

"Eric, damn it—"

"Your mother *is safe*. Being one of them *makes* her safe. You, me, we're not one of them. We're not safe. In other words, we're leaving the way we should have left earlier today. Together."

"Yes, but—"

He kisses me, the touch of his lips to my lips, instantly bringing me down two notches. "Together," he murmurs. "And once we're alone on that plane we'll talk about everything."

Talk.

About the baby.

About the past.

About the secret I kept from him.

"I'm not sure a plane where I'm trapped and forty thousand feet in the air is a good place to have that conversation."

"But I am," he says. "It's exactly the right place to have that conversation. It's exactly where you belong. With me. You belong with me now, Harper."

He says that now, but what if he changes his mind when we really talk about what I left on his voicemail? What if he hasn't even heard it? What if he hates me when he hears all the details?

"I can't get on that plane with you."

Chapter Forty-Five

Harper

Eric and I are still huddled together, that talk we're going to have in the air between us, when the SUV stops without warning. "What's happening?" I ask, jerking out of Eric's embrace, the reality of being trapped in a warehouse and on the run, now coming back to me with a jolting force.

"This is it," Adam calls out from the front seat, placing us in park. "Private airport and private plane."

Eric squeezes my hand. "We're all good, princess. I promise. All is as it's supposed to be."

"Did you—have you listened to your voicemail?"

"I did, about ten times." He kisses my hand. "We're okay."

He only allows me a fleeting moment to absorb that information and feel relief before he says, "Now we get the hell out of here." He leans forward to speak to Adam in a low, muffled voice that I don't try to understand.

Instead, I eye a runway with the plane waiting on us.

The plane that will take me away. Take *us* away.

The plane that will leave my mother behind.

Do I really dare to leave her behind?

Could I even get her to leave with me if I tried? No, the real question is: could I ever get her to leave with *us* if I tried? That's the key here. She's definitely not going to agree to go anywhere with Eric and who am I kidding? She won't leave my stepfather.

I have to leave her here. I have no choice.

Adam opens his door and gets out of the vehicle as Eric settles back into the seat with me. "Adam's going to clear the plane."

"Clear the plane?" I ask incredulously. "Surely you don't think someone is waiting on us here."

His hand comes down on my leg and he squeezes. "Relax, sweetheart. He's doing his job and doing it well by being paranoid.

The safest place we can be right now is on that plane, in the air. And this was our plan anyway. We were going to give them space. Get away. Make the family feel safe. They'll let their guard down. The Walker team is watching."

He's right. I know he's right and I can't let my mother's decisions make me a fool, any more than I can my miscarriage and where our talk will lead us. Yes, we'll be trapped on that plane in our own swampland of pain and history, but we'll both be alive.

"Harper."

At Eric's softly spoken prod I shake myself and refocus on him. "Yes?"

"I promise you, your mother is safe. If there's a shift in where she settles in all of this, Adam will be here to get her out." And then as if he's reiterating my earlier thoughts, he adds, "She wouldn't leave if we asked. You know that."

"Maybe if she hears what happened tonight, that'll change."

His hands come down on my arms, those blue eyes of his connecting with mine. "You can't tell her. You don't know how she'll react or what danger she'll put herself in. We need to stick to the plan. Let them get comfortable. Let them lead Walker Security to whatever is going on here. All that's happening right now, is that we're making sure whoever thinks we're a problem, thinks we're not anymore."

"You mean whoever thinks *I'm* a problem."

"We're one, baby. They know that. I came here for you."

But we're not one or he wouldn't have left. *Only he didn't leave*, I remind myself. "You really think this is all Isaac?"

"He's involved, but he's not the mastermind."

"The mastermind of what?"

"We don't know yet, but we will." There's a knock on the window.

"We're clear," Eric says. "Let's move."

He opens the door and exits the SUV, cold air gushing in through the open vehicle. I resist the chill, but my realization that we couldn't even afford the time for me to pack has me worried we might have been followed. A thought that has me quickly scooting across the seat to catch up with Eric. He's waiting on me and all but pulls me out of the backseat, a hint of urgency radiating off of him as I settle onto the pavement, but not the cloak of darkness. The night is bright, illuminated by a full, rather ominously looking orange moon. I shiver as a cold gust of wind envelopes me, glancing up as I do to find a star shooting dart across the sky.

Eric pulls me close, under his arm, setting us in motion toward the plane, while his big body is a shelter against the wind; shelter that he doesn't seem to need, considering like me, he has no coat, not even his suit jacket he left in the warehouse. We start walking toward the plane, and I quickly scan for the star again. It's gone, but I make a wish anyway: *Please keep everyone safe and alive.* It's the only wish that matters. It's the only wish I'd dare make. We cross the tarmac and Eric halts us by the stairs where Adam awaits. "I'll plug into the internet in the air," Eric says. "Update me."

Adam, who is big, broad, and the definition of tall, dark, and deadly. "Of course. And our team will have support waiting for you when you land."

Eric inclines his chin and refocuses on me. "Let's get inside, baby." He urges me up the narrow stairs and I begin the climb, eager to escape the wind. Relieved with Eric at my back, a protector that I never expected him to be, and never would have asked him to be. A protector to my mother, who hasn't been kind to him. A protector to—

I stop at the top of the stairs and step into the plane, backing up to let Eric join me. "What about Gigi?"

His teeth clench. "What about her?"

"She and I—"

"Don't finish any sentence that begins that way. Not with you and Gigi connected. I'm not in the mood." He pulls me roughly to him. "Walker's watching everyone." He turns me to the plane. "I need to talk to the pilot," he says. "I'll be right there. Go to the back of the plane."

With that gruff order, I pant out a breath. This is not starting well. I run my fingers through my hair and start walking down the narrow path, eyeing the fancy plane with luxury cream-colored recliners and tables left and right without really seeing it. I'm focused on the engines firing up already, a sign we're wasting no time getting into the air. A sign of urgency, of a sense of danger. This hastens my pace, all the way to the rear of the plane, to a set of recliner-style seats I assume will allow us to lay back and sleep, as if I could sleep right now.

I claim one of them and sit down, shivering again and not from the chilly air coming out of the overhead vents. From the evil at play in this family, in my life. I hug myself, trembling in that kind of deep, soul-wrenching way that comes with a fever and illness, but isn't this family just that? An illness? A sickness I can't escape, but Eric had. Until I went and pulled him back into this.

Eric joins me almost immediately and he must notice me shivering because he pulls a blanket from an overhead bin. When I expect him to hand it to me, he doesn't. He wraps it around me and settles on one knee in front of me, his hands on either side of the blanket.

"The Gigi thing—"

"I know. I just—I'm not used to war games, and death isn't exactly my friend."

"No one is going to die. And I shouldn't have left you tonight," he says, and I know he's not talking about the plane. He's talking about back at the office. He's talking about our fight. "I *didn't* leave, not for long. I went back for you and I'm here now, but I fucked up. I let Isaac get to me tonight."

"What did he say to you?"

"It doesn't matter what he said. I listened to him and I reacted rather than asking you questions first. And I regret it. You could have been hurt. I keep telling myself Adam was there, watching you, and you would have been fine, but just thinking about what could have happened to you guts me." His tone is guttural. He's affected. He's worried. *I'm* affected and worried. I have questions. I have fears, and not just about the attack, but the attack is what he's brought to my mind. I'm suddenly back in the dark warehouse, firing that gun.

The plane starts to move.

"Buckle up," he orders. "We'll talk in the air. We're flying through a storm the pilot hopes we'll get past quickly." He stands up and when he would move away, he leans down and brushes his mouth over my mouth and his lips are warm and wonderful. "No one is going to hurt you," he promises. "I won't let that happen. I got you now. You're with me." But even as he issues that vow, his hands fall away from me, and every warm spot he's created goes cold as he moves to his seat next to me and across the tiny walkway.

I inhale and replay his words: *When I think what could have happened to you.* And: *No one is going to hurt you.*

Ice slides deep into my already chilled bones, turning them brittle. I can feel myself quaking inside, like some kind of internal tremble, and I can't seem to breathe. He really thinks those men were there to kill me.

Chapter Forty-Six

Harper

I grip the arms of my seat as the small private plane lifts off and climbs to the higher altitudes with jolts, jumps, and shakes, with only one thought: *Oh God, please don't let us crash.* I'm terrified and not because I'm an amateur flier. I'm not. I've flown. I've even flown in bad conditions, but nothing like this, with the plane jerking, violently pulling and pushing, but I can surmise why pretty darn quickly. Pilots don't take off in conditions like this. Eric paid this one, and I suspect paid him well, to get us off the ground. Considering the conditions, I can only assume that he felt it was far more dangerous to stay where we were than travel in treacherous weather.

We jerk violently to the right and I stop analyzing Eric's reasoning for taking off in this mess. I focus on praying that we survive the powerful gust of wind, punching us from both sides. The plane seems to hopscotch and my white-knuckled grip tightens right as we jerk sharply left and then drop a good two feet that leaves me gasping.

Eric reaches over the small aisle and grabs my hand, his touch strong and warm. The minute he tightens his grip on me, I breathe out the air trapped in my lungs. I breathe when I thought I couldn't. That's the power this man has over me, and it's almost as terrifying as this flight.

He rotates his chair to face me when I'm pretty sure it's supposed to be locked. Next, he does the same with mine, and turns me to face him. My seat tries to sway with the bumping of the plane, and he quickly holds onto it while leaning in and locking me back into place. Now we're closer, and thanks to his long legs, our knees touch, while those blue eyes of his hold mine, his hands settling on my knees. "I've flown through hell and back with a lot less skill controlling the plane. We have a military pilot. A man who flew in a combat mission while under heavy fire. He's good. Really damn good."

"Which is why you paid him to take off in *really* bad weather," I say and I can't keep the accusation from my tone.

"Yes," he says. "Exactly."

We rock and sway. I grab his hands. He presses them to my legs and covers them with his. "We're safe."

"You paid him to take off when he normally wouldn't because you thought we'd get murdered on the ground."

"He wouldn't have taken off if he thought it was too dangerous. He goes down with us, remember?"

"I see how you avoided the part about us getting murdered. And as for the pilot, people do crazy things for money."

"Money does him no good if he's dead. He goes down if we go down," he repeats. "Let's talk and get your mind off the flight."

"I'm *not* talking about what we need to talk about while fearing for my life."

"All right then. We have four hours in the air. Let's start with something simpler."

"Define simpler," I say cautiously, and the weather seems to answer, the plane leveling out, nice and steady.

"You wanted to know about my tattoos. Let's talk about my tattoos." He releases me and starts rolling up his sleeves, displaying his incredibly intricate ink as he does. It distracts me. It has my attention, right up until the moment that the plane jerks again. I jump and Eric grabs my legs again. "I got you."

He has me. He does. I know that, but for how long? How long until this man is gone? How long until he breaks my heart? Because he will and yet when I'm with him I can't seem to care. Except now. Reliving six years ago has cut me open, and I'm still bleeding, and as much as I hate to associate with this word—fragile.

"I got you," he says again, his eyes warm. I'm warm too now. "I know I haven't done the best of showing you that, but I'm going to be better."

"I don't know what to say to that," I whisper.

"Say you believe me. Say you trust me."

"Say *you* trust *me*," I demand. "You didn't trust me when Isaac of all people lied about me."

"I told you. This thing between us is unfamiliar territory. I'm used to trusting people and not getting burned. Right or wrong, and it was wrong, a shield is my sword."

I breathe out a shaky breath. "I know that. I do. And I'm not without guilt. I should have told you everything a long time ago."

"I didn't make you feel like I'd believe you. Grayson always says you get what you give and I did." He holds out his arm, displaying his powerful forearm and colorful ink. "Ask me anything, Harper."

My gaze rockets to his and for a moment, I study that handsome, rugged face, looking for the meaning behind his offer and what I find is vulnerability. These tattoos are more than ink to him. They're his life. They're his secrets. They're a look into his soul. He's offering me a window into that world and trusting me not to abuse it.

My attention immediately settles on his left arm, on the rows of numbers banding its width, and stacking on top of each other, some with images and others without. I run my fingers over a row of nothing but numbers. "This one," I say, looking at him again. "What does this one mean?"

"It says, 'everyone has a price.'"

My lips tighten. "You mean me."

"Everyone, Harper, not just you, but the truth is, that you, at least in part, inspired that tattoo."

My gut clenches, throat tightens. He still thinks that I stayed at Kingston for power and money. "You think it was about money."

"No. I know why you stayed, and you've paid a price and that price was years of your life."

"To protect my father's creation, his empire." Emotions tighten my throat. "His memory."

"I told you," he replies softly. "I know why you stayed and I get it. I stayed for a long time, too. I wanted to be a Kingston, but the price for me became too high."

"Was there a price you paid for leaving?"

"You. I left you behind, but no matter how many regrets I have about that now, that was how it was supposed to happen. I didn't know me like I do now. I wasn't the man I am now."

I think of my miscarriage, and how that baby wasn't meant to be, but I wanted it to be. I wanted it badly. I swallow hard and look at another tattoo, a grim reaper with numbers next to it. "This one," I say, before it hits me that this could be about his mother, but it's too late. I've committed to the question, and he's told me to ask anything. "What does it mean?" I ask, meeting his stare.

"You would pick that right now, wouldn't you?" he teases.

"If you don't want to talk about it—"

"Tuus mors, mea vita," he says. "Latin for 'your death, my life.'"

His mother.

I was right.

This is about his mother.

My heart bleeds for the young man who lost a parent and so very brutally. "What does it mean to you, Eric?"

"It's meant a lot of things to me at different times in my life, but ultimately 'kill or be killed' is the meaning it's taken on in recent years. It's about survival."

Maybe I was wrong, I think. Maybe it wasn't about his mother at all. "Did you get it when you were in the Navy?" I ask.

"No. You can't tell now, since it's surrounded by the rest of my ink, but it was one of my first tattoos. I got it after my mother committed suicide." He glances skyward and seems to struggle with what he's about to say before he fixes me in a turbulent stare. "My mother wrote those words to me in her suicide note. *My death. Your life.*"

Emotion balls in my throat. "Oh God. I'm sorry I chose that tattoo."

"I'm not," he says, squeezing my hand. "You want to know me, you have to know her and how she affected who I am. Harper, I protect myself but I also protect those I care about, the way she did me. She made the ultimate sacrifice for me. When another person would have fought for a cure to cancer, for more time on Earth, she fought for me. The way I'm fighting for you. The way I'm *going* to fight for you." The plane quakes and then immediately enters calmer air once more. The plane is steady, the flying smooth, but I'm in knots. His mother died. He has no real family left, but I was carrying his child. I don't know what that means to him but it meant, it *means*, so very much to me. It's time to talk. We have to have this conversation no matter what the outcome. We have to talk about the child we lost.

Chapter Forty-Seven

Harper

"I need you to know that I would have called you if I hadn't miscarried. I swear to you, I would have, but what was the point once—once I lost the baby?" I choke up and try to turn away, but my seat is locked and Eric is holding my legs.

I look down at my lap, at our hands, and Eric catches my face, forcing my eyes to his. "Tell me. Tell me everything. Forget you said anything on my voicemail. I want to hear it again."

"What did Isaac tell you?"

"It doesn't matter what Isaac told me. It matters what you tell me."

"Because I didn't tell you when it happened?"

"You told me why. I understand why."

"Mostly on voicemail, though. I didn't know if you would believe the baby was yours, and it was. I hadn't been with anyone else. And I thought you'd think I had some Kingston agenda for telling you when you could do nothing to change what happened." The plane shudders a moment, as if warning me to stop now.

"I might have," he admits. "I don't like to believe that I would have, but I saw you on that stage with the family at the party, and I left believing you were one of them. And that means manipulative and self-serving actions. In my mind, at that point in my life, I left you before you burned me."

"I know," I whisper, my throat thick. "I know that. I knew that. That was why it just didn't make sense to call you, but I wanted to. You were the only person who it might matter to like it did me. I didn't tell anyone."

"But Isaac knows because he was there when it happened," he confirms.

"Yes."

"Tell me," he urges, a gentle but forceful push to his voice. "I wasn't there then. Let me be here for you now." He hesitates. "If you can."

It's as if a blade pierces me with emotions, but I beat the pain down, into that hollow place where I don't feel all of it with such sharpness. "I will. You deserve to hear the story, but I want you to know that I was going to tell you. I almost told you back at my house, in my bedroom when we were—when you thought something was wrong—"

"The condom," he supplies, following my lead. "You were thinking about this when I was putting on the condom."

I nod. "Yes, then, and several times that night. God, how I wanted to just tell you, but we kept having visitors and problems come up. I couldn't find just one good moment alone with you that felt like the right time to talk about this."

"I'm here now. *We're* here now."

It's another prod and I don't make him push me harder. "I didn't know I was pregnant. Honestly, I didn't even suspect it. I was late starting my period, but I've had that happen on occasion and I was working long and hard hours."

"You didn't have morning sickness?" he asks.

"Yes, but I didn't know it was morning sickness. I was barely sleeping. I had no reason to suspect I was pregnant. I thought I was just pushing myself too hard. We didn't finish what we started that night. I didn't think I *could* be pregnant." My lips purse. "Of course, I found out in a brutal way how wrong I was on that." I squeeze my eyes shut and when his fingers brush my cheek, I look at him. "I was cramping, so I thought I was finally going to start my period."

Suddenly I'm back in the past, back in my office, and reliving that night all over again in vivid color.

"I was sitting at my desk, sorting through a stack of files and I couldn't find the one that I needed. Frustrated that I couldn't finish my report without it and finally get out of there, I knew I had to hunt it down or miss the critical deadline for the production department. I stood up and rounded my desk when a punch of cramps hit my belly. I slouched forward as another punch hit me and then radiated through my womb." I close my eyes and for a moment I'm there. "Oh god," I whisper, just like I did that night.

Eric's hand comes down on my hand and he squeezes. "We don't have to do this."

"We do," I insist firmly. "We do." I launch back into the story. "I tried to move, but my feet were heavy, like they were planted in the ground. I looked down and blood was seeping through the skirt of my cream-colored dress. I just stared down at it as if it wasn't real, as if it was happening to someone else but then the cramps radiated through me again. I tried to get to my desk and my phone, but I just couldn't. The pain was extreme, and the blood just started pouring like a faucet. It scared me and I started screaming for help."

"And Isaac came to help."

"There was no one else in the building *but* Isaac, and there's nothing between me and him. There never has been. I wasn't lying about that. I haven't lied to you." Now I'm the one squeezing his hand. "Please tell me you know that."

"I know."

My mind goes back to us outside of the Kingston building, and him pretty much telling me to go to hell before he left. "You didn't know earlier tonight."

"I *did* know," he promises. "That's why I came back. *I did know.* I told you. I let Isaac fuck with my head. I let me fuck with my head." His thumb strokes my palm, tingling sensation sliding up my arm. "We would have made a beautiful baby together."

Tears well in my eyes. "We would have, wouldn't we?"

"Yes. We would have. We still could." I can't even begin to revel in the commitment that statement suggests. "I don't know if I can."

"You don't know you can't. It wasn't our time."

"Do you even want kids?"

"I didn't. I don't know, Harper. You've made me think about a lot of things in my life a little differently."

"Well, if you do," she says, her voice breaking on the words, "then, I might not be the girl for you anyway. They said I had a problem with my uterus."

"Don't put that pressure on yourself or us. If you can't, you can't. We'll get dogs and treat them like our kids."

"Yes, but—"

He leans in and kisses me. "If you can't, you can't. I want you, Harper. Just you. Like I have never wanted anyone in my life." He kisses me then, our tongues colliding in a kiss that is as tender as it is sexy and sultry, and I feel each stroke everywhere. My nipples ache. My sex clenches. My entire body is humming. Some part of me knows I need to talk to him about what happened in Denver. Some part of me knows we need to talk about what he believes his brother is really doing. Some part of me knows that if someone tried to kill me tonight, they will follow me to New York City, but right now, I just want him to keep kissing me. I just want him to drug me the way he drugs me with his touch, and when he unhooks his seatbelt and mine as well, I let him pull me into his lap.

I let him turn and lower the seat and ease me into the chair beside him, the two of us facing each other, his lips parting mine, his breath fanning my cheek, my lips. "We can't do this here," I say weakly.

"I pulled the curtain to the front of the plane which means we'll be left alone," he promises even as he caresses my skirt up my legs. "And since I don't have a condom," he adds, "I say we roll the dice."

"What?" I try to pull away but his hand settles on my lower back, holding me fast and close, "What if I get pregnant again? We just—"

He kisses me and cups my backside, molding me against his thick erection. "Quam quae potest esse diligentissima," he murmurs next to my lips. "Another one of my tattoos that means—"

"What is meant to be," I whisper, "And I'm thankful now that my father taught me Latin."

"Yes," he replies. "What is meant to be. This is our time, sweetheart." And then he's kissing me again, and I have no protest left in me. This *is* our time, but that doesn't mean that we'll end up together. What is meant to be might be the end of us, and that thought has me throwing caution to the wind. I kiss him with all that I am, like these will be the last few hours we'll ever share, and I don't know why I fear that it is.

Chapter Forty-Eight

Harper

We're different now, the events of the day changing us and who we are together though I can't say how. Every touch and kiss just feels taut with underlying emotion, deeper, more intimate, more vulnerable and yet more confident and sure.

I tug at his shirt, but the space is too small for me to free it from his pants. Instead, my palms caress the flex of his hard body beneath his clothing. He responds to my desperation, a low, gruff sound of hunger rumbling in his chest. I revel in the depth of his arousal, in my ability to drive him wild, to drive him further. He palms my ass and squeezes the thick ridge of his erection against my belly when I want him inside me.

His hand slides up and under my skirt, over my thigh and there is something about this man's touch that can be gentle and rough in the same moment, and it's fire and ice, and wicked torment. And I like it. "Harper," he whispers, his lips traveling my jaw, down to my neck, distracting me for a brief moment before his fingers are under my panties, stroking that wet heat that drenches me and now his fingers. I pant with the flick of my clit, and then he's pressing inside me—one finger, two, his mouth closing over mine, tongue licking my tongue, even as he does wicked things to my body.

I grab his arm, fingers twining in his shirt, sensations rocking my body, and I can't stop what comes next. His thumb is working just the right spot while his fingers pump all the right places, and I am floating in that beloved place that is as much pain as it is a promise of pleasure. I tumble into a shuddering, quaking, incredible release, and when my body collapses in sated satisfaction, Eric leans in, his lips at my ear. "I'm learning all your little sweet spots. I'll know all of your secrets."

Those words are not an accident.

He's telling me he believes that I am still keeping secrets. And I am, but not the kind he wants to know. Not the kind he *needs* to know and I have to be strong enough not to tell him. Because they're really not my secrets at all. They're a part of his life he doesn't even know, but knowing would be nothing but glass raining down on him, cutting him with a thousand broken pieces.

Chapter Forty-Nine

Harper

I'll know all of your secrets.

Eric's words don't linger in the air and fester in my mind for long at all. He rights my clothes and kisses my temple. "I need to log onto the internet and get an update."

It's the kiss on my temple that undoes me. It's something a man who cares about you does. He cares about me. He came back for me. The only secret I had that was mine, he now knows. The rest, what I've held back, and he's obviously sensing, is history that serves no purpose besides hurting him and eating me alive. Okay, maybe I do have a secret. No, it's more of a gray area where I didn't tell him everything, but I didn't lie. It just wasn't necessary that he know the rest of the story. And that story matters zero in present day.

Zero.

It serves no purpose but to hurt him, I repeat in my mind, because my guilt could easily make me selfish. My clear conscience would make me feel better but at his expense.

He shifts and the recliner lifts.

A few minutes later, we end up at a half-moon-shaped booth. I slide into the seat and he walks away to grab a briefcase. It's then that I jolt with realization. "I have nothing with me," I say as Eric joins me. "And I'm not talking about clothes. My phone and computer and all my work. Eric, anything I'd researched and found they'll find. Whoever they are—Isaac, I assume."

"Isaac's involved," he confirms, sitting down next to me. "Of that, there's no doubt, but I'm guessing my father is as well." He scoots close to me and removes a MacBook from the briefcase. "I left my things in my rental as well. This is Walker equipment. They wanted us to have a way to communicate with them on the ground." He keys up the screen.

The MacBook beeps with a message and then messages explode with back-to-back beeps. Eric scans the messages and I'm suddenly alarmed. We're in the air. My mother is on the ground. What if something goes wrong?

"What's happening?" I ask, scooting closer and trying to see over his shoulder. "Is everyone safe?"

"Yes," he says, typing a reply before he glances at me. "My father and Isaac showed up at the warehouse and apparently had a blow up in front of the building."

"Because I'm still alive? Or because your father found out Isaac tried to kill me and went nuts?"

He stops mid-sentence of whatever he's typing and focuses on me. "Maybe the latter. I don't know." He stops there, but his expression says there's more, it's ripe in the air.

"What do you and Blake think?"

"Undecided. The Isaac thing could have been meant to get me out of the picture before your attack and I don't like how that reads."

"Meaning?"

"They wanted to end you, and they knew I wouldn't let that happen."

"So you had to hate me enough to leave and not care anymore."

"Yes, but they had to worry that if you ended up dead, I'd come back for revenge. Then again, I let them get away with hurting my mother." He cuts his stare.

"You were a kid and you followed her wishes."

He narrows his eyes on me. "What are your wishes, Harper? What do you want to happen to the Kingston family?"

It feels like a test, but I don't even know on what subject. "I don't want to hurt anybody, but I don't want *them* to be able to hurt anybody either."

He rotates to face me fully. "I'm going to do what I promised to do and ask you a question before I assume the answer. I ask. You answer. Don't hold back. Be one hundred percent honest no matter the consequences."

Unease slides through me and I bristle. "Because you have to say that or I'll lie? I told you my secret and it meant carving myself inside out to do it."

"What else, Harper?"

He can't mean my knowledge of his past. That's not this. There'd be no way that was possible. It's not a secret. It's just knowledge.

And I'll have to have a gun to my head to willingly hurt him with that information. "I don't know what you're talking about."

His jaw tics. "Why did Kingston wire large sums of money into an account in your name that you later closed?"

Suddenly, I feel as if the floor of the plane is opening up and sucking me into the turbulence.

Chapter Fifty

Harper

My hand is at my throat as I turn away from Eric, trying to calm down. "That didn't happen."

He slides his MacBook in front of me. "What is this? Look at it," he orders.

I draw in a breath and focus on the screen, on a bank account in my name, that is now closed. Worse, there are several large wire transfers into the account. I'm trembling with adrenaline and fear, as I twist away from Eric, trying to calm down. He catches my arm and turns me to face him.

"Talk to me, Harper. Be honest, no matter how bad it is."

My gaze rockets to his. "Be honest? That again. And again. And again. Stop calling me a liar."

"I am not calling you a liar".

"Semantics. Be honest. Don't lie. Same thing as calling me a liar. So here's my 'not a lie' explanation. I have two bank accounts. Checking and savings. I've had the savings since I was ten. I've had the checking since I moved to Denver years ago. I don't have, nor have I *ever* had any account that received wires."

"That bank account says differently."

My hands are shaking harder now with his accusations, and I positively hate him right now. I jerk my arm from his grip. "I need a bathroom." I don't wait for approval or direction.

I scoot out of the booth and hurry down the small walkway toward what I think is my destination. When I find the small alcove, I grab the door there and enter a space that is as compact as most airlines, despite this being a private plane. I shut the door and I do what anyone would in here. I go to the bathroom. I wash my hands. I act like normal activity will make this go away right up until the point that the normal activity is over. Now I'm just standing in a tiny space, staring at myself in the mirror. How have I given this much of myself to this family to end up here?

Eric knocks on the door. "Harper. Open up."

Anger surges in me and I yank the door open to find him big and intimidatingly male, filling the doorway and the entire exterior space. It doesn't make me back down. "I thought you wanted to talk about the miscarriage, but obviously, you didn't get me up here, trapped in a cage, to talk about a baby that meant nothing to you. You brought me up here to corner me about a bank account that isn't even mine. You don't *want* to trust me. You want to prove I'm the damn princess you so eagerly hate. You wanted me to be her so badly that you carved her name on your body." I shove against him. "Move. I need to get out of here."

He shackles my wrists and in a quick second, I'm against the wall next to the door, and he's all but suffocating me with muscle and man. "Don't bully me. I don't like it."

"You're pushing me in ways you don't want to push me, Harper."

"What are you going to do? Kill me? Or just tell me to be honest again?"

His eyes glint hard, anger burning deep and dark before he releases me and starts walking away.

Shocked at his abrupt departure I swear my knees go weak and I need the wall for support. Right when I feel as if the floor of the plane is opening up, about to suck me out, Eric is back, his hands pressed to the wall on either side of me. "This is not how this was supposed to go."

"This is exactly what you did to me with Isaac. You look for me to be a liar. You want me to be a liar. *Stop* doing that to me. Actually, just stop everything with me. If we're not a couple, maybe it won't disappoint you that I'm not a liar."

He pushes off the wall, dives frustrated fingers through his hair and then presses his hands to his hips. "I keep fucking up with you."

"Yeah. You do. It's *not* my account."

He studies me all of two seconds. "I believe you."

"Well in this case, I don't believe *you*, but just pretend I'm innocent and maybe we can find another way that account got in my name."

"Damn it, Harper."

I step closer, and point at him. "Don't *damn it, Harper* me."

He catches my hand and I'm back against the wall. "I'm sorry."

"Fuck you."

"*I'm sorry.*"

"*Fuck you.*"

He lays his forehead to mine. "Harper," he whispers. "Forgive me. This all came out wrong."

I press on his chest, his heart thundering beneath my palm, probably with the knowledge he's a certifiable asshole. "I'm just not ready." I lift my gaze and let him see the burn in my stare. "I need a minute."

He studies me several beats, eyes lifting to the ceiling, as if it's a sky filled with a rainbow of answers, and then catches my hand and leads me down the aisle. I don't fight him. It's my turn to say damn it, because I can already feel myself softening, letting him back inside. It's a stupid thing to do, but I'm just stupid in love with this man. There's no fighting it or how badly this ends for me.

But I'm going to give it a go a little longer, because right now, I want to yell at him.

He halts at the booth and motions for me to sit. I draw a laden breath and huff it out, before I do as he's basically commanded. *He's damaged*, I tell myself, cut from a mold forged in suicide, death, and betrayal. He's pain and heartache, and he'll etch those things into my soul before this is over. And I can't stop it from happening.

I stay on the edge of the booth, forcing him to sit across from me. He could technically slide around but then I'd just get up and he knows it. So, he finally acts like the man he is with a genius IQ and stays where he's at.

Our eyes lock in a collision of unspoken angry words that I mentally rein in, and focus on what matters right now. "Pretend I'm innocent," I start again.

"Do not say that again. I told you—"

"You believe me. Right. Let's pretend you do. How can anyone open an account in my name?"

His jaw tics, and several seconds pass before he says, "There are hackers like Blake Walker who have the skills to do it."

His Mac begins to ping with rapid shot messages again, and he pulls it in front of him, engaging in an exchange for a full minute before he looks at me again. "One of Blake's men followed one of the men who attacked us at the warehouse. He's tailing him now. No word on who he is yet." He types another message, followed by another and then turns his Mac to face me. "Read the messages.

Blake's going to make the bank account history disappear. By the time we're on the ground, it won't exist."

I don't want to read the messages, so I don't. I also don't want to be a part of any of this, but that's not as easily solved. "It disappears," I repeat, not daring relief just yet. "Just like that?"

"He's one of the best hackers on planet earth," he explains. "So no, not just like that. Just like Blake. We're damn lucky to have him working with us."

"Do you know what those wires were used for?"

"Not yet. Blake's going to have us go to their facility when we arrive in New York City and we'll talk all of this through and come up with a master plan. Exactly why we need to get some sleep." He shuts his Mac.

"I'm being framed, right?"

"Or just used. We can't know for sure. That's what we'll work with Blake and his team to figure out." He stands up and offers me his hand. "Come on. Let's lie down. We need to be alert when we land and if we rest right now, we only have about three hours to sleep."

I stare at his hand, tormented by how much I want to touch him and how much I shouldn't. Once I do, I'll melt like a buttery conquest. "Harper," he prods softly.

I don't look at him.

He kneels beside me. "Forgive me."

My gaze jerks to his. "Why would you think that of me?"

"It's not nearly as bad as you think it is. I made you feel you couldn't talk to me about the miscarriage, but I thought we were past that. When I found out about the bank account, I didn't think you intentionally did bad things. I thought you were still holding back, afraid I'd judge you."

"You did. It's not my bank account."

"I know that now, but I thought you just didn't want to tell me how deep you got fucked by this family."

He captures my hand and brings it to his lips, kissing it, and my body trembles, and not from anger this time. From his damn wicked mouth and those luxuriously blue eyes. "I thought you didn't trust me enough to go all in with me. After all we just talked about, I overreacted. I told you. This is all new to me. The things I feel for you are not familiar."

And there it is. The money shot that softens me to mush. "You made me feel really bad."

"I'm understanding that now." He stands and guides me to my feet, catching me to him, and molding me close. "I'm crazy about you. Don't let me fuck it up."

I press my hands to the side of my head and curl my fingers around my hair. "You confuse me."

"Sleep brings clarity to most things." He turns me toward the back of the plane and smacks my backside.

I rotate to face him. "That's not okay."

He laughs. "That's not what you said the last time I did it." His hands settle warmly on my waist and he walks me backward until we've reached our destination, the two side-by-side recliners. If I stand here with his hands on my body, I'm going to melt and after what he just did, he's not getting that reaction, this easily. I claim my seat and he's quick to slide into the recliner next to me.

For a few beats we both sit there, facing forward, a pulse between us, but somehow, in unison, we lean our seats back and turn to face each other, the intimacy between us a bubble of warmth I want to live inside, get lost inside, but I'm not sure I dare. The world around me is a warzone, and it's impossible to think straight while dodging bullets, perhaps quite literally.

That's when a thought hits me and I turn away from Eric, raise my seat and press my hands to my face.

He's upright in an instant. "Harper?"

I twist around to face him. "If they framed me with that bank account, and who knows what else, maybe when you showed up they got spooked. Maybe that's why those men came at me. Maybe I was a get out of jail free card. If I died and was framed for whatever this is, then it would have ended for the rest of them." Another thought hits me. "Oh God."

"What is it? What are you remembering?"

"What if Gigi sent me to get you so she could frame you for my murder in some way?"

Chapter Fifty-One

Eric

Harper unhooks her belt and stands up as if she's coming out of her own skin with the idea of Gigi betraying either of us, as if that is some novel idea. I have no idea why she wants to believe the best in that woman. I thought it was her being naïve at one point, and maybe it is, but I'm coming to understand that part of her only exists because she's just such a damn good human being.

Not something I can say about myself.

I'm on my feet, moments after her, stepping in her path and catching her waist before she can escape. "Where are you going?"

"I can't just sit in that seat. I'm losing my mind right now. This family is like the plague. The bad stuff just multiplies."

"I warned you about Gigi."

"I know that times about a hundred right now. So, do you agree? Do you think she set us up?"

"Evil doesn't disappear. As you said, it multiplies and it all blossoms from her. She's the matriarch of the family."

The plane starts to quake around us again and she grabs a hold of my waist and hangs on. "Can this flight be over already?" As surely as she asks the question, the plane jerks, this time violently. I catch the ceiling, and mold Harper close, holding onto her, the way I plan to hold onto her from this point forward.

The extreme jolts ease, and I act. "Let's sit back down," I say. "We need to buckle up."

The plane drops and I have to grab the damn seat to keep us from tumbling. The minute I regain my footing, I rotate us and plant Harper in her seat. Another rumbling of the plane beneath my feet has my hands planting on the arms of her chair. "Eric," she breathes out, grabbing my shirt as if she's trying to protect me, not steady herself. Like she could hold onto me and keep me from flying if we jolted much more. "I won't let them use me to get to you."

She says those words with such passion and emotion that I wonder how I ever doubted her, but of course, I know the answer. *They* are why I doubted her. I let them get into my head and I judged her the same way they judged me: by where she came from. "They don't get to use either of us anymore, Harper. No more." The plane calms for a moment and I quickly buckle her seatbelt, and sit down, securing myself as well.

She glances over at me. "I thought we were through the storm a long time ago?"

"Sorry, sweetheart, but not likely anytime soon. We have storms riddling the entire flight path."

"Kind of like our entire lives right now."

"Once we're in New York, we're in control. That's where I have a world of resources at my fingertips. Grayson, the Walker headquarters."

"What happens when they come for me in New York City?"

"They won't be that foolish," I assure her, and I believe that to be true. "They know I'll be waiting. They know I'll be ready, especially after tonight."

"Desperate people do desperate things."

Like my mother, I think, with a punch in the gut. "They do stupid things, too, sweetheart, and that's what we're counting on."

The plane settles into a smooth ride again, at least for now, and Harper reclines her chair. I follow her lead and she rolls to her side facing me and rests her head on her hands. "Gigi's an old woman, Eric. I really felt sorry for her."

It's the first time she's spoken that woman's name without me wanting to rip it out of her mouth. Instead of looking for the bad in Harper, I need to be thankful for the good. She might be all that saves me from hating the world. Well, her and Grayson. The two saints and the sinner. Grayson would laugh his ass off if I said that to him.

I shift to face Harper, and brush her hair from her face. "I was hard on you over, Gigi. I've been hard on you in general. I'm kind of an asshole."

"You can be," she teases, but turns serious quickly. "But it's okay. I know that you have walls a mile high. And I get why."

"They're only inches high with you."

Her eyes twinkle. "That's not even a jump."

"No, it's not, but I think I might need to jump a few feet to overcome that asshole mark."

"You're tall and smart. I have confidence in you."

"That makes me a very lucky man." I kiss her hand. "Sleep now. We only have a couple of hours until we land."

"How can I sleep? The plane. This damn family. My mother back there with them."

"Your mother is safe."

"Can we warn Walker Security that Gigi might be involved? What if me leaving has them turn on her?"

"You know Walker is already watching her. They're damn good. They've thought of everything we've thought of."

"How can you be sure? If this was your mother—"

"You're right," I say. "You're absolutely right." The plane is calm enough, for the moment at least, that I unbuckle and walk to the table where I left the MacBook in a compartment under the wooden top. I grab it, hold on as we shake a good thirty seconds and then make my way back to my seat. Once I'm secure again, I pull up the MacBook and try to connect but this time it's a no-go. I show Harper the message I'm getting. "Sorry, sweetheart. It's just not going to happen." I shove the Mac into a pocket by my chair and turn to Harper. "Adam's in charge in Denver and he's damn good. He'll protect your mother with his life. I promise you this. Rest, princess."

"Princess?"

"I like that name for you," I say, my voice rasping with about ten emotions I can't name. "You're *my princess*, not theirs. Not ever again. They don't get to define us, remember?"

"But you—"

I lean in and kiss her. "Want you like I have never wanted in my life. Now rest. You won't get to rest when you're in my bed. Not the first night. Hell, maybe not the first month."

A faint smile touches her lips but doesn't quite reach her eyes. She's a ball of fear and worry, and the only way I make that go away is to end the family I should have ended a long time ago. I cup her face and my thumb strokes her cheek. "Shut your eyes and think of something that makes you happy."

"Ending this would make me happy."

"Then I'll end it, just to make you happy."

She gives me another half-smile. "Just to make me happy?"

"Yes, princess. Just to make you happy."

Her hand settles on my princess tattoo. "Maybe princess isn't such a bad nickname. Not when you say it like you just did."

"How did I just say it?"

"All low and rough and sexy."

"Sexy, huh?"

"Yes," she whispers. "Everything about you is sexy." Her cheeks don't heat this time. She's not flirting. She's just being raw and real, and fuck, I need raw and real. I need *her*.

"Show me," I reply softly, "when we get to my bed. Sleep now, while the air is calm."

Her lashes lower and seconds pass before she whispers, "I can't believe you really came back."

I'm going to change that, I think. I'm going to make sure she knows that I won't just come back. I won't leave. Ever. I lay there and watch her for a good thirty minutes until I'm certain she's asleep. Then and only then, do I grab the MacBook and try Walker again. This time I connect easily and go live with Blake.

Anything new? I type.

Nothing urgent enough to discuss while you're in the air. Everyone is safe and secure. We're gathering data to review with you when you arrive. Anything I need to know or relay to Adam?

We suspect Harper is being set-up as a fall guy who ended up too dead to defend herself.

My thoughts as well, he replies.

Isaac tried to break me and Harper up today. He told me some fucked up shit that was all lies. Harper suspects Gigi wanted to have her killed and set me up as the killer.

What do you think? he asks.

Gigi is an evil bitch, I reply, and I know that's all Blake needs to hear, but I add, *Keep her the fuck away from Harper's mother.*

He doesn't immediately answer, and my fingers thrum the seat. What the hell is going on? A bad feeling claws at me and I'm about to nudge him when he finally goes live again.

Plot twist, his message reads. *Harper's mother is at Gigi's house. I'm sending Adam to the door as a maintenance man to check on her.*

Fuck, I think, barely holding back verbal reaction.

My gaze lands on Harper, beautiful in slumber, her dark lashes half-moons against her flawless skin. She's trusting me to take care of her and her mother or she wouldn't be asleep. Damn it, I have to act, and I'm about to piss Harper off again. sets hard and I type a reply to Blake: *Get her mother out of there and I don't care how you do it. Adam needs to throw her over his damn shoulder if that's what it takes.*

Chapter Fifty-Two

Eric

The alarm on my watch beeps and my eyes open, and for a moment, I stare up at the airplane ceiling, clearing the numbers cluttering my mind. It's a process I learned in the military, a way I take control of my mind from the moment I start my day. Beside me Harper murmurs something and I rotate to face her only to find her dreaming and sound asleep. She's so fucking beautiful and too good for the likes of me. If I'm honest, part of me pushes her to prove she's as human and damaged as the rest of this damn family, because then we'd make more sense. But I'm coming to believe that it's our differences that pull us together that can make us both stronger and better.

She's mine now, even if she doesn't know it yet. Mine to *protect*. Nothing else can matter until I ensure she's safe. A thought that has me sitting up and checking for an internet connection again with no success. I store my MacBook in the seat pocket and lay back down, reaching out to caress Harper's cheek. She doesn't wake up. Right now, she's with me, in the air, safe, and some part of her knows that.

Some part of her trusts me the way I told her I need to trust her. The problem is that I'm a fucking hypocrite. I've demanded honesty from her but I haven't told her everything. I have my own secrets. Things she will not like, but I'll have to share with her. And I'll have to pray she can read past my history and see how she's changed me. I need to build trust with her and damn it, that means keeping my promise to keep her mother safe, but I'm not on the ground. Adam is. I'm trusting Adam to keep my promise to Harper.

Adam is the one protecting her mother.

Adam

Denver, CO

A master of disguise.

It's what I do, a skill I learned while on the road with my mother and her boyfriend, along with their pack of criminal friends during most of my youth. I'm dressed as a repairman in a blue jumpsuit with a pair of brown contacts over my blue eyes. My black hair is slicked back. I ring the bell of the stucco home wrapped in ivy and wait for an answer.

A mid-thirties brunette I know to be Celia Ramirez, Gigi's housekeeper of five years answers the door. "Yes?"

"There's a gas leak on the street." I show her a clipboard. "We need to check the lines running in and out of the house to assure we aren't on the verge of a catastrophic event."

"Oh God," Celia says. "That sounds terrifying. What do I need to do?"

"I'll need access inside to determine where the pipes might be under pressure. From what I can tell from the maps, it's the kitchen and the backyard that need attention."

"You want to come in?"

"That is necessary, yes."

"I can't just let you in. Can you prove you work for the gas company?"

I shove a card at her that will ring Blake. "Call. Make it fast. Time is critical."

She grabs her phone from her pocket and dials the number on the official-looking card complete with the gas company's address and logo. She speaks to Blake and her eyes go wide, proof he's laying it on thick. A moment later, she disconnects and waves me forward. "Come in, please." She backs up and allows me my entry.

I enter inside the house, entering a towering foyer with a fancy chandelier above my head and I decide it would make a good weapon, should one need one. Cut it, drop it. Someone gets it in the head.

"This way," the woman says, pointing down a long hallway, and hurrying ahead of me.

Our destination is just beneath an archway where I find a living room with expensive, Regency-style furnishings that scream "grandma."

"The kitchen," she says.

She indicates a door and I enter the kitchen with her on my heels. The kitchen layout is expensive and as expected; high-end tile, stainless steel, a dramatic island. "How do you look at the pipes?" Celia asks from behind me.

I reach in the bag on my shoulder, pull out a fake gadget that does absolutely nothing, and hold it up. "This little baby will snoop out a leak. I'm going to stick this behind each appliance." I hold up a hand. "I don't have to move anything. I just have to let it sit for a few minutes."

"I see," she says tightly, probably fretting about her need to pick up her kids in half an hour. "I guess I'll check on you in a few minutes."

With a nod, I set my bag on the island, and after another moment of hesitation Celia exits the kitchen. I stand there, listening to her footsteps fading, and when they disappear, I cross to the back door and crack it open. I plan to sneak around the door, just outside Gigi's office and try and put eyes on Harper's mother. But that plan shifts immediately.

Not only is a fire crackling in a massive stone fireplace, but Gigi and Danielle, Harper's mother, are standing in front of it while Celia, who clearly tracked them down via the office patio door, explains the gas leak.

The chat with Celia is short and she departs, which means she'll be coming back here sooner than later. "Answer me, Gigi," Danielle demands, her tone low and clipped, but I can hear her clearly. "Why would you convince Eric to come here?"

"I didn't convince him," Gigi snaps. "He hates me. Harper convinced him. Your daughter knows we need help even if you don't."

"We don't need help," Danielle says.

Gigi laughs. "Are you playing dumb or are you really that stupid?"

"My daughter's smitten with him. He's rich and good looking and that's all she sees."

"Like my son who you married? Sounds like you're two of a kind. Mother and daughter."

"Stop being a bitch," Danielle pops back. "*Stop.* I love your son. I'm protecting him. You're protecting you."

"You seem very afraid of Eric. Why is that?"

"Your son doesn't want Eric here."

"Eric is my son's child. He's my grandchild. He's more a part of this family than you will ever be."

"Now you're just being a bitch. Eric's our enemy."

"Seems to me none of us know who our real enemies are, now do we?"

"Why does that feel like a threat?" Danielle quips back.

"Why do you see threats that no one else sees? But you want a threat," Gigi adds. "I might be old, but I protect what's mine. Everything you think is yours has always been mine."

Footsteps sound behind me and I shut the sliding door to face Celia. "All clear in here. I was about to head outside." I don't wait on her to reply. I reach for the door again, only to have it open as Danielle, a pretty brunette, who's the spitting image of Harper, runs smack into me.

"I'm so sorry," she says. "I'm—" She blinks up at me. "I just need to get by."

I step back as she swipes at her cheek, as if hiding tears, and then darts away. I hit a button on my phone that sends a message to my man outside the house. He'll follow Danielle while I monitor what Gigi does next.

I lift a hand at Celia. "I'll be fast."

She nods. "I'll be back again in a minute to check on you." She quickly follows Danielle.

I exit to the backyard and Gigi has her back to me, and thanks to age-related, poor hearing she doesn't know I'm here. She sits in a chair by the fire and punches in an auto-dial number. "I need to speak to you," she says into the phone. "Where are you? Why aren't you answering my calls?"

She disconnects and just sits there. And continues to sit there as if she knows whoever she called will call her back. I need to know who she called. I enter the kitchen, shut the door, and text Blake: *Who did Gigi just call?*

His answer is instant: *Kingston Senior.*

I frown. That is the last person I expected her to call. Kingston Senior is supposed to be in combat with Gigi, in a war for stock and control, and pissed as fuck Gigi brought Eric into the mix. There is more to this picture than meets the eye.

Chapter Fifty-Three

Eric

W e're about to touch down and incredibly, Harper has yet to move. "Harper, sweetheart, wake up." I stroke her hair. "We're landing."

Her eyes go wide and she tries to sit up, but she gets caught in the seatbelt. "Any news?" She frees herself and reattaches her belt. "Is my mother okay?"

"No news," I say, wishing like hell that wasn't the truth. I hit the button to raise her seat. "The internet has been out for the past few hours."

"Hours? It's been hours?" She runs her hand through her hair. "I need to know she's okay. I can't believe I even slept."

"Your mother is fine. We have eyes on her with Walker Security. And you slept, because you were exhausted, with good reason. It's not been an easy twenty-four hours."

"Did you sleep? Please tell me you did. I don't even remember us laying down to rest."

"I did," I say, amazed at how she worries about me. No one worries about me. I don't let them close enough to even think about me. The descent is faster now and I glance at my watch and then back at Harper. "It's one in the morning. We'll make it to Blake's offices before sunrise, talk with him for a few hours, and then go try to get some more rest." We hit the runway and I grab Harper's hand, lacing our fingers together. "In my bed, Harper."

"I wonder what your bedroom looks like. Do you secretly have a fetish for pink?"

"The only fetish I have is you," I assure her, pleased that she's, at least momentarily, forgotten the danger on the ground. "Okay, not the only one, but I don't want to scare you off."

She laughs. "Oh, do tell. I'm not scared at all."

"We'll see, won't we?"

"Will we?"

My phone buzzes with a text, signaling we're now at tower level, and I glance down to find a message from Adam that reads: *Call me.*

I dial his number and he answers in one ring with, "About damn time."

A reply that sets me on edge, or rather, more on edge than I already am. "We're on the runway. Talk to me."

Harper grabs my arm. "Is that Adam? Is my mother safe?"

"Is Danielle safe?" I ask, relaying her worry.

"Yes," Adam says. "Danielle's safe."

I glance at Harper and give a nod. She breathes out in relief and settles into her seat.

"But there's an interesting twist," Adam adds.

"I'm listening," I say, choosing my words cautiously so as to not alarm Harper.

"Danielle fought with Gigi. Gigi then called your father and I got the impression it might be the two of them plotting against you and Harper. He never returned her call, but he did something far more interesting. He got on a plane to New York City. Your father is on his way to you and Harper."

What the hell? I think, biting back the words for Harper's benefit. "What else?"

"He was so anxious, he chartered a plane. I'll let you know when he's on the ground. He's a couple hours behind you."

We exchange a few more coded words and disconnect.

"What's happening?" Harper asks, leaning in close. "What just happened because I can tell you were choosing your words cautiously and that makes me nervous all over again."

More like, what the hell *is happening?* I think as the numbers in my mind start to spin, looking for my father's angle, and one word keeps coming to me over and over, wanting to be recognized: Murder. There is murder in the air and I need to keep Harper close and safe.

Chapter Fifty-Four

Harper

E ric's fingers drag through his hair and he looks skyward, and I am reminded of what he said about triggers that create a paralyzing influx of numbers in his mind. Whatever is wrong isn't about my mother. It's about him.

My hand goes to his hand, and I turn it over, pressing our palms together but I don't push him to talk. He doesn't look at me, his lashes lowering, his expression tightening. I wait, silently letting him know that I'm here, until finally, his eyes open, but he doesn't look at me. "My father's on his way to New York City."

It's an odd development, unexpected even, but what strikes me now is Eric's mood, his edginess. He's a literal warrior, a SEAL who has taken on enemies and the world, including this family, even his father, and yet right now, his father hangs in the air between us like a nuclear bomb about to drop and blow holes in him.

I unhook my belt, and settle on my knees in front of him, my hands on his calves, and I search his handsome face that is all hard lines and shadows, his expression unreadable. "Why is he coming to New York City?"

"Why do you think he's coming?"

"I don't know," I say. "You tell me."

"To fuck me if he can." He's intense. He's big-time intense.

"I know that we're new," I say. "I know that I haven't spent every day of the last six years with you, but I've experienced your reactions to your father to some degree, and it's not like this. What else is going on?"

He cuts his stare, unhooks his seatbelt and his hands flatten on his knees. I have this sense he's coming out of his own skin or perhaps drowning in a sea of numbers.

The exterior doors to the plane open and I'm confused, not sure what to do next, aside from just trying to be here with him, the way he decided to be here for me when he followed me back to Denver. I capture his hand in mine and kiss it, and there's surprise in his eyes that I really don't understand. A moment later, he's standing, pulling me to my feet, and kissing me with such torment, I'm quaking inside.

His lips part mine and I'm left panting when he says, "I need you. You know that, right?"

He speaks those words with a deep raspy voice that I feel like a vibration through my body. He needs me. I never thought I'd hear those words from this man. "I need you, too."

The minute I speak those words, the tension in his body eases, his expression softens. "Show me when we're finally alone. Come on. Let's get out of here." He catches my hand and leads me toward the door, and I hurt for him. My bond with my father was special. His bond with his father is poison, even more so than I'd ever imagined.

We exit the plane side by side and travel the narrow, double-wide stairs into the dark, cold night. I block out the weather as best I can without a coat for protection and manage to glance at Eric's watch, confirming the one a.m. hour. It's a brutally cold New York City morning, damp and biting, and far more impactful than the dry, high-altitude weather in Denver. I thought I'd never leave Denver, but I realize now I've allowed the beauty of the city and the beauty of the family I once knew in my father and mother, to seduce me, to hold onto me. I didn't want to let go of what I'd lost in my father, so I held onto what I had left of him. But I have history and memories the Kingston family can never take from me.

The wind gusts again and Eric throws his arm around me, pulling me close. An SUV pulls in front of us and halts, and I thank God, for the blessed relief only seconds away.

By the time we're at the vehicle, a big brute of a man meets us at the rear door and holds it open. "Savage," Eric greets as I climb into the back of the vehicle. "Good to see you, man." It's a comfortable, easy greeting that speaks of trust, and right about now, trust is good.

The two men talk for a full minute, their voices muffled, before Eric joins me inside, and Savage shuts the door behind him. "We're going straight to my apartment after all," Eric announces.

"I thought we were going to the Walker offices?"

"They're coming to us. Grayson's wife, Mia, took the liberty of grabbing you a few necessities. They're stopping by as well."

"Should they do that? You said my attackers were professionals. What if coming near me, and us, puts them in danger?"

"Grayson already knows what's going on. He won't stay away. If I'm in trouble, he's in trouble. That's how we operate."

Friends. That word is hollow to me. I have no friends. My life has been this family and therefore it's empty.

"The harder I push Grayson away," Eric continues, "the closer he'll step, which is why I need to see him now, today, and convince him all is well." He glances over at me, "Your mother went to see Gigi tonight."

The whiplash of the subject change and the content of that change jolts me. I twist around to face him. "And?"

"Adam was there at the time, pretending to check the gas lines. He said she was bitching about me, scared of what I might do. She was angry at Gigi for recruiting me."

Confusion furrows my forehead, "Wait. Does that mean Gigi has been forthright with us?"

"There's more."

"Of course, there is," I say. "What did he do?"

"She called my father right after your mother left. She didn't talk to him, and still hasn't, but the message she left sounded pretty damning to Adam. Like they've been planning something together."

"I'd like to think they came together to save the company, but that doesn't add up. He's the reason she wanted you to help."

"More like planning the end of us."

It's a bitter statement for a bitter action.

Eric's phone rings and he snakes it from his pocket, glancing at the number and then me. "Adam."

He answers the call, has a back-and-forth conversation I can't make heads or tails of and then disconnects. "Your mother is at home in bed asleep," he says, and his phone rings again. He answers with, "Blake," and they settle into what feels like a non-eventful conversation, simply because I can't figure out any of the details.

I settle against the soft leather of the seat, confused by this new development with Gigi. Something isn't adding up. Thinking back, she absolutely told me his father had no idea she was asking Eric to come to Denver, or rather that *I* was asking Eric to come to Denver. Did she lie to me?

It's not hard to believe she might have done that and more.

Eric disconnects his call and I jump on the chance to talk to him before he gets another. "Your father can't know about the attack."

"And you base this on what?"

"You're his son. You were being set-up."

"I'm his bastard son."

"Your head always goes there, doesn't it?"

"His sure does. That's the point."

I decide to ignore that statement and move on, "If he has knowledge or connection to my attack, make me understand why your father would come here and risk aligning himself with a murder plot."

"He wouldn't," Eric says. "But he's not here to help us, either. He's here to serve himself. He's here to protect himself."

Or Isaac, I think. "And hurt us?" I ask.

"Yes. And to hurt us."

I'd argue with him but he knows his father better than I do. In six years, I've never even shared a cup of coffee with that man alone. "Coming here makes him look guilty. Maybe that's the idea. Maybe someone else baited him into coming here."

"You're reaching. Why are you protecting him?"

"He's your father."

Eric's lips thin and he cuts his stare before he looks back at me, and his gaze has gone from hot to icy cold. "How have you been with this family this long and you don't see how evil they are?"

"I know how evil they are. Whatever it is that you think is going on, just say it."

"My father's the kind of man who could easily sit next to us, sip a drink, and watch while we each take a bullet he paid to put in us, but it doesn't stop there. He'd take one himself just to be sure he looks innocent. He's that devious. It's a mistake to assume he's here to do anything but end us, which is exactly why I'll end him first."

"End him? What does *that* mean?"

He cuts his stare again, and I grab his arm, pulling him around to me. "*What* does that mean, Eric?"

Chapter Fifty-Five

Harper

"What does that mean?" I repeat, pressing him. "End him? End *your father*?"

Those blue, blue eyes of his, such intelligent eyes, meet mine. "As we said in the Navy: All in, all the time. It's war. It's us or them. Me or him. I have to be willing to do whatever it takes to make sure it's me and us. I'm all in."

"You're avoiding a direct answer," I accuse. "You want to end him how?"

He shackles my arm and pulls me to him. "I want this fucking family out of my life and yours," he says, his voice low, rough. "And I want it to happen now."

"I do, too, but the right way."

"And what exactly is the right way, Harper? Do we let them kill me, but not you, or vice versa?" I shove against him and pull free, pointing at him. "Don't be an asshole."

"Just a bastard?"

"What is *wrong* with you?" I demand.

"It's called being born a Kingston."

The SUV jolts to a sharp halt that shoots me backward. Eric catches me and pulls me to him and our faces end up close, his breath warm on my lips. "I got you, remember?"

"And I have you. That's why I can't let you do something you'll regret."

"I'll do whatever it takes to end this," he says softly. "To protect you and if you hate me for it, hate me."

"It's almost like that's what you want. Like you subconsciously don't know how to be happy."

The SUV starts moving again and then immediately halts. "Fucktard," Savage growls. "Red light means stop."

I push out of Eric's arms and sit back against the seat, and he does the same. We don't touch. We don't talk. A sense of foreboding consuming me. I don't know why we were even talking in front of Savage anyway, but obviously Eric not only trusts him, he approves of his plan.

There's a loud honk and Savage growls again. "Shoot that finger, you bastard. We both know that if I get out of this Escalade and Green Beret'd your ass, you'd be sucking your thumb."

Bastard.

I hate that word and it sits as heavy as a boulder in the air between me and Eric.

We start moving again and after five minutes of awkward silence, we pull to a stop in front of a building. The doors to the SUV open on all sides, as valets attend to our service and the cold air has me hugging myself. The minute I'm out of the vehicle, and under a canopy, standing next to a portable heater, Eric catches my shoulders and walks me to him.

"We fight too much," he says softly, for my ears only.

I nod. "Yes, but I don't think we're done."

His hand settles on my lower back, fingers intimately splayed, as he leans in close, his lips near my ear. "How about I lick your pussy until you forgive me?"

I gasp softly and just that easily I'm wet and clenching my thighs together, but for a smart man, his plan is not smart at all. I ease back and glare at him. "This, what you're doing right now, is *not* going to work. I'm not going to be distracted."

His lips twitch. "We'll see."

It's right then that the doorman approaches Eric. "You wanted to see me, sir?"

"Yes. I need to have my car brought up to the top level." He palms the man a large bill. "Keep it there for the next twenty-four hours."

"I will make it so," the man agrees, before walking away and Savage joins us. "Tips delivered. Keys handed off. Where do I get a good whiskey? I know you got the good stuff, Eric, and you owe me a bottle."

"That I do," Eric replies tightly, and tilts his head my direction. "I got drunk and let him beat me at pool. The final bet was a bottle of Macallan 25."

It's evident, they're friends and after a life of being nothing but a bastard to his family, his life full of people who care about him. A part of me envies him this as I do not have that circle of my own. and yet, I'm also happy he escaped the Kingston curse, though I'm not certain he believes that's true or possible. Eric has a mental fixation on the Kingston family I'm not sure he sees any more than he does his own fortune.

It's in these black spots that this conflict with his father and family has led to an explosive situation, one that has already turned dangerous.

A gust of wind undoes me. I shiver and hug myself. "Can we go upstairs and you can both drink while I roast by the fireplace?"

Eric slides his arm around my shoulders. "Sorry, princess. I forgot we're more used to the bitter New York cold than you are." He turns us to the building door and we enter the lobby of elegant white tiles and red cushioned chairs to make our way to the elevators.

Savage punches the call button.

Once we're inside a car, Eric punches in a code, draping his arm back around my shoulders and leaning me into him, no question to anyone around us that I'm his woman. And I like it, I do, but I cannot lose focus on where he is mentally right now, and how skewed by a bitter childhood his decision-making is at present.

The floors tick by and Savage hums, "We Wish You a Merry Christmas," when Halloween hasn't even arrived, and despite him looking like the hot, but mean Obviously he doesn't just feel the sexual tension between me and Eric, he feels the tension, the war, that is barely contained. A guy who'd never even consider singing a Christmas carol. He's trying to calm our energy, distract us from the words spoken in the SUV.

While I actually really appreciate his efforts, I tune out Savage and his song. I'm thinking about how completely done Eric is with this family. So am I but in contrast I haven't suffered at their hands, while he's been a literal victim of mental torture. They played on his need for family, for belonging. I remember a point where he denied being a part of them and turned around not long after and said he was done denying that he's a Kingston. I hope like hell he doesn't think that gives him a free pass to act like a Kingston considering the Kingstons just tried to kill me. Is that what he means by "end" his father? Does he intend to kill him? Does he believe he's the one who ordered the hit on me and now he wants revenge?

I turn in Eric's arms, and search his handsome, unreadable face, trying to understand where his head is right now. He gives me no hint. I simply don't find my answer, and I can't demand one with Savage in the car. But I can feel the press of time with his father arriving. He's here to see Eric and he's going to reach out to him sooner than later. If it's sooner, I will have no influence over Eric, and I don't want to think about what comes next.

Avenging his mother is unfinished business.

And I truly believe that in his mind, it's an unfinished equation that will drive him insane until it's finished. Together, we have to find a way to finish it that doesn't get bloody.

Chapter Fifty-Six

Harper

The elevator dings, and the doors open.

Savage exits first, and when I would follow, Eric catches my arm and turns me to him. "I love that you are sweet, and good, and right, even when everyone else is doing everything wrong. I'm not thinking you are one of them."

"I know that. You know I know that."

"Do you?"

"I think you get confused sometimes. I think—a lot of things."

"*Trust me*, please, to only do what is necessary. If I was going to fly off the handle and go for blood for revenge, I would have already done it." I can feel the doors shut at my back as he adds, "Okay?"

"I have way too much to say to that to be able to articulate it in an elevator, but I trust you. I would never have come to you if I didn't."

Something flickers in his eyes, something dark and stormy that I do not understand. He captures my hand. "Let's get out of here." He maneuvers us, and punches the button to open the door. There's a shift in him now, as if he's closed himself off again, and I have a bad feeling I should have stayed in that elevator and finished our talk.

Savage is standing at the apartment door at the end of a long hallway, looking exceedingly bored, and holding up a wall, his arms and feet crossed. "I'm guessing he wants that drink," Eric murmurs.

"He does have a way of getting his point across," I agree, but we're speaking empty words, while other, more important conversations wait to be had.

We join Savage, and he pushes off the wall. "You have a houseful of assholes in there waiting on you."

"Who?" I ask.

"Our men," Savage answers, and Eric keys in a code at his door, and opens it.

"You hacking my door now, Savage?" Eric asks. "If you hacked my locks, I'll have to kill you."

Savage chuckles and I get the feeling that despite Eric's stern tone, this is some shared joke between the two of them. "You'll have to kill me another day," Savage replies. "Grayson used his key."

That announcement is a nugget of welcome information. Grayson is not only here, he's close enough to Eric to have a key, and as a bonus, it's already clear to me that he's a voice of reason and morality. Eric opens the door and pulls me in front of him, his hands scorching my waist, as he leans in close to whisper. "Welcome to my home. I hate that we're not alone."

My breath hitches with emotion and I reach up and touch his face. "Me, too," I whisper, and in this moment, there is only me and him, and him and me. There is us and I can almost hear his wicked thoughts, and feel his hands on my body in places he's not touching. Savage clears his throat, and Eric shoves the door wider, his hands falling away, when I wish I could pull them back.

I enter a narrow hallway with gorgeous gray and blue Chevron parquet hardwood beneath my feet. A glance up and the wall above the walkway steals my breath, because in the center is a magnificent painting of a jaguar.

Eric steps to my side and catches my fingers with his, his eyes alight with mischief. "I saw that painting and just had to have it."

Because it reminds him of his enemy, his family, I think. "I have a love-hate reaction to everything about it."

"I suspected you would. Now, you meet my real family."

Grayson, I think.

He means Grayson.

He kisses my knuckles, something warm and yet turbulent in his stare as Savage steps around us and heads down the hallway. "Has he been here before?" I ask.

"Never," Eric replies. "But he's Savage. He's—"

"Comfortable everywhere," I say and it's a relief when we both laugh. It's a light, welcome moment that carries us down the hallway with lighter steps.

"Come on," he says, guiding me forward.

In a few short steps, we pass an archway to my right, where I discover a long, mosaic-topped dining room table, and while it compels me to stop and admire it, I do not. That's for later, when all of this stuff with his father has passed.

Voices lift ahead and we clear the walkway. A moment later, we step into Eric's open-concept living room that connects to a kitchen by way of a granite island; it's a room of warm colors and masculine décor, with gray leather furnishings, high-beamed ceilings and one wall that is nothing but windows. It fits him. I really think maybe I do, too.

Savage and another man, one of the Walker team, I assume, are huddled up near a bar to the right of the kitchen. Two other men, both also casual in jeans and T-shirts, sit on the couch in deep conversation. Grayson is one of those men and he and the stranger to me immediately stand and start walking toward us, joining us in a few short steps.

"What the hell are you doing here, Davis?" Eric demands, focusing on the "other" man.

"I'm your damn friend," Davis replies, his cursed rebuttal a contrast to his refined good looks and chiseled features. "I know you forget that, asshole," he snaps. "But I am."

"I don't have friends," Eric quips back and the energy between them tells me that this is just who they are together. They push and pull. They fight. "Right, Davis? Isn't that what you're always telling me?"

"Well then," Davis comments dryly, "I'm an enemy watching your fucking back." He glances at me. "Sorry. He just pissed me off and the word 'fuck' summed up how I felt too well to miss the opportunity to use it. I'm Davis. A close friend, attorney, and confidant to Grayson." He glances at Eric. "And you, asshole."

Grayson smirks, amusement in his eyes. "They really are friends," he assures me. "I promise you. And welcome back to New York, Harper." He takes my hand and covers it with his other hand, warmth in his touch that is all about the welcome he just expressed. "I'm glad you're here with Eric."

"Me, too," I say, and when he releases me, I look at Eric and repeat the words, "Me, too," and with good reason. These men are his friends. I want them to know that I'm one hundred percent on Eric's side. I'm not a Kingston. I'm not a damn princess.

Eric touches my cheek, approval in his eyes before he glances at Grayson. "My father is on his way here."

"I heard," he confirms, "and I think we should talk about where that leads you."

"Me, too," I chime in again, squeezing Eric's hand, but he doesn't look at me.

"We'll talk, all right," he replies, his tone steel, almost brutal. "What do we know about my father's trip?"

The group of us spread out and form a circle to the side of the couches, and Savage and the man he's been talking with—a tall, dark-haired man with long hair tied at his nape—join us. "This is Blake," Savage says, indicating the other man. "One of the founders of Walker Security. That means one of my bosses. He's also a world-class hacker. I'm not. I'm still just brute force me."

"The one who hacked me to freedom," I assume.

"If you mean I got rid of the bank account that was created in your name," Blake says, "yes. That was me."

"Thank you. Thank you so much," I say."

Blake gives me a nod and then focuses on Eric, getting right to business "We know your father had an argument with your brother at the warehouse before he booked his trip. When he left the warehouse, he called no one but his assistant, who booked his trip. He hasn't communicated with anyone in transit. At least not on a known device that we're tracking. He could have burner phones or unregistered electronics."

Eric eyes Savage and Blake. "Let's step outside." He doesn't wait for their agreement. He starts walking, decisively, determined, as if he has a plan and he's setting it in motion and that's enough for me to decide this could be trouble. I can't let this meeting happen before I talk to him. I don't know Walker Security. I don't know what they'll do or agree to. I don't know where Eric's endgame lands him, or where his head is right now, but I know that I don't want to find out the wrong way and too late to stop a disaster.

I dash forward and I place myself in front of Eric, planting my hands on his chest. "We need to talk before you say another word to anyone."

His eyes narrow and glint hard. "Why?"

Why is easy to me, but I can't say any of my reasons in front of an audience. Because he blames his father for killing his mother and now for my attack. Because I think he's secretly wanted to end that man for his entire life. He hates his father far too much for me to let him make any decisions tonight, when all those old wounds have been cut open to bleed anew.

For now, I need a reason to get him into another room alone and I make a fast decision that now is the time to put it all on the line. Now is the time for me to stop holding back and I act on that decision before I can back out. "Because I need to tell you something. I need to talk to you."

He studies me for several long beats, his expression unreadable, before he takes my hands and starts walking across the room without speaking a word to any of the men in the room. His strides are long, calculated and rapid enough to have my short legs struggling to keep up. Once we're on the stairs, he places me in front of him and I hurry forward, hyperaware of him at my back. Hyperaware of the box I just shoved myself inside, and how easily a box can be cut open and destroy me with him.

We travel up a winding set of stairs and when we reach the top level it's a few steps until we enter a pair of open double doors. I have about ten seconds to take in a massive gray leather bedframe on a pedestal, his bed, that I should have been introduced to in a far different way than I am now.

I rotate and he shuts the doors.

Another ten seconds before Eric has placed me against a wide wooden bedpost and steps in front of me, his powerful thighs caging mine, his palms flattening on the door on either side of me. "I'm listening."

He's listening.

And now I need to talk.

Now I need to tell him what I brought him up here to tell him.

Officially, my time is up.

Chapter Fifty-Seven

Harper

My heart races, no it's more of a gallop that wants to punch through my chest.

Eric is staring at me expectantly, anger ticking in his jaw, and I know why. Not because I interrupted his meeting, not because I wanted to talk. It's because I lured him up here with a confession and now, he thinks I have been hiding things from him when I have not.

So I just stare at him, a doe in headlights.

He's beautiful. He's gifted. He's damaged in ways that I wasn't equipped to understand six years ago. In ways that I can never fully understand, and the truth is some of the darkness in him, is brutally sexy to me. It's also terrifying with his talk of ending his father.

"Talk to me, Harper," he urges, his voice low, almost gentle, but tension radiates off of him, almost as if it pings off the walls and slams right back into him.

I press my hand to the solid wall of his chest and his heart thunders under my touch. Because of my touch? Because of what he's about to do to end his father? "Whatever you were about to tell Walker Security to do down there, please don't."

He offers no denial. His hand comes down on top of mine. "Why would you protect my father?"

There's an accusation in that question that pisses me off, even though I know I brought it on with the promise of some revelation. But I thought we were past him believing it was something that somehow linked me to his family, and pitted me against him. "Are you really serious right now? I'm not protecting your father," I say. "I'm protecting *you*."

"Me? How are you protecting me, Harper?"

"There are some things you can't come back from."

"What do you think I'm about to do?"

"Tell me. What are you about to do?"

"Whatever it fucking takes to get that man out of our lives once and for all."

"Kill him?" I challenge. "Would you *kill* him?"

"Kill or be killed, sweetheart." He is cold, hard, decisive. He's made up his mind. He has a plan and it's a plan I have to change.

"No," I hiss, bunching his shirt in my free hand. "No, you will not."

"You don't want him to die."

Again with his damn accusations. "I don't want *you* to die. Do you really think you could live with killing your father?"

"Live with it? I'd sleep like a baby if that man was gone. What don't I know *again,* Harper? What did you bring me up here to confess?"

"Confess?" My anger ignites all over again. "I have nothing to confess. You already know what I have to say. There is no secret. There is no *again.* I *hate* that you just said that to me."

His jaw spasms and he looks right, seeming to struggle before he fixes me in a turbulent stare. "You know you teased me with a secret to get me up here."

"I was desperate. *I'm sorry.*"

Anger boils in his eyes. "Don't throw out taunts about secrets with me, Harper. Not now. Not after what we went through tonight."

"Me? Look who's talking. Don't you accuse me of keeping secrets and taunting you. I never taunted you and I never kept a secret that I wanted to keep. I promised you on the plane that I have no more secrets."

"But then you turned around and used the promise of another one to get me up here."

I ball his shirt as tight as possible in my hand and step into him. "I said I had something you needed to hear."

"I'm still listening," he says. "I'm still waiting."

And here it is. That moment of truth I committed to when I brought him up here, and I don't hold back. "I have needed you since the moment we met and no amount of time or space would ever erase the impact you've had on me. You *affect me.* You scare me. You own me in ways I don't want to be owned, and yet I do with you. If you do this, if you go at your father in the way I know you want to tonight, I'll lose you again. And I don't want to lose you again. I just found you."

He doesn't immediately reply.

He stares down at me, his eyes hooded, his expression inscrutable, seconds ticking by in which I start to fear I've said too much. I start to fear I've asked for too much. Time and his silence close in on me with such heaviness that I can't breathe, but then he's molding me to him, his fingers splayed on my lower back. "I've been obsessed with you since the moment I saw you across that pool, Harper. You affect me, too. You belong with me and I'm *not* losing you again." His mouth closes down on mine, brutal and punishing, hot and seductive, long strokes of his tongue caressing mine until I can barely breathe. When he finally relents, his hand moves roughly over my breast, and his lips linger above mine, his breath hot, and his voice a near growl. "You're mine now, Harper. I own you. No one gets to take you from me. You understand? No one."

His emotions pound on me, punishing me like his kiss, the way he wants to punish them. "Eric—"

"They tried to kill you tonight. I believe that. You aren't the one who ends up dead."

"If you kill your father or your brother, you could go to jail. Then I do lose you again."

"I'm way better than a common criminal, sweetheart. I won't go to jail."

Those words punish me yet again. He's brutal. He's a killer. And I love him. I do. I love him. "What if Walker screws up?"

"Walker won't know. I handle my own dirty work. I'm going to take care of this and then I'm going to come back up here and fuck you in my bed just like I promised. And the word 'again' applies because I'm going to fuck you, lick you, and kiss you, again and again." His fingers tangle in my hair, rough and erotic. "You're never going to want to leave my bed. That's a promise." And then he's kissing me again, sealing that promise with a deep, demanding stroke of his tongue before he orders, "Stay here," he orders, and then he's walking away.

I'm instantly cold, ice in my veins freezing every inch of me. I can't let him leave. I dart forward and place myself between the door and him. "You will not kill anyone. That's an order."

He tangles his fingers in my hair again, his fingers biting. "You will not say those words again. You will not speak of murder. You will not speak of any of this. Understand?"

"No. No, I don't understand. You will not—"

He turns me toward the door, pressing my hands on the hard surface, framing my body with his. "You will not repeat those words. Ever."

"I'm not agreeing to that," I pant out.

He shoves my hands over my head. "Damn it, Harper. You will listen to me." He buries his face in my neck. "You will listen or I swear I'll make you listen."

There's an erotic promise in those words that shouldn't turn me on, not in the context he speaks them, but they do. They so do. "Make me then," I challenge, welcoming whatever that means, my sex aching, wet. My nipples puckered and throbbing. I want whatever he's offering. I want him here with me.

His hands slide over my waist, cupping my breasts, pinching my nipples through my shirt and bra. "I should," he whispers. "I really fucking should, but I'm not going to. Not like this. Not when I'm like I am right now. *Fuck.*" He pushes away from me, leaving my sex aching and drenched, my body screaming for some unknown pleasure it's been denied.

I rotate to find him standing with his back to me, his hand pressed to his neck. "Fuck," he curses again, turning to me. "What the hell are you doing to me, woman?"

His eyes are dark, tormented, his body a hard line of edgy need. I want to understand that need. I want to understand this man. I want to satisfy the burn in him for revenge, and I know only one way to do that. To satisfy another need in him, to drive him over the edge, and then bring him down, and then maybe, just maybe, he'll let go of his anger to see a solution that doesn't include murder. Maybe I'll save him and us. That means now, before he puts something in motion I can't stop.

"You can't leave this room yet," I say. "I won't let you."

"You can't stop me, Harper."

He's wrong. I can and I will.

Chapter Fifty-Eight

Harper

I'm still against the door of Eric's bedroom, my body all that's stopping him from leaving this room and acting on his promise to end his father. My declaration that he's not leaving the room between us. His declaration that I can't stop him, right there with it. And he's right, of course. I can't stop him. Not if he really wants to leave. The man is six-foot-two or three at least, and a wall of solid, hot, hard muscle. He has that control. He is, in fact, one hundred percent in control of the physical equation. He's in control of what happens next if he wants to be, and that's a problem because I know, *I know*, that if I let him leave this room right now, I won't be able to stop him from acting against his father. I don't know the right move to make to deal with the hell we're in, but I know with certainty that making any move right now, in his current state of mind, is not a decision made of the genius he was born with.

It's emotional.

It's passionate.

It's about pain, revenge, and anger.

It's about the attempt on my life that I can't think about right now. If I crumble, he'll act out. He'll lash out. He'll protect me at all costs, and the costs could be too high. He'd do all this for me and that affects me on so many levels, in so many ways. No one but this man would do anything for me, and the fact that he would is a realization that warms me, but also comes with responsibility for how I affect his actions.

I'm suddenly ravenous to tear away Eric's physical control, to find the man beneath all those emotions and all that powerful anger. Desperate to save him the way he saved me because I know no matter what his claim, he'd regret the actions he's planned against his father. He might be a genius, but he's still just a man, and a man I want the chance to know; all of him, all of the broken, damaged

273

pieces beneath his perfect surface. I'm not letting him out of this room until I know what is really in his head or until he at least promises me to wait to make any decision that doesn't involve us naked in his bed.

I go to him and I don't give him time to react, my hands catching at his waist. "You say I belong with you."

"You *do* belong with me." His tone is absolute, his voice and eyes pure steel.

"That means *you* belong with *me.*"

"Yes, Harper. It does." He says those words without hesitation, his voice low, a raspy hint to it, that says he's affected and yet, he doesn't touch me.

A charge hums from him, like a ball of anger spinning in the air, faster and faster until it combusts. Like years of anger and pain that have collided into this moment, this piece of time and I understand. He walked away. He made his own future and yet still they came for him—God, *I* came for him. They've pushed his limits and he needs to find them again.

I need to find them for him.

I drop to my knees and caress the thick ridge of his erection. He's hard, thick, pulsing beneath the stretch of his zipper. He wants me. He needs me like he did on the plane and I believe now that he just needs a release. He needs to fuck or be fucked. No. He needs to take and I need to give.

"What are you doing, Harper?"

"Giving you a reason to stay in this room with me." I reach for his belt and tug it free.

He catches my shoulders, finally touching me. God, I didn't know how much I needed him to touch me, to prove to me that he's here, he's still in this room with me. "People are waiting on us," he warns, staring down at me, his eyes hooded, heavy.

"They'll wait," I say, unzipping his pants, aware that he hasn't pushed me away or pulled me to my feet. "We both know what you need right now."

"What do I need, Harper?"

"To take a pause. To breathe again. To get out of your own head."

I reach beneath his pants, my hand finding the hard, warm flesh of his erection as I ease him from his clothes. And the fact that he doesn't stop me empowers me. As does the carnal look on his face as he watches me. I like that look, oh yes, I do. Just as I like how hot and hard he is in my palm, and the way liquid pools at the tip of his cock. Boldly, I catch his stare before I give him a long, sensual lick.

He shuts his eyes, his lashes low, his body tight, but he's not touching me again. He's trying to maintain control. He's trying to keep it as his own and that I don't like. I lick his cock again, swirling my tongue all over him, around him, up and down, and when I suck hard and deep, a soft breath escapes his lips. A breath he tries to control but can't. Encouraged now, I take just the tip of him in my mouth and suckle hard, but I don't take more, I make him want and need, but he can't have it, not yet. Not until I get what I want. Not until he's one hundred percent in the moment.

I lick and swirl, thrusting my tongue down the underside of him, and finally, his fingers tangle in my hair. Finally, he's all in. "Holy fuck, woman," he growls. "You know you're killing me. Take all of me."

Take all of him.

Oh yes. I will.

Heat pools low in my belly and my nipples pucker and ache. I want and need just as he does. I want his control. I want his revenge. I want his anger. I want it all right here, right in this moment. I suck him deep and hard. I suck him and clutch him and move up and down him.

"Yes," he murmurs. "Deeper, Harper."

Harper.

I have no idea why him using my name right now has me on the verge of orgasm, but it does. I've never been this wet and hot from giving a blow job. My lips tighten around his shaft, and I slide all the way to my fingers where they grip him. He thrusts into my mouth and a salty-sweet taste touches my tongue. He's close. He's right there where I want him and I pump my hand against his next thrust, and repeat. Again. Again. And then again until the muscles of his thigh that are now under my palm lock up, even as his fingers tighten in my hair.

"Deeper," he demands again. "More."

More.

He wants more, and more works for me. My breasts are heavy, my sex dripping, I'm so very wet.

I pump my hand again and stroke my tongue low and high. He pumps into my mouth and then he's shuddering, the salty taste of his release exploding in my mouth, a low groan sliding from his lips. And incredulously, I come. I come with him and I didn't know that was possible, but I do. And when it's over, my forehead is on his stomach, my body weak. The next thing I know, I'm on my feet, Eric's hands on my shoulders, his eyes locked with mine.

"If you're trying to make me fall in love with you, Harper, it's working, but that doesn't save my father or that family. You can't save them. Not this time." He sets me away from him and this time when he heads for the door, I can't stop him.

I whirl around just in time to watch him exit the room.

Chapter Fifty-Nine

Harper

He's falling in love with me. I'm shellshocked at his confession but I don't allow myself to revel in his words. I don't stand in the bedroom and hope for the best. I'm out of the room and on Eric's heels in the blink of an eye. I don't call after him, though. Not yet. Not with a houseful of people and I doubt I'll stop him at this point anyway. He believes he's protecting me. Now, I need to protect him. He clears the stairs before I do and by the time I'm around the corner, Eric is following the Walker team toward the front door.

Now I call out. "Eric!"

Much to my relief, he stops walking but he doesn't turn, tension tracking his shoulders down to his fingers where they curl into his palms at his sides. I'm not discouraged. I hurry forward and I step in front of him, planting my hand over his chest, holding him right here with me. "Where are you going?"

"You knew I needed to talk to the Walker team."

"Talk? Just talk? Or make plans that you can't come back from?" I don't give him time to reply. "Promise me you won't take any permanent actions until we can talk."

"We already talked," he replies, his expression inscrutable. "And you know where Walker falls in all of this."

"That's not even close to a promise. I need a promise, Eric."

There's a flex in his jaw before he's suddenly dragging me to him, his hands firmly on my waist. "Bastards don't make promises they actually keep."

"Then don't be a bastard, because we both know that's your choice. You told me your promises matter."

"I swear to you, princess, if you—"

"Don't finish that sentence and turn yourself into a bastard by choice. If you do, we're going to end up fighting right here in the middle of all these men. I'm trying to protect you."

"What the hell do you think I'm trying to do for you?"

"Protect me. I know that. *I know*. Make the promise."

He cups my head and kisses me. "I promise," he says. "For you. *Only* for you." His voice is low, gravelly. Rough. "I won't be long."

I don't get to ask him where he's going or what he's doing. He sets me aside and heads for the door, but I let him leave this time. He made a promise and I trust him to keep it. The door opens and shuts behind me and that's when I find myself in the spotlight. Grayson and Davis are standing in the living room, watching me.

"That was something to observe," Davis comments.

"What are you talking about?" I ask, confused.

"You," Davis replies. "Eric. I'm not used to seeing him invested in a woman."

"He's known me a long time," I say, closing the space between the other two men and me. "For all kinds of reasons. I'm his stepsister. I'm his—"

"Woman," Grayson amends, his voice low, but no less absolute. "You're *the woman*. I saw it in his eyes when he looked at you. And I saw him in your eyes when you looked at him. I knew the day you came to the office." He motions toward a bar on the wall next to the patio door. "Drink?" He doesn't give me time to reply to his stunning revelation. He walks to the bar and Davis joins him, but my gaze locks on that door next to them, on the patio entrance.

Eric had planned to talk to the Walker men out there before we went upstairs. Instead, he left with them. He made sure I couldn't interrupt this time. He promised me he wouldn't do anything permanent before we talked, and yet, he didn't go to the patio. He left the apartment.

He promised me.

He wouldn't break his promise.

Grayson hands me a glass. "Drink. It'll help calm your nerves. You've been through a lot tonight."

"I'm not worried about me."

"Let Eric do what he needs to do to make sure this ends sooner rather than later."

"He wants to end it by ending his father."

"He's wanted to end his father for a very long time. He didn't do it. He has reasons not to do it."

"Because of his mother, I know, but he believes they tried to kill me tonight, Grayson. He wants his father dead."

"He promised you he'd talk to you before he did anything permanent. I heard him."

"That's all you're going to say? He wants to *kill* him."

He eyes Davis and Davis nods. "I actually need to deal with a client at the office. I may or may not be back." He glances at me. "He's intense. It's contagious. Drink the drink." He turns and walks away.

I frown and eye Grayson. "Did he just tell me I'm wound too tightly?"

He chuckles. "I do believe he did." He motions to my drink.

"I know. Drink it. It'll help. I'm following the theme going on here, but I'm not a good drinker. I need a clear mind right now for Eric."

"Eric isn't going anywhere without you. You were attacked. You could have ended up dead. He is not leaving your side. His father is safe for the night. He's not on his way to kill his father. He's still in an airplane."

"Do you believe he'd do it?"

"Not tonight, and I know him well. By morning, he'll decide death is too good for him."

"How can you be so sure?"

"Because I met him when he was still bleeding out over his mother's death, and even then, he didn't go after the family. His mother's wishes meant too much to him."

"They went after him through me. They went after *me*. He knows this. He's not going to let that go. I feel it. I see it in his eyes."

"He promised you that he wouldn't act. You proved you have the power to affect his decisions."

I down my drink. "You just put the world on my shoulders."

"No," he says. "The world is on his shoulders and has been for a very long time. You can ease that pressure. You can make him let go of the past once and for all."

"I'm part of his past. I'm part of *them* and he hates that."

"He's a part of them, too, but both of you can choose to walk away."

"*They won't let us,* Grayson. I believe in my heart that they tricked me into setting him up for my own murder." Saying that out loud to someone other than Eric twists me in knots. "I need another drink. No. I need Eric here. Now." I reach for my phone and remember that I don't have it. "I have no phone. I have no purse. I have no clothes."

"My wife, Mia, is bringing you some necessities, including a new phone."

"Because Eric's like a brother to you and you're protecting me to protect him."

His eyes warm with that statement. "Eric is my brother."

Brother.

That word radiates through me and I walk to the bar myself, refill my glass and down it again. "I believe he's hit a limit," I say when Grayson offers me his glass to fill. "If you really love him like a brother—"

"I do," he says, taking the whiskey in my hand from me.

"Help me stop him."

"What are you suggesting?"

"I don't know, Grayson. I just know if he does this, he'll lose sleep. He'll feel pain over it. Even if he doesn't get caught—"

"I wouldn't get caught."

At the sound of Eric's voice, I whirl around to find him standing a few feet away and relief washes over me. He's back. He's already back.

"And I told you, Harper. I would sleep just fine if he were dead, but I don't plan to kill him or anyone. That would be too gentle a punishment." His cellphone rings and he pulls it from his pocket to glance at the number. His expression is stone, his entire body more stone than man, as he allows seconds to count down before he answers the call.

He takes the call, gives a clipped greeting, listens several seconds and then says, "When?" Another few beats pass and he adds, "I'll be there." He disconnects the line and cuts his stare, seeming to think, perhaps calming his mind a moment, before he says, "I'll be back," and turns and heads for the door.

Warning bells go off in my head and I run for him, planting myself between him and the door, watching him slip into a jacket. "Who was that, Eric?"

"My father." He opens a drawer to the foyer table, pulls out a gun, checks it, and sticks it in his pants.

"You need a gun?"

He faces me, his stance wide. "Would you rather me go without one after what happened at the warehouse?"

"You're not going to meet him. Not tonight. Sleep this off. Think about what comes next."

"I don't need to think."

"You aren't going to meet him."

"Yes," he says. "I am." And once again, he sets me aside, opens the door, and leaves.

I try to follow, but Savage steps in my path. "Sorry, honeybunch," Savage says. "I can't let you leave."

"Move, Savage, or I swear, I'll hurt you."

"You do appreciate the ridiculousness of that statement, I'm sure." He steps back just enough to indicate another man with sandy brown hair and lots of muscles, standing beside him. "I brought back-up. This is Smith. He's going to be your regular doorman."

Smith gives me a nod, confirming that I'm outnumbered. I grimace and turn back to the apartment. Grayson appears in the foyer. "He went to meet his father. He won't kill him, right?"

Grayson's eyes darken. "That's not his plan."

"That's not a no."

"It's the only answer I have for you."

Chapter Sixty

Eric

The past...

Jennie pulls her giant truck to the edge of the trailer park and stops. "I have to let you off here." She looks at her watch. "Hurry. You have to go. I'm *so* late to work, it's insane. If I get fired, my mom will be pissed and we won't be going out this weekend."

"We aren't going out this weekend," I say. "You know that. I'm staying with my mother."

"You're only sixteen. You still have to live."

"What part of *she's dying* do you not understand?"

"I can't date a guy who can't ever go out."

I cut her a look. "Then don't date me." I open the car door.

"Eric, damn it."

I don't reply. I get out of the truck. "Thanks for the ride." I slam the door and slide my backpack onto my shoulder. I have homework that will take me all of about thirty minutes. I can do it in the morning before class, but my mother likes to see me open books. I'll open them for her.

I start down the road that leads to our trailer, and just that easily, I'm already done with Jennie. I don't need anyone in my life right now but my mother anyway. I don't know why I tried. My mother is what matters. My mother who can't die. We have to find another treatment. There has to be a way to pay for it. I'll volunteer as a guinea pig. I'll let them study my brain. I know my mom doesn't want that, but she'll have to understand.

I turn the corner to our street and the sight of ambulances and fire trucks slams into me. My heart explodes in my chest. My stomach knots. Numbers begin to pound at my mind. "Mom. Mom!" I charge forward, blood pumping through my veins and in my ears. "Mom!" I run and run and I don't stop until I'm right on the edge of the yard and only then because a monster of a police officer catches my arms.

"Son," he orders. "You need to stay right here."

"I live here. I live here! This is my home. You can't stop me from going into my own home."

"Are you Eric Mitchell?"

"Yes." Tears start streaming down my cheeks. "I need to see my mother. She's sick. She's got cancer. She needs me. I'm her son!"

The officer hits a button on his arm and says, "Get that social worker here now."

"Social worker?! I don't need a social worker. I know she has cancer. What's wrong? Is it a reaction to the chemo? *What's wrong*?!"

"Son," he says, his voice vibrating with an undercurrent that touches his eyes. With something he doesn't want to say. "Son, your mother—"

"She's dead. She's dead, isn't she?"

He doesn't have to reply. I see it in his face and the numbers attack my mind, diving at it like sharp blades.

My knees go weak and I fall down, grabbing my head and in a tunnel of pain, I hear, "Get me an EMT tech! Now!"

I black out.

No. I don't black out. There are numbers.

11111

77777
88888

99999
11111

They won't stop. God, make them stop. I sit up, ramrod stiff and find myself in the back of an ambulance. "Easy, son," a male voice says, and I bring him into focus, sitting next to me. "I gave you something to calm you down."

"I don't want to calm down." I sit up. "I want to see my mother."

A woman with long brown hair in her mid-fifties appears at the end of the truck. "Eric, she's gone. I'm sorry."

My throat goes dry, the cotton sensation all but choking me, and I try to find the numbers again, the ones I control but I can't find them. "No. No, that isn't right."

"I'm afraid it is. Your mother's gone, son."

My mind tunnels through empty space and for the first time in my life, I need to count, I need numbers and math, and there is nothing but white noise. "How?" I hear myself say, but my voice is distant, the world is distant. "How did she die? She was getting treatment."

"She was in a lot of pain. I'm sad to report that she took her own life. "

"No. No, she was fighting. *She was fighting!*"

"She was tired. She wanted more for you, too. She left a letter. I called your father and—"

"I don't have a father. I don't fucking have a father!" I try to get up, but the EMT holds me down, my head spinning with the damn drug he gave me.

"I want to see the letter," I whisper.

"At my office," the woman says.

"Who are you?"

"Evelyn Minor. Your social worker." She holds out a hand. "Come with me."

Two hours later, I sit in her dingy office with a scuffed desk and yellow chair, the letter in hand, but no numbers in my head. That drug the EMT gave me makes me dizzy again as I start reading:

My dearest Eric—

I had to do this. I had to do it because I love you with all my heart and soul. I did this for you. It was time for you to get on with your life. It was time for your father to claim you. Make him. Accept him. He can help you make the most of your gifts. He can get you the help you need to control it. Don't fight him. Don't lash out at him. Do this for me. Do this so that I know I left you behind better than I brought you into this world. Please, son. I beg of you. I need you to do this. For me. Do this for me.

Before I can read on, the door to the office opens and in walks a man in a blue suit, his brown hair slicked back. I know him. I don't want to know him. Jeff Kingston, the man my mother claims is my father, ignores the social worker and steps in front of me, towering above me. "Looks like your mother got her way," he bites out. "You're with me now. Let's go."

"Excuse me," the social worker says. "But there's paperwork and—"

"Fuck your paperwork. Sue me if you want to. He's coming with me." He motions to me. "Get up. Come with me. Now."

No words of sorrow or sympathy.

Just a command.

And I have no choice but to follow it. It's what my mother wanted and she's gone. She's dead. She killed herself and any version of me that I knew.

Chapter Sixty-One

Harper

Present day...

I'm still standing in the foyer of Eric's apartment with Savage and Smith at my back preventing my exit from Eric's apartment. Grayson is in front of me, dismissing my worries about Eric and his father. "I thought you were the level-headed brother Eric values," I say to Grayson. "He doesn't plan on killing his father, but *hey, if it happens, it happens,* is not level-headed."

"I didn't say if it happens, it happens," Grayson replies, his tone cool but his voice is still low.

"You aren't worried at all. If you are, you hide it well."

"I know Eric well enough to know that he'll do the right thing."

"The right thing? How do you define the right thing when staring into the face of a man who just tried to frame you for the murder of your girlfriend? Call him. Call him now so he'll answer and let me talk to him."

"I'm not going to call him," he says. "He needs to focus. Someone tried to kill you. He could be the next target."

"All the more reason for him to be here. Call him."

There's a knock on the door and then it opens. "Hi," a female voice says.

I whip around to find a gorgeous brunette, in a floaty green chiffon dress standing inside the foyer with bags in her hands. "Shopping trip successful. My favorite personal shopper worked miracles and got the stores to open for me. Did you know that Apple has a twenty-four-hour store in Manhattan? Amazing. Oh." She laughs. "I guess I should introduce myself. I'm Mia. Grayson's wife. Nice to meet you, Harper." She sets the bags down. "I brought you some necessities."

The door shuts behind her and I give her my full attention, but introductions are the last thing on my mind. "Tell him to call Eric."

"What?" She blinks and eyes her husband. "What's going on?"

"Someone tried to kill me and frame Eric," I say, not sure what she knows. "Eric wants to 'end' his father, and now his father is here, in the city. He went to meet him. I couldn't stop him."

Mia looks between me and Grayson. "End him how?"

"Kill him," I say. "I think he wants him dead."

"He won't kill him," Grayson bites out. "He's got this under control."

"He was quaking, literally, after he found out about his father. That is not under control."

"Quaking?" Grayson demands.

"Yes. His entire body was trembling, and I know it was one of those attacks he used to have trying to come back."

He narrows his eyes on me. "You know about the attacks?"

"Yes. I know. He isn't good right now."

"My God, Grayson," Mia says. "If he's that bad and she's as bonded to him as you told me she is, then let her call him. Get him back. Make sure he's okay."

Grayson stares at Mia, seconds ticking by before he pulls his phone from his pocket and punches a number before handing it to me. "It's ringing."

I eagerly accept the phone and listen as the ringing continues, and then goes to voicemail. "Eric," I breathe out. "Please come back. Don't meet with him tonight. Talk to me. Be with me. Take a breath and just think. *Please*. I need you and I don't want to lose you." I hang up and redial, but it goes to voicemail again. This time when the line beeps, I say, "Please come back to me, now, before you meet with him."

I disconnect and hand the phone back to Grayson before I walk into the living room, barely seeing the room, my destination the floor-to-ceiling windows. I stop at the glass and stare out at the inky night, not a star in the sky. There is just the darkness eating away at Eric, and holding us captive.

Chapter Sixty-Two

Harper

Fifteen minutes after Eric leaves me in his apartment with Grayson and Mia, I'm fretting and then fretting some more over where he is and what he's doing. Still glued to the window, the eerie fog has thickened, consuming all remnants of the city lights. The way this family consumes both Eric and my mother. "He's one of the strongest people I've ever known," Grayson says, stepping to my side.

"But he's human."

"Barely," he replies softly. "More so with you in the picture."

It's an odd thing to say and I can feel my defenses bristle, my arms folding and I bring him into view. "You don't think he's human? I thought you were his best friend?"

"Part of being his friend is seeing him clearly."

"And yet you just said he's barely human."

"He doesn't think like you and me. He lives with numbers first, and people second."

"Those numbers are his wall, his shield he hides behind and inside. And while it's hard to explain why, I know him. I understand him, and in his mind, those numbers tell one story over and over. The Kingston family killed his mother, the only person he's ever loved, besides you. Distance and your friendship allowed him to bank that, to compartmentalize his pain, but they pulled him back into their world. They brought it to the surface." My fist balls on my chest. "And I helped them." I turn back to the glass and press my hands to the bar there. "I came here to get him. I helped set this in motion."

"You didn't know you were being used."

I can't even look at him for the guilt spiraling inside me, a sharp blade that won't stop cutting me. "I should have known. I knew the family couldn't be trusted."

"My understanding is that's exactly why you went to Eric. Because you knew they couldn't be trusted and you felt he could help. And he is helping. He's the reason you're alive right now."

"I have coffee," Mia exclaims, joining us, two mugs in her hands, one that she hands me and another that she hands Grayson.

"Thank you," I say, accepting the mug. "I think I'm going to lose my mind if I don't calm my nerves. I'm really worried." I eye Grayson. "He told me he hasn't had an attack in years."

"Not since college," Grayson confirms.

"But he did today. Driven by the emotional trigger of his father. That was obvious."

He eyes Mia and seems to share a silent conversation with her before he refocuses on me. "The last time I saw him like that, he left Harvard the next day. He knew Isaac was pushing his buttons. He put distance between the two of them. He removed the triggers."

This comment doesn't take me to a good place. "And yet he knew his father was a trigger, and he just went right to him."

"He's not a college kid anymore," Grayson reminds me. "He's a man who walks into problems, rather than away from them. I know this. I see it every day."

"Is that good or bad?" Mia queries, crossing her arms in front of her. "Because if he really cares about Harper, and they, the Kingstons, I assume, tried to hurt her, well, I'm worried. What if the numbers in his head calculate the odds of them succeeding next time as too risky. He might take the action, but the wrong action. We both know how much he hates that family." She looks at Grayson. "A man held me at gunpoint and you tried to get him to shoot you instead of me. Think about Eric doing the same."

I don't know what she's talking about, or who held a gun to her head and I don't ask. I can think of only one thing. She just said that Grayson tried to take a bullet for her. "Eric's trying to take the bullet for me, too." I take a sip of my coffee, just to do something, anything, to keep from losing my mind and it doesn't work. I'm going to crawl out of my own skin. "I need the phone to try to call him again."

Grayson breathes out, scrubbing his jaw and dialing the number before handing it to me. It rings and rings, and I walk to a coffee table and set my mug down. The table is black stone—a part of the black theme to the room and it feels like a theme. He lives in darkness and numbers, and it's not okay. Voicemail picks up and I leave a message he may never hear. "I need you to come back here alive right now. I need you, period. I do. Come back so I can tell you that in person." I disconnect and dial again, and again, and every time, I land in voicemail.

When I finally hand Grayson his phone back, Mia comes to the rescue. "Let's busy ourselves unpacking. It'll distract your mind."

"I have such a bad feeling about this night," I whisper.

"He *will* be back and safe," Mia promises me.

I need her to be right.

No.

I just need Eric. Here. Now.

Eric

In the short time it takes for me to get an uneventful update from Adam, and exit my apartment building alone, my phone rings with a call from Grayson. "Sorry, brother," I murmur. "Not now." I hit decline. If anything important is happening, the Walker team will contact me

I place the phone on mute and cut right, walking toward my father's hotel, bypassing the use of a hired car with a driver that might remember my travels. I push through the fog-laden, cold night for another three blocks and once I'm at the hotel, I dial my father.

"Back of the building in the alleyway."

He snorts. "I'm not meeting you in the back of the hotel."

Just the sound of his voice cuts me all the way to my black soul he helped create. "You afraid of the dark? Good thing I'm not or Harper would be in a dark warehouse dead right now."

"I heard what happened, son. Why do you think I'm here?"

"You mean you ordered someone to kill her." It's not a question.

"You're confused, son," he says, using a familiar snide tone, "which is why we need to talk. Here. Now. In my room."

"Not a chance in hell. You have five minutes and then I'm gone. Back service door." I disconnect the line and a notification pops up with a voicemail from Grayson. I ignore it and head down the alleyway toward the back of the building. If my father won't come to me, I'll go to him, but on my terms, in my way. I walk to the rear of the building, finding the alleyway dark, with a dim overhead light spiraling down on a dumpster. I take a position in a dark corner by the door I've named, where I'll wait to discover how desperate my father is to talk to me.

Three minutes pass and I become aware of someone else in the alleyway and he isn't my father. A man, based on his build, dressed in all black steps behind the trashcan and disappears. Waiting on someone, and of course that someone is me.

Chapter Sixty-Three

Eric

The past...

I leave the social worker's office on the heels of my father, who never looks back at me. When we get to his fancy car, he flicks me a look. "Backseat."

His message is clear: I don't belong in the front with him. I want to punch him. I want to hurt him like I know he hurt my mom. God, I want to kill him. He must see it in my face, too, because he charges up to me, grabs my shirt and shoves me against the car. "You got a problem with me, boy?"

"You're an asshole."

"Yes. I am. I'll teach you how to do it just like me and then maybe you'll belong with us. Right now, you don't. You forget that—you won't like the results. *Backseat*." He releases me and walks to the front of the car.

I consider leaving, but my mother's letter is still in my hand. She wanted this for me. She wanted him for me. I get in the car and when I settle into the backseat, my "father" says, "People die. You're going to have to deal with it."

A swell of anger and pain fills my chest and I cut my gaze to the window. He starts the engine and I fight the burn of tears in my eyes. I won't cry in front of him. Once we're moving, I open the letter again and the first thing I read is: *You will not fight your father. You will not go after him or anyone in the family. You're smart enough to do it. You're smart enough to hurt them, but DON'T DO IT. That is my final wish. That is my plea to you. Don't do it. Because family doesn't hurt family and they're your blood, they're your family now, until we meet again one day in a better place.*

Present day...

My father did exactly what I expected.

He hired someone to shut me up, if not kill me.

If my mother were alive, if she'd written that letter she wrote me so many years ago, knowing what I now know, she'd have changed her tune. She'd have shown the side of her that was a fighter. The side that went after a DNA test and forced me on the Kingstons. She'd tell me to fight back. She'd tell me to win.

I stand in the dark corner, and I reach in my pocket and pull out a quarter, focusing on walking it through my fingers to calm my mind. Taking myself to that place I went all those years ago when I had to kill or be killed. It was natural then, an instinct that didn't require honing, but I'm not in that place anymore. I'm in the one that came first. The one where my father lives, which makes this not quite as simple as the "kill or be killed" warfare presents. I'll still kill if I have to, but I want answers.

The alleyway is an unmoving box, not even a shadow flickers. I listen for the enemy, and the man behind that dumpster *is* an enemy. Seconds tick by and turn into minutes and he doesn't move, but neither do I. Anyone my father hired worth any salt knows my skill level. Knows I'm here, watching this fool, waiting to act. One of us has to make a move and I decide what the fuck. I'm game. It's been too damn long since I played a game like this one and I find I missed the hell out of it.

I flip the quarter into the center of the alleyway, and it lands on the pavement and then clanks as it wobbles. It's an invitation. Come get me. I wait and wait some more, but there is no impatience in me. I don't need to move to feel relief. The numbers in my head are running and running for me, calculating risk, assessing my next move. I don't even flinch when the other man must decide he doesn't like his odds, and darts out from behind the trashcan and starts running. Smart man. The odds were against him, but that hasn't changed. I might still be wearing a portion of a suit, but I'm fast and I run behind him, yanking him back and shoving him against the fence in thirty seconds.

"What were your orders?"

"Fuck you," the man growls.

I smirk. "My mother was good and kind, unwilling to hurt anyone. In many ways, I'm not my mother's son." I knee him and he groans. "I'm my father's son," I add, "and I suspect she knew that when she asked me not to go after the Kingston family. She knew if I did, I'd destroy them. That's who you're working for, right?"

"Fuck you again!" he shouts.

"Again it is," I say, giving him a repeat knee, this time with such force that when I let him go, he crumbles to the ground. He groans and moans, and when a homeless man wanders into the alleyway, I point at him, telling him he's next if he doesn't back off, and he runs away.

My would-be attacker rolls to his back and I press my foot to his crotch. "What were your orders?"

"To scare you."

"We both know that's a lie." I pull up his shirt and eye the gun there, complete with a silencer. "Who sent you to kill me?"

"Your father," he bites out and then tries to spit at me, like a fool. Obviously, my father doesn't know how to hire a good killer, which works for me right about now.

I reach for my phone and snap a photo of him and then grind my foot into his crotch. He screeches and rolls to his side. I grab his wallet. "You're lucky I don't want a mess to clean up tonight. I know who you are. I know how to find you. We'll talk soon. That's a promise." I stand up and start walking.

When I step out of the alleyway, Savage joins me. "I didn't ask for your help," I say, cutting left toward my apartment.

"You didn't need it either," he says. "Which was kind of disappointing. I haven't had a good brawl in like three days." He doesn't wait for a reply. "One of our guys followed you. I caught up. I'm your front-line guy until Adam gets here. And there's no interesting movement back in Denver. I just talked to him."

I open the wallet, glance at the name on the ID that reads Joe Melton, and then hand it to Savage. "He was sent to kill me tonight. I took a photo to confirm the identity matches the driver's license. I'll shoot it to Blake since I have his number." We cut across the street.

"Who sent him?"

"My father," I say, "who I'm going to leave squirming in his room, hoping I'm dead for the time being." I pull my phone out to listen to the messages, and the minute I hear Harper's voice, her soft pleas undo me yet again tonight. I go warm the only way her voice can make me warm, and then instantly cold with the certainty that this attack on me confirms that the warehouse attack on her was, in fact, an assassination attempt. We reach my building and I stop to face Savage.

"Find out what you can on the guy who attacked me. Make sure your team knows that I believe we're dealing with hired killers. And I need an hour alone with Harper."

"Understood," he says, giving me a mock salute.

I enter the building, and suddenly, I can't get to Harper soon enough. I will not feel as if she's safe until she's with me. I head for the elevator and dial Grayson to make sure there's nothing I need to know when I get there. The phone rings. And rings. And rings again. I try Mia's phone in hopes that she's with Grayson or at least talked to him. She doesn't answer. My heart starts to race. What if that amateur back there was a distraction and I fell for it? Fuck. Everyone I care about is in my apartment. I start running for the stairs.

Chapter Sixty-Four

Eric

I call Blake on my race up the apartment building stairs. "Get in touch with your man. I need to know my apartment's secure and everyone inside with it."

"Hold on," he says, without asking why.

In the time it takes for him to reply, in the dead space that is my seventeen flights of stairs, I die over and over again. The idea that everyone I love could be in trouble, and that I let it happen, guts me over and over again; a blade for every floor I have to travel to get to them. My mind starts playing a series of numbers. They calculate the odds of me being set-up. The odds of Harper, Grayson, and Mia lying dead right now, which are too high. The odds of them being held captive at gunpoint. The odds that I can save them if they are kidnapped, which are all too slim. I don't like any of the numbers. I reject them all. There's a reason Grayson and Mia aren't answering their cells, that the numbers in my head fail to offer me. It doesn't matter that the numbers never fail me.

Blake finally returns to the line. "Eric," he says, his tone grim. "Our man isn't answering."

Those words gut me all over again, as in it feels like I'm literally having my heart pulled from my chest as Blake adds, "Savage is on his way up and I'm sending back-up."

"I'm about to exit to the hallway," I say. "I'm going silent." I disconnect and finish my upward charge and approach my floor, pulling my gun as I do, opening the door a mere crack when I want to explode into the hallway. I scan and find the floor clear, but there's no man from Walker Security standing guard at my door either. Adrenaline and dread swell inside me and I shove open the stairwell door, exploding into the hallway and running until I'm at my door. Once I'm there I pull my key from my pocket and unlock the door. I then aim my gun and kick it open, to enter the foyer.

"Harper!" I shout, moving into the room and finding the living room empty, but no one there with guns or dead bodies either. "Harper! Grayson!"

"Eric!"

At the sound of Harper's voice, it's like an angel singing me out of the hell that the past few minutes have shoved me inside. And when she appears in the doorway that leads to my office, her dark hair in a beautifully disarrayed mess around her shoulders, that swell of emotions inside me from minutes before now includes relief.

"Oh God!" she exclaims, eyeing the gun, stopping in her tracks. "Why do you have a gun? What's happening?" She looks wildly around the room.

It's then that Grayson and Mia exit the office, both in safe condition. "Oh God," Mia gasps, echoing Harper from moments before.

"Oh shit."

That male voice draws my attention back to the office, where a man now stands, holding a gun. A man that I recognize as Smith from Walker Security. "Why the fuck are you not at the door and why is no one answering their phones?" But I know even as I ask the question. My office has crap for service. It always has. It's like a cold spot in a room, haunted for about ten reasons no one but me has ever known.

"My phone didn't ring," Smith replies.

"I asked to talk to him," Harper interjects. "I was desperate to reach you. I was driving everyone crazy. Grayson went and got Smith because he was trying to confirm that Walker had eyes on you to make me feel better."

"Fuck," I grind out, scrubbing my jaw, and lowering my gun, still focused on Smith. "Get an extra man on the door," I snap. I'm agitated, still feeling the effects of fear for what I'd find when I got here. Still feeling that rush of adrenaline.

By the time the gun is in the band at the back of my pants again, Harper is in front of me, wrapping her arms around me. "I was so worried about you," she exclaims. "So incredibly worried."

She doesn't even begin to understand what worried means right now. I cup her head and close my mouth down on hers, and I don't give a shit who's watching. I kiss the fuck out of her, drink her in, drug myself all over with her, and it's a high I can't get enough of. "We need to have that talk I promised you."

"Yes," she whispers. "We do."

"Sounds like our cue to go home," Grayson says.

I shift Harper to my side, but don't let her go. "Keep Walker with you."

Grayson nods in understanding. "Call me."

"I will," I confirm as Mia rushes to Harper and gives her a hug to add, "Call me, too."

Smith and I exchange a look and I lean down and kiss Harper. "I'll be right back." I press my lips to her ear. "Wait for me in the bedroom. Be naked when I get back." I don't wait for a reply. Smith and I fall into step behind Grayson and Mia and when they exit the apartment, we stay inside the foyer.

"We both know you fucked up," I say. "Don't do it again." I don't wait for a reply. I move on. "I need to know where my father is right now. I need to know who he talks to or who he sees. And somehow, get a bug in his room, even if that means using room service to do it. Just make it happen."

"We're resourceful," Smith assures me. "We'll get it done." He turns and leaves.

I lock the door and stick my gun in a table off the entryway. I have another upstairs. I want this one ready to say hello to anyone at the door that shouldn't be here. Once it's sealed away, I exit the foyer, and walk the path to the stairs, starting the climb; blood rushing in my ears, pulsing through my body, just thinking about touching Harper, holding her again, after thinking I might have lost her. A feeling I never want to experience again.

Harper appears on the second level, at the top of the stairs, waiting on me, still dressed, and looking like she's ready to launch ten questions at me that I don't want to answer right now. I catch her by the waist and walk her backward until we're in my room where I shut the door, and then plant her against it. "You scared the fuck out of me." That swell of emotion is back, pounding at my chest, radiating through my voice. "Don't ever do that to me again."

Her fingers curl around my shirt. "*You* scared *me*. Don't do it—"

I twine my fingers into her hair and drag her mouth to mine. "Don't talk," I order. "Not now. Not Yet." And then I'm kissing her, and she is sweet, so damn sweet. The kind of sweet a Kingston destroys, but I'm not a Kingston. I'm just the bastard son.

Chapter Sixty-Five

Harper

Wе kiss each other as if every moment has a way of feeling like it will be our last. And I know he feels it, too. It feeds our emotions, defines us as a couple, and it drives our passion to an intensity that is as addictive as he is to me.

I really feared for him today and just knowing that he's here, that he's alive, undoes me, drives me. I don't want to know what he did or didn't do to his father right now. He didn't kill him. He promised me he wouldn't. What matters now is that he needs me and I need him and that need runs deep into my soul.

There's a desperation between us, the intensity of the burn we share swelling into an inferno like I've never experienced, like nothing I believe this man lets anyone know he can feel, but he lets me. He claims me with every touch and lick, and yet, he denies me more.

He tears his lips from mine, placing an intolerable space between my mouth and his and I'm overwhelmed with the pulse of his emotions, the self-hate in him. The part of him that blames what happened to me in that warehouse on himself. "Eric, I don't know what you think there is to hate in you, what you think will scare me away, but it won't. I'm here. I'm not going anywhere." *At least until he shoves me away*, I think, which I feel him doing now, even as he holds me close.

His eyes narrow, his scrutiny deep, as intense as the way he'd kissed me, and try as I might, his expression is impossible to read. I search, I probe, and I'm still trying to read him when suddenly he's kissing me again, licking into my mouth, testing my words on his tongue. I sink into him, absorbing his hard body into mine, clinging to him, meeting him stroke for stroke, trying to answer him, trying to show him that I'm here. I'm not going anywhere. He can't scare me away.

There's a low, sexy rumble in his chest that I feel everywhere. It's that moment of no return for him, that moment where he snaps, where he needs to claim and possess, rather than think. He wants me. He doesn't want me to leave. He doesn't want me to walk away. I feel that in him now, but I also feel his torment. He thinks I *should* leave and no matter what he claims, I think he'll walk away for me. But even as I feel that niggle of uncertainty trying to work me over, he lifts me and distracts me.

In a few long strides, he carries me to the bed, a driven man with a purpose and I'm that purpose. But he doesn't lay us down. He settles me on the edge of the mattress just long enough to remove my clothes. His own shirt follows, and his naked torso is sinewy muscle, his skin a brilliant inked canvas of male beauty. I'm still drinking him in, when he pulls me forward. My hands plant behind me, sinking into the mattress, catching my weight, even as he spreads my legs.

He drops to his knees and before I even process what he intends, his mouth closes on my sex and then he's suckling, stroking his tongue over me. I pant, and with one more lick, my elbows soften, and I allow the cushion to absorb my body. My reward is his fingers, teasing my sensitive flesh, stroking, and then pressing inside me. I arch into the feel of him stretching me, pumping into me, my fingers closing around the blanket beneath me, and oh God, he's good at this. So very good, his tongue's erotic play tantalizing in all the right ways, too right.

I'm embarrassingly already on edge, already right there in that sweet spot of no return. I tumble over the proverbial ledge, my body quaking, and there is no doubt Eric owns my pleasure and my body. He owns all of me. The only thing missing is him inside me. The moment my body calms, the ache of emptiness remains and he knows, of course he knows what he's done to me. How he's pleased me and left me craving more.

He's already on his feet, undressing, and I sit up just in time to find his cock is jutting between us, thickly veined with arousal. My eyes meet his and the punch of erotic heat between us steals my breath. In another moment, he's laid me back down on the mattress. My arms wrap his neck, and he's on top of me, the weight of his body pressing into me.

"I'm not just going to fuck you, Harper," Eric promises. "I'm going to make love to you."

Love.

It's the second time he's used that word in one night, and it's not without intent, and I feel it in every part of me. Love is bittersweet, filled with promises of happiness and heartache. It's scary and powerful. And after watching my mother lose my father, I never wanted it in my life. And then he came along.

My walls erect. I need to protect myself. Heat rushes up my neck. "I thought you needed an outlet tonight? I thought you needed to fuck me?"

"You took care of that on your knees earlier."

He's naked on top of me, his cock pressed between my legs, and I can still feel the heat in my cheeks.

In the back of my mind, this is what I want, but he is a force of nature, and I'm afraid to believe it's real. This could be us riding the adrenaline of all of tonight's emotion. I can't have him be all in one moment, and not the next. "Fucking me is safe."

"Fucking you is perfect," he murmurs, brushing his lips over mine. "And I *will* fuck you, Harper." His fingers gently wrap strands of my hair with a soft, erotic tug. "Every which way you'll let me and as often as you'll say yes, but there's more for us." And when he kisses me, it's with a sultry, sexy caress of his tongue that seduces me and tears down my walls.

I moan and tangle my fingers in his hair.

Forget safe. It's overrated.

He presses inside me, and the sultry kiss becomes the sultry sway of our bodies. He kisses me all over. My neck, my shoulder, my nipple. Every inch of me is alive and lost in sensations, in the mix of naughty things he whispers in my ear that still take nothing away from the lovemaking. It's not until after we crash into release, our bodies trembling as one, before we calm, that realization hits me.

We didn't use a condom.

Chapter Sixty-Six

Harper

E ric shifts us, rolling us to our sides, facing each other, and the wet rush between my legs sends a wave of panic through me. My fingers curl on his face. "We didn't use protection. I don't think I can get pregnant, but—"

He leans in and kisses me. "Stop freaking out. If you get pregnant, we get pregnant. I'll get you something to clean up. I'll be right back." He pulls out of me and rolls off the bed. I don't move, waiting for him to bring me a towel or tissue.

The "we" in his reaction sets my belly to fluttering for all kinds of reasons. It stabs at my heart, too, with a memory of cramping in my office. I always feared how he'd react to the news of my pregnancy, but I'm not sure it would have been as negatively as I thought back then.

Eric returns and hands me a towel, I press between my legs. "I need to go to the bathroom," I say, and when I would move away, Eric catches me to him.

"Stop freaking out, sweetheart."

"Do you even want kids? And God, I don't want you to answer that because either answer could be problematic. If you don't, and I'm pregnant, then we have an issue. If you do, and I can't get pregnant, then you need another woman."

"I do not want or need another woman. Never once did I think about having kids until I found out about your pregnancy. I want you, Harper. If that means we have kids, we have kids. If we don't, we don't."

"You say that, but—"

"I don't want a child to inherit this Kingston hell. So should we use a condom, yes, because I want closure first."

Which we may never get, I think. He may never really feel this is over. But I love him and I can live with that. "I understand."

"This isn't about us, Harper. It's about them."

My gut twists but I nod. "I know."

He studies me a moment, and I don't know what he sees, what he wants to see. "Go to the bathroom, but don't go run to the bathroom."

I curl my fingers on his face, overwhelmed by what I feel for him. "You're an amazing man. I wish you knew that." I kiss him and then roll off the bed.

I hurry into the bathroom, and shut the door, leaning against the hard surface and staring down at my belly. I don't think I can have kids, and even if I can, I don't think this is the right time. Eric and I are finding each other, and he's still trying to learn to love himself. He doesn't need that pressure right now and I don't want the pressure of thinking we end up together for a baby, not because we chose that option.

I give myself a mental shake.

I need to let this go and find out what happened tonight with Eric's father. I quickly clean up and take the liberty to dig in Eric's closet, and pick a T-shirt, and tug it over my head. It's big and long, but even clean, it smells like him, and I like it. For just a moment, I survey his well-organized closet, and imagine my things here and my emotions need a U-Haul. They are just so full I need to cut them off until later. It's time to go back to Eric.

This sets me in action and when I open the bedroom door, he's sitting on a chair by the window with his pants on, and cellphone at his ear. The instant he spies me, he disconnects and stands, closing the space between us.

His hand slides under my hair, his fingers resting on my neck. "As much as I love you in my shirt, you need to get dressed."

"Did something happen?"

"Blake and Savage are downstairs and I know how upset you were tonight. I don't want to leave you in the dark. I want you to come down with me."

I'm surprised and pleased, but also concerned. "Thank you for that, but what happened with your father?"

"Get dressed and we'll talk before we go down."

I nod and we quickly pull on our clothes, sitting down on the end of the bed when we're done. Eric doesn't immediately speak and I cover his hand with mine. "What happened?"

He draws in a heavy breath laden with emotion I cannot read when he's facing forward, not looking at me. "He's alive," he says flatly, before he tilts his stare to me. "I'm not sure he meant for me to be right now, though."

My eyes go wide and I slide down in front of him on my knees. "What does that mean?"

"I refused to go to his room. I told him to meet me at another location. He sent a goon. It could have been an attempt to scare me, but he knows that wouldn't be an easy task to complete."

"What happened? Tell me everything."

"I left the guy he hired holding his balls in pain and came back here but this is war. I got ahead of all of this, Harper. We need to wear a condom until this is over. We can't bring a child into this."

My throat tightens. This is what he does. He lifts me up and tears me down, but logically he's right. I know he's right. "Yes. I agree."

"This won't be forever. I'm going after them. The way I should have a long time ago." Anger and bitterness vibrate through his words and I'm suddenly rocked by the secrets I've kept from him about his mother. Things I've already decided I have to tell him but not now, when those things could be triggers. *Not until this is over*, I think. I don't dare. So I focus on just how this ends.

"What comes next?" I ask, aware I won't approve, but I'm not sure it matters anymore. It feels like someone is going to die, and I don't want it to be Eric or my mother.

Chapter Sixty-Seven

Harper

"There are two Navy sayings I live by. No plan survives first contact. In other words, have a backup plan to your backup plan. We need to go downstairs and meet with Blake and his team and figure out what comes next." He stands and takes me with him.

"What's the other saying?"

"Don't run to your death. It's the one that kept me alive tonight."

It's those words that shoot a biting chill down my spine. This isn't just a family soap opera filled with drama anymore. It's combat and there are bullets coming at us from all different directions. I hug myself with the impact of that reality, and remain that way as we walk side by side, down the stairs.

Once we're in the living room, we locate Savage and Blake hanging out in front of the fireplace, flames licking at the glass cover, between them.

"Ho, ho, ho," Savage says, greeting us. "I came back bearing gifts. Or one gift." He motions to Blake. "I brought the hacker extraordinaire. I tried to put a bow on him, but he refused."

"He's not fucking joking," Blake grumbles. "He tried to put a bow on me because he's a crazy person."

Savage's phone vibrates with a message and he glances down at it. "Duty calls. Too bad it's not a woman." He eyes Blake, and they exchange a look I can't read, before Savage heads for the door.

I'd laugh if I wasn't still reeling a bit from my conversation with Eric upstairs. I'm on edge and it's all I can do to force myself to sit on the couch while Eric perches on one of the arms.

Blake surveys me with concern. "You okay?"

"He's okay," I say, motioning to Eric "and that's all that matters to me."

"That wasn't an answer," Blake comments, "so I'll take that as a 'no' and after what you've been through, I get it. I don't like it, but

I understand." He doesn't press me, and shifts his attention to Eric. "You really think your father wanted to have you killed tonight?"

"I've been thinking about that. My father isn't stupid enough to send someone that beneath my skill level to kill me. He knows who I am. He knows *what* I am." His cellphone rings and he pulls it from his pocket. "Speak of the devil himself." His lips press together. "My father." He declines the call.

"You're not going to take it?" I ask.

"Let him wonder what I'm doing right now."

"I don't understand what's happening," I say. "I agree with your assessment. He's too smart to be stupid, but if he wasn't trying to kill you, then why attack you tonight? It makes no sense. That action puts us on guard. It keeps me, and us, here. You'd think that they would want me back in Denver with you by my side. That's how they get to me and blame you."

"He doesn't believe I'll let you go back to Denver," he replies. "The playing field has shifted, and it's now New York."

"But how can he believe he can get to me or you here?" I challenge, holding out my hands. "We're well insulated."

"Baiting me," he replies. "Somehow, someway, he plans to bait me into doing something that backfires. He knows that emotional stress used to set off the savant in me, and it would become debilitating. I think he came here to trigger me which used to be a lot easier. If he made me breakdown, and need intervention, I'm an easy mark to blame for all their sins. Hell, he might have even hoped I'd kill the guy he sent after me."

Everything he just said, I believe. This assessment fits what I know of his father and how he operates, but I'm still left trying to pull a few pieces of the puzzle together.

"So at this point," I say, "do we believe Gigi called my father, because they're working together? Or not? Maybe Senior is negotiating with her now." I hold a hand up at Eric. "I'm not saying she's a good guy, but rather self-serving. She was cut out. She acted because of that, but she might even be back in the circle now.

Eric and Blake exchange a look, before Blake says, "I don't think we have the real picture yet which is why we need to talk about the unions."

"The unions?" I ask. "You think this is somehow connected to them?"

"I do," Blake says. "I have a bit of data that points me in that direction, I'll email to Eric, but nothing I could hang my hat on yet."

Union involvement makes sense, considering Isaac tried to link me to them.

"That said," Blake adds, "the union's involvement is not good news."

"No, it's not," Eric agrees grimly.

This jerks my gaze to Eric. "What does that mean? What do you two know that I don't know?"

"The unions are still connected to the mob," he explains. "You piss them off, you die. You steal from them, you suffer before you die. If the Kingstons got on their radar, they may want to shift that blame, and we're the targets. And it fits. Isaac was scared when he came to Harper's the other night. Really fucking scared. The kind of scared you are when you've fucked over the mob. And you don't fuck over the mob, or anyone powerful, without a plan to cover your ass."

"We were that plan," I say, following where he's leading.

Realization hits me and I can feel the color drain from my face. "The money in the account in my name. It could be mob money. It could look like I stole from the mob."

"We handled that," Blake assures me. "There's no connection to you."

"That we know of," I say. "We don't know much of anything, it seems to me, right now."

"They'll have to come through me to get to you," Eric says, "and that won't go well for them."

"That's plan A," I say. "What's plan B? Because as you said, no plan survives first contact."

"Plan B is to turn the mob's attention to everyone but us."

"How?" I ask.

"I could always sell them my stock."

It's not a bad idea, I think. "And plan C?"

"People die in plan C, sweetheart, so let's not talk about it."

"Okay then," I say. "We won't talk about it." I glance at the window. "I think the sun is coming up, we've been at this so long."

"My father needs to be frozen out," Eric replies. "Waiting makes him nervous, and a nervous man in trouble makes stupid decisions."

"And we're watching," Blake says, giving me a wink. "And we're badasses." He lifts his chin at Eric. "Not as badass as your savant right here, but badass enough. And yes. We all need sleep. Call me if you need me. I'll lock up on my way out." He heads for the door.

Eric pushes off the arm of the couch and helps me up. "Let's go shower and get some sleep."

I nod, and he slides his arm around me and that's how we walk up the stairs. We don't even talk. We stand under a hot shower together, each deep in thought, and for me, the exhaustion is to the bone. And yet, when we climb in Eric's bed, and he folds me close, my head on his chest, his hand on the back of my head, I can feel us both thinking.

For me, it's a replay of plan C.

The one where people die.

Chapter Sixty-Eight

Harper

I wake to the warm wicked wonderful scent of Eric and roll over to discover he's gone. I sit up and scan the room and he's nowhere in immediate view. A glance at the clock tells me it's only ten in the morning, which still means we slept maybe four hours, or I did. I can't help but wonder how long he's been up and what might have lured him out of bed.

Worried now, I throw away the blanket and push to my feet, and pad my way to the bathroom. Eric's not present, but I take a quick break to pee, and then use his brush to right my messy hair. I then dig around for an extra toothbrush. When I hit the jackpot in a cabinet, I put it to fast use. Hopefully the shopping bags Mia left me will have something I can wear, because for now, I'm stuck in Eric's shirt.

Exiting the bedroom, I walk to the railing overlooking the lower level, and find Eric alone, sitting at the island with a Rubik's cube in his hand and a coffee cup by his side. A fresh T-shirt and damp tendrils of hair on his brow tell me he's showered and dressed, and I slept through it all.

I watch him sip his coffee and then starts fiddling with the cube, turning it and turning it, his mind working to solve a puzzle. I'm not sure I should interrupt him and when I glance right and find all the bags Mia brought sitting on the floor, I decide to shower and dress first. I snatch them up and make two trips to the closet, that's how many they are.

Turns out Mia thought of everything, and I don't even have to dig through all the bags right now to find what I need. I find several outfits, all in the correct sizes which must mean Blake hacked my shopping records. There's no other way they'd know my size. I try on a few things and then head to the shower with shampoo and conditioner in hand.

Once I'm showered, I dress and snatch up the bags I know hold make-up and a flat iron. Twenty minutes later, I'm dressed in black pants and a black sweater, with my hair flat ironed, and my make-up lightly done. I spray on a jasmine perfume from FRESH I found in one of the bags. All of this must have been thousands of dollars, and I am sure Eric paid the bill. I'll pay him back because I will not allow him to feel I am with him for his money.

I rotate with the intent of heading downstairs only to find him standing in the doorway, holding a cup of coffee. "Hi," I say, and point to the cup. "Is that for me?"

"It is," he says, closing the space between us and offering it to me. "How'd you sleep?"

I sip the coffee, the cream sweet on my tongue. "Good until I found out you were missing. Did you sleep at all?"

"A few hours," he says, backing up and allowing me to enter the bedroom. I join him and we sit in a couple chairs by the window.

"That's not much," I say, not sure I believe him at all. As if confirming my point he says, "I don't need a lot of sleep."

I set the cup on the table between us, cross my arms in front of me, and study him, noting the dark stubble on his jaw. "Is it the savant thing? Was your mind obsessing with numbers?"

"Always numbers. You know that. Which reminds me." He pulls a phone from his pocket and offers it to me. "This is new, but it's not registered to you. I don't want you traced."

"Thank you. I hadn't even missed my phone. I guess that was my mind's way of surviving all this. I just cut it all off for a while." I set the phone next to my coffee. "Any news?"

"Nothing yet this morning." He reaches in his pocket and hands me a credit card. "For you."

I don't reach for it. "What is that?"

"Use it for whatever you need."

"I have my own money. I don't need yours."

"You don't have your purse, but Mia says you have a purse in the bags."

"I'm not taking the card."

"Take it, sweetheart."

"Eric," I breathe out. "Please no. As it is, I need to pay you back for all of the clothes."

"Stop," he says. "I know you aren't with me for my money, but if you're with me Harper, you have to accept that I have it, you have it. And I like it that way. Take the card. *Please.*"

I draw in a breath and accept the card, but his hand covers mine. "I like it this way."

"I'm not sure I do."

"You will. In time. Move in with me. Stay here in New York."

"My mother—"

"We'll get a second home in Colorado, and you can visit. You cannot live your life for your mother. I have never asked anyone to live with me. Come on, sweetheart. Say yes."

I say the first thing that comes to my mind. "I'm scared."

"Of me?"

"Of us. You could hurt me so badly, Eric."

"Then I'm scared, too."

I laugh. "You are not scared."

"I'm scared shitless of losing you. *Say yes.*"

"I can't believe I'm doing this. Okay. Yes."

He leans over and kisses me. "I'll get a mover to pick up your things."

"I think I need to find a job first."

"You already have a job. I talked to Grayson about it. Put the card in your pocket."

"You don't think it's weird for me to work for you."

"You'll work for Grayson, not me."

My new cellphone buzzes on the table and I frown. "I thought this wasn't connected to my old phone?"

"It's not," Eric says. "Check it."

I pick it and read the messages: *This is Blake. Put this number in your phone. Eric's father called your phone. Check your messages.*

My heart skips a beat. This can't be good. "It's Blake," I say, glancing at Eric. "And he said I have messages and should check them. I glance down quickly and dial in my phone number, to get to my mailbox, but my mind races. His father is such a bastard. He really is trying to trigger Eric. He's cruel and evil. I consider not telling him what's going on, and I decide that's wrong. We've had too many secrets between us.

"You need to read the message from Blake, Eric." I offer him my phone.

His expression darkens and he takes it from me, scans the message and then hands it back to me. "Play it."

"Eric."

"Play it, Harper. Yes, I know this is all about fucking with my head. It won't work. Play it."

I nod and punch in my retrieval code and then hit the speaker button. His father's voice fills the line: *Listen to me, Harper. I'm here in the city for you. If anything happens to you, your mother will never forgive me and I love her too much to see her suffer you as a loss. Eric is not a good person. He's dangerous and anything you think you know about what's going on, you don't. Come to my hotel. The Ritz, room 1101. Find a way. I'll be here for twenty-four hours. Come sooner than later. I worry for you every moment you're with him.* The call goes dead and my eyes are locked on Eric's impassive expression but a moment, a fleeting second, I see a stab of pain in his eye, before they turn to ice, a bitter winter ice.

Chapter Sixty-Nine

Harper

I don't speak, I don't even think about opening my mouth.

I hold my breath, waiting on Eric's reaction, and it's in silence that I can feel the vibrato of his anger, and while it's soundless, it screams in my head.

His eyes, blue ice and steel, fix on me. "What do you want to say to me?" he asks.

"That was the act of a desperate man. He's afraid of you. He's seen the tide shift. Now he's the bastard, and you are the king."

He doesn't reply. He simply stares at me. Seconds tick by and I look down at his watch—black leather, a black face, red hands—and I can almost hear the tick before my gaze lifts to Eric's again. He pushes to his feet and steps in front of me and I answer his silent request. I'm on my feet instantly.

We stand there, inches separating us, him towering over me, close, so very close, but he doesn't touch me and I burn for that connection. I have this sense that there's a question between us, and while I don't know what it is, I know his father willed it into existence. I press my hand to his chest, and breathe out with the heat of his body beneath my palm. I want to tell him I love him, and I think he needs to hear it, but there's one reason I don't. "I'd like to say something to you right now, but I won't let him have the moment or be a part of it."

Another second, or maybe it's three, pass us by and then finally he's touching me, his hand on the back of my head, his mouth crashing over mine; punishing me with his bittersweet, brutal kiss, laced with ten layers of emotions. And I know then that no matter how much he doesn't want his father's actions to hurt, the pain is a wild river running far and wide.

Desperate to drive away his pain, I don't just kiss him, I devour him, my hands sliding all over his body and in a haze of lust, we tug at each other's clothes. I end up against the wall, him pressing inside me, and in some far part of my mind, I can hear my gasp and pant. He lifts me off the ground, my legs wrapping his waist, and he thrusts into me. I lose myself in the wildness of it all, in the thick pump of his cock inside me, the ravenous way his gaze rakes over my naked breasts.

He devours me in every possible way, but he isn't alone. I'm right there with him, living the moment, feeling the passion. My hands cling to his arms.

Thrust.

Pump.

Fuck.

If we were making love earlier, we're fucking now, and it's what we both need.

It's wild, hard, and fast, and it's not long before my sex is spasming around his thick cock and he's quaking as he fills me, that condom he claimed we needed nowhere to be found. When it's over, he buries his face in my neck and holds me for long seconds, still standing, still holding me, perhaps a little too hard. Whatever demons he was trying to drive away are still alive and well and in this room with us.

Eric lifts me off the wall and walks us to the bathroom, sitting me on the sink and handing me a towel before he pulls out. He literally presses the towel between my legs and my cheeks heat. "We didn't use a condom."

"No, we did not." He strokes hair behind my ear. "Motivation to fix this so we don't end up with a kid destroyed by a fucked-up family." He steps away from me and walks to the other room.

My heart bleeds for him and I scoot off the counter and follow him. I find him by the chairs, already dressing. At this point I'm naked and I don't even care. I cross the room and grab my clothes, only to have Eric finish up and sit down. Now he's watching me dress, and a wave of silly shyness overcomes me. He was just inside me with his hands all over me.

When I'm finally pulled back together and would sit to get my boots back on, Eric catches my hand and walks me to him. "You're beautiful."

The compliment sets my belly to fluttering. "Thank you."

"I wasn't fair to you. I said no condom, then I changed my mind, and insisted we needed a condom, but just fucked you and didn't give two shits that we didn't have one. I'm sorry. After what you went through, I know that's not what you need from me."

Emotion wells in my chest and I press my hand to his face. "Thank you for saying that, but it's okay. It's not the right time and I really don't think I can get pregnant anyway."

"I think you can, which is why I shouldn't have done what I just did. A baby doesn't belong in a warzone and I want some time with you, Harper, without all the rest of this."

"Me, too," I say and my stomach grumbles. I laugh. "I clearly need to eat." I search his face. "You okay?"

"I'm good," he says, but his tone is hollow.

I'd say more, but I'm not sure that's what he needs from me right now. I back away from him and grab my boots, sitting down to pull them on. By the time I've laced them up, he's got a cube in his hand, and I know he's calming the numbers in his head. "Replay the message."

I'm not sure if that's a grand idea, but I don't fight him. I reach for my phone and hit the replay button:

Listen to me, Harper. I'm here in the city for you. If anything happens to you, your mother will never forgive me and I love her too much to see her suffer you as a loss. Eric is not a good person. He's dangerous and anything you think you know about what's going on, you don't. Come to my hotel. The Ritz, room 1501. Find a way. I'll be here for twenty-four hours. Come sooner than later. I worry for you every moment you're with him.

The message ends and I want to talk about how I reply to his father, but there's a tic in his jaw, and his grip on the cube is white knuckled. This is when his magic happens, when he plots big business and big personal matters. I sit back, and just choose to be present.

A full five minutes later he asks, "What did that message mean to you?"

It's a question I've been sitting here thinking about and my answer comes quickly. "He's desperate. Things aren't going his way so he's trying to turn the tide. He thinks turning me against you will be how he does that. He'll probably try to use saving my father's company to do so, but he'll fail. What does it mean to you?"

"Ten things," he says. "Twenty. Nothing."

I glance down at his inked arm, at one of the only words written out in letters, not numbers: *Honesty.* It resonates with me and this moment. It's everything he wants in his life, a contrast to the lies that represent the Kingstons, his father specifically.

It's how I understand what he's saying. "It's a lie. He might not even want to meet with me. It's a distraction."

Surprise flickers in his eyes, followed by approval. I've understood him correctly and this pleases him. "Yes," he confirms, "and he's putting a lot of effort into the lie. He's scared."

"Of what? The mob?"

He pushes to his feet and offers me his hand. "Let's get you some food."

I stand and say, "What's he scared of?"

"Me," he says. "He's scared of me."

Chapter Seventy

Eric

The past...

Only half an hour after my father pulls me out of that social worker's office, I'm at the Kingston mansion. He parks in the garage and calls over his shoulder. "Get out."

I want to punch the window. I want to scream. I want to hit him. I don't get out of the car. Meanwhile, my "father" is already walking into the house. I want to turn and leave. Instead, like the puppy dog I am tonight, I relent, and get out of the car. I have no choice. I have nowhere else to go. I close my hand around my mother's note, and glance around the garage, suddenly aware of the collection of three sports cars and several motorcycles, all more expensive, I'm certain, than the trailer I've called home these recent years.

I hate this place already.

"Get in here!" my father grumbles, leaning out into the garage door from inside the house.

I hate him.

He probably thinks I'm planning to steal one of the cars.

I don't want anything from this man.

I cross the garage and enter what turns out to be a stairwell. My father disappears out some door at the top as I start climbing. Once I'm at the door he'd departed, I exit to a foyer and he's not even there. A plump older woman wearing an apron greets me.

"Hello, Eric," she says. "I'm Delia, the housekeeper. I'll show you to your new room." There is grief in her—sadness for me. She knows about my mother.

"Thank you," I say tightly, wondering if the rest of the world feels pity for me. I don't want pity. My mother didn't accept it when she was sick. She'd be ashamed if I accepted it now.

Delia heads up a winding wood-railed stairwell, but she doesn't leave me behind like my father. She waits on me. When I join her, she gives me a warm look. "You can do this. I know you can."

I don't want to ask what she means. I see it in her eyes. She's telling me I can survive because I believe she did at one point as well. Survive what, I don't know, but she survived. I suddenly like this woman and I'm happy to know her.

At the top of the stairs, we turn right and enter a doorway that leads up again. It's a loft room, a place where I'm here, but not a part of this house. This works for me. I have to be here, but I don't want to be a part of this house.

"I'm going to get you some clothes," Delia says as I sit on the plaid-covered bed, with the low part of the ceiling above me. "Are you hungry?"

"No. I'm not."

"I'll bring you food anyway." She turns and leaves, a part of me smiles inside at her stubbornness that reminds me of my mother. I decide right then that my mother sent me Delia. Somehow, someway, from heaven above, my mother is watching me through her. And I believe in heaven, because I can't mathematically prove it doesn't exist, and because she believed in it. Right now, I need her to be there, not in the ground, dead and gone.

Once the door shuts, I pull out the note in my pocket and read a line and another and another: *No matter how hard it is for you, and I know you, it will be monstrously hard, turn your cheek to the insults and attacks. Don't let anyone make you fight. That's not control. Losing your temper because someone else can bait you is weak. You are not weak. Dream big and live big. Use your gifts, don't let them use you anymore than you let anyone bait you into throwing them away.*

Be the man I know you can be.

Not for me.

For you.

I look up and Delia is in the room, and I don't remember her entering. She's hugging me and my cheeks are wet, my heart cold. It's ice that is brittle and breaking.

Chapter Seventy-One

Harper

I've barely had time to pour a cup of fresh coffee when Blake arrives, bearing gifts. Fresh bagels. He hands them off to me and then motions to Eric. "Let's chat a minute."

Perhaps I should be worried about being left in the dark, but I'm starving and so tired that I just don't have it in me to fight about it. They walk into the living room and I choose an everything bagel, slather it with cream cheese, stuff my face.

I take a bite and my phone beeps where it's sitting next to me. Apparently, it's been set-up to alert me to the messages and I literally cringe at the idea of another message from Eric's father, though I do think it would speak of desperation, which is interesting. I punch in my code and find a message from my mother instead: *Your stepfather needs to speak to you. Please call him. I don't understand what's going on with you and why you would disrespect Jeff by ignoring him. Eric has been a horrible influence and I'm worried. Please call Jeff and let me know you've done so.*

I set the phone back down, my teeth grinding together. My jaw tenses. My mother is a puppet to a master, and it's gone no place good. And if he thinks using her to call me again looks any less desperate, he's wrong. I take a bite of my bagel, and for the first time in my life, I'm not sure I want to go back to Denver. I'm not even sure I want a place here and a place there. I feel like there is nothing but evil growing in that city, but right here, there is a seed of something special with Eric.

I'm glad I said yes to staying. I'm sad my father's creation is gone, but I can't save it, and as Eric said—I'm my father's legacy. And the best thing I can do right now, is create my own, and that starts by helping us shed the Kingston shackles which brings me to Eric's father. We have not even talked about me going to see him.

I glance up as Eric walks into the room, followed by Blake. "Why is your father here?"

"To protect what he believes is his," he says, stopping on the opposite side of the island.

"Your history says that you'll leave and wash your hands of them. Why come after you now? He even managed to get rid of me. There's more to it."

"I believe he's trying to draw the attention to himself. He's the distraction."

"It's my job to figure out what he's doing when he thinks we're looking the other direction."

"Well then we need to make him think this is working," I say. "If I go to see him—"

"No," Eric says firmly. "You will not go to him." His tone is absolute, a wall I intend to bust through to make him see reason. "If I go to him, he'll see weakness. He'll feel empowered and act. I have to do this," I say. "I'm going to do this."

"That's not happening," Eric replies. "The end. No more conversation."

"Eric—"

"No."

I glance at Blake. "Blake," I plead.

He just points at Eric. "What he says."

"He's desperate. My mother left me a message ordering me to call your father, Eric. I'll call her back and convince him I really have turned against you."

Eric rounds the counter and pulls me hard against him. "If he hurts you, I go to plan C and then you're gone and I'm in jail the rest of my life. Is that what you want?"

"No. But why—"

"Because I said. And because I know how hardheaded you are, so that won't be enough for you, I need you to trust me, *really* trust me. I'm protecting you."

"I'm protecting you," I counter.

"*I* protect *you*," he counters. "That's just how it is."

I laugh. "Really? Did you just take that caveman attitude with me?"

Blake whistles. "I'll just get a bagel and pretend Eric's not about to get his ass kicked by a hundred-and-ten-pound female."

Eric releases me and faces the island, pressing his hands to the granite, and speaking to Blake. "Is your wife as bullheaded?"

"Worse," he says, finishing off a bite of a bagel. "And she's an ex-FBI agent who carries a gun."

"I'd like to meet your wife, Blake. Maybe she can give me tips."

"We walked right into that one," Blake comments, disapproval in his tone.

"*I* need to buy us time," I say. "He gave me twenty-four hours to make contact, and nearly eight are gone. He'll have a move planned when I don't show up."

"He probably has a move already in play and it won't take twenty-four hours for us to find that out," Eric says, pushing off the counter and facing me again. "You haven't called him. You haven't called your mother. That tells him that you're talking to me, not them."

"Then I need to call him now."

"What you need to do is listen to me."

"Okay. Then I'm listening. What are you going to do, right now, to distract him?"

"What he doesn't expect. What I never give him."

"Which is what?"

"Me. I told you, Harper, this is all about me. He wants me."

"You said he fears you."

"Which means he needs to control me. He's attempting to do so through you. He needs to know if he goes after you, he gets me." He pulls his phone from his pocket and punches in a number. A moment later I hear, "It's Eric. Let's meet."

My heart zips and zags. *Is that his father?*

"Your hotel room," Eric says. "Yes, coffee in your hotel room works." Eric disconnects. "I'm going over now."

I catch his arm. "The last time you went you were attacked."

"That was at night in an alleyway. I'm going to walk in there, in my Kingston Motors shirt and have a civil conversation with the man. Like fathers and sons should do."

It's only then that I realize he's changed into a Kingston shirt, I'm shocked he even owns. "Not this father and son."

"Today we do."

He turns away and starts to walk.

I dash around him and plant myself in front of him, hands flattening on the hard muscles of his chest. "So you can walk into a trap and end up dead? I forbid it. I'm not going to lose you. I just got you back."

He drags me to him, that spicy dominant scent of him teasing my nostrils and wrapping me in the almighty force that is this man. "Princess, you're not getting rid of me today, or this easily. If you run, I'll run after you."

"You can't do that if you're dead. I forbid you to do this."

"If you want to forbid me, do it while you're naked. I'll listen a whole lot better."

"Fine. Yes. Let's get naked. Am I supposed to complain about getting naked with you?"

"No. You most definitely are not."

"Then let's get naked."

"Not now, sweetheart. When I get back." He kisses me, his hand on my head, a deep, passionate kiss, a promise on his tongue that lands on mine. He'll come back. He's not leaving me. With those promises, he parts our lips, and for long moments, seems to just breathe me in before he releases me and turns away. He starts for the door, and this time there's no stopping him. His strides are too long and determined.

When I turn to Blake to appeal for help, he's on his feet. "Savage is waiting on us downstairs. We're going with him. We've got his back and Smith has yours. He's in the living room." And then he's walking away, and disappearing around the corner. There's no stopping Eric now. He's gone and it feels bad. It feels like he's not coming back.

Chapter Seventy-Two

Eric

The past...

It's one day until I turn twenty-one, mere days before Christmas, and three weeks before I join Isaac in law school, and I know he's hating that shit. Younger brother tested out of high school, fast-tracked through college, to jump right into law school, years before he can escape my term. Then again, he hates my job at Kingston, my role that grows while he's off turning pages in a book.

Despite my preference to stay at my own place for Christmas and just eat a damn frozen pizza, my father has demanded my presence, so I'm here. I enter the house and I can hear Isaac and my father speaking in muffled tones, too muffled for me to make out the words. And I don't want to make them out. The best days of my life are those where Isaac is gone and so the fuck am I. Every time he comes home, we have issues.

The voices seem to be coming from the den and that's exactly why I head toward the kitchen where Delia will be making the mac n cheese that I love. I make it a few more steps when I hear, "Eric."

At the sound of my father's voice to the left, I halt, and for a moment I fight the wave of darkness inside me. These are the days I hate him all over again. These are the days that I forget our working relationship. I forget our bloodline. I remember the man who told me to "get over" my mother dying.

"Son," he bites out, and I don't like that word. Not most days. Never when Isaac is here. Never on a holiday when my mom is gone.

Nevertheless, I rotate to find him standing in the doorway of his den, only slightly underdressed for a day of fucking with our heads. His dark hair sprinkled with gray, his jaw shaved clean, because that is all that's acceptable. He's in a dinner jacket, a button-down shirt starched as crisply as his spine is stiff, and of course, dress pants.

My jaw is not shaved clean. It's sporting a three-day stubble I embrace. And I'm damn sure dressed like my mother had us dress for every holiday: comfortable in jeans and a blue sweater, because comfortable, she'd said, is how a holiday is supposed to feel.

"Join us for a smoke and the whiskey your brother brought me," my father orders.

I brought him nothing. I figure the games he'll play today are his gift. I start walking in his direction and he disappears into the room.

In too few steps, I enter the den, which by most standards is a welcoming room with walls of books so high a ladder rolls across one wall. Brown leather couches and chairs rest on top of a heavy oriental rug that decorates a dark wooden floor.

Isaac's standing by the fireplace, a smoke in one hand, a glass in the other, and holy fuck, he's dressed like my father. A little clone boy. Clown boy is more like it.

"Celebrating my national chess win," he greets me like it's not been months since we last saw each other, "by kicking father's ass in chess."

"Smoke, son?" my father asks, and the way he emphasizes "son" isn't to ensure Isaac knows that's what I am. It's to piss him off and it works. His eyes glint hard steel.

"I'll pass on the smoke," I say, walking to the couch that faces Isaac and sitting down.

"Well, have a glass of this fine whiskey your brother brought me. I think it's about ten grand?" He eyes Isaac.

"Fifteen," Isaac says, his chin firm.

"I'll take a glass," I reply and that's the thing about the holidays. I feel my mother's loss. I feel the loss of who I once was. I didn't read my mother's letter for a reason this morning. I didn't want to contain myself. And I don't obviously as I add, "I always like the taste of wasted money, just to make sure I don't forget how smooth stupidity can go down."

"Fucker," Isaac snaps, and motions to the small table by the couches with a chess game setup. "Play. It's better than our conversation."

"Sure you want to do that?" our father asks. "He's a genius."

"I'm a national champion," Isaac bites out. "And no idiot."

Apparently, he is.

Most definitely he is.

My lips quirk and I sit down at the table. My father hands me the expensive whiskey, amusement in his eyes. I down it and set the glass aside. Isaac joins me and sets his smoke in an ashtray, his glass by his side. "You start us off," he says.

No harm in starting things out. I do it. I make my move. He makes his and so it continues, and with every move, I back him into a corner. With every move, I end the game in my favor. When it's done, he stands up and so do I, and he's postured to beat my ass. I give him a deadpan stare. He glowers and then turns away, storming from the room.

My father steps in front of me. "You taught him something important today. What lesson, Eric?"

"Not to underestimate your opponent."

"No. That's not the lesson."

He turns and walks away.

Chapter Seventy-Three

Eric

T he minute I exit the building, Savage pushes off the building and falls into step with me. "I'm your Huckleberry, you badass got your back Huckleberry. Blake's on live feed."

"Where's Adam?"

"Oh fuck," he growls. "You SEALs. You think no one is as good as you are. He's still in Denver. He doesn't trust anyone else to handle what you need handled there. You want me to call another one of our fin-wearing, belly-flopping guys to be back up right now, or do you think you can live with me?"

I arch a brow in his direction.

He arches a brow in mine.

"I simply wanted to know if Adam still had eyes on Isaac."

"Oh that," he says dryly. "Yes. He does and he has his lifejacket by his side with his little arm tubes, too, just in case he has to dive in and save someone."

I surprise myself and laugh. "You're a piece of work, Savage."

"And I don't even need fins to swim." He drops that joke and turns serious. "Why are we walking?"

"I planned to clear my head and think, but you keep talking."

"Right. What are we doing?"

"Apparently not clearing our heads and thinking. I've decided it's time for me and my father to have a heart-to-heart."

"I heard that shit. I guess my job is to make sure neither of you kill each other."

I don't comment. He doesn't know my history with my father or he'd know how true that possibility is. Lord only knows, I wish the fuck it wasn't what it is. I wish like hell I hadn't been that man's little bitch, at one point in my life, but I have been. For years, he knew how to work me, how to rattle me, and that's what he wants now. To break me and set me up.

He'll need an army, a whole lot of ammunition, and luck, to do it.

We cut a corner, and Savage grimaces. "It's cold as a motherfucker out here and you don't have a coat on."

He's right. It's cold, but my shirt sends a conflicting message to my father, one of loyalty to the brand, that may or may not include him. I want to be sure he sees it the minute I walk in the door.

Savage's phone rings. He grabs it and answers. "Savage here. What the fuck do you want?" He eyes me and then listens again before he hangs up. "Adam says that Isaac hasn't exited his house since you left Denver. It's reading off to him. He's going in for a closer look."

It's not off to me. Isaac had a fight with his big bad boss, and father, and now he's sulking like the little bitch he is and always has been. He's probably been told to stand down and wait on daddy to call him with the "all clear" because I'm dealt with. I'm about to be dealt with, all right. I don't voice any of this to Savage. I'll let Adam confirm Isaac's tucked in bed or washed up in a bottle.

A block from the hotel, I stop at the entrance to a coffee shop. "I'll be right back." I don't wait on Savage to reply.

I walk inside, order two hazelnut lattes, just the way my father likes them, one for him, one for me to hold. When the coffees are in hand, I exit the coffee shop and hand one of them to Savage. "You can drink what you want of that one, but I need the cup at the hotel."

"You're taking your father coffee?"

"Of course. I want this to be a cordial meeting." I think of the lesson my father was speaking of when we ended that chess game between me and Isaac right before I started law school: *Never fight a war as the underdog.* I've let myself act like the underdog with him. I never was.

Which is why I focus on the lesson my mother taught me: *no regrets.*

I pull my phone from my pocket and dial Harper. "Eric!" she exclaims, answering on the first ring. "What's happening?"

I almost smile with her excitement and I would if I wasn't headed to see my father. When the fuck was anyone ever this damn glad to hear my voice. "Nothing yet, but you remember you said you had something to say to me earlier?"

She's quiet a moment. "Yes?" she asks, a tremble in her voice.

"I fucking love you, woman. Time isn't going to change that and I would have rather said this in person. I'll tell you again when I see you in person."

"I love you, too, but why are you saying this now? What are you going to do? Forget whatever it is. Come back, and tell me you love me in person."

"I'll be back soon. Be naked when I get there."

Savage looks at me. "Oh shit. No one confesses love on the phone unless they're about to do something stupid. You're going to choke him out."

He smiles.

I don't.

Chapter Seventy-Four

Harper

"What are you about to do, Eric?" I whisper, adrenaline shooting through me.

I set my phone down and rush to the living room to find Smith watching TV. Even before he sees me, he's on his feet facing me.

"Eric called me right before he went in to meet his father. I think he's going to do something stupid."

"Savage is with him."

"Will Savage stop him from doing whatever craziness he's planning?"

"Savage is the kind of guy who'll take over."

"Take over? Eric won't let him take over."

"He'll take over," he repeats.

"No. He won't. Eric won't let that happen."

"I know Savage acts like a goofball, but he's a literal surgeon, and yes, I said surgeon with a medical license. He's also a former mercenary. He'll take care of him. Eric will be back without an irreparable blemish."

"Irreparable blemish? Are you trying to make me feel better?"

"I don't make promises I can't keep. It's a thing here at Walker. We tell things as they are. We're honest. I can't tell you that they won't end up banged up, but I can assure you they'll end up safe, in one piece, and without any damage that they can't come back from."

"You're killing me."

"No," he says. "I'm protecting you, like Savage is protecting Eric."

"You remember he's a genius, right?"

"Quite clearly."

"He can outsmart Savage," I counter.

"First, surgeon and mercenary. Remember? And why would he want to outsmart him? Savage isn't a man who needs things sugarcoated."

"You're not making this better."

"They'll be back soon."

Frustrated and feeling helpless, I re-enter the kitchen, just in time to find my cellphone ringing. I rush forward, grab it and find my mother calling. Apparently not only are my calls forwarded to this phone, Blake even set-up my phonebook. I hit decline. I can't take it. I'll confront her over my attack, and I have no plan after that. I don't know if we want to tell her about all of this or not. I need to talk to Eric first. I stand up and start to pace.

Another ten minutes pass, and my phone rings again, and this time it's Gigi. I don't like the timing, and how close it is to when my mother tried to reach me. I don't want to take the call at all. I feel like this woman set me up to be murdered, but I also fear there might be something she says, that if ignored, could become even more dangerous.

I hit the answer button. "Hi, Gigi."

"What is going on?"

"You tell me. Because it sure seems like you know more than I do about everything."

"I know nothing."

"Why is Eric's father here in New York City?" I demand.

"He's—what?"

"Don't tell me you don't know."

"I didn't know. Honey, I *didn't know.*"

"He knows you used me to get Eric to Denver."

"If he went fishing, you can't give him the fish. Keep your mouth shut."

And yet, Adam says she called him and I decide to roll the dice and see where I land. "Someone tried to kill me last night. Eric saved me."

"What? No. Who? Why? Oh my God." She sounds panicked. "Oh God."

"Gigi?" I say urgently, afraid she's having another heart attack.

"He did know. I'm sorry, I lied. I told him after I sent you to get Eric because—it doesn't matter. He knew Eric was coming but—Oh God."

"Gigi, talk to me. Are you okay?"

"I didn't want to see either of you hurt. I don't want that."

She's breathing heavily. Really heavily. "Gigi, I want you to call an ambulance or I will for you."

"No. No. I'm fine. I need to call my son right now. Don't call a damn ambulance. I'm not the one who's about to need medical help." On that feisty note, she hangs up.

I breathe out. What just happened? Who is on whose side?

I could make all kinds of assumptions from her statements, but right now, I need to do something more productive. I need to help. I consider calling Eric again, but my conversation with Gigi will just piss him off more, and he might really kill someone.

I dial Blake. "Hiya, Harper," Blake says. "You got something for me?"

"Gigi called. I told her I was attacked, and she panicked and said that yes, she told Eric's father that I helped get him to Denver. She was upset and said no one was supposed to get hurt. She hung up after saying she needed to call her son. I'm not sure if I just made things better or worse."

"I think anything you do to create a reaction; we can observe is good. I'll call Adam."

"And Eric? Is he okay?"

"He just went into the hotel. He even stopped and got coffee for his father. I don't think you have to worry. He's not going to kill him with coffee."

"I'm so confused right now."

"He has a plan. Trust him, like he asked you to. I'll text you when he's on his way back to you. Gotta run." He disconnects.

And now all I can do is wait and pray for the best. And lose my mind, one second at a time.

Chapter Seventy-Five

Eric

Savage sips from the coffee I've just handed him. "Your father likes a hazelnut latte," he observes. "I would have taken him for more of a black coffee, no cream or sugar kind of guy."

"My father's the kind of man that sweetens his drink and pisses in yours."

"Ah. Gotcha." He downs another swig. "I'm sweetened up and caffeinated. Ready to fight. What's the plan? Kill him? Punish him? Tickle his feet until he pees himself? Or just piss in his coffee? I can do that right now, if you like?"

"I'd get the honors on all of the above," I say, offering nothing more. My plans are my plans. I don't need anyone else inside them, crawling around and fucking them up. I start walking toward my father's hotel. Savage falls into step with me. "Decision yet to be made, aye?" he asks. "I get it. He's your father, but he sent a hitman to kill you."

He knows as well as I do that that man wasn't sent to kill me, but rather Harper. He's looking for answers that I'm not going to give him. "My father has a funny way of showing love."

"Love by way of a hitman. Your family is more fucked up than mine."

He hits about ten nerves with his "love by way of a hitman" comment that shoots me right back into the past. Into the day my mother killed herself, and as far as I'm concerned, my father was her hitman. What an appropriate time for me to walk into my father's hotel and head toward the elevator to pay him a "loving" visit.

My cellphone buzzes with a text message and I grab my phone and glance down at a message from Harper. *I talked to Gigi. Please call me.*

I stop walking and eye Savage. "Give me a minute." I step to a vacant seating area to our right and dial Harper.

"What about Gigi?" I say when she answers.

"She called and I told Blake about it but after pacing about, I think you need to know before you talk to your father."

"Tell me."

"She had a panic attack when I told her I was attacked. Eric, she wasn't acting and she didn't know your father was here. She hung up with me to call him and she was pissed. I'm not misreading this."

"She set us up."

"I'm going to use your own words on you right now. What if she didn't? I know you hate her, but being a bitch and arranging a murder are two wildly different things. What if she was set-up, too?"

"You're suggesting my father used her to get me to Denver, and she played an unwitting role in all of this." It's not a question. I'm simply letting her thoughts calculate in my mind.

"Isn't he the only person that could use her that way? Which means he has to be the mastermind behind the attempt on my life."

It's logical with one flaw, the one that has my father desperate enough to bury the problem I believe Isaac created. That's why he was at the warehouse before he got on a plane and came here, but nowhere in that equation, or any equation I've created, does my father use Gigi to get me to Denver. Gigi is playing Harper and that's not something she will want to hear.

"This changes nothing," I say. "My plan is still my plan."

"And that plan is what? Because I feel like you called me and told me you loved because—"

"Because *I do*, Harper. No other reason."

"Gigi set me on edge. I have a bad feeling in my gut right now that I didn't a few minutes ago."

"I'll be back soon," I say and disconnect. The call from Gigi changes nothing. In fact, it solidifies my plan.

I rejoin Savage and motion to the elevator. Once we're inside, I eye him, aware that I don't have the room number or a key to get upstairs, but he does. Or he better. I pay his team too damn much to have them be anything but prepared.

"Eleven," Savage says, handing me a keycard. I accept it, put it to use, and pocket it, facing forward.

Savage doesn't ask any further questions. I don't offer any answers or commentary. We arrive at our destination and I cut him a look. "Stay by the elevator."

"You sure about that?"

"Yes." I motion to his cup. "I need that coffee."

He takes another drink and hands it to me. The doors open and I exit the car and start walking. The hallway is long and my mind counts out the steps without my permission. Ten. Twenty. Fifty-two and I'm at the door. My hands are full. It's a good reason to pause. I went years without seeing my father. I could do without seeing him now.

I use my foot and knock on the door.

My father answers in sixty-one seconds to be exact. "About time," he grumbles, appearing in the doorway, his gaze downward turned. "I ordered an hour—"

He looks up and stops speaking, shock sliding over his face. "Eric."

We stare at each other, two bulls in a stand-off over the same red flag and that flag is power. In some way, shape, or form, a play for power has always been between us. Not love. Not friendship. Not father and son. Power. It's always been about power.

Today that power is mine and we both know it.

It was mine the minute I decided to change my routine. The minute I showed up here and faced him instead of walking away.

"You wanted my attention," I say. "You have it and I even brought coffee." I offer him the heavier cup, the one Savage hasn't been drinking from, *his* cup.

He says nothing, but he accepts the coffee and steps back, offering me entry into his suite. I move forward into an elegant living area, with a desk to the right and a television to the left. He motions to a door at the back of the room to the left. I've been in enough Ritz Carlton hotels to know that will be an office where he wants to sit behind a desk and play the power card.

I sit down in a chair, letting him know this is how we're doing this: my way, not his.

He grimaces. "Okay, son. Have it your way." He claims the couch, his spine stiff, his tone formal, but he's dressed in his casual gear which for him is a crisp white button-down shirt and dress pants, with his thick head of hair neatly styled.

He glances at the cup in his hand, smirks as if this is a peace offering and he's won a war, before he takes a drink. "Now what?" he challenges but his eyes go wide and he trembles, and then he's grabbing his throat, gasping. He's choking.

Chapter Seventy-Six

Eric

The coffee cup falls from my father's hand and crashes to the floor, splattering with the impact, liquid droplets hitting my face and arms. Choking sounds come from my father's throat, fear etched in the eyes of a man that feels no emotion. A desperate plea for help swims in the depths of that fear, directed at me. I wait to feel remorse. I wait to feel panic over the potential loss of my last living parent. I feel none of those things. In fact, I have several seconds in which I contemplate letting the bastard die and burn in hell.

Part of me wants to squat in front of him and say, *Everyone dies. Get over it.* But somehow Harper flashes into my mind. Harper looking up at me with love in her eyes, with expectations that I be better than my father.

He falls to his side and starts to jerk, his vomiting a sure sign that he's been poisoned. There isn't much I can do for him here and now, but besides get him help and make sure his throat remains clear. My jaw clenches and I set my cup down on the table, standing up, and charging to the door. I yank it open to find Savage exactly where I expect him to be, by the door, despite me telling him to stay at the elevator. "Get an ambulance here now," I order, knowing his team will bypass the millions of questions I don't want to answer right now.

Savage curses and I'm already turning away when I hear him directing his team to order emergency services. I race back inside the room and Savage catches the door as my father rolls off the couch onto the floor, crashing between the couch and the coffee table. I walk to the table, move it and flatten him on his back, kneeling by him to rotate him to his side, pressing his shoulders to the couch and pulling his leg forward. "An ambulance is on the way," I tell him, not so much to comfort him, but out of obligation. He damn sure didn't comfort my mother through her cancer.

I've done what I can do for the man. He's now in a recovery position, a position that prevents him from choking to death, despite all his groaning and panting. Savage kneels beside me and eyes the coffee cup on the floor. "Do I need to get rid of that?" he says, obviously as aware as I am that poison is the culprit in my father's ailment.

"Genius doesn't mean stupid," I snap. "No, you don't fucking need to get rid of the coffee cup."

"Fill me in here, man, and do it like I'm stupid. I'm in this room with you trying to cover your ass."

I settle back on my haunches, my hand on my knee. "He took a drink. He started choking."

"Like I said. Do I need to get rid of the fucking coffee cup?"

"And like *I* said. No, you don't need to get rid of the fucking coffee cup. He started choking in ten seconds."

He frowns, clearly seeing that as a timeline that doesn't connect.

"What you need to do," I add, "is to think beyond the obvious."

His eyes narrow on me and he seems to get the message. He reaches for his weapon and stands up as I do the same, reaching to draw my Glock from the back of my jeans where I put it. I motion Savage to the right, down a hallway to what I believe is the bedroom. I go around the couch to the office, where I find a pot of coffee on the desk, as well as condiments and a half-eaten pastry. I pull my phone from my pocket and shoot photos to prove these items exist.

I don't linger to search the office. Instead, I exit the doorway and cross the living room, traveling down another hallway. There's a bathroom to the right that's clear and untouched. A few feet down, there's a dining room with a conference table as the centerpiece. I walk past it into a small kitchen and check for evidence. I open the refrigerator, but it's empty. I rotate and retrace my steps, returning to the living room as Savage returns from his portion of the search as well, and gives me an "all clear" motion.

The doorbell to the suite rings. Savage and I both put away our weapons and Savage, standing just beside the door, doesn't wait for approval he wouldn't need. He opens the door.

The EMT crew—two men in uniform—rushes in, asking for details even as they kneel beside my father and start administering rescue services. Blake walks in moments after I finish delivering the update. "Join me in the hallway," he orders softly.

I nod but I look at Savage and make sure that Blake can hear. "Office. Pastry. Coffee. Recent. I need to make sure that doesn't disappear."

Savage nods and Blake and I walk to the hallway, stepping to the side of the doorway. "We have about sixty seconds until law enforcement gets here," Blake says, "Talk to me."

"He was poisoned and the only reason he's alive is because I decided to show up to talk. He's alive because I called the EMTs."

"Did you poison him?"

"If I decided to kill my father, I wouldn't have second thoughts and call the EMTs. I also wouldn't make myself the prime fucking suspect."

His lips thin. "That's not a fucking answer. Give me a direct fucking answer."

"I didn't kill my father."

"Did you try?"

"Had I tried, he'd be dead, Blake. I brought coffee. He drank his own before I got here, along with eating a portion of a pastry, but I can promise you he's not going to test positive for poison. I only know what I witnessed."

He narrows his eyes on me, and it's clear that he thinks I just confessed to setting this up. I open my mouth to respond to the assumption, but it's right then that a rush of activity erupts at the end of the hallway, shouts lifting in the air. Blake and I both eye the force of three officers rushing our way and Blake lowers his voice. "This conversation isn't over."

"The one you're having with yourself or the one you're having with me?"

He glowers and we both turn to greet the officers. It's chaos from there, and I answer a few questions before the EMTs exit with my father on a stretcher. "I'll be at the hospital," I tell the lead officer. "You can ask me anything you want there." I don't wait for his approval. I follow the EMT and confirm that my father is indeed stable. Had he been alone at the time of his incident, he'd be dead.

I follow the emergency team into the elevator, standing next to my father, but I don't look at him. I text Davis, not because he's an attorney but because I want to head off bad press for the company and Grayson: *Need you. Meet me at the St. Francis Hospital ASAP. More soon. Can't talk.*

Oh fuck, is his reply. *Need you? What the hell is happening? On my way. Call me if you can before I get there.*

I inhale and stuff my phone back into my pocket, my gaze falling on my father's pale face and I once again wait to feel anything but hate for this man, but I don't. I hate him. If he dies, I won't grieve, but he won't die. Because I, the bastard son that I am, saved his fucking life, by calling for help. But if I find out that he's the one behind the attempt on Harper's life, he'll wake up and wish he'd died today.

Chapter Seventy-Seven

Eric

I ride down in the elevator with my father and two EMTs, my mind calculating the who, what, when and why of what just happened in that hotel room. All the while my father's heartbeat on the monitor pounds a steady beat. The risk for him will come down to the type of poison, some of which can cause rapid and fatal organ damage.

Nothing about my father being a target makes sense.

Who benefits from him dying?

Me because I hate him.

Isaac because he gets rich.

Harper's mother also gets rich.

I swing back to Isaac, and how damn scared he came off when he came to Harper's house. I think he needed a fall guy. Harper and I didn't work out.

Isaac did this, but that means he hired a professional.

The elevator doors open and I eye the EMT to my left. "I'll meet you at the hospital," I say, not about to ride with them. To do so would seem insincere, an actor in a movie of lies, and right now, the last thing I need is more lies.

Nevertheless, I follow the EMT crew, exiting the building behind them, but the minute I spot the press, I cut into the crowd, dialing Davis as I start the short walk to the hospital. "Where are you now?"

"I just got to the hospital," he says. "Grayson said you needed us."

"Exit the front of the hospital and go right. Walk a block down." I eye the corner. "There's a Starbucks." I disconnect. I don't care about making a showing at the hospital. I care about getting to Harper before her mother or the press gets to her, which means I need Davis to do damage control.

I finish the short walk and Davis is arriving at the coffee shop at the same time I am. He meets me at the right side of the entrance and buries his hands in the leather jacket he's wearing over a T-shirt and jeans. "What the hell is going on?"

"I went to see my father. He took a drink from the coffee I brought him and started choking. I called an ambulance."

"Holy fuck, man." He scrubs his jaw. "Does Grayson know?"

"No. Go to him. Help him do damage control. Keep this away from Bennett Enterprises."

"That's impossible. You're heading up a bid on an NFL team, Eric. You're high profile right now."

"Just do it. Make it happen."

"You need an attorney, a criminal attorney. Call the guy Grayson was going to use for that big scandal he was in last year."

"*I'm* an attorney," I remind him. "And there's nothing they can charge me with. I'm not going down."

"You're that sure?" he queries.

"Talk to Grayson. Do what you need to do to distance me from the company."

"I thought you weren't going down?"

"Don't push me, asshole."

"You're negotiating the NFL deal right now."

"You just said that. Move on. I saved my father's life. Paint a picture in our favor."

My cellphone rings and I grab it from my pocket and curse. "Fuck. It's Grayson." I answer the line to hear, "I called Reese Summer, that powerhouse attorney—"

I don't ask how he knows what's going on. I know. The Walker crew knows him. They do work for our firm, too. They called him. "Eric?" he presses, when I don't immediately reply.

"I don't need a powerhouse attorney," I say. "That makes it look like I *need* a powerhouse attorney. I'm an attorney. You need to stay away from this," I order, and *it is* an order. "Davis is coming to you. He'll help you do damage control." I hang up and focus on Davis. "Go get him under control."

"He tried to hire that same attorney I suggested, right?" He doesn't wait for an answer. "You do need a powerhouse attorney. You handed your father a drink and he all but keeled over. He might die."

"Go to Grayson," I order.

"I'm going, but we're going to talk about this." He steps forward and pats my shoulder. "Because we're friends and, genius or not, you're being stupid. You're fucked right now, man." With that positive reinforcement, he walks away and Savage, who was obviously following me, steps to my side.

"I have good and bad news," he announces.

"The bad news is your team told Grayson what was going on. What the fuck?"

His lips thin. "I'll get back to you on that. Right now. *This*. We have security footage of a man entering your father's room to deliver the coffee," he says. "No one at the hotel recognizes him. That's good news. It lends to a suspect other than you."

"What's the bad news?"

"He resembles a man we picked up on camera loitering around your building last night."

Suddenly my father's poisoning isn't a singular event. "There's a hitlist," I say, "and I just happened to be there two times, at the right time, to save Harper and my father."

"I'm thinking the same," Savage agrees.

"Harper's on the list," I say and I start running.

Chapter Seventy-Eight

Harper

Antsy and going crazy, I search Eric's cabinets and find hot chocolate, which I make. I actually really love that he has hot chocolate, and I try to imagine him at the grocery store making the decision to buy that hot chocolate. It's such a humanizing thing to buy and I feel like often people see the genius not the man, and it's destructive in ways I don't think they understand.

I boil some water in the microwave and make the sweet beverage. I even find marshmallows. He's a kid in a man's body and I love it. I really want to know this side of Eric. I sit down at the island in the kitchen with the bag of marshmallows, the cup and drop a handful inside. I snatch a pad of paper and pen I find in a drawer and I start writing the numbers and letters from that sequence we'd been given by the man by my house. I write them over and over, and they feel familiar. I eat half the bag of marshmallows trying to find the memory in my mind. There's a memory. There are also enough marshmallows in my stomach to perhaps make it explode.

I stand up and start to pace, and when I spy a Rubik's cubes on a shelf I grab it, and start spinning it. What do those numbers and letters mean? What do we deal with all of the time? Parts. VIN numbers. Bank accounts. Badges. I stop walking. A badge. Could it be a badge number? I don't have my computer, but I saw one in the office. I hurry inside and locate the MacBook on top of the wooden desk. I power it up and use my access codes to enter the Kingston system. I pull up the employee badge numbers and type in our mystery sequence of letters and numbers. Nothing. I sigh. Blake checked this of course, anyway. I wasn't going to find anything, but something about this premise of a badge number feels right in my mind.

Frustrated, I decided maybe I'll just ask Smith if he has any ideas. I'm close to something. It's worth a try and I have to do something to keep my mind off the fact that Eric is with his father. If I let myself get lost in that thought, I'd picture his father dead right now.

I enter the living room and oddly Smith isn't here. "Smith!" I call out but there's no reply.

Nervous now, adrenaline pumping through me I walk toward the front door, and wonder if he's in the hallway. I open the door and no. He's not here either. A chill runs down my spine. Something feels wrong about this. Something feels very wrong. I shut the door and lean against it. I lock the door, my instincts shouting at me. I dial Eric, but he doesn't answer. Smith had to go to the bathroom. He took a bathroom break. I race about and check that theory and it's a no-go.

I dial Blake, and he doesn't answer. I don't have Smith's number.

On alert now, in a big way, I grab the coat Mia bought me and put it on. My gut is telling me to run and I don't know why. If I open this door and he's still not out there, I'm listening to it. I'm leaving. I'll hide. I'll go to the Walker offices. I google their address and find the walk will be short. I have a plan. I'm probably being paranoid, but I can't seem to fight this need to escape.

I open the door again and this time I'm not alone.

Chapter Seventy-Nine

Harper

"Eric," I breathe out and any relief I feel is momentary as I take in the hard lines and shadows of his face, and the blistering anger in his eyes. "What's happening?"

"Where the hell do you think you're going?" He backs me into the apartment and shuts the door.

He's angry, really angry, which makes me angry. "Smith was missing. You weren't answering your phone."

"Smith was at the end of the hall talking to me. I didn't answer because I was already here."

"And I knew that how? What is going on?"

"Where were you going?"

"Somewhere safe."

"Because you're not safe here with me?"

I blanch. "What? What are you talking about?"

His lashes lower, torment crossing his handsome features.

"Eric, talk to me."

"I need you to stay where I tell you to stay. Do you understand?"

I'd normally bristle at such a possessive demand, but I can all but feel the emotion vibrating off of him. "Is he dead?"

He pulls back to look at me, searching my gaze, his stare probing to the point that I swear he can see straight to my soul, and I hope, I pray, that he finds himself there. Because he is. He's a part of me, all of me, in ways I didn't know were possible.

The powerful muscles of his neck bob and he cuts his gaze before he releases me and moves away. I rotate to find him halting at the window, his hands pressed to the glass.

I was right. His father's dead.

My fist balls over my thundering heart. This can't be happening. I don't want him to go to jail. The very thought has me stepping to his side.

He pulls me in front of him, presses me against the glass. "What do you want to say to me?"

"Why are you so angry with me?"

"I thought you were running," he surprises me by admitting.

Relief washes over me. His father must not be dead. "Why would I leave you?" I ask wrapping my arms around him. "I *love* you. I can show you on my phone. I googled the address to Walker Security. I was going there. The only place I'm running—is to *you*, Eric."

"God, woman," he murmurs, and he dives his fingers in my hair, inhaling as he does. "I love you, too."

"Then why would you think I'd do such a thing?"

"You thought I went to kill my father."

"Did you?"

"No, but we need to talk." He captures my hand and guides me to the couch and sets me on the cushion, while he claims the table directly in front of me.

My throat is tight, nerves dancing in my belly. "What happened?"

There's a nervous energy about him. He sighs heavily as if working up to the words that follow. "He wasn't dead when I left him. He's in the hospital and we have to go there."

My eyes go wide. "What happened?" I repeat.

"I took him coffee. Playing nice when I knew he wouldn't expect that from me. We were in the living area of his suite, he took a sip, and that was it. He started choking."

"Did he have a heart attack?"

"If he did, it was drug-induced. I know what poison looks like and it was definitely poison. And no, it was not in the coffee I gave him."

"I didn't think it was, but who and how?"

"A hitman."

"What?" I blink and air lodges in my throat. "What—I—what does that even mean?"

"There was video footage of a man at my father's hotel door, delivering him a tray and no one in the hotel knows who he is. Walker saw him here, too, on the camera footage outside the building."

My mind races with the possibilities this creates. "Does this mean, that at the warehouse—"

"Yes. I think so. There were several of them that night, which means this is not one man, but an operation. I just happened to be there at the right time and place."

"You wouldn't have been if I hadn't left you those voicemails. Isaac made sure he got rid of you. He made you hate me. He has to be behind this. He didn't think he could kill you, so he was going to blame you."

"I'd bet my money on him. Yes."

"You took your father coffee, Eric. The police are going to blame you."

"I'm willing to bet the drug won't show up on any test. Not unless I'm being framed and that's not likely, not at this point. And if I wanted him dead, I wouldn't have called an ambulance or did what I could to ensure he kept breathing."

"You made me think you were going to kill him. You saved his life by showing up." No sooner than I say those words, does my heart jackhammer.

"Will the assassin go after my mother?"

"Your mother is well protected. I know how important she is to you."

"I know you do," I whisper, aware that he lost his mother, that he knows how much I fear losing mine. "But we're talking about assassins here, Eric. They came at me. They got to your father."

"They won't get to your mother."

"But do you think they'll go after her?"

"At this point, we have to assume yes, and protect her."

"The minute she knows your father's in the hospital, she'll come here. She'll come right to the assassin. Maybe that's the plan. Does she know about your father yet? If she does—"

"We won't let your mother come here. And no, she doesn't know yet. I talked to Savage on the way over here. Blake is controlling the flow of information, using their connections to law enforcement to help us. He's talked to the police about the man he caught on film. They know about the safety concerns."

"Are we all targets? Is that what's happening? Your father was distracting us while he tried to fix what couldn't be fixed because the union or the mob, or whoever they've pissed off, was already too angry? They now want everyone who is a Kingston dead?"

"That idea has crossed my mind," he agrees, "but the mob wants to get paid. They don't get paid if we're all dead."

"Isaac and Gigi seem like prime suspects."

"Again, I'll put my money on Issac."

"So what's next?"

"We protect everyone and wait and see what Isaac does next."

"And if he does nothing?"

"A son who does nothing while his father is dying—that is something, not nothing."

His phone buzzes with a text and he snakes his phone from his pocket, glancing at the message and cursing. "Grayson's at the hospital." He shoves his phone back into his pocket. "He's trying to make himself a damn target for the press, the police, and anyone who wants to burn me."

"Isn't the Walker team watching over him?"

"Yes, but that's not the point. He's making their job harder."

"He loves you the way Isaac was supposed to love you, Eric. Of course, he's there. Of course, he doesn't care about being a target. Just like I don't care about anything right now but protecting you and my mother."

"Grayson has an empire to protect and everyone inside that empire that depends on it for their livelihood." He punches in an autodial on his phone and in what can't be more than one ring, he says, "Blake, keep the press away from Grayson." He listens a moment. "No. Not here. I'll come there." He pauses. "Yes. Fuck. I'll bring her." He disconnects. "The police called Isaac. Walker still has eyes on him and we need to go to the hospital."

"What was that about bringing me? Blake wants you to bring me with you?"

"Yes. I don't want you in the middle of that mess at the hospital, but he's right. You need to be there showing concern."

My cellphone rings in my pocket and I check the caller ID. "Gigi," I say urgently. "Gigi's calling me."

"Let it go to voicemail. We need to leave."

I nod and shove the phone back inside my pocket. Eric snags my hand and pulls me to my feet. "Go get your coat and whatever else you need. We need to leave now."

I hurry away and we're at the door in a blink. He yanks it open and Savage and Smith are waiting on us on the other side. "No news," Savage says, without being asked. "On anything, including your father's condition."

"What about Denver? Anything there?"

"Nothing," Savage says. "All is quiet."

"Then let's get to the hospital," Eric says.

"What about calling Isaac?" I ask. "What do we know about his reaction?"

"Nothing," Eric says, pulling the door shut and locking up. "I'll call him when we're on the road."

A minute later at most, we're moving down the hallway with Savage and Smith front and back. We don't take the elevator either. We head down the stairs and none of us speak during the walk to the lower level, where we exit the building. We exit a side door of the building that I didn't even know existed and there's an SUV waiting on us there.

Eric and I slide into the backseat of the vehicle and Savage climbs behind the wheel with Smith in the passenger seat. We have two men protecting us, despite Eric's skill. I definitely don't feel like anyone is dismissing the threat of the hitman.

I turn to Eric. "Why did Blake want you to bring me to the hospital?"

"The police have questions for both of us and I'd rather them ask there than at my apartment. Once they're here, they'll start taking liberties."

"Hasn't Blake shown them the footage of the assassin?"

"Yes," he confirms, "but that doesn't erase guilt. I could have hired the killer. We might have hired the killer."

Us.

Oh God.

Nerves erupt in my stomach and my hand settles on my belly. "We're suspects." It's not a question.

"Yes. We're suspects."

"But you don't inherit anything from the Kingstons."

"I have no idea what's in the will."

I glance over at him. "You might inherit?"

"It would be just like my father to pit me and Isaac against each other, even from the grave."

My lips part with a brutal realization. I now know why I'm a suspect. "My inheritance. The Kingstons might have borrowed it, but if your father dies, it reverts back to me immediately."

Chapter Eighty

Harper

N o sooner do I announce the bombshell about my inheritance than Eric is pulling me around to face him, the leather of the SUV cradling us. His voice low but firm. "Don't turn yourself into a viable suspect or the police will as well. Think about all the people that benefit from my father's death. Isaac. Your mother. Me, perhaps. Who knows who else."

"But I'm the one he took from. Why are you not worried about this?"

"Because it's not that much money, Harper."

"It's millions. It's a lot of money. It's motive."

"You have me and I'm worth a whole lot more than those millions and that's not arrogance. That's a reality the police will look at for you and me."

"You. Not me."

"Motives are everywhere, Harper. I blame him for my mother's death. For all we know he promised to disinherit Isaac after that warehouse incident. They fought, and we have it on camera. My father threw around that threat to disinherit all the fucking time."

"To you?"

"To Isaac. He told him he'd give it all to me, a good dozen times that I remember. My point is there are motives everywhere you look. Don't volunteer information and answer with as little as possible. And remember, I offered you a job and a paycheck to rival and exceed what you have now. I offered to make sure you didn't need that trust fund."

Realization hits me. "My mother. If Isaac knows about your father, she must, too."

"Yes. You need to call her." He releases me and faces forward. "Savage. We need—"

"To make sure Harper's mother stays locked down?" He glances over his shoulder. "We've already talked to Adam about that."

"She's not going to agree," I say. "I know her. She's not going to listen."

"We have a plan," Savage assures us. "Blake's brother, Royce, is calling her as an FBI consultant, which he is, and telling her that she's on lockdown until we catch the person who poisoned her husband. Adam will show up as one of Royce's employees, which he is, to protect her."

Eric's attention shifts to me. "What do you think? Will it work?"

I nod. "I think it might." I grab my new mini-Chanel purse the personal shopper picked out, which I don't even remember bringing with me but clearly, at some point, I did. I even stuck my phone in it. I grab it and stare at the missed calls. "She called," I say. "I didn't hear it ring." I punch the voicemail and play it on speaker: *Your father. I need to talk to you about your father.* I grind my teeth at her calling him my father again and Eric's hands close down on my leg, understanding in the touch, as my mother adds: *Why is he there with you? He's in the hospital. He's—call me. The FBI won't let me leave. Call me now! Oh God. They're calling again. I have to go. Just—call me. This is Eric's fault. Somehow it's his fault and you're sleeping with him!*

The line goes dead and Savage whistles. "That was some heavy shit." Smith elbows him and Savage growls. "Keep your fucking hands to yourself."

"They're calling again?" I ask, eyeing Eric. "Who are they?" I punch in the call back button for my mother.

"Probably Royce," Savage replies.

"He's right," Eric says. "It's likely Royce."

"Royce is not a they," I say. "I guess she means the FBI." The line rings and rings and goes to voicemail. "She's not answering," I say, feeling panicked now. "Why is she not answering?" I redial.

"I'm calling Adam," Smith says. "He's got eyes on her."

"Don't panic," Savage adds. "She's safe. We have her."

I get voicemail again and look at Eric. "I'm freaking out here."

"Easy, princess," he says. "She's safe. I'm sure she's safe."

"Please be right." I look toward the front of the truck. "Smith?! Anything?"

"No answer," he says. "Adam must be talking to her. I'll call one of the other men on the ground there."

"And just to complicate this intense moment," Savage interjects, "we're not only at the hospital, we have uniforms at the side door that already spotted us. And for the record, yes, our fuckhead team should have warned us."

"You're not making me feel good about my mother and your team," I say, punching in her number again.

"I have Adam on text," Smith announces, looking back at us. "He's standing with your mother now. She's fighting with him, but he's got her under control."

I breathe out and sink back into the leather seat. "Oh thank God."

"We're about to be in the hot seat with the cops," Savage warns. "Stay where you're at. We'll come around and get you."

"Don't volunteer information," Eric instructs.

"Yes. Okay." He studies me a moment as if weighing my reply and state of mind which is shit right now, and he knows it. But he also seems to accept that fact as inevitable and reaches for the door. I inhale, preparing myself for whatever hell follows, wishing this was just over, but Eric takes my hand and it reminds me I'm not alone anymore. I'm not alone for the first time in a very long time. Eric has somehow become so much to me in such a short period of time. Then again, we've been there, a presence in each other's lives, for six years.

Eric helps me out of the SUV, and into the cold night air, I don't want to escape nearly as much as I do this night. Savage takes his position in front of us and Smith behind, which reminds me again that there's an assassin hunting at least one of us, and that would be me.

We reach the side entrance of the hospital, some sort of service entrance, and Savage enters the building first. Eric and I join him only to have two police officers step in front of us, crowding Savage and forcing him to step aside.

One of the officers is mid-fifties with what looks like an oddly fitted toupee on his head and crinkles at his eyes. The other younger, thirties maybe, with curly brown hair.

Eric steps forward, taking me with him, and assumes the obvious. They know who he is. "Any word on my father?" Eric asks, the question is his only greeting to the officers.

"He's in ICU," the older of the two officers answers. He's mid-fifties with what looks like an oddly fitted toupee on his head and crinkles at his eyes. "They're running tests, but it appears it might be a heart attack." The man's words drip with accusation, as if the heart attack was a product of Eric's making.

Eric's hand flexes ever so slightly against mine, but his expression is unreadable, unchanged. His tone is steady, unaffected, as he asks, "And the man my security team found on the security footage?"

"We're looking into it," the younger officer announces, his keen eyes falling on our connected hands and then on me. "Perhaps your stepsister might recognize him."

And there it is. The next slap, and accusations, of what will likely be many. We're a tabloid party waiting to happen. The potential headlines run through my head, taunting me with implication that two stepsiblings have come together for sex, scandal, and murder.

Chapter Eighty-One

Eric

The stepsister comment is getting really fucking old and adolescent. I don't directly reply to the asshole cop who made the shitty comment. I don't defend mine and Harper's relationship. Too often in high-profile cases, and this will be one, law enforcement tries to take the heat off themselves and put it on other people. The incestuous headlines they're already starting to frame would do that—if I let them get away with it.

I drape my arm around Harper's shoulders, making it clear that I won't cower and neither will she. In fact, I plan to attack. I glance at the cop's nametag. "You know, Officer Marks. I admire a good cop as much as I do my former SEALs," I say dryly, my gaze meeting the gaze of the cop that just goaded us. "Bravery and sacrifice are qualities to admire. Unfortunately, there are those who serve who use power trips to feed their egos. Like you, officer. You might inspire me to file a harassment charge and I have to tell you, our firm would enjoy taking on a case against the bad eggs on the force. They put the good cops in danger."

"Are you threatening me?" he asks, and a threat lives inside that question.

"Quite the opposite. I'm trying to protect the many good men and women you put in harm's way. Now if you'll step aside, I need to go check on my father." I guide Harper around the two men and we've made it all of a few steps, with Savage and Smith framing us, when Officer Marks smarts off again. "Why?" he demands. "Why go check on him at all? Word is that you hate him."

I stop walking and rotate to face both men. "And yet I still saved his life."

"That's still to be determined," Officer Marks says. "He could die."

"Which is why I need to get to talk to the doctors." I turn away from both men and pull Harper closer, kissing her temple as we turn a corner. "Don't freak out," I whisper, sensing she's doing that and more. "We had to control them, not the other way around."

"Fuckers," Savage grumbles. "Talk about a couple of bitch cops and I like cops. I like cops a lot. Just not those two assholes."

"Amen to that," the normally silent Smith chimes in. "Amen to that." He points to an elevator and we all pause while he punches the call button.

I press my hand to Harper's shoulders, lowering my voice. "If this was a professional hit, there will be no poison in his system and this is over, at least from law enforcement's standpoint."

"Why are they even looking for it?"

"I told them what happened. It reads like poison, but professional hitmen do not leave evidence."

"What if they did?"

"They didn't. Act like you have nothing to fear. You don't and weakness to those cops is like blood to a coyote. It draws them in and makes them attack."

She nods. "Right. Got it. Play the game."

"Play it our way, not theirs. Our way. Own every conversation with them. Got it?"

She inhales and lets it out, calmness sliding over her beautiful face. "Yes." She sounds stronger now. Even stronger as she adds, "No fear."

"No fear, sweetheart. Exactly." The elevator dings and the doors open. "Come on." I lead her into the car, looking forward to the day I can just be with her, minus this damn family drama, determined to make that day come sooner rather than later.

Savage and Smith follow us into the car and right before we're sealed inside, the two officers step in front of us, the older one catching the door to keep it open. "Is there a reason you need two bodyguards?" he asks.

"You're assuming they aren't our friends?" Harper asks. "Because we have no friends?"

"Exactly," Savage says. "You think I can't have friends? I'm a good friend." He runs a hand down the scar on his cheek. "Saved a friend's life getting this." He scowls at the officer's hand on the elevator. "Why the fuck are you holding the door?"

Smith pulls his phone from his pocket and holds it up. "Recording. Is there a reason you're holding the elevator door?"

The officer holding said door curses and releases it. The minute we're sealed inside, I lean in close to Harper, my lips by her ear as I whisper, "My hero."

"They're really starting to piss me off." She rotates in my arms. "What happened to reassuring us and protecting us?"

"Exactly," Savage snaps, the giant brooding man himself adding, "We need protecting like everyone else. We have real feelings."

We all laugh and I kiss Harper while the car halts and the doors open. Savage and Smith exit first and I lean in close to Harper and whisper, "I'll show you how real my feelings are when we finally get home."

She doesn't laugh or smile. She presses her hand to my cheek. "Yes. You will." It's a promise, that isn't about playful flirtation. She's talking about what's going on with my father. She's talking about how real this is about to get. He could be dying. I have to face that and she thinks that's going to be brutal, which means when it's not, because it won't be, she'll think *I'm* brutal. It's not a good thought, but I am who I am, and I've already decided that Harper has to face that reality. A savant and a bastard. That's who I am and with that comes baggage. And a little brutality.

We exit to the hallway and Smith and Savage assume guard posts there at the entrance to the floor which is open to a waiting room. Davis, Grayson, and Mia are waiting for us here and immediately greet us, all wearing casual clothing and worried looks. "He's in ICU," Mia says. "And they won't release further details to us. What's going on?"

Grayson eyes me. "Get an update and then let's talk."

Davis and I exchange a look in which Davis tells me he can't hold Grayson back. He tried. There is no damage control. Grayson won't have it. I look at Grayson again. "The part where I told you to stay out of this—"

"Landed on deaf ears," he replies. "We're friends. You're in this, I'm in this."

"I didn't do this," I tell him. "You need to know that, but the press—"

"I know," he says. "Check on your father. We'll deal with the press later—*together.*"

My lips thin and I eye Savage and Smith. "Protect them. Keep them the hell away from the police and the press." I give the entire group my back, and start walking toward a nurses' station.

Harper is by my side in a flash, her hand on my arm, her steps matching my steps and it feels right. Like she belongs by my side. Like she has always belonged by my side. "Stubborn man," I bite out.

"Stubborn friend," she whispers. "And friends are hard to find."

"Which is why I was trying to protect him."

"Which is why he wants to protect you," she reminds me.

I grunt at that and flag down a nurse who turns out to be an aide who leads us toward the ICU. In a few short minutes, she's left to find us a nurse, and we're standing outside a glass-enclosed room where my father lays in a bed and monitors track his breathing and heart rate, which is too slow. "And there he is," Harper whispers, glancing at me. "How do you feel?"

"I don't," I say honestly. "Not a damn thing."

"There you are," a fifty-something nurse with bright red hair greets, stopping beside us. "I heard his son had arrived and wanted an update. I'm Kasey. I'm your father's nurse. He's stable. The police aren't allowing me to offer more details." Someone calls her. "Sorry. I have an emergency. We'll tell you more when we can." Kasey rushes away and leaves us alone again.

"That didn't sound good," Harper says, hushing her voice and stepping closer to me. "I think we need an attorney. A criminal attorney and a good one."

Savage joins us before I can reply and I don't ask how he got back here. He's resourceful. "Interesting update," he says. "Isaac called Gigi and told her about your father, Eric. She immediately rushed to the airport, but she didn't get on a plane to New York City. She got on a plane to Italy. She's running."

The wicked witch herself, but wicked enough to have her own son killed?

Chapter Eighty-Two

Harper

G igi ran?

I'm stunned.

She left while her son lays in a hospital bed. My hand goes to my neck, the sterile smell of the hospital suffocating me, when moments before it had not. This makes no sense. That woman loves her son. He was the king of the empire that she created. A million thoughts charge through my mind, and I can barely make sense of them. I wonder if this is how Eric feels when he's attacked by numbers, consumed in the chaos of it all.

My eyes meet Eric's. "I know you hate her. I know this makes sense to you because of that hate, but it doesn't make sense to me. Why would she run? It makes her look guilty."

"Or afraid. You said she sounded panicked when you talked to her, right?"

"Yes. I think she thinks she's next. She thinks everyone in the family is going down. She thinks someone is coming for them. Or us. For all of us."

"I'm still not a hundred percent convinced we're not the fall guys for something this family has gotten into."

"You think Isaac and Gigi were the ones setting us up? Not Gigi and your father?"

"My father's in a hospital bed. That doesn't spell guilt to me though there's no question, he was here to protect himself. Maybe that means he was turning on the family. As for Isaac, my first instinct is always to blame that little prick but he has limits. He's not smart enough to plan any of this alone."

My eyes go wide with a memory. "Gigi made a comment about you getting your brains from her."

"Nothing about me came from that woman but the bottom line here is I do believe she knows exactly what's going on."

"Then we have to talk to her."

"Agreed but right now, I need to talk to Davis and get us out of here. And I need your help. Talk to Mia. Make her understand how dangerous this is for Grayson. She'll get him out of here. Just get them away from this. Even if it means you leave with them."

"I can't leave. I'm not leaving you, and as you said—if we don't deal with the police, they'll come to us. We need legal counsel."

"I'm an attorney surrounded by attorneys," he argues.

"But you don't want Grayson close to this. A Bennett attorney pulls him in."

"If we need a criminal law expert, outside the firm, we'll get one, but there is nothing to protect ourselves from right now. It's a heart attack."

"They didn't say it was a heart attack."

"They will."

"You don't know that."

He kisses me, a hard press of our mouths. "Trust me." His voice is low, rough, a demand and question all at once that only Eric could make possible. "I'm asking you to trust me to protect you and us. Help me protect the only other people other than you that matter to me. Grayson and Mia."

My heart squeezes with the realization that they are all he has, or they were. He now considers me a part of a small, intimate group of people he allows in his life. "I so need to be right here with you right now, but yes. I trust you and I'll come through for you."

His eyes darken, warm, seem to soften and then harden again. "Go now. I need to know they're out of this."

I press to my toes and kiss him. "I'll ask Mia to have coffee, but Grayson will—"

"Be right by my side. I know. And Davis will be, too, and he, like me, protects Grayson."

"Because he's a friend?" I ask, wondering why he denies Davis that title.

"He's not Grayson." His reply is flat and curiously hard.

I don't know what that means, but I don't push. Not now. I'll understand at some point. "I'll get Mia to help." I turn away and all but walk right into Savage.

"Just a wall hanging out," he says, when I stop dead to avoid blasting into him. "I'll keep him safe while you're gone."

Yes, please, I think, ridiculously relieved to have Savage stay by Eric's side. Eric can take care of himself.

I step around the beast and head toward Mia and Grayson, who are standing in a waiting area just around a corner, and in deep conversation with Davis. "What's happening?" Mia asks the minute they spy my approach.

"He's stable," I say, joining them. "That's all they'll tell us."

Davis discreetly steps away, headed toward the ICU, but Grayson fixes his attention on me. "How much trouble is he in?"

"He didn't do this," I say. "I'm certain of it."

"Who did?"

"I'll let Eric share his theories on that," I say, "but Grayson, as long as you're here, he won't think his way out of this."

"As long as I'm here, he'll be forced to think beyond his damn family, and find a way out."

I blink. "I don't understand."

"When a Kingston is involved, that brain of his goes swimming in shark-infested waters where any productive thought dies. He needs reasons to think outside those waters. That's me and that's you. You'll stay close to him and so will I." He starts to walk away to follow Davis, and I catch his arm.

"Wait." He turns to look at me. "His thoughts aren't the only thing that goes swimming in those shark-infested waters. If you force his hand, if you put yourself in harm's way, he'll find a way to end this and I'm not sure either of us want to know where that leads him. You don't know—"

His jaw clamps down. "I might not know the entire situation, but I do know him. I know him far better than you think I know him. He won't go to that dark place when I'm with him. He won't go there when you're with him either. Keep him close. I damn sure am."

"You said he was fine at the apartment."

"His father wasn't lying in a hospital bed, either." He pulls away from me and starts walking, and it's clear to me that Grayson really does know Eric, even better than I do. Because he has seen the dark side of Eric that I have sensed, but rejected. And he's worried that dark side will dictate Eric's actions.

"Coffee?" Mia suggests, as if she'd read my plan.

I force myself to turn to her. "Yes," I say, battling a need to go to Eric, but remembering my commitment to him as well, to use

Mia to get Grayson out of here, though I'm not certain that's smart right now. I manage a weak smile. "Coffee is good."

"I know where the coffee shop is. I was here for a client's mother a while back."

I don't move. I don't want the coffee. Damn it, I have to talk to her. "Great," I say. "Lead the way."

"Of course," she says and we start walking, but suddenly I just know Eric is near. I stop and turn to find him, Davis, and Grayson, entering the waiting room we just left. They huddle up and start talking and as if he senses me looking at him, his attention shifts, and suddenly I'm captured in his intense stare.

Seconds tick by and I can't explain it, but the world just shuts down, it shrinks, and pulls us together. There is so much between me and this man, so much to learn, to know, to experience. So much to lose and I have a horrible feeling that's where this is headed.

Pain.

Loss.

Goodbye.

I need to do something I'm not doing.

What? What do I need to do that I'm not doing?

Chapter Eighty-Three

Harper

*P*rotect Grayson and Mia, I tell myself. That's what I need to do and with that, I force myself to turn away from Eric, and rejoin Mia, and the two of us fall into step together, and round a corner that leads us toward an elevator. A few minutes later, we're sitting in a desolate cafeteria at a tiny table, with coffee in front of us, her keen eyes studying me. "He really matters to you."

"He really does. And that's why I'm going to get straight to the point. Grayson's right. Eric is swimming in shark-infested waters, and while Grayson feels he needs to be with him to protect him, I believe that any risk or backlash against you or Grayson is what will send Eric over the edge."

"Define over the edge."

"He'll protect you and Grayson at all costs. He needs room to breathe. If Grayson's by his side, he won't breathe. He'll feel the pressure to end this before Grayson gets in too deep. And I mean, end it however he has to end it."

She sits back, looking as if she were punched in the chest before she leans forward. "However he has to end it?"

"Yes. However, he has to end it."

She lifts a hand. "I'm not going to try to define what you might be implying. The bottom line is that Grayson loves Eric like a brother. He doesn't want Eric to feel alone. He won't leave his side."

"Eric doesn't feel alone. He knows he has Grayson. He speaks of him as blood, family. A brother. He can't lose him. That's what Grayson needs to understand. Eric can't lose him. He can't be a part of taking him down in some way. And you need to understand how dangerous this is, Mia. They tried to kill me and we don't know who 'they' even are. Now his father was poisoned. Eric has every reason to believe that danger is a living, breathing monster, ready to attack at any moment. He won't sit back and let Grayson get hurt."

"What do you want me to do?"

"Get Grayson out of here. Even if it's just for now. I know Grayson feels that he needs to be here but now, now is not the time. He's putting himself on the wrong radars and that's putting Eric on edge. Please. I beg of you. Pull him back."

"I don't know if I can," she proclaims solemnly.

"Try. Please."

"I will. Yes. Of course, I will. I want everyone safe. I want everyone past whatever this is, but I know him. Give him a few minutes with Eric to feel good about where Eric is mentally right now, and then I'll get him out of here, somehow, someway." She tilts her head and studies me. "In the meantime, let's talk about you. They tried to kill you. Your world is shaken to the core. How are you?"

"I'm okay if Eric and my mother are okay. That's the bottom line for me."

"You were attacked. You're going to have to slow down and think about you at some point or the reality of it is going to sideswipe you. You're going to have to deal emotionally with your attack, but for now, I get it. You've banked it. You've put it in a place and buried it because you care about other people. Because it's survival."

"I feel fine. I do. I'm fine."

She gives me a keen look. "Are you convincing you or me?"

"I'm fine," I repeat firmly, and I am. I have to be.

"How's your mother handling things? Is she coming here?"

"God, no. We're not letting her come here if we can help it, and she's not a friend to Eric. He doesn't need that right now."

"Is that a problem for you two?"

"No, it's not. My mother needs to open her eyes and see that Eric is the one helping her, not the opposite."

"Sounds like we need to sit down with wine rather than coffee."

"Well, wine would be good, but I can't afford to be anything but sharp right now. Please. Get Grayson out of here."

"Okay. I'll go, but I need to ask you something. I need you to be honest." She leans in closer again and lowers her voice. "Did Eric do this?"

I hate that she's asking me this again. I hate that her doubt reflects Grayson's doubt. It hits me then that maybe, just maybe, Grayson's shift in position on Eric, is him seeing Eric and what's happened today with too much reflection on their youth. "I already answered that question. No." My tone is firm and absolute. "No, he did not do this."

"That was a fast and sure answer."

"And an honest one."

"I like real and honest." Her eyes soften the way her voice did moments before. "You're good for him. He's different with you, not so shut off and reserved. That's how I'll get Grayson to step back. Eric has you and you're his Mia." She stands up. "You coming back with me?"

"I'm going to get Eric a coffee and then I'll be there."

She nods and when I stand she hugs me. "You're family now, too. If you need me, I'm here for you." With that, she's gone, hurrying toward the cafeteria exit, and disappearing into the hallway.

I walk to the register and pay and with my cup and an extra empty cup in hand, I head toward the coffee bar and prepare a fresh coffee for me and Eric, doctoring his the way I've already noted he prefers. I've just finished up, both hot coffees in hand, when I turn to find a tall, muscular man with a salt and pepper beard standing in front of me, or more like towering over me. I jolt to a halt, all but toe to toe with him. His lips curve, a hint of evil in that barely-there smirk. "It's way past time that you and I have a talk, Harper."

Chapter Eighty-Four

Eric

"Friendship is the hardest thing in the world to explain. It's not something you learn in school. But if you haven't learned the meaning of friendship, you really haven't learned anything."

— *Muhammad Ali*

Grayson, Davis, and I are standing in the waiting room when Grayson receives a phone call. "It's our friendly investor who stabbed us in the back over the NFL deal." He hits the decline button. "I'll talk to him tomorrow."

The NFL deal that represents the dream Grayson and I have shared for years: owning part of a team. It's our pet project together and yet I haven't thought about it in twenty-four hours. I'm a shitty right arm man and friend, while Grayson is as solid a friend as anyone could ask for. "I promised you that I'll handle it tomorrow," I say. "I will. We won't lose this deal. You have my word."

Grayson's hand comes down on my shoulder. "We're a good team. I can carry some of the weight."

"I need to speak to Eric," Davis says. "Alone."

"At least you plot against me behind my back, openly and honestly," Grayson says with a chuckle, a man confident enough to know when to step away and fear nothing. And with that, he simply walks away and leaves me with Davis.

"I don't want this hell I'm living to stain the firm," I say, the minute he's out of hearing range. "I need you to distance him from me right now."

"NFL," he says yet again. "We're negotiating the purchase of an *NFL team.*"

"How many times are you going to say that, Davis?"

"*You're* negotiating the purchase of an NFL team. That's un-fucking-believable. It's damn near a wet dream. You did this, Eric. You made it happen. I can only do so much in these circumstances, but that said, I'll do everything I can."

"I'm not coming to the office. That'll bring the press to the doorstep of the company."

"We're going to get press. We get lots of bad press. Many times and many ways, outside of this situation. Don't assume our weakness. We have always managed to come out on top just fine."

"This is different."

"The difference is that you're acting like a little bitch, running scared."

My jaw sets hard. "Don't push me, Davis."

"Don't make me. I say own the fuck out of this. Don't walk away. Don't stay away. That makes you, and us, look like there's something to hide. And we don't even know if this is an issue yet. There's no charge. There's no problem."

"There's a fucking assassin on the loose. That's a problem. They went after my woman. They went after my father. What happens when they go after Grayson? I don't need him to be on the radar of the wrong people."

He blanches. "An assassin?"

"Yes, Davis. I don't have time to give you the details right now, but I need Grayson and Mia out of this."

"Do I want to know the details?"

"No. Don't ask."

A muscle in his jaw tics. He wants to push for more but seems to think better of it, at least for now. "Okay, you had me at assassin. I'll find a way to get them out of the city without them connecting the dots to you, but that means I need to use the NFL deal to make it happen. You have to step back."

"Meaning what?"

"If Grayson thinks there's a targeted meeting for that project, and that he's handling it for you, he'll go."

He's right. The NFL deal is the only way to get Grayson out of here. "I can make that happen. I'll make a few calls. You press him to take over. Tell him you think I'm too distracted. Be an asshole. You're good at it."

He smirks. "Yes, friend. I'll be an asshole, just for you."

Mia joins us then. "Where's Grayson?"

"Where's Harper?" I counter.

"She's grabbing you coffee and—"

"She's alone?"

"Yes, but—"

"Safety in numbers, Mia," I say, and I'm already walking. Fuck. I have a bad feeling right now. Why did I let her and Mia go anywhere without protection? Why did I discount an ICU floor as a danger zone? My heart thunders in my ears, numbers pounding at my mind, calculating the odds that Harper is in danger, but the numbers aren't what sets me off. It's a gut instinct that tells me she's in trouble.

I start to jog toward the cafeteria.

Harper

In the seconds after the bearded man steps in front of me, time seems to stand still. Adrenaline pumps through me and fight or flight is nowhere in sight. I want to run. I want to scream. I do neither. I just stand there, my mind racing, and my feet planted on the ground.

Is he here to kill me?

Is he the assassin that put Eric's father in the hospital?

I force myself to inhale deeply and reach deep to a lesson that my father taught me about calming myself and making rational decisions. I ground myself by focusing on the mundane details around me, rather than my death. The first thought I have is that the cafeteria smells of pizza. The man in front of me like coffee, the way I smell when I sit in a Starbucks for hours to catch up on work. These random observations work, as they always did in my professional life. My pulse steadies. My gaze sharpens on the man.

"Who are you?"

"Let's sit down and talk," he replies, and it's not a question. It's an order.

Now that he's spoken again, I'm hyper-focused on him, just him, and I drink in every detail I can. The fine lines by his eyes aging him to early forties. His beard neatly trimmed. His cheekbones high, a scar across the right side of his face. His eyes a teal-blue. He towers over me a good twelve inches. He's in a black designer leather jacket, wearing black jeans. I don't know what's on his feet because I'm not looking down and giving him the chance to come at me. Voices sound to the left, and the tension in my spine eases ever so slightly. He can't kill me here. And would an assassin walk up to me like this?

No.

That's illogical.

Isn't it?

"Who are you and what do you want?" I ask, wishing like hell the coffee cups in my hands didn't have lids on them.

"Excuse me," a female voice says to my left. "Do you mind if I grab a napkin?"

I'm standing in front of the condiments and supply area. It's a good public place to be but I can't block the path to others using the area. I step slightly to the right, in front of the creamer, giving the woman room to grab her napkin, but I don't look at her. I'm not leaving our public location. I'm not giving him a chance to grab me.

The woman moves closer and she messes with the napkins and doesn't seem in a hurry to leave. It's odd and I have this sense that she's listening in, that she's intentionally crowding us but I'm pretty okay with that right about now.

The man steps with me, maintaining a position that is far too close to me and directly in my path. "Who are you and what do you want?" I repeat softly. "Answer now or I'll start screaming."

"Is that the typical way you respond to people who wish to speak to you? Screaming?"

"You have ten seconds," I say. "Ten. Nine—"

"Detective Wright," he says. "Consultant for the FBI."

I don't even know what that means but I'm pretty sure it means he's a liar. "Badge," I order.

"Consultant," he repeats, and reaches in his pocket to offer me a card. "That's all you get." My hands are full and he holds it up for me to eye.

"It looks real, but anyone can make a business card."

"Call it in," he says. "But do it after we talk." He reaches down and takes my cups, walking to the trash and dumping them. He returns and hands me the card. "Do you know what you're in the middle of, Harper?"

Harper.

The way he uses my first name bothers me. Don't FBI agents usually use your surname? "If you're in a rush to talk to me in private," I say, that very idea setting off warnings, "don't waste time speaking in code."

"Everything is not what it seems and if you don't open your eyes, and see with them, your stepfather won't be the only one in the hospital."

"Is that a threat?"

"It's a fact and a warning. Open your eyes. Look beyond the obvious. Your time is up."

Male voices sound and one of them is Eric's. "Eric!" I call out, and the man in front of me growls low, guttural. He grabs my arm and pulls me to him. "Bitch, you should have waited to hear me out. You should have let me help you. You should have fucking listened to me. Now there's a price to pay."

Chapter Eighty-Five

Harper

Just when I am certain fight is my only way to get away from the bearded man, the woman who'd crowded me by the coffee supplies appears beside us and grabs his arm. "Let her go. Now. We have to go."

Wait, what, I think. *She's with him*?

The bearded man, the FBI consultant, if I believe his lie, hesitates, but he releases me and then cuts right toward a stairwell. I whirl around, desperate to ensure no one else is coming at me, my gaze catches on Eric, the sight of him running toward me, a mix of relief and panic. He's too far out to be impactful right here and now. And this is a now situation. The woman darts past me and I reach for her arm but fail. I don't even think. I charge after her. I have to catch her. She has answers we desperately need to end this nightmare. I take off running, but I'm not far when Eric catches up to me, and yanks me around to face him. "What the hell are you doing? Stay here." He's barely spoken the words before he's launching himself forward.

I don't stay. I spy Savage and shout his name, waving as I hop around like a fool. "Savage! This way!" Eric disappears around a corner. I start running after him, afraid of losing sight of him.

I actually catch up right as he enters the stairwell, but I make it no further. Savage grabs my arm and now he's yanking me around. "Stop. What the fuck are you doing?"

"Does Eric have a gun?" I demand. "Tell me he has a gun."

"He has a gun. Talk to me. What just happened?"

"That man told me—"

Eric bursts through the stairwell door. "No one is there. They must have exited a flight up." He eyes Savage. "Get someone looking for them. A tall man with a beard and a short brunette."

Savage grabs his phone and makes a call while Eric crosses the space between us with lightning speed and pulls me to him. "What the hell happened?"

"This man came up to me and he claimed to be FBI. Or a consultant for the FBI. He gave me a card and I'm paraphrasing here but he warned me that I needed to open my eyes. That everything isn't how it seems and if I didn't figure that out, people would die."

Eric scowls. "Holy fuck, why did I let you come to the coffee shop alone?"

"You didn't. I went with Mia and—"

He kisses me, his hand coming down on my head and his tongue licks into my mouth, the taste of fear on his lips. "You go nowhere without me until this is over. Do you understand? Nowhere without me." His voice is low, rough, guttural. "Nowhere, Harper. Do you understand?"

"Yes," I breathe out. "Yes, of course. You don't go anywhere without me either, understand?"

"We stay together," he agrees.

"No one has seen them," Savage interjects, "but we're looking. What the hell are we dealing with here?"

Eric's arm wraps my shoulder, his big body sheltering mine as he turns to face Savage. "Tell him everything. Tell us both everything. Start from the beginning. Pretend I know nothing at all."

I relay every detail I remember about the encounter, down to the color of the man's beard, and Savage is the one scowling when I finish. "FBI? No. We're connected to the FBI. Unless this is a rogue agent, and I doubt he'd have a partner if he was, he wasn't FBI."

Which isn't a surprise to me. I knew in my gut he wasn't FBI, and as I stand here now, I'm not rattled the way I was after the warehouse, but I don't take the time to truly analyze that. "He gave me this." I hand Savage the card.

He shoots a picture of it. "I'm texting this to Royce. He's well connected with the Feds. I'll have answers for you in about ten minutes." He types a message and sends the photo and then hands me the card.

Eric grabs the card and studies it a minute. "What do you want to do right now?" Savage asks. "Stay or go?"

Eric shoves the card into his pocket and turns to me again, his hands on my shoulders. "We go. We'll have Walker deal with the police and our reasons for leaving."

"If they come to the apartment doesn't that bring attention to you by way of bad press that bleeds over to Grayson?"

His lips thin. "We aren't staying. We need to regroup." He eyes Savage and the other man nods and makes a call before he says, "I have men waiting to escort us out when you're ready to leave."

"What about Davis, Mia, and Grayson?" I ask.

"We have a man with them now," Savage assures us. "We'll escort them out of here and stay with them at their homes."

Smith joins us then, and in a few seconds, he's taken up a position behind us while Savage leads the way. Eric keeps me close the entire walk to the elevator, and even inside the elevator car, he uses his big body as a shield. He's afraid of an attack. This man is willing to take a bullet for me. That understanding for me is as good as another proclamation of love, because, yes, he's a SEAL. Yes, he's lived to protect the innocent, but it's more with us. There's a history, a family he hates, and yet, he's always been right here with me, even back on that first night. He warned me away from them. He kissed me and that memory reminded me every day after that there was more out there.

We arrive at the rear door of the hospital and Savage clears the way before we exit. I climb into the backseat of the SUV with Eric by my side. No one is in the driver's seat yet. We're alone and once Eric seals us inside, his fingers tangle into my hair. "Don't fucking scare me like that again." His mouth closes down on mine, his kiss wicked and hungry, an edge to him that I understand. Not once, but twice now, he's come to my rescue. Not once, but twice now, I could have died. I don't know why this hasn't affected me yet. I don't know why it hasn't shaken me to the core, but it has him. I feel that in the way his hand presses between my shoulder blades, molding me close. I feel it in the desperate edge to his kiss.

He's touching me and I'm touching him and it's as if this vehicle doesn't exist. I need him. God, how I need him and my hands slide under his shirt, over warm taut skin, when there's a rap on the window. Eric curses and drags his mouth from mine, his fingers wiping away the dampness there. "Give me just a minute."

"Hurry," I whisper, and somehow my hand is in his pocket closing around that business card I'd given him.

He kisses me again and exits the SUV, shutting the door. I stare down at the card and scoot to a spot where the hospital lights beam down on the writing there. I run my hand over the name. I was freaked out by that man, especially when he grabbed me but I wasn't afraid in the way I was back in the warehouse. Maybe it was because people were around me and us. Maybe I felt safer, as I had help nearby.

The man's words come back to me: *Everything is not what it seems and if you don't open your eyes, and see with them, your stepfather won't be the only one in the hospital.*

Open my eyes and see with them. As if there's something staring me in the face that I'm ignoring. I flip the card over and my eyes go wide. There's another code on the back, another message. He obviously meant for me to have it, but why not just tell me what it means? Why not just tell me what I need to open my eyes and see?

Chapter Eighty-Six

Harper

I don't move. I sit there in the SUV, the heater cranked, the soft leather hugging my body, all signaling warmth and comfort, but the card in my hands sends a chill down my spine. No matter what the message on the back of the card means, it spells danger. Again a number and letter sequence, and I stare at the combination and will my mind to find an answer there. The first clue was given to Eric at my house. Now this one was given directly to me. Even I, who am not a savant, can see myself as the common denominator. And that man, the FBI consultant, or whoever he was, told me to open my eyes, as if the answer to some big question is right in front of me. As if I should understand the message. Frustrated, I'm impatient for Eric to return to the vehicle.

I open the door to my right and shove the card into my jacket pocket, aware that we are likely being watched and I don't want anyone to know that I've already discovered the message on the card. The minute I step outside, I find Eric standing a few feet away, not with Savage as I expect, but with Blake, who I didn't even know was here, but the two of them together are exactly the pair I need right now.

Blake to hack the code with a computer.

Eric to hack the code with his mind.

The instant I step onto the curb, the attention of both men shifts to me, their attention sharp, disapproving. They want to shove me back in the SUV. Eric even sways my direction, but I hold up a hand and start walking toward them.

"The card the man gave me," I say without preamble as I join them. "I grabbed it from your pocket, Eric. There's another message on the back. The same kind of message we received back in Denver. Just numbers and letters. I don't want to show it to you here and risk someone knowing that we've seen the message. It seems like it buys us time to figure it out before they expect some sort of action."

They, I think.

Who are *they*?

We need to find out.

"Good decision," Blake approves. "Is there a chance that he's actually an informant or friend?"

"The man grabbed her and threatened her," Eric snaps, and apparently just the idea requires that his hand slide around my waist as he pulls me to him. "He's an enemy. The end."

"I guess that means he wasn't FBI?" I ask.

"You guessed right," Blake confirms. "No one at the FBI knows him."

"And on that note," Eric says. "I'm taking her back to the vehicle. I don't want her out in the open until we figure out what the hell is going on."

He doesn't wait for Blake's approval. He starts to turn. "I need a copy of the message," Blake calls out. Eric doesn't stop moving. He simply lifts an agreeable hand and leads me back to the vehicle, his actions protective, possessive. He places me between him and the SUV and then opens the door, his body once again sheltering mine, but I fear for him, not me. That's just it. I'm not scared and maybe that's some mental coping mechanism, a way to block out my warehouse attack. Mia wasn't wrong. Eventually, I'm certain I'll have to face that trauma, but that time isn't now.

I settle into the soft leather of the backseat again and this time when Eric enters, we aren't left alone. Savage claims the driver's seat. "Home?" he asks over his shoulder.

"Yes," Eric replies. "The sooner the better."

Savage places us in motion. "Where's the card?" Eric asks, but before I can respond his cellphone buzzes with a text.

He snakes it from his pocket, eyes the screen as another message pings, and then glances at me. "Adam had to get a doctor in to calm your mother down. She's worried about my father. They gave her Xanax and she's sleeping."

It's then that I step back and realize the hell my mother must be going through. "She lost my father," I say, my hand settling on my knotted belly, "and I've forgotten that to her, this is her worst nightmare. She's preparing to lose the man who became her second partner in life. I've forgotten how much your father means to her."

I look at Eric. "She needs me and I've let the poison of this family allow me to forget that."

Eric squeezes my knee. "You're protecting her. *We're* protecting her. Every time you get the chance, you remind me how important protecting her is to you."

"But I wasn't there for her today. I didn't—"

"You were attacked and almost killed. That was less than twenty-four hours ago and even then, you were worried about her. You have not thought of yourself at all. She's safe. The medication will help her cope and as a bonus, the sedation keeps her there with Adam."

"Adam's a badass," Savage chimes in. "This isn't a bad thing. It's good. He'll keep her safe and cozy. They're going to be so safe and cozy they'll have cookies and cocoa when she wakes up. You can bet on it."

I know he's trying to make me laugh. I do and I appreciate it, but it's not going to work. Not when the magnitude of being hunted and forced into hiding has set in. Eric squeezes my knee again and when I don't look at him, he leans across me, his cheek pressing to my cheek, his lips at my ear. "We're going to get through this. We're going to protect your mother."

"But not, I fear, without her suffering," I whisper.

He pulls back to look at me, still leaning over me, creating the façade of being alone. "Then we'll help her recover." It's not a sugarcoated reply. It doesn't promise me everything is going to be peachy for my mother. She's in love with his father, after all. No one knows more than Eric how much pain his father can cause. No one knows more than Eric that I can't save her from some parts of this.

He strokes a strand of my hair behind my ear, repeating his promise. "We'll help her and we'll do it together. You have my word." His phone buzzes with another text message and reluctantly Eric eases back into the seat and scans the incoming message, while I savor that word "together" and the raspy, affected tone he'd spoken it in, for just a few seconds longer.

Seconds that end as Eric announces, "Isaac wants to talk." He sticks his phone back in his pocket. "I'm going to let him squirm."

"What if squirming makes him do something stupid?"

Savage halts us in front of Eric's building. "Adam will be there to kick his ass. Blake said he's waiting on a text from you two."

"We need to shoot him a photo of the message on the back," Eric explains.

I pull it from my pocket and hand it to him. He turns it over and when he would shoot a photo, he goes still, suddenly more stone than man. He's just staring at that combination of numbers and letters, and while he's not moving or reacting, I have a sense that it's familiar to him and not in a good way. "What is it?" I ask, grabbing his arm. "What does that mean to you?"

He doesn't look at me. He shoots a photo and sends it to Blake, then sticks his phone and that card inside his pocket. "Let's go upstairs," he says, reaching for the door, and opening it. He actually gets out of the SUV and he still has not looked at me. I'm right. He knows what that message means and it's a problem for him. It's a problem for us. A big enough one that he doesn't want to tell me. Maybe he doesn't plan to tell me at all, but that's not happening. He's not only going to tell me, he's going to tell me the minute we're alone.

Chapter Eighty-Seven

Harper

Eric and I step into the elevator and Savage actually tries to follow us inside, but I'm not having it. I rotate on him and point. "No. I need to talk to Eric alone. Go take care of the truck or something."

"One of my men—"

"You aren't getting on this elevator, Savage," I say.

He holds up his hands and backs away. The doors shut and Eric keys in the security code to his floor. I rotate to face him. He stares down at me, his eyes hooded, shielding him from my probing stare, and I don't believe this is an accident.

"I know you know what it means." It's all I say, all I can say about the message on the back of the business card when I'm certain that we're being recorded.

His hands come down on my arms and he pulls me to him. "Not here. Not now." His voice is low, rough, an edge to him now that is one-part power, one-part anger, and I'm not sure why.

I rest my palm on the hard wall of his chest, and his heart thunders under my touch. He might seem cool and calm on the outside, but he's not. "You know what it means," I whisper. It's not a question. It's a fact. He knows. I know he knows.

"I know a lot of things," he says. "None of which we're discussing in this elevator."

My eyes narrow on him, on the hard lines of his face, the sharpness to his features I've never noticed until this moment. His defined cheekbones. His square jaw. His steely eyes. "Why are you angry?"

"I have a lot of reasons to be angry, don't you think?"

"Of course, you have reasons, but this, this that you feel right now, is different." The elevator halts and dings, announcing our arrival at our destination, while frustratingly cutting me off before I can press him for more, but it's also the promise of privacy.

The doors open and he captures my hand and starts walking, leading me down the hallway toward his apartment. We don't speak, but I can almost feel Eric shutting himself off, caging himself in a place where I don't exist. He not only knows what that message means, he really doesn't want to tell me. We reach the door and I can't get inside the privacy of his apartment soon enough. What does he know? Why is he this on edge?

He unlocks the door and I quickly walk inside, rotating to face him. "Tell me that message isn't about my mother."

"It's not." He shuts the door, locking it, and then shrugs out of his jacket, hanging it on the coatrack a few feet away, and I get the impression that it's all show. He's avoiding me. He's occupying space that he doesn't want filled with something else.

"That's it?" I press. "You aren't going to say anything else?"

He faces me, his legs spread wide in this alpha, controlling stance, hands settling on his lean hips. "It's not about your mother," he repeats.

He's going to make me ask the question. He's going to make me push. "Then what—"

"It's about me." His statement is hard and flat, and it sits between us like a concrete block.

"You?"

He cuts his gaze, looks skyward, and then to my surprise, he walks away, heading toward the kitchen that connects to the living room.

I shrug out of my jacket and hurry after him tossing it on the couch as I pass it by, and continue my pursuit. Eric rounds the island and opens the fridge. I'm standing with my hand on the island counter, facing him when he shuts the door and removes the cap off a beer. He offers it to me. "It's a good time for a drink."

I don't want the damn beer but I take it. He opens the fridge again and grabs another bottle, twisting off the top, as he had for me. Only this time, when the top is gone, he tips back his beer and downs half of it. I set mine down untouched. "Talk to me. You're scaring me."

He fixes me in a hooded stare, his handsome face all hard lines and shadows, as he orders softly, "Drink the beer, Harper." He downs another swallow of his own.

"I don't want the beer."

He sets his bottle down with a solid thud, then closes the space between us, a predatory intensity about him, as he drags me to him. "Then what do you want?"

"Answers. I want you to talk to me. I want you to—" He tangles rough fingers into my hair and drags my mouth to his.

"No talking," he commands. "Not now. Understand?"

"No," I whisper, his breath warm on my cheek, his body hard against mine. His cock thick against my belly. My sex clenches and my nipples ache. I want him, but this is a distraction. This is him avoiding conversation.

"Eric, please—"

"I like that word," he murmurs, and then he's kissing me, and the first taste of him is passion, the next demand, possession, and yes, anger. He's angry. He's outright pissed for the first time since the hotel room in New York City when he came to me and wanted to drive me away. Only I don't think he ever wanted to drive me away. He wanted to drive away the hell of his past. He wanted to drive away the family he would deny if they'd just go away. He's in that place again. He needs to drive them away, and as much as I want to know what's triggered him, there's a shudder that slides through his body, and I understand what it means. He's on the edge of that cliff the savant in him can lead him to, the numbers in his head beating at his mind and his emotions. Whatever that message I was given says it's personal to him, really damn personal.

My gorgeous, talented, gifted man needs me right now. He needs this escape and I will not deny him. He turns me and presses me against the refrigerator, my back to the steel surface, his hands sliding over my breasts, cupping them, even as his tongue licks into my mouth. I reach for his shirt, but he's already caught the hem of mine and it's over my head in about two seconds. He tosses it and his eyes meet mine, dark shadows in their depths that do nothing to hide the war that rages inside this man.

I want to ask about the message again, I want to ask what it says, what it means, but that is not what he needs right now. That is not what comes next and we both know it. "I know what's happening right now. I know what you're battling. I want to be here for you. What do you need right now?"

"More than I deserve from you."

"What does that even mean?"

"It means I should walk away, but no matter how many times I think it or say it, I won't. I know I won't do it." His body quakes, almost as if he's experiencing an internal tremor that I can physically see.

I press my hand to his chest. "What do you need right now? Right this minute. Say it. Tell me. Take it. Do it."

His hands grip my wrists, and he pulls me close. "You don't want to know what I need right now. You don't want to see me like I am right now. I don't *want* you to see me like I am right now."

"And I don't want you to hide this part of you. *What do you need from me right now?*"

He shuts his eyes, a turbulent, tormented look on his face, his grip almost too hard, but somehow, I wish he'd hold on tighter. "Eric," I whisper.

He opens his eyes and looks at me. "Go to the living room and undress. Wait for me there."

Chapter Eighty-Eight

Harper

"*G*o *to the living room and undress. Wait for me there.*"

Eric watches me, waiting for me to obey his command.

But this isn't about control. I know that instantly. It's about trust and for reasons that stretch beyond the Kingston family, but most certainly rooted in their very existence. So yes, his order is daunting, but it's not one that I will refuse him. I don't believe he would ever hurt me. In fact, he's proven that he'll protect me. That he'll include me in his life, down to making the decision to spare his father, the man who he blames for his mother's death. With these things in mind, I don't let him wonder what I would do if I walked into the living room, where I could still back out.

I stand right there in the kitchen and shed every last inch of what I'm wearing down to my socks. Once I'm naked, vulnerable with this man beyond the fact that I'm wearing nothing and he's still dressed, vulnerable in how much I've fallen for him, how easily he could hurt me, my chin lifts with a realization. "I don't hesitate with you, Eric," I say. "One day, I hope you won't with me either."

I'm still in a mental box he's created labeled "Kington" which translates to pain. It's why his first instinct over my miscarriage was distrust, but I forgive him because I understand him. My need to touch him is all encompassing and I press my hand to his chest. "I know you hold back. I know you do, and it's okay. I know what this family has done to you. Just as I know the real love of a family, and I want to be yours."

He stares down at me, his eyes shadowed, half veiled, and he doesn't move. He's more stone than man, more muscle than heart. With another realization, I let my hand fall away. He wanted me to go to the living room because he needed a moment to compose himself and step outside whatever savant-related episode he's battling. As much as I want him to face this with me, as much as I want to understand this part of him, he's not ready for me to see all of him.

He still needs space. I have to understand that.

I step away from him, oblivious now to my naked body. I'm thinking about him. I'm thinking about his walls. I'm thinking about the space between us that this family creates, and while they are why we met, they may well be why we're divided. I make it all of two steps and suddenly he's captured my arm and pulled me back to him. In an inhaled breath, I'm pressed close to him, one of his hands splayed between my shoulder blades, molding me against his body, while he tangles the fingers of his free hand into my hair, wrapping the strands tightly, roughly.

"What are you doing to me, woman?"

"What are *you* doing to *me*?"

"I was going to push you. Push you so fucking hard, I probably would have pushed you away."

"Do it. Try. Push me. If that's what you need, if you need to push my limits, and your own, to deal with whatever is going on inside you, then push. I'll push with you. I can handle it."

"Can you?"

"For you, I can handle anything, Eric."

"What if I turn you over my knee? What if I spank you and fuck you and spank you again? What if I take everything, and destroy you and us."

His words shock but they don't horrify. He's testing me and I understand all the ways he needs to test me. I understand all the reasons he doubts me. I won't fail. "Nothing you just said to me would destroy us."

His phone rings and he grimaces, his mouth coming down on mine, hard, demanding, the taste of anger on his lips all over again. He's still so very angry and I still don't know why. I sink into the kiss, welcoming his emotion, the pain that's hidden deep in the depths of it. The torment I believe he lets me taste. That's his naked truth. That's his path to me and mine to him.

I reach for his T-shirt, and he drags it over his head, tossing it, the logoed cotton that reads "Kingston Motors" somehow appropriately hitting the ground. "Don't wear that shirt again," I order. "It doesn't fit you. And I'm not talking size, and we both know it."

"And it does you?" he demands, his fingers tightening around my hair.

"No. No, it never did, but you do."

I barely finish those words and he's kissing me again, a deep intensity to the stroke of his tongue that is somehow both wild and controlled. I'm wild but not in control. I have this insane feeling I'm about to lose him if I don't get close enough to him, if I don't feel him deep enough. If I don't let him know how much I hunger for him. My hands are all over his body, caressing the taut flesh beneath my palms, that beautiful ink that tells his story, drawing me in, making me hunger for more. I need more. And he touches me and kisses me like he wants all of me, but he already has me.

Somehow, I end up on top of the island and Eric's low, rough declaration of, "I need inside you now," has me fumbling with his pants even as he manages to drag them down.

And then he's there, between my legs, thick and hard and pulsing, pressing into the slick wet heat of my body, driving into me, stretching me. He thrusts deep, settling in that deepest spot inside me and for a moment he's staring down at me, studying me like he means to see my soul. "I will push you. I will take more than you want me to take and push you harder than you want to be pushed."

"You can try," I challenge. "But it still won't drive me away."

His thumb stretching to my jaw, tilting my mouth to his. "Remember you said that." And then he's kissing me again, taking me in that kiss, and in a thrust of his cock that rockets sensations through me. Taking and taking, but I am, too. I arch into him, lifting my hips, and soon he's cupping my backside, arched over me, forcing my hands to the counter behind me. I'm not oblivious to the control this gives him. I'm not naïve to him needing this, but I want him to have what he needs. I want to heal the hundreds of cuts that bleed from his soul, and I will do anything to make that happen. The way he almost gave everything when he risked his life to save mine in that warehouse.

That is my last coherent thought as sensations rock my body, and his hand cups my breast and pinches my nipple. I arch again, lifting into his thrust and we shatter together, our bodies quaking, trembling and then finally collapsing. We come back to the present with a pounding on the door, and somehow, it feels as if the devil himself is our visitor. Somehow, I just know, maybe because of the fierceness of the pounding, that whatever is on the other side of that door is a problem and not a small one.

Chapter Eighty-Nine

Harper

I'm still naked on the island, with Eric leaning over me, when yet another pounding sounds on the door. "Damn it," Eric grounds out. "What the fuck."

"It must be because you didn't answer your phone," I say.

"Yeah, fuck probably." He lifts me and sets me on the floor. "Or it's Savage being Savage and over the top about everything."

I laugh. "There's that, too."

He grips either side of the counter. "Eventually I'm going to get you alone and keep you naked for an entire weekend." He kisses me and when he would release me, I catch his hand.

"Are you okay?"

He cuts his gaze sharply but then he's back, and I'm staring into his clear blue eyes, the storm banked at least for the moment. "When I'm with you, I am."

It's a reply every woman would welcome from this man, and I do. Of course, I do, but it's not quite a direct answer. It's avoidance I want to poke holes in, but I'm naked and we have a guest at the door, so I let it go. And for now, only now, I let Eric go, too. He scoops up my clothes and sets them on a barstool. I clean up and start dressing as he adjusts his pants, and then grabs his T-shirt. It's then that my gaze catches his tattoos, rows and rows of letters and numbers inking his arms and chest to total completion. Ink that tells his story and that's a story that after today, I know I don't fully understand. Just like the row of letters and numbers on the back of that business card tells a story. One I'm now reminded that Eric understands in some way that I don't. And now, we have company to distract us, which isn't well timed.

Eric isn't going to tell anyone but me what that message means, and he doesn't even want to tell me.

I finish dressing and pull on my socks and shoes to find Eric watching me. "We need to go shopping so you have some things of your own."

There's a pinch in my chest, with the thought of my cute little house in Denver, that will never feel like home ever again. I can't believe how fast my life has changed. Everything I knew was there. Now everything I want is here. My eyes burn for no good reason and I cut my gaze, afraid Eric's going to misread my state of mind. Eric steps in front of me and tilts my gaze to his. "I don't want you to go back." He pauses as if for effect. "Ever."

This is what I want to hear from him, maybe even needed to hear from him, I realize. I don't want to go back to Denver; I just don't want to leave my mother behind, but as I study this handsome, brilliant man, I set that aside for now. I'm focused on him and the undertone to his words. I'm focused on a hint of trepidation in him, the uncertainty I think I see in his eyes. Does he really think I'd leave him? Does he really think I'm anything but one hundred percent here with him? Yes, I decide. He thinks I'm going to leave, if not now, one day. He thinks I'm somehow too good for him and this tells me that my man, my beautiful man, is so very damaged by this damn family.

There's another knock on the door. "Maybe it's urgent," I say, starting to get concerned. "If it's Savage he knows we're safe now and he's still being pushy."

"Right. I'll go." He's already walking toward the door.

I hug myself and step deeper into the kitchen to watch him close the space between us and the entryway, all long-legged grace and confidence, but there's a sharpness to his spine, a tension in his shoulders. The connection between us got him out of his own head, but it was short-lived and we never dealt with whatever set him off.

There's nothing I can do about it now though. Eric's already opening the door and Savage steps inside, and just the brute size of the man is a force when entering a room. "Grayson's in a hired car that just pulled up downstairs," Savage announces, shutting the door. "I tried to call and warn you. We couldn't stop him from coming. He said it's critical that he talk with you."

Eric grimaces, his hands settling on his hips. "I thought you were taking him home?"

"We did," Savage confirms. "He made it all the way into his apartment and then he figured out that you weren't joining him and he wasn't having it. He said he needs to talk to you in private, one on one."

I hug myself a little tighter now and digest this news. Grayson was worried. I know that. He had reason to be worried but this feels over the top. Or is it? Would I let Eric get away with shutting me down if I was worried? No. I wouldn't. Well, outside of sex on the kitchen island, which distracted me, but that wasn't meant to replace conversation. And yet it has. I can't talk to him now.

Eric runs a hand through his hair, an act of utter frustration that he rarely displays. He's a man of control and between myself and Grayson, we're practically wrestling it from his grip. That can't sit well. "Bring him up when he gets here."

Savage's phone buzzes with a text message and he glances at it and then Eric. "That would be now."

Eric's lips thin. "Of course it is. Is Mia with him?"

"No. Grayson made her stay with one of our men and," he glances at me and then Eric again, "he seems to really want to talk to you alone."

Eric turns away from Savage and just leaves him standing there. He walks right by me, through the living, to the bar area just beside his patio door. Shutting us out, claiming an empty space that I believe he lives inside far too often. Eager to fill that space, I cross to join him, watching as he pours himself a drink.

"Talk to me," I whisper, aware of Savage nearby, and wishing he'd just step back into the hallway.

"Not now," he says softly, and he still doesn't look at me. "Later."

The doorbell rings and he downs the amber liquid, setting the glass on the bar before he turns to me, his hand cupping my neck as he drags his mouth to mine. "There's much unsaid and undone between us, too much, but not for long." He kisses me, a deep, drugging kiss that is over too soon. Suddenly, he's set me aside, and he's gone, his long legs eating away the space between him and the door again.

Something in his words, in his manner, guts me, cuts me, burns me but I can do nothing but feel his pain. I can't stop it. Not now, and part of me wonders if I'll ever be able to. I pour myself a drink and down it, another type of burn—the whiskey-induced kind—following, first in my throat and then settling in my belly. I might regret that decision later, but right now I need to come down. I turn as Grayson and Eric enter the living room. "Harper," Grayson greets.

"Hey, Grayson," I say and without further preamble, I add, "I know you two need to talk. I'll go upstairs."

"We'll step into my office," Eric replies. "You stay here if you like. We won't be long."

They won't be long. Eric doesn't want to talk to Grayson any more than he does me. I nod and the two men cross the living room and enter the office, the same office where Eric had cursed out Smith for leaving the door unguarded. I wonder who is at the door now. I wonder what it would be like to live without this kind of drama, without the Kingston imprint on our lives. I watch Eric and Grayson disappear into the room and shut themselves away. Once I'm fully alone, I pour a splash more of whiskey into my glass and down it, choking with the burn that slides along my throat.

Once I arrive at Eric's bedroom, I pause at the doorway to stare at the massive bed, his bed. The bed he wants me to share with him again tonight. The one he wants me to share with him and call my own. I'm so deeply entrenched in this man's life and he in mine, that there's no turning back. Whatever comes next, no matter how good or bad, it's in motion. I inhale with the odd sense of foreboding that follows, rejecting it entirely. I'm here with Eric. He's got men protecting my mother. We're okay. We will stay okay.

Entering the room, I sit down on the chair in front of the window, staring forward without really seeing what's beyond the glass. Eric's voice lifts through the vent on the floor by the wall. "The bearded man gave her this," I hear him say, and I assume that Eric's now handing Grayson the card. "We received a similar message in Denver."

"From who?" Grayson asks. "The bearded man? He was there, too?"

"A different man. He parked in front of her house. When I approached him, he drove away and threw a message out of his window."

"Numbers and letters," Grayson says. "It reads like a message to you but this message seemed to target her. Was the other one the same?"

"Same format, different letters and numbers."

I stand up. I shouldn't be listening. I need to just leave the room, but then Grayson says, "What do they mean?" And that question plants my feet.

"Yes," I whisper. "What do they mean to you, Eric?"

"I haven't figured out the first one," Eric replies to Grayson. "But this one, the one Harper was handed at the hospital. This one is personal."

"Explain," Grayson presses and I hold my breath, waiting for what comes next, my stomach in knots.

"It translates to a saying we had in the SEALs. *If you ain't cheating, you ain't trying.* It means to win, you have to break the rules."

Grayson's silent for several beats and I imagine him studying Eric, before he says, "And you think that means someone knows what rules you were going to break with Kingston."

"Don't you?" Eric challenges. "It's a fucking threat. They want me to do something for them, pay them off in some way, or they'll tell Harper."

"Then you tell Harper. That's why I came here. You have to tell her."

"Tell her I betrayed her? Tell her I lied to her? Hell no. That's not happening."

"We both know it's not that simple. Explain it to her but tell her. Before someone else tells her."

Not because he loves me, I think. Not because he trusts me. Because someone else might tell me. Because someone else knows. This reasoning guts me more than the secret, the lie, that is obviously between me and Eric.

"She'll walk away," Eric bites out, his voice low, rough, guttural, "and I can't, *I cannot,* let her walk away."

And I can't breathe.

I can't breathe and my heart is beating so fast that I feel like I'm going to pass out. The voices go silent, or my heartbeat blasts over them, I don't know which. I don't even remember the moment that I exit the bedroom. I don't remember the walk down the stairs. I'm just standing at the office door. I open it and Eric and Grayson turn to me.

"I was upstairs. I heard you talking. I wasn't trying to, but—" I turn to Eric. "Tell me. Tell me everything. Is nothing between us real? Is this all a lie? Why can't you afford to let me walk away, Eric? What is this really all about?"

Part Three: The Empire

Chapter Ninety

Eric

Only moments before, I stood here in my office, in a heated conversation with Grayson, with no idea that Harper could overhear from the bedroom upstairs. No idea that I was jeopardizing our relationship.

With Harper staring at me, caging me and Grayson inside my office and demanding answers, my world shifts and spins, the ground no longer solid beneath my feet. I'm not solid without her. It's a realization that shakes me to the core.

She stares at me.

I stare at her.

A million unspoken words fill the space between us with her pain and accusations pulsing through it all.

"Harper," I say softly.

Her response is to cut her gaze sharply, as if her name on my lips guts her, while her attention lands hard on Grayson. "We need to be alone." Her voice quakes and trembles. "We've needed to be alone and—"

"Understood," Grayson says, and I can feel his gaze on me as he says, "I'm going home, but we need to finish the conversation." I'm not looking at him though. I'm focused on Harper, and Harper only, the woman I want in my life and could easily lose.

Numbers punch at me and my hand goes to the Rubik's cube on my desk. I don't pick it up, but I mentally solve the puzzle, each block I turn, taking me down one notch and then another.

Grayson moves toward the door and Harper steps into the room and out of the archway to allow his exit. He pauses next to her and waits for her to look at him. She resists, her attention on the Rubik's cube that I know she knows my mind reaches for. I know she knows I'm mentally trying to work through how to make this right with her.

"Harper," Grayson finally says, compelling her attention.

She jerks her gaze to his, and then and only then, with her focus, does he say, "It's not what it seems at first glance. There's a reasonable explanation for what you heard. Listen to it all before you react."

She swallows hard and nods but doesn't speak. I notice the delicate line of her neck in profile, which might seem like an odd observation to some, but to me, it's about how easily it would be to those who didn't know her well, to assume her to be as delicate as her petite, feminine body. They'd be wrong. She's strong; strong enough to walk away from me no matter how much we might share.

Grayson grips her shoulder, a gesture of support and friendship that I appreciate in this moment. It's him telling her that she's family now. It's him telling her the confession she just overheard, the secret I appear to have kept from her, means nothing and it doesn't. It's not as big of a deal as she might appear, but I didn't tell her, because I knew how she'd react. I didn't know if I'd get her to hear every part of the story.

Fuck.

I think about in the kitchen, naked, fucking without a condom again. Maybe some part of me allowed that to happen. Because she's the only way I'd have a child is with her. Her child. *Our baby.* A beautiful little girl with her dark hair and blue eyes. It's not something I deserve or want. My child might well be like me, a savant, a freak, and I don't wish that on anyone, let alone my child.

The door firmly shuts as Grayson leaves, jolting me out of my thoughts, back to this room, and the confession she overheard. Harper leans against the wooden surface of the door, as if she can't hold herself upright, as if she's that shaken by what she overheard. Her hand goes to her belly, obviously trying to calm a reaction to the stress. She's that affected by what she's feeling, by her obvious belief that I've betrayed her. And I have. I hate it, but I have. I don't want her to feel these things and yet, I can't deny the pain I've caused her.

I step toward her, but she holds up her hand. "No." Her voice is rough, a tremble of emotion. "No, I don't think clearly when you touch me. *Talk to me*, Eric, like you should have already." Dark hair falls over her face and I want to shove it away, but she does it herself with an angry swipe of her hand.

I want to touch her. I want to pull her to me and force her to stop fucking thinking so much but that's not the answer. She's right. We have to talk. She deserves honesty. "You think this is a big lie, but it isn't. This is not some shocking revelation."

"That's not what you said to Grayson."

I scrub my jaw. "I was angry with the Kingston family. You know that."

"Okay," she says. "And since that's not news to me, keep talking. What do you really have to say to me?"

Too much. Not enough. Too fucking much. I walk to the sunken alcove that frames the only window in the room, folding my arms in front of my chest. I don't know what to say to her and seconds tick into a full minute before she steps to my side. My side, where I want her to remain. Together, the way it should be, we stare out of the glass. "This skyline," I say finally, indicating the jagged edges of buildings and the ocean that is our view, "this damnable skyline is what I thought would make me forget the mountaintops of Denver I always loved so damn much."

"But it didn't? It doesn't?"

I turn and lean on the inner wall of the alcove and she does the same, facing me. I meet her stare, I let her see the truth she questions in my eyes. "There are times when my mother is in my memories—times when I wanted the mountains back. When I wanted what I couldn't have. Times when I wanted to destroy every Kingston that lives and breathes."

"Past tense?"

"For the most part, yes but I have nightmares, Harper. They come and go and all of them are either about my time living with the Kingstons, or about my mother, and how that family all but held a gun to my mother's head."

"How often?" she asks, sounding worried. "How bad?"

"Not often, not any more, and as for how bad? Bad. Really fucking bad. So much so that I usually take a week off at the office, hole up in here and get a grip on myself. I still work, but I'm absent from the rest of the world to avoid any exterior triggers."

"Grayson knows?"

I nod. "Yes. Grayson knows."

Her lips thin and her expression tightens. "What else does he know that I should know?"

"The last time it happened was right after I heard about the second Kingston recall. The company was weak, ripe for an attack."

"An attack?" she asks. "By who?"

"A lot of people, but in this case, I'm referring to me. I set out to weaken them and take them over. Grayson knew. It was a business move, nothing more, our path into the automobile industry, or that's how I painted it."

"And Grayson believed that?"

"No, Grayson believed it was personal but if it finally gave me closure, he wanted me to have closure."

"What about all those morals you say he possesses?"

"He's a businessman and it's not like someone else wouldn't have done it, had they seen the opportunity. We both knew we'd treat the employees and the customers better. We'd make them all safe. We'd make them all more secure."

"And I was a Kingston. Is that where this is going? It didn't matter if you hurt me?"

"Yes," I admit. "Exactly. I had plans to ensure your trust fund was defunct. You'd never see it. I did that because I didn't want the Kingstons to have a way to use it to save themselves, which is exactly what they did. They used your money and—"

She tries to move away. I catch her arm. "Harper. Damn it, you agreed to listen. To hear me out."

Her eyes are fire and pain. "You tried to destroy me. Didn't you?" Her voice trembles with barely contained anger. "Is that why my trust fund is gone? Was I supposed to come to you and beg for help? *Was I?*"

"No. No. *And no.* Listen to me. I told you I wanted to ruin them. I told you I included you in the Kingston family. I never held that back."

"Did you take actions to destroy me and my mother?"

"I prepped a plan. I didn't act, but I was close. I even negotiated with the banks that Kingston uses for their credit lines to strip them away. Now, ask the next obvious question."

"Why didn't you do it?"

"You. *You* are the reason I didn't do it."

"You say that now but—"

I drag her to me. "Ask Grayson. I was sixty seconds from pulling the switch but you stopped me."

"Me? You hadn't seen me in years."

"I did. I had. I went to Denver to finish the takeover. I was at the bank when you walked in. You fought with Isaac. I didn't know why. I couldn't hear you, but you fought with the same fierceness I always felt when I fought with him, when I believed I was right and he was wrong. When something mattered to me. Watching you with him made that night in the cottage come back to me. That conversation you and I had about your need to protect your father's empire came back to me. You're the reason I backed out of the takeover. I know it sounds impossible. I knew it then, and I know now, but I fell hard for you the moment I met you, harder than I wanted to admit. That's why I never forgot you. That's why I tattooed you on my damn arm."

"Fell for me? You hated me enough to try to destroy me then. That wasn't a long time ago. It's present day and now you dare to say you love me?"

"I never hated you and I would have told you all of this but the events of the past week have been lightning speed."

"You're only telling me now because someone else knows. You're telling me because the message on the back of that business card made you believe that someone else knows about your plans to destroy me."

"Do you think I want you to know what a vengeful asshole I was? I am? I didn't, but I *would* have told you."

"When?"

"After you agreed to stay here with me. After I saved your mother so you believed I would."

Her fingers curl on my chest. My hand comes down on her face, tilting her gaze to mine. "I know this is happening fast, Harper, and I'm not an easy man to understand or live with. This savant thing is hell. I'm hell sometimes in ways you don't know yet, but I don't want to do this without you."

"Do what without me?"

"Everything. Anything." My voice lowers, a tremble in the depth of my words that I can't control. "I'm sorry. Forgive me. Stay with me."

Harper doesn't immediately respond, her intelligent eyes searching my face for the sincerity in my apology, and my desire to have her with me. "Stay because I can't live another day, let alone another six years, without you," I add softly. "Stay because I hope like hell you feel the same." And with that confession, I wait, I hold my breath, and pray that she doesn't walk away from me and us.

Chapter Ninety-One

Harper

I'm reeling. I'm confused.

Eric and I stand in that alcove of the window in his office, the warmth of our bodies doing nothing to wash away the coldness of what he'd planned to do to me and the Kingston empire. "You tried to ruin me," I whisper. "I still don't even know what to do with that information." I step back, force away his touch, and lean against the stone wall behind me; needing the extra support as I search his handsome face, probing his blue eyes that tell a story I need desperately to understand. "It all feels like a lie. We feel like a lie."

"We're *not* a lie." He steps toward me and presses a hand to the wall just above my head, but he doesn't touch me. I want him to touch me. I want to push him away. I'm a conflicted mess where this man is concerned.

"*Nothing* I have told you is a lie, Harper. If I wanted to ruin you, you know me well enough to know I would have. I stopped before I went too far."

"I can't get over how far you took it. You met with bankers."

"But I *didn't* do it."

"You should have told me on your own. Not because that message I was given at the hospital forced you to. Not because I overheard your conversation with Grayson."

"What you overheard was pieces of a bigger picture, not the full picture. It's been a crazy few days. I would have told you."

"Grayson didn't believe you were going to tell me."

"Grayson doesn't know all that's transpired the past few days. He doesn't know how much either of us have had to digest. He doesn't understand the extent of this war which we're in together. *Together*, Harper, and fuck, I want to touch you right now, but I feel like you don't want me to. I would have told you. I swear to you on my mother's memory, God rest her soul."

"No." My hands come down on his chest, heat and emotion spiking between us with the connection. "No, don't do that. Don't swear on your mother's memory. I believe you. I have to believe you would have told me because any other place my mind goes is not a good place. I don't want to believe that you saw my visit as a way to attack that family."

"I was done with them," he replies, his voice a snap of barely contained anger. "I went back for you. I saved that damn family for you."

"Saved them from yourself?"

"Yes. You saved them from me. If we're going to be honest here, *you* saved them from me more than once, at least where my father's concerned."

"How do I believe I have that power? Why would I have that power?" I shake my head. "I don't know how I have that power."

"And yet you do. There are only three people in my life who have ever been able to pull me back when I'm charging forward: my mother, Grayson, and you."

"I want to be able to do that for you, but we just talked about trust on the plane. You say you would have told me—"

"*I would have.*" His words are low, rough, emotion-laden in ways he doesn't do emotion except with me.

"But you didn't want to. I heard you say that to Grayson."

"Of course, I didn't want to tell you, Harper. But I would have worked through my resistance and done what was right. And telling you was what was right."

You didn't trust me and what I'd do with that information. That was clear in what you said to Grayson. You didn't trust me or us. I need us to be more than that or I can't do this."

"When this family gets out from between us, we will be."

"They don't get to be between us, Eric. That's not how this works. No excuses. No secrets. You trust me. I trust you."

His eyes sharpen. "Are you sure you can live with those terms, Harper?"

The implications of that question are clear. He believes I have another secret. Maybe I do, but it's not like his. I duck under his arm and walk toward the desk, whirl around to face him, even as he faces me. "I want that kind of trust with you."

His eyes narrow on me, those damn intelligent eyes that see everything. He knows I didn't say yes. He knows I just avoided a direct answer. Damn it, I want to tell him what I found, what I saw, what I know about him, but now more than ever, I fear it will only make things worse. "I really do want that kind of trust with you, Eric."

He pursues me, closing the space between us, and this time, he doesn't stay hands off. His hand slides around my back and settles low, molding me close. "Does that mean you're staying?"

I could resist, and torment us both with a battle, with a breakup, but he's right. There's so much going on in our lives, so much that has tried to divide us, so much keeping us apart even as we've held on to each other. I've never believed for one moment he wasn't flawed or that I knew everything there was to know about him. He is a beautiful, broken man, but I think he's less broken when he's with me. As I am with him. And those things matter.

"Yes," I say. "I'm staying but I'm still angry with you."

He strokes my hair behind my ear, and his touch shivers through me, his finger settling beneath my chin and tilting my gaze to his. "Be angry with me, but don't leave me. I will not be okay without you."

"I will not be okay without you either, which is a terrifying thing to confess after what you just told me."

"That was the past, the part of our story that brought us together. Without it, we wouldn't be here right now."

He's right. Much like his tattoos, we are a dramatic story filled with heartache and happiness, created over time, even years before we met that first time at his father's house. And when his lips brush mine, I tell myself we will leave the heartache behind and find our happy ending.

Chapter Ninety-Two

Harper

Thirty minutes later, we're in the living room, on the couch, a bottle of wine between us, our glasses full and plates ready, waiting on our Chinese takeout to be delivered. We also have the two coded messages we've been given, and not one, not two, but three Rubik's cubes in front of us. I grab one of them and eye Eric. "I thought you didn't need to solve these to focus anymore?"

"I don't *have* to use them," he explains. "I can focus without them, but I've trained my mind to turn off the outside noise the minute I pick one up."

"That's something you learned in the military, right?"

"Yes. When I went into the Navy, I was just another enlisted soldier to the government, but as they discovered my 'gifts' as they called them, they called in several specialists to work with me. One, a woman named Karen Montgomery, a grumpy old lady is a more precise description, honed my thinking process. She was a bitch, but she was a good bitch. Good at heart. Good intentions. To her, being the bitch was her job. She was about protecting me. She was saving my life and teaching me how to save other people's lives."

"Do you ever talk to her now?"

"She had a heart attack during one of our training sessions."

I blanch. "What?"

He nods. "She smoked like a chimney and drank like the sailor she was. And she was no spring chicken." He gives me a sad smile. "She grabbed my arm right before she died and made me recite a formula for her. Anyway, to her I wasn't a freak. I really was gifted."

The freak he still sees himself as to this day. And there it is. His self-hate. The hate I want to reach inside him and yank away, never to be seen again. "You *are* gifted, Eric."

"I was in hell when my first cube was put in my hand," he says, picking one of them up and looking at me. "There were times when the data that I had access to literally brought me to my knees. I couldn't slow it down. That didn't feel like a gift. It felt like a curse."

"Look at your success. Look at your life. You have to see that your curse is a gift now."

"I'm not like everyone else to the rest of the world."

I reach out and cover the cube in his hand. "I like you just how you are."

His lashes lower, a shadow sliding over his face, and when I might press him to look at me, to talk to me, the doorbell rings, no doubt our food. Eric immediately untangles our grip, sets the cube on the table and gets up. Shutting me out. Shutting me down. The doorbell was simply the vehicle he used to do it but I remind myself talking about how he got to where he is now, means talking about that past. That means his father, his mother. His tortured youth. Maybe he's not shutting me out. He's instinctively protecting himself.

There's a difference.

My gaze lowers and lands on the two messages, and once I'm looking at them, I set aside my talk with Eric. They have my focus and I will them to mean something, but they just don't. My cellphone buzzes on the coffee table and it's my mother. I want to answer, but I don't know what to say to her. I twist around to find Eric already walking back toward me, bags of food in his hand.

"That's my mother calling," I say. "What do we want her to know?" My phone stops ringing.

Eric sits down with me, placing our order on the table. "The best thing we can do, and the safest for her is to keep her out of this for as long as we can."

"I *am* my mother's daughter. In other words, that won't work for long. She won't be put off. Your father is fighting for his life. He's her husband and he might be a horrible person to us, but he is the man she loves."

"Be honest. She's under protective custody until we know exactly what happened to my father."

"Which translates to catching the assassin. How do we do that?"

"I hope like hell he does come for us," he says. "Then I don't have to hunt the bastard down."

"Because we'll be dead?"

"You underestimate me, princess."

I think of the man in the warehouse, and how easily Eric handled him. "I'm not underestimating you," I say. "I saw what you can do, but that's no surprise to anyone anymore. I'm assuming that after the warehouse incident, the assassin won't either. He'll have a plan."

"And it won't work." He motions to my food. "Eat, sweetheart. We've had a hell of a couple of days. We both need to take every chance we can get to eat and rest."

I nod and set my phone down, but I find it curious that my mother hasn't called back. "Can you ask Adam what's going on with my mother?"

"Of course." He snags his phone from his pocket. "Eat while we wait."

I nod and we unload the bags and dig into our food. "I never got to tell you about my talk with Mia. She said she'd talk to Grayson and convince him to back off."

"And not long later, he showed up here," Eric comments. "Obviously, she failed, but I have a plan B. Davis is going to get him out of town."

"Grayson isn't going to go."

"He'll go because he'll think he's handling the NFL deal on my behalf. He needs to feel like he's helping me."

"He was right when he told you to be honest with me." I put my fork down and turn to him. "I hate that he trusted me more than you trusted me."

"He had nothing to lose. I have you to lose. Which is an example of how one answer is not the only answer. It's often different if you look at it from another perspective." His fingers close on my knee. "What you just said about my skills no longer being a surprise. What if my father didn't hire the man who attacked me in the alleyway? What if it was the assassin? What if he was testing my skills?"

"But he knew where you were."

"He could have been following me."

My cellphone buzzes with another call from my mother. "I think I need to take the call."

Eric tunes out this comment. Instead, he grabs the business card the bearded man gave me and stares at the message on the back. "What if it wasn't about a secret I'm keeping from you?" He looks at me. "What if that was my guilt driving how I saw the message?"

"What are you saying?"

"The SEALs consider ourselves brothers. What if this message was telling me that the root of our problems is my brother?"

"That feels obvious. Doesn't it?"

"The man told you to look at what was right in front of you and this message," he holds up the card, "ties me to Isaac. Fuck," he says softly and then pulls his shirt off, tossing it to stare down at his arm. "Somewhere on my body is the link that ties those two messages together."

My phone buzzes with a text message. My mother has given up on calls, apparently, and I glance down to read: *Does Eric know?*

My heart sinks. Oh God. His father must be dead.

Chapter Ninety-Three

Harper

I stare up at Eric, still standing above me, his shirt off, the ink etched on his body highlighting taut skin and well-developed muscle. Ink that tells a million stories, one of which perhaps solves our puzzle, but right now I'm looking at the jaguar covering one shoulder. The black ink, the blue eyes. The symbol of everything Eric hates about his life, perhaps even about himself. But his father is a part of him. His father has been his only parent still living for more than a decade of his life.

Eric sits down and takes the phone from me, his gaze lowering to the message. He frowns and looks at me. "Does Eric know what, Harper?"

I grab his arm. "Your father—"

"I'd know before your mother. Walker is tapped into the hospital activity and law enforcement."

I'm afraid to let relief take over. "What else could it be?"

"Call her."

"Call Adam. Please. Call him before I call her. I want to know what I'm getting myself into. And it's weird that she hasn't said anything else. No more calls. No more text messages." My fist balls at my chest. "She might be falling apart right now. I need to go to her, Eric. I know it's dangerous but—"

"We'll bring her to us if necessary." He reaches for his phone that's sitting on the table and dials Adam on speaker.

"Yo, man, what's up?" Adam answers.

"I've got you on speaker with Harper. What the hell is going on?"

"I have no idea what you're talking about. Isaac is still holed up in his house. I went to check on him and he's doing a lot of pacing and not much more. I'm watching him myself. Harper's mother is loopy on the drugs but fine. I have Jesse, one of our best, with her."

"She sent me a text message," I say. "It says, 'Does Eric know?'"

"What? That's odd. Hold on." The line clicks as he obviously mutes it.

"Should we call Blake?" I ask.

"That's what Adam's doing right now, I promise you. He's communicating with Jesse and Blake."

I nod and stand up. Eric pulls me back down. "Relax, baby. All is well."

The endearment does funny things to my stomach, perhaps because it's new. Perhaps because there is such tenderness in his face and his voice when he says it. "Baby? You never call me baby."

"Would you prefer princess?"

Adam comes back on the line. "Your father is fine, Eric. No change. Your mother is awake for the first time in a few hours, but she's struggling with the effects of the drug. She's drunk on Xanax. He knew she was calling you. He has no idea what the message is about. We can take her phone."

"No," I say. "Not yet. Let me call her."

"Just shoot me a text," he says. "Let me know what you need and want on this."

"Will do," Eric says, disconnecting the line. "Call her. Let's find out what it is that she thinks I know or don't know."

I have a horrible feeling this might be about the secrets I've kept from him. A really horrible feeling. My gut twists and I desperately want to tell him before I call her, but there isn't time. There's too much going on, too much danger in the air for me to delay. I dial my mother, but I don't put it on speaker phone. She answers on the first ring. "Harper! Harper. God. Harper. What if he dies? What if he dies?" She starts to sob. "And they won't let me go to him."

I inhale and let it out. "They're trying to keep you safe."

"I need to be there with my husband and my daughter. Are you safe?"

"I'm safe." It hits me that she knew I was here when I didn't tell her I was here. "How did you know I was here, mom?"

"Know? You told me."

I did not, but she's drugged. Obviously, she's very drugged. "What was that text message you sent me about?" My eyes meet Eric. "*Does Eric know? Does he know what?*"

"I—I don't want him to know. He can't know."

"Know what, mother? What are you talking about?"

She starts to sob again. "It would be bad. Oh God. What if he knows? What if he's the one who did this? What if it was him? What if—"

I stand up, angry now, certain this is indeed about the dirty deeds this family has done to Eric. Certain I have to tell him. I walk toward the window, my voice low, but my fury palpable. "He didn't do this, but my God, mother. He has every right to hate this family. Can you imagine if they'd done to me what they did to his mother and him? How can you not see what they are? How can you not understand what they've done is evil?"

"It was all Isaac. Isaac did it all, not your father."

"He's not my damn father and Isaac didn't do half the shit this family did to Eric. It was Gigi and her damn son. Your husband. And you're close to both of them. Please tell me that you didn't have any part of any action against Eric. Because if you did—"

"Why can you not see how much he can take? Why can you not see that he can take everything? Why? Don't you know—"

"He doesn't want your money. He has his own. Far more than you will ever have. Tell me you didn't—"

"Does he know? Is that what this is about? Is he coming for us because he knows?"

I frown. She keeps saying that. "What is it that you think he knows?"

"You know what it is. You know. I told you."

"You weren't sure when you told me. Then you said you were wrong."

"I am. I just—I didn't want you to hate your father so I—I told you I was wrong. I know you knew it was true, though."

Bile rises in my throat. It's true. I can't believe it's true and she's still with that man.

"Did you tell him?" she demands. "Did you tell him because you imagined yourself in love with him? He's your stepbrother. He's—"

"Stop! Will you just stop? I don't imagine myself in love with him. I *am* in love with him." One of my hands presses to the glass. "I love him."

"He doesn't love you. He loves power. He's using you to take everything. He's taking the love of my life and now he's taking you and all we've worked for."

The love of her life. Suddenly that isn't my father. Emotions well inside me. Anger. Pain. More anger. "I don't even know who you are right now," I say, my voice low, taut, when I want to scream

421

at her. "Take your Xanax, mother, and go to bed." I disconnect, trepidation enveloping me. I don't know how I tell Eric what must be revealed. I think to this point I've reasoned away telling him because I wasn't certain of the facts. But I can no longer deny the truth as reality. But how do I do this? No. I can't tell him. Oh Lord, help me and him, I *have* to tell him.

Eric's hand settles on my waist, warm, strong, and perfect. I don't want to tell him. I don't even know if it's safe to tell him. I rotate to face him, taking in the handsome lines of his face. His firm jaw. His full mouth that can be both brutal and gentle, sometimes within the same few minutes. My gaze lands back on that jaguar tattoo and my hands settle on top of it. "I wanted to protect you."

His eyes narrow, the blue sharpening with sparks of amber. The air sharpening with his sudden shift in mood. He doesn't touch me, a charge crackling off of him. "What does that mean, Harper?"

Chapter Ninety-Four

Harper

I try to catch my breath, but I can't. I'm almost wheezing with the effort. I think I might be hyperventilating and I've never hyperventilated in my life. Eric's hands come down on my arms and he turns me, pressing me against the beam dividing the window. "What is bad enough to make you react like you are right now? And what happened to no more secrets?"

"I wasn't sure it was real. I said that, didn't I? I'm not sure if I did or didn't but that's the case. My mother told me years ago and then she played it off like she was wrong about it. Now, she thinks that I told you and that you tried to kill your father because of it."

"Harper," he warns, his expression stormy, intense, dark.

"I need to tell you. I do, but I need a plan first." My eyes go wide with the only solution possible. "I tie you to the bed to tell you and let you calm down before you take action. Or not tie you down. I think you need your cubes. Lots of cubes. Like a dozen and to be locked in a room. Can we do that? Can we do those things?" Tears start to burn in my eyes. My fingers flatten on his chest. "Please. I'm begging you. I need you. We need each other, remember?"

"Yes. I remember, Harper, but whatever this is, I probably already know. Just tell me and let's deal with this."

"No. No, you don't know this or your father would be dead right now. You wouldn't have saved him. God. He didn't deserve to be saved. I convinced myself this wasn't real. I convinced myself he didn't do this because if he did, that means my mother accepts what he did. It almost makes her guilty. I knew I'd lose her. I knew—"

"Harper," Eric says firmly, tilting my gaze to his, and only then do I realize that tears are streaming down my cheeks. "You need to take a deep breath, sweetheart. It's going to be okay. I'm certain, I know more than you think I know." His thumbs stroke the tears from my cheeks.

"Not this." I grab his hand. "Not this. I can't tell you this without you letting me lock you in a room or something first."

"Trust me—"

"I do. And I want you to trust me, which is why I knew I ultimately had to tell you this but when you hear what it is, you'll know why I didn't want to. You'll know why I thought it's unchangeable but painful, so why cut you that way?"

"Just tell me."

"Let's go get naked upstairs." I wrap my arms around him. "Let's just go fuck and fuck some more. Forget this. You can't change it. I can't change it."

"Harper, I need you to just tell me."

"No." I laugh and it's not with humor. I sound a little crazy. "No. This isn't a good idea. I was smart to not tell you. I was holding it back to protect you."

His jaw sets and voice firms. "You're going to tell me."

Panic rises inside me. "Let me off the window." He doesn't move and I push on his chest. "Let me off the window!"

"Harper—"

"Eric. Damn it. I'm suffocating."

His eyes glint with a mix of steel and storm clouds. He wants to push me. Oh God, he's *going* to push me. I reacted emotionally. I did this. I opened my stupid mouth. And there are so many prices that will be paid for this. "It's nothing I did. Let me off the window. Please."

His jaw flexes and the next thing I know I'm over his shoulder and he's carrying me across the living room. I don't even yelp. I can't seem to process anything for the ache in my chest and the blood rushing to my head. By the time he lowers me onto bed and then comes down on top of me, my head is throbbing.

"Tell me."

"And if I don't?"

"You will."

My fingers curl on his jaw, the rasp of stubble beneath my skin, tenderness filling me for this man. "This is a motive for you to kill your father. Right now, if you get accused of killing him, if he dies, I can say under oath you didn't know this. Wait until we know if you'll be blamed."

"Harper, *princess*—"

"I hate that name. It makes me feel like you think of me as one of them."

"You with me now. That name is about you and me, not them. Harper, I need you to tell me. I promise you, I will not leave this apartment after finding out. I'll stay right here with you."

"That's not enough."

"It's all I have. My word. My word to you, and a vow to make that mean something to you now and forever."

"Please don't hate me for not telling you."

"I don't. It's clear you were protecting me."

"Say it again. Promise me you will not leave after I tell you, but more so, tell me you'll confirm the information, and take a step back, a week, days, to think before you act."

His eyes meet mine. "I promise."

"And I'm not saying this to protect your father. If this is true, he is worse than I ever dreamt he could be. He's a monster. I'm saying this to protect you because you don't deserve to end up behind bars because of him."

He rolls with me, pulling me on top, telling me he's in control. I lean over him, and I draw in a breath, praying telling him is not a mistake, but I have to. He has a right to know. He has to know with my mother running her mouth. "It was—about six months after my miscarriage and my mother called me. She was in a panic. She'd found something that freaked her out. I met her at their house, and she said she'd seen notes in your father's files. She was looking for some property lease and—"

"What did she find?"

"Just keep in mind that she told me she was wrong. She read the document wrong."

"Harper, you're killing me here."

"The document was about a cancer trial that your mother was trying to get into."

He doesn't blink. "Why would my father have that document?"

"Then you know about the program?" I ask.

"Yes. I know about the program. It was her best hope. It was what we were hoping for, but she killed herself before she got in."

Dread fills me for all I must tell him. "Yes, well when I heard your father had documents related to the trial, I thought that meant that your mother mattered to him as well. That she was more to him than we realized."

"But?"

"My mother found proof of a payment to someone who worked at the facility. She thought he paid extra to get her into the program.

But then she found a note from the man the check was written to that read: *As requested, decline issued."*

He goes stiff, his jaw so hard I think it might shatter. "Are you saying that my father paid off someone at the treatment facility to ensure my mother didn't make it into that trial?"

"Yes. Later my mother said she misunderstood the note. That she found another and it explained that money wasn't a factor in acceptance into the study. It was first come, first serve. But today. Today she made it seem like—"

"He paid to keep her out of the trial," he repeats. "And she knew she'd been rejected the day she killed herself."

"Yes," I whisper. "Yes, I think so. Eric—"

He shoves his fingers through his hair, his head dipping low, his emotions cutting, jagging, and tunneling through the room. He's trembling and I'm not even sure it's from the numbers in his head. It's pure, white-hot fury.

Chapter Ninety-Five

Harper

E ric squeezes his eyes shut, but he doesn't immediately move. He's on top of me, his big body steel that seems to hum with his emotions. My hands close around his arms. "I hate them, too. I hate them and—"

He shifts then, his body suddenly lifting from mine, and I am ice, brittle to the bone with his withdrawal, terrified I've made the wrong decision by telling him about his mother. It's truly terrible timing, but when would be the right time for something like this? The minute he's standing, I'm sitting, holding myself up on my hands. Watching as he turns away, his shoulders bunching, his hands going to his waist, and I watch his body shift with the inhalation of a breath he holds, tension radiating off of him. Aware that the savant in him reacts to emotions, I'm afraid that anything I say or do might trigger a reaction he won't have otherwise.

Slowly, I scoot to the edge of the bed where I can be ready to do whatever he needs me to do. Ready to stop him from leaving any way I can manage. It won't be easy, but I have to win. There's no other option. He steps forward and I stand up. He takes two steps and I take one, only to have him stop dead in his tracks. I stop just as abruptly, holding my breath, not sure what to expect. A full attack, as he described after his mother passed? Anger? Pain? A charge toward the door to leave? I just don't know. I have no idea what to expect.

Will he hate me for not telling him sooner?

Will he hate me for staying with the Kingstons after I found out? For justifying what I learned as my mother talked craziness?

Will he hate me?

That's the bottom line.

Have I lost him? God, I can't lose him. I love him. I love him so much that it hurts to think about never touching him or kissing him again. It hurts to think about losing the chance to find out all we can be. I don't even know how he likes to spend the upcoming holidays he once spent with his mother, now that he's here in this life he created for himself. And as silly as it might seem, right now, that cuts terribly. I want to know everything about this man. I want to scream this at him. I want to kiss him. I want to rip the rest of his clothes off and make him stay in bed with me until the rest of the world forces us to leave. And yet, I do none of these things because they don't feel right.

Waiting feels right. Giving him space to decide what comes next feels right.

Several beats pass and we just stand there, neither of us speaking, but I can feel his awareness of me just behind him. Just as I'm intensely aware of him, so very aware of him. I've been aware of him on some deep, soul-searching level since the day I met him. I'm a part of this man. He's a part of me and he has to know that. He has to see that. I sway toward him and my fingers ball by my sides. I flash back to the day my mother told me what she'd found years ago now. I think of the moment I picked up the phone to try to track down Eric and then set the phone back down. And I did so for one reason: I didn't have the facts. Technically, I didn't this time either, but he had the right to know.

I need to say or do something.

Finally, when I think my knees might buckle from the intensity of the waves of adrenaline surging through me, Eric holds out a hand, a silent invitation to join him. My heart squeezes with this sign of unity. He's not pushing me away. He's not withdrawing. I step forward and press my hand in his and the minute my palm touches his palm, his fingers close around mine. I'd feel relief if it wasn't for the way his body hums. He's on edge. He's barely holding it together, and yet, he's holding my hand.

He walks me toward him until I'm by his side, and I think—I really do think—he's telling me something. He's telling me that he's not doing this without me. Seconds tick by when we would be shoulder to shoulder before he looks at me. "Come with me."

"Where?"

"Downstairs."

"Why downstairs?" I ask, nervous about how near the door we'll be there.

"The view. The cubes. The space I need to be in right now with you."

"With me?"

"Yes, Harper. With you."

"I'd like that."

"Good," he says simply, and he starts walking.

Together, we walk down the stairs and we say nothing. Together, we walk into the living room where we sit down again, where we'd been when this all started, where our food still sits. I close the lids and take it all to the kitchen where I store it. When I come back, Eric is standing at the window with a Rubik's cube in his hand. I don't close the space between us. I just know on some level that he needs me to be here, but that he needs space. Instead, I sit on the couch, pick up one of the cubes and hold it in my hand, watching him. Time passes by, told in the darkening of the sky, the disappearance of stars, the shift of the city lights beyond the window where he stands, the window that frames this room on top of the world where we hide. Where he thinks. Where the man, who is like no one I have ever known, thinks through what comes next. Right now, the storm is at bay. Right now, every bullet I feared might fly remains locked and loaded in a weapon that is this man. Right now, he's more savant than man, and it's the man that will hold that weapon.

I don't know how much time passes, but suddenly he goes from standing there to pressing his hands on the glass, his chin on his chest, and I have this sense he's emerged from a tunnel. He's here. He's present. He's made decisions and those decisions are where trouble could emerge. This is where the man takes control. This is where this woman, *his woman*, needs to be ready to take control.

I set down the cube and stand up, hurrying across the room. Once I'm behind Eric, I wait, giving him time to face me, but I have this sense of him waiting on me, on him willing me to come to him. I slide between him and the bar running in front of the window, in almost the exact spot where he'd demanded I tell him everything. I don't touch him. He doesn't touch me. We just stand there, staring at each other, so close we could touch. So close that we are fire and there is no ice to be found. That's how we operate. That's how we ignite when we're near one another.

He reaches up and caresses my cheek, goosebumps lifting on my skin with that touch, tingling sensations sliding all through my body. "Princess," he says softly, and that word is both silk and blade to me. It cuts in so many ways.

I want to tell him to stop calling me that damn name again, as I have before. I want to tell him to never call me that again. His hands are suddenly on my upper arms, his eyes holding mine. "That name is on my body forever. Your name. To me, it means Harper. It means my heart."

His heart. He's my heart and I'm bleeding for him right now. "I didn't tell you. I wanted to but—"

"I wouldn't have wanted to tell you either."

"Would you have?"

"I'd like to say yes. I'd like to say that you deserved to know, but I would have battled with that decision."

He's okay. I can tell he's okay. My hand settles on his chest and his heartbeat is steady. "How are you okay right now?"

"I already knew they'd done something to trigger her decision."

"You thought Gigi had." My fingers curl on his chest. "Your father—"

"Is born of the same cloth. I knew that."

"Everyone wants to believe they have a parent that cares about them."

"I had that. I still do. My mother will always be with me. She's always dictated many of my decisions. She's always been my moral compass, not Grayson. She just spoke through him." There is more to that statement. Something he hasn't said. Something he doesn't want to say.

"Eric—"

"They have to pay." His voice is hard. His emotions are checked. This is about control and he has it. "You have to know that," he adds, and then repeats. "They have to pay, Harper."

I could fight him on this. I could bring up my mother. I could say so many things, but the truth is, my mother hid this from Eric. My mother hid this from law enforcement. I have to trust Eric right now. He needs to know that I'm with him, the way his father knows that my mother is with him. She's made her choice. Now I have to make mine. And so, I ask simply, "How?"

The Kingston family is evil. They have to pay for their sins but at my agreement, surprise flickers in Eric's eyes. He expected a battle of wills, but mine is his. "Aren't you going to tell me to save your mother?"

"I think this family has told you enough. You don't need that from me, too."

"What about your mother?" he repeats.

"I don't even know who she is anymore, Eric. How can she know what he did and still protect him? I told you, I let myself believe it wasn't true because if it was, any shred of anything between you and your father would be gone. Today I lost her." I lift a hand. "I'm sure our phones are going crazy." I try to duck under his arm and he catches me to him.

"You don't want to talk about your mother," he says.

"Not now. I'm having a hard time accepting what she's become. Then again, can a person become evil? Or is it just who you are? Are you born that way? Maybe she was always like this, I just never saw the truth."

"Let's hope like fuck not. I've got that man's blood running through me."

"You're nothing like them."

"Yeah, well if I act like them, check me. Check me hard." He laces the fingers of one hand with mine. "I need to change this fucking shirt. I'll meet you in the kitchen and we can heat up our food." He kisses my hand.

"Yes," I say. "Sounds good."

He walks away, and I turn to the window, the horizon streaking the sky with hues of yellow and orange. I want to hide here, disappear for days with Eric, and pretend no one else exists. But there's no escaping the world outside. Most people seek shelter in their families and call them their moral support. We need bodyguards and weapons to face ours. We might as well call them serial killers.

At the very least, just killers.

Chapter Ninety-Six

Eric

The food is hot and we sit at the kitchen island, eating our food, and sliding into a debate over what is really going on with both our families.

One thing we both agree on—the Kingstons want to end us. I grab the beer she set on the kitchen counter and chug it.

"Are we sure this is about the mob at all?" she asks, taking the beer from me. "That's my point. Did they find out that you tried to end them?" She takes a swig from the bottle. "Is that what set this off? You said you talked to bankers."

"My father was poisoned. Without that piece of the puzzle, I'd buy into that theory. Whoever wanted me, and you, out of the picture wants him gone, too. Blake believes the mob's involved. So do I."

"Then we're back to how Isaac got them in trouble with the mob. He set you up not once, but twice. He had to have convinced your father to come here. That made the hit on him look like it came from you."

"My father isn't convinced to do anything. He didn't come here at Isaac's direction. I told you. He was distracting me."

"From what? What is so big he has to personally distract you?"

"My father didn't choose to involve me in anything. He knows I'm a problem for him. Most likely, Isaac got them in trouble. He's a two birds one stone guy. Solve the problem and pin it on us, therefore he gets rid of us."

"Or maybe he was going to ask you for help."

"Never. He would never ask me for help."

"Maybe he was. Maybe that's why Isaac had him poisoned. Of course, maybe Isaac just wanted the money he'd inherit to pay off the mob."

433

"My dumb ass brother is just that—dumb. I know for a fact my mother was a genius who let it cripple her. I am who I am because of her genetics and thank fuck. In other words, you overestimate Issacs's skills. If it was as simple as what you suggest, my father would never have involved me, and Gigi didn't plot to kill her own son. She's a bitch, but that man is her world."

"Okay, but what if Gigi knew what Isaac was into? Maybe she even believed your father knew but he was too prideful to ask for your help, so she did it herself through me. You're a savant, a genius and a billionaire. She's smart enough to know who to call with the brains to help. We need to find Gigi."

"She's on a plane to Europe."

"I know, which is my point. She's running when her son, the man you said is my life, could be dying. We need to know what she knows. Why would she run?"

"The mob is every reason she needs to run, sweetheart. I guarantee you, she doesn't believe Isaac put a hit on my father. She believes it's the mob and that means she thinks they'll come after everyone in the family."

"Or Isaac needs everyone dead to inherit and pay them off. We need her to just tell us, Eric. She's scared. I think she'll tell us."

"When she's on the ground, if we can reach her, we can try."

"Can we just go to her?"

"We should have stopped her from leaving, but we didn't. And we need to be right here, in front of the police, and the problem."

"Can Walker just get someone to confront her? Do they have resources to do that from Europe?"

My cellphone buzzes with a text and I snake it from my pocket, glancing at the message and then at Harper. "We may not need Gigi. Isaac can tell us when he gets here. He's about to get on a private jet on his way here."

"He's not going to talk to you."

She's wrong. He will. I'll make him. "I'll handle my brother."

"Why is he coming here now?"

"He looks bad if he doesn't show up."

"And my mother. Doesn't she look bad, too?

"Blake's handling law enforcement. He's protecting her. She's sedated. They know. Walker is respected and known to only support those they believe to be innocent."

"I kind of got that feeling." Her gaze falls to my arm and then lifts. "Who knows what your ink means?"

"No one, and yet, I get where you're going with this. The message on that card was on my arm."

"And just before I told you about your mother, you were searching your ink for clues."

I huff out a breath. "I always radiate toward a puzzle and that leads me to my ink. I need to sit and think. That's not how I come up with answers." I cup her face and kiss her. "I need you, sweetheart, but I also think independently. It's a savant thing. It's a singular process."

"Yes, okay. I'll try every way possible to reach Gigi."

She won't reach her but I don't say that. I brush my knuckles over her cheek and I walk toward the couch, where I sit down and somehow end up with a cube in my hand without consciously picking it up. My mind is already working, tossing around numbers, but at the same time, going back to the same place I went to when I was talking to Grayson. "What does the message mean?" Grayson had asked.

My answer had been "It translates to a saying we had in the SEALs. If you ain't cheating, you ain't trying. It means to win, you have to break the rules."

"And you think that means someone knows what rules you were going to break with Kingston?" he'd asked.

"Don't you?" I'd challenged. "It's a fucking threat. They want me to do something for them, pay them off in some way, or they'll tell Harper."

It *was* a threat.

Or was it a warning?

The more I think about the messages, the less likely they feel like they're from the mob. The mob isn't warning us. That's not how they operated. They'd just get in our fucking faces. I stare down at the message on the back of the business card and look down at my wrist where the saying is inked in letters and numbers.

Gigi is back in my mind.

She's at the center of all of this.

She told Harper I get my brains from her, and while I don't believe that, not for a minute, someone like me, another savant, could see the random codes in my ink. That particular saying that was on the back of the card, and anything to do with the Navy is about honor, courage, sacrifice, and brotherhood to me. The SEALs are my brothers. Isaac is not my brother. Years ago, I remember telling her as much. They are my brothers. Isaac is not.

Could Gigi be warning me about Isaac?

Did she pull me into this because she knew he was going to try to kill her son, his father, *my* father to inherit and pay off the mob? Of course, Gigi would know that I'd never save my father, so she'd need Harper to get me involved. That theory would assume that she knew about me and Harper, but again, there could have been cameras from the cottage. And Harper could have given off signs about me that she didn't realize she gave off.

Gigi tried to save the family by using me to do it. Isaac thought it was Harper. He came at her and me. Maybe, and this is reaching, my father did come here for help. It's far-fetched, but I have to set aside the personal baggage between me and my father and look objectively about all of this. If Isaac tried to end our father, he'll try to finish him when he's here. He'll try to finish me and Harper.

I'll finish him instead.

I slide the first message that I have yet to understand in front of me. I need to break the code before Isaac gets here.

Chapter Ninety-Seven

Eric

The pad of paper in front of me is filled with numbers and equations, pages deep, when I text Blake for a copy of my father's will and other random documents he might not think are important, but I do. I set my phone aside and just as I reach for my pen again, Harper slides a steaming hot cup of coffee in front of me, right along with a bag of peanut M & M's. "In case they help. I remember you said they're part of your process." She offers me a shy, beautiful smile, and I wonder how the hell I let her go for an entire six years. "How long have I been sitting here?"

"Two hours." If the fact that I've ignored her for that time bothers her, she doesn't show it. "I left Gigi three urgent messages," she continues, "but Blake tells me she's still in the air."

"If Gigi was going to tell us what was going on, she would have told us before she left."

"Or she left and put distance between whatever this is and herself before she tells us. If we believe she's the source of the messages, then she clearly wants to tell you."

We don't know it's Gigi, though the numerical odds sway heavily in her direction.

Harper motions to the pad I've been writing on. "Anything worth sharing? If it doesn't disrupt your thoughts." She glances at all the numbers and letters on the page.

"Assuming Gigi sent me the messages, and that she was warning me about Isaac, message number one should be easy to figure out. It should somehow tie to that warning. It should represent something that we both touched that has somehow come full circle."

"But it doesn't?"

My lips thin. "I don't know yet."

"Why didn't she just tell us?" Harper asks. "These messages—"

"Must expose something she doesn't want anyone else to know."

"But she hates you."

"And yet she convinced me to come back to Denver through you. I assume the messages boil down to one of a few things. She hates me, she is not about to give me the satisfaction of gloating, therefore she remains invisible. More likely, she'll somehow expose herself or my father in some way. Or, and this is not hard to believe, she's trying to prove I'm not as smart as is claimed."

"Why would she need to prove such a thing?"

"She's a Kingston. Who fucking knows."

"Maybe she told the mob you were smart enough to make them billions, too. And they said prove it."

"The mob doesn't test you. They just tell you to write a check." I pick up my pencil and start writing, the numbers in my head driving me back in time, processing everything I know about Isaac and the company. Every deal he touched that I touched as well. I'm looking for something Gigi, assuming she sent the messages, wants me and only me to know. Something she thinks will make me protect her interests, and my father's, which translates to hers. I lose myself in the numbers and when I finally come back to the present, I blink the room into view and find it shrouded in shadows, a lamp I don't remember turning on, glowing on the end table, and Harper lying on the couch next to me with a blanket pulled over her. I don't even remember her lying down.

I scrub a hand through my hair and grimace. And I ignored her for what? I don't know what that fucking message is telling me. I squat down next to Harper and she doesn't move. She's that secure. She's that safe with me, and unbidden, I'm back in the past, I'm in the trailer a few nights before my mother died—no—killed herself because of this damn family. We'd been watching a movie with the lights out when a shadow had passed the window.

I jolt with the large shadow. My mother grabs my leg. "Shh," she murmurs and when I nod, she stands up and walks to the television, lowering the sound.

She then points at me and mouths "stay" before she walks to the cabinet in the corner and shocks me by pulling out a gun I didn't know we had, ready to fight. I stand up. "What the hell is that?" I hiss in a low whisper.

"Survival and we're survivors."

"This is about that family you say I belong to, isn't it?" I demand. "I don't want—"

Someone bangs on the door. "It's Richard. Open up."

My mother's lips thin. "Go away, Richard. We're done."

"He wants to make you an offer. I can shout it through the door or you can come out here."

My mother squeezes her eyes shut and then walks to me, handing me the gun. "If he comes in the door, shoot him." And then she leaves, exiting the trailer. I run to the window and open it, listening, but they get into a car. I sit down with the gun and I wait only ten minutes. After that, I head to the door, and I plan to go get my mother any way I need to get her. Only she walks back in, looking flustered.

She takes the gun. "Let's get ready for bed." She starts to walk away and I grab her arm.

"Mom," I plead.

"We're good, honey. I'm going to get into that study, beat the cancer, and we'll be just fine."

I blink back to the present and remember my mother sleeping on the couch that night with the gun in her hand. She was ready to fight. She didn't want to kill herself. She didn't want to die. I later found out that Richard was my father's "fixer" who died not long after my mother in a car accident, which I found out when I tried to confront him about what happened that night.

My phone buzzes with a text and I grab it to read a message from Blake: *The computer system at the hospital was updated to read heart attack on your father's chart. The early drug testing is clear of toxins.* Only it wasn't a heart attack. It was poison. Just like I doubt Richard really died from a car accident. I consider my mother's suicide. That was real. She made that decision, but a Kingston might as well have been holding the gun. They did everything they could to keep me out of this family and ironically, I believe Gigi really did think that I was the only way to save it. She's a fool. The only saving I'm going to do is of Harper.

I reach down and stroke her cheek. She blinks awake and catches my hand. "Eric."

"Yeah, baby."

"Any luck?"

"A few leads. It's late." I glance at my watch to read midnight. "Let's go to bed."

"Bed with you sounds pretty perfect," she murmurs groggily.

"Good. Because bed with you is always perfect." I scoop her up and start carrying her toward my room, our room now. The room we're going to share in the kind of peace that comes only one way: with the end of the Kingston family.

Chapter Ninety-Eight

Eric

I sleep three hours and lay in the bed holding Harper for another hour, finding the numbers in my head easier to control when she's with me. Almost as if she's my Rubik's cube, which isn't as crazy as it sounds. As I was trained, it's about finding a way to ground myself and calming my mind, and Harper does that for me.

I'm fairly certain it would sound ridiculous to anyone but me. Or Harper. I don't think it would be ridiculous to Harper. She seems to understand me in ways no one else, not even Grayson, has ever understood me. I inhale the sweet scent of her, motivation to solve the puzzle I can feel my mind on the verge of solving.

I grab my cellphone, read an hour-old text message from Blake: *Isaac is not only in the city, he's holed up in a room at the same hotel where your father was poisoned. Some people might be scared of that hotel. Not him. Interesting.*

Interesting is right, I think. He's stupid enough to think that staying at the hotel makes it look like he's not guilty. He's wrong. The police are going to see this just like I do. Isaac isn't scared because he set-up that hit. The blood tests might be negative, but their suspicions were too juicy a morsel to just let go.

By sunrise, I've showered and despite it being a workday, I dress in jeans and a shirt, with every intent of staying away from the office, and Grayson. I glance through the bags Mia brought Harper and while she brought her plenty of items, I'm sure Harper wants things she picked out herself. We'll have to go shopping today.

I exit the bedroom with Harper still completely knocked out. On one hand, I'm pleased that she feels safe here, but on the other, I worry that when she wakes, the adrenaline rush of her attack is going to hit her. Eventually, it will, and I want nothing more than to hold her and help her ride the wave to get through it. But it's also a luxury we can't afford right now. Not with my father in the

ICU, Gigi on the run, and Isaac here in New York City, but at least he's a means to an end.

He's in the monster's lair and I'm that monster.

I've just finished brewing a second pot of coffee when my cellphone rings with an unfamiliar number. I answer it on the first ring. "Eric Mitchell."

"Mr. Mitchell. This is Detective Rider. I thought you'd like to know that your father had a heart attack."

"All right," I say. "I'm not sure that constitutes as good news. Why are you really calling me?"

"I'm fairly certain that you, like myself, believed he was poisoned. Walker Security showed us the man on the security footage that entered your father's room."

"Did you find him?"

"No."

"Was my father poisoned?" I press.

"You tell me. We're waiting for additional testing. Perhaps we can chat today. Should I come to you? Because I can't seem to find you at the hospital."

"I saw a couple of your uniforms who seemed to be more interested in accusations and slander than protecting me and my family."

"It's their job to ask questions."

"But not to harass innocent citizens which is a distinction that cost the police department millions upon millions of dollars. Find the man."

"Who's the man?"

"You want me to do your job? Wait. Yes. You do. And I expected that, which is why I hired Walker Security. We'll be by the hospital later today. You want to talk to me, find me when I get there."

"Which will be when?"

"When I get there." I hang up and dial Blake. "Do you know a Detective Rider?"

"I met that prick last night. He's chasing a promotion and thinks taking down one of the Kingston family, and its car empire, is his ticket."

"Of course, he does," I say dryly, right as there's a knock on the door. "Who the fuck is at my door and how'd they get past security."

Blake laughs. "It's me and Savage," Blake says. "And we have donuts."

"Let yourselves in. We both know you have the code." I disconnect and about thirty seconds later Blake and Savage are sauntering across the living room, both dressed in jeans and Walker Security shirts.

Unfortunately, they're not alone.

Grayson's with them, which Blake conveniently left out, and thank fuck his perfectly-fitted, gray pinstriped suit tells me he's headed to the office. "Where the hell are the donuts?" I ask.

Savage pulls a bag out from behind his back. "Donut holes because we're dealing with so many assholes." He laughs. "Get it?"

"You're a fucking idiot, man," I say, taking the bag from him. "And for the record, I like éclairs. They don't come with holes." I head to the kitchen with a bark of Savage's laughter at my back. "Coffee's on the house," I say, motioning the men to the pot.

"Don't mind if I do," Blake says, walking in that direction with Savage joining him.

Grayson steps to the island across from me as I pop a donut hole in my mouth. "How's Harper?"

"Sleeping and staying."

"Staying," he says, his eyes sharp. "That's good news. Did you tell her?"

"Yes," Harper says, her voice floating down from above us at the railing. "He told me. And yes. I'm staying."

I glance up as she heads down the stairs, dressed in a black skirt and an emerald green blouse paired with knee-high boots. "Glad to hear it," Grayson says, rotating to greet her. "For how long?"

"She's moving in with me," I state, not giving her time to change her mind. "She's not going back to Denver." I watch Harper, waiting for her reaction.

She rounds the island and stops beside me, her arms wrapping around me as she says. "No. I'm not going back to Denver." She pushes to her toes, kisses my jaw, and then glances at our company. "What's happening?" she asks softly. "Why is everyone here?"

"For the coffee," Savage says, as he and Blake join us with cups in hand.

"Everyone has coffee but me," Harper says, rolling with the punches. "I hope that and the donuts means this is a power breakfast that makes this all go away." She moves to the coffee pot.

"We're peeling away the layers," Blake assures her.

"What layers?" I ask. "Get to the point. Did you find something in the documents I had you pull?"

"You're not in the will," Blake states. "I'm sending you the documents soon. As for anything that connects dots between you and your brother, I've got plenty of data, but nothing that stands out to me. You can let that mind of yours go to work."

"Where's Gigi right now?" Harper asks, stepping back to my side, coffee cup in hand.

Blake's lips thin. "Gigi got off a plane in Europe and disappeared at a private airport, where she diverted to at the last minute. Unfortunately, we didn't have a man in position at that airport. She's sneaky and she's gone, at least for the moment."

"My God," Harper says. "What are we into? What makes a woman her age run and hide with this kind of determination? She's literally got to be afraid for her life."

"Which makes sense," Blake replies. "She must know what we know. Her son was poisoned. She must think she's next."

"Who inherits? Isaac?" Grayson asks before I can.

"The oldest living biological child," Blake states.

I frown. "But it doesn't state Isaac's name?"

"The verbiage is likely an attorney-inserted basic clause," Blake replies, "especially considering you're years younger than Isaac."

"I've never found the Kingstons don't do anything without purpose, especially something this important. Is there another sibling?"

"He fucked around with my mother," Eric says. "It's hard to believe she was the first and last woman he did that with."

"Or," Savage offers. "Did your father plan to kill off Isaac? I mean, he is a pain in the fucking ass and a pathetic representation of his bloodline."

I press my hands to the island. He's not wrong.

Chapter Ninety-Nine

Eric

My cellphone rings before I can respond to the bombshell, if it even is that. I grab my phone from the island and glance at the caller ID. "Speaking of the pain in the fucking ass himself," I say and hit decline.

I lean across the island and look at Grayson. "Go to work and stay away. I'm not sure why Blake, and Savage, the fucktard himself, let you come up here."

"He pays us a lot of money," Savage replies, "and he means you no harm."

At least he's honest, which I value in a person, probably because the Kingstons are all big fat liars. Which is why I stay focused on Grayson. "I can't do what I need to do while I'm worried about you."

"And what exactly is it that you think you need to do?" he challenges.

"Whatever the situation calls for. You need to understand that one moment of hesitation could mean someone ends up dead. I can't be in a position where I hesitate because of you. Where I frame words or actions to protect *you*."

"Then let me take Harper with me."

"No," Harper says immediately. "I can't go. I appreciate it very much, Grayson, but my mother is involved in all of this. And they came at me. That makes me a target who doesn't need to be by your side."

"Take Mia out of here," I repeat. "At least give me forty-eight hours, Grayson."

"I'm not leaving, but we'll lock down with protection." He pushes off the island and looks at Blake. "Lock us down. Two days." He glances at me. "But I want updates."

Relief washes over me and I give a firm incline of my chin. "Done." I eye Blake, who motions to Savage.

"At your service," he says to Grayson. "Actually, Smith will be your man. I'm just going to escort you to him."

Grayson gives me a quick piercing stare meant to be a command and then heads for the door. He's the only fucking guy on planet Earth that can give me a look like that and I'll just take it. And listen. "Gigi knows what this is about," Harper says, lowering her voice. "We *have* to get to her."

"We don't need Gigi. Isaac is here and knows everything."

"On Isaac," Blake interjects. "We have proof that he's been meeting with Nicholas Marshall, the young, newly-minted prince of the mob, who's known to have a long history with the unions."

"Newly-minted, meaning what?" Harper asks.

"His father died," Blake says. "He took over." His eyes meet mine. "Sound familiar?"

"Isaac isn't working alone," I say. "He and Nicolas have a plan to rule the world together."

"Exactly my thought," Blake says. "And about that wording in your father's will, I tried to pull your birth certificate and Isaac's as well. I found yours and it reads as expected. Isaac's is another story. It's sealed, and there's no online record. I've sent a man to get hard copies any way necessary."

Harper turns to me. "What the heck is this?"

My mind is chasing the messages we've been given. "Good question," I say, walking to the coffee table, grabbing the message I haven't decoded, and staring down at it. I sit down and search for birth certificate numbers in the state of Colorado but this one doesn't connect any dots there. The format and digits don't add up.

My phone buzzes with a text message and I grab it to confirm that it's from Isaac and as cordial as I'd expect from him: *I'm at the hospital. Where the fuck are you?*

Harper sits down next to me and I show her the message. "At least it's a controlled environment," she says. "No one can get hurt."

I snort. "He doesn't have a chance in hell of hurting me."

"I was more worried about him," she replies.

"I second that notion," Blake interjects, joining us and clearly aware of what's going on. "You and Isaac don't need to be alone." He eyes Harper and then me. "Not after her attack and I speak from experience. I lost a fiancée once. I lived for revenge for years of my life."

This statement explains a lot to me. It tells me why I'm comfortable with Blake. Why he doesn't push back at places that would earn him a hard push out the door, though he got close after my father's attack. I stand up and pull Harper with me. "Can you handle knowing what you know, and standing in front of him like you don't?"

"You mean will I hurt him? You'll be there to protect him, right?"

My lips quirk. God, I love this woman. I glance at Blake. "Can we have Savage to stand between us and him if it comes to that?"

"Maybe I better come along," he says dryly. "Savage loves revenge a little too much, even someone else's."

"I'll take Savage," I say, sliding an arm around Harper. "Let's go to the hospital."

Blake nods and makes a call to alert his team. "Savage already handed off Grayson to Smith. He's meeting us downstairs."

Harper and I head for the door, and I help her pull on a jacket. "I'll take you shopping today," I promise softly while Blake takes a hint and steps outside.

"I'm not worried about shopping," she says. "Though at some point we have to talk about my apartment and my things."

"I'll make sure I get in touch with the service we talked about today."

She inhales and lets it out. "Yes. That's—yes, okay." She cuts her gaze.

I catch her chin. "What is it?"

"I'm excited about our new life, I am. It's just—it's daunting to realize that everything that was mine when I left is gone. It's like I spent years of my life building nothing."

"We can sell this place. We can pick out a place that you want, that feels like ours, not mine."

"No. Eric, I love this apartment. It's stunning."

"I want you to feel like it's yours."

"It will in time. This has all just been a whirlwind. A crazy whirlwind. I'm starting over. And I *need* to start over. This is the right decision and a happy one, but I can't revel in that until this storm has passed. I feel like the happiness is hiding in the clouds, just out of our reach. And a tornado is waiting to erupt and just destroy everything."

"Hiding in the clouds, *within* our reach." All the sudden, numbers blast through my mind and I count out the digits in that first message, before my lips quirk. "You're brilliant, baby."

"I am?"

"Yes. You are." I kiss her and open the door to find Blake waiting. "I know what the first message means."

Chapter One Hundred

Eric

The answer was right in front of me the entire time, and my mind was too damn muddled with Kingston nonsense to see what was right in front of me.

At this point, Blake and Harper are standing in front of me with expectant gazes. "It's a birth certificate number from Chicago, Illinois," I say and text Blake the way that number breaks down. "I just sent you the exact certificate number."

"And you know this how?" he asks.

"How I know is simply how my brain works," I say. "Harper said something completely unrelated, and I went there. There is no other way to explain to you how I came to that conclusion, but I did. That's a birth certificate from Chicago, Illinois."

Blake stares at me as if I've grown three heads, but Harper—Harper just accepts what I've said and moves on. "Who was born in Chicago?" she asks. "Not you, right? And I've heard Isaac talk about being born in Denver."

"I don't know the answer to that question," I say, draping my arm around her shoulder. "Now Blake gets to do his magic and find out."

She twists in my arms to look at me. "Is there another sibling?" she asks again. "Have you ever gotten the idea that's possible?"

"Never," I say, "but they tried to bury me. My mother didn't let that happen. They could easily have succeeded with someone else."

"What if—what if that sibling is the one coming after you or both of you?" she continues. "Or he bribed Isaac? I could keep going. There are so many possibilities."

"All of which I'll be discussing with Isaac," I assure her. "But there are other possibilities. Mob connections. The secrets Gigi might know but didn't feel safe sharing don't have to be as direct as another sibling."

"You really believe this is Gigi?" Blake says. "She's sending the messages?"

"She told Harper that I inherited my mind from her. She very specifically told her that."

"And maybe she wanted me to repeat it?" Harper asks.

"Yes," I say. "That's what was throwing me off with the message until now. I was looking at it with normal logic. But it wasn't written by someone who thinks like everyone else. It was written by someone who thinks like me."

Harper reaches for her purse and grabs her phone. "And if you got your genius from her, that means her. I have to reach Gigi."

"Her phone is dead," Blake says. "And it's not pinging at all."

"Damn it," Harper grumbles, and I slide my arm around her again. "Let's get to the hospital and let Blake work."

"Yes," Blake says. "Let me work. I'm damn eager to dig into this and figure out what the fuck this is we're dealing with."

"I'll grab my bag," Harper says, darting away.

A few minutes later, Harper and I are standing beside the SUV we're going to travel in with Savage and Blake. "I can get the name that's attached to that birth certificate quickly," Blake says, "if it's not sealed like Isaac's. Assuming I do, I'll text you the name in case it helps you with Isaac." He eyes Savage. "Don't let him kill Isaac."

Savage glances at me. "I'll do it for you. Just say the word. I can't stand that little bitch."

I don't think he's completely joking. I know he's a surgeon and a mercenary which doesn't compute in any equation in my mind. A man who can kill and heal is a strange creature, but then so am I. Whatever the case, I don't look at him. I don't want to encourage him. If anyone gets to kill Isaac before this is over, it's me. And I don't think that's what Blake or Harper wants to hear. "Hurry up with that name," I say, opening the back door for Harper.

She moves in front of me, but when she would climb inside, she turns to face me, her hand planting on my chest, under my coat. Her hand is always on my chest and I swear every time my icy heart warms. I want to end this and figure out life with this woman minus the damn Kingston family.

"Do you think Gigi's dead?" she asks, trepidation in her voice, and I know now it's not about her love for Gigi. It's about that sweet, caring part of her, that even the Kingston hate hasn't destroyed, and I'm not going to give it a chance to finish the job.

"The odds are not in her favor." I brush her hair from her face. "Get in, baby. If I can get answers out of Isaac, I need to do it and get this over with."

She doesn't even sway that direction, let alone move. "How bad is this going to get between you two?"

"Get in," I order. "Assassin, remember?"

Her eyes go wide and she climbs inside. I quickly follow and eye Savage. "Give us five, man."

Savage glances back at us and says, "It's a lovely day in the neighborhood," and he gets out.

I think a lot of people think he says things that make no sense but he makes sense to me. Every time, and with every bad joke, there's a meaning. And there's a lot of fucking anger beneath his surface, which I know because I have it, too.

"I'll push his buttons," I say, answering Harper's question. "He'll lose his shit. If I estimate correctly, there will be a detective or two around to witness it all. I don't need to kill Isaac as Blake suggested to get revenge. Isaac is really damn good at burying himself alive."

"I know you think you know what to expect with him, Eric, but he came here for a purpose. It feels like some sort of set-up. Like there's a play going on and we're in the third act, but we're the only ones who don't know what comes next. We don't have the script."

"I'll be careful. I'll be cautious. Is that what you want to hear?"

"Yes. Can you say it again?"

I angle her direction. "I will be careful. I will be cautious. I will not kill him unless he makes me, but if he does anything to even remotely attempt to hurt you again, there's no saving him."

She wets her lips and then kisses me. "Killing him gets way too complicated, and complicated might delay the goal I've set for myself."

I inch back to look at her. "What goal?"

"Licking every tattoo on your body."

My cock thickens, the idea of her tongue on my body stirring a blast of dirty thoughts that I find far more appealing than dealing with my brother. "Is that right?"

"Yes," she says, her hand sliding low and stroking my zipper. "So let's go get this over with so I can get started." She tries to pull away, but I hold her fast and easy, my mouth closing down on hers, my tongue stroking deep before I say, "Do you know how much I want to take you back upstairs and keep you naked and in our bed for days on end?"

"I'd like to be naked with you and in *our bed* for days on end. Yes, please."

I kiss her again, a firm press of my mouth to hers. "Let's go so we can get home." I knock on the window.

Savage climbs back inside and another man I do not know joins him. "This is Adrian. He's a badass. He eats too much and talks too much, and tells really bad dad jokes, when he's not even a dad. But he shoots straight in every meaning of that statement." Adrian lifts a hand and Savage glances over his shoulder at us to add, "Regarding Grayson's protection, I trust Smith. I know he got off on the wrong foot with you, but he's good, man. Really good. And Grayson is layered with surveillance and backup. Also, Blake told us to hold a moment. He has something for you."

I nod and Savage turns his attention to the front, leaving me with Grayson on my mind, which is why I text Davis: *Grayson was just at my apartment, pushing to be more involved in what is getting dirtier every moment. Get him the fuck out of town.*

His reply is almost instant: *Tomorrow. If I push the NFL negotiation today, he'll be suspicious. I'll get him out of here tomorrow.*

Considering the decoded message and Isaac showing up here, that doesn't feel soon enough. There's a knock on the window and Savage calls out, "It's Blake," and then rolls down my window.

"That record is sealed," he says. "Whatever this is, someone wanted it well buried."

Just like Isaac's birth certificate, I think. "Tell me you can get to it."

"I can," he assures me. "I already have a man in Colorado working on Isaac's birth certificate. I'm sending someone to Chicago. By morning, you'll know whatever secrets those birth certificates hold."

I nod and he steps back while Savage rolls up the window. By morning, we'll know the secrets Gigi was trying to expose, but right now, morning feels too far away. My gut says I need answers, and I need them now, but only one person can give those to me—and that's Isaac. Fortunately, that's the very person I'm going to visit right now. Unfortunately, as much as I'll enjoy watching him make a fool of himself with law enforcement watching, they'll also be watching me, and anything I do to him.

Chapter One Hundred One

Eric

The traffic is light and ten minutes later, Savage pulls us to the side door of the hospital. "Here we go," Harper murmurs, but I don't allow her to wallow in the nerves attached to that statement. I open the door and exit the vehicle, guiding Harper to her feet beside me.

Adrian, a tall, dark-haired man, is in front of us almost instantly, alert and ready for trouble. "I'll park and Savage will walk you inside. I'll be close."

I give him a nod, and Harper sighs. "I hate we need protection."

"Better to need it and have it than need it and not have it like Isaac," I say, as Savage joins us.

"Onward and forward," he says, motioning us toward the building, which is a short few steps.

We start walking and Harper's fingers grip the leather of the jacket I pulled on as we left the apartment. "Just remember," she says, "if he's not guilty, he may be emotional. If he is guilty, guilt is an emotion, too, and it's a brutal one. Both things will magnify his reaction to you by one hundred. It's kind of like being at a family Thanksgiving meal and knowing someone will say something that will become an ordeal."

It's wise advice I digest, but also laugh a bit about the analogy. "Family on Thanksgiving, huh?"

"My father had a few crazy brothers who I loved, but they were as crazy as him."

"Where are they now?"

"They died together in a car accident the year before he did."

If not for the threat, I'd halt and talk to her about this. She lost everything in a matter of a year, and I judged her and gave her hell for clinging to the company that was her father's. I glance down at her. I reach over and squeeze her hand. "I'm sorry I didn't know that."

We arrive at the hospital door and somehow Adrian is on the other side. "Your brother is in your father's room. Apparently, your father's doing better now. Still in ICU, still unconscious, but expected to live."

"How very disappointing for my brother," I say dryly.

"Be interesting to see what comes next," Savage replies just as dryly.

"Agreed." I urge Harper forward, comfortable letting her go ahead of me with Adrian, obviously on his toes.

And as I expect him to, he blocks for her, as I step into the hallway with Savage at my rear.

"Obviously they think the assassin is back," Harper whispers.

I don't sugarcoat the danger, which will not do anything to help her stay safe. "I doubt he ever left," I say, guiding her toward the elevator. "A man sent on a mission to kill doesn't leave until the target is dead."

"But there's a problem for Isaac," Savage says, as we stop at the elevator and he punches the button. "If someone dies right after Isaac showed up, all eyes will be on Isaac."

"It won't matter if it's another heart attack," I say. "And maybe that's the idea. Isaac stands right next to him while it happens. Kill in plain sight."

Harper's eyes meet mine. "Are you going to let it happen?"

Having her even asking that question pisses me off. She knows what he did. She knows he kept my mother out of treatment. "Damn straight I am. He's not mine to save, just like my mother wasn't his to save. Are you going to tell me I should feel differently?"

She studies me a long, intense moment before she steps to me, pushes to her toes, and kisses me. "You know I do. So stop directing the anger at me."

I don't care who is around. I don't care what the fuck they think. "I thought you could handle me?"

"I can."

"We'll see about that. Later. When we're alone."

The elevator dings and the doors open to display two men, one of whom is my brother. The other, I don't know.

"There you go, detective," Isaac says. "Ask and you shall receive. Just what you were looking for. My two incestuous stepsiblings."

I consider the merits of beating his face in right here and now, fuck the witnesses, and the badge. But that's emotions driving me, and I stomp them down and let the savant in me take over. No face beating. Not right now. Instead, my lips quirk. I have another plan for my brother. One I'll enjoy far more than he will.

Chapter One Hundred Two

Eric

I saac and the detective exit the elevator and to my surprise, Harper steps right in front of Isaac. "Do not say that to me again," Harper snaps, responding to Isaac's snarky "incestuous stepsiblings" remark. "We never lived together. It's a title, one you didn't mind every damn time you tried to get into my pants."

My lips quirk and I catch her hand, pulling her back to me. "Easy, sweetheart. Emotions are high right now. Remember what you said about that." I nod at the detective, a man in his mid-forties, wearing a blue suit with a black tie at half-mast. He's also sporting a three-day stubble that screams television cop. "Detective Rider, I assume," I acknowledge.

"I am," he confirms. "And you're Eric Mitchell. Good to see you by your father's side."

I smirk at the repeated jab. "No one expects me to be by my father's side. I'm not going to pretend otherwise."

"And why is that?" he asks.

"Because I wasn't his golden child like Isaac here."

"Who inherits should your father die?" the detective replies.

"That's a callous question," Harper chimes in. "Has he taken a turn for the worse?"

"He's the same as he was when he arrived," the detective replies. "One foot in the grave and one out. I simply want to know who inherits, should both land in the dirt."

"I was never under the impression that I'm going to inherit," I say. "Thus why I made my own money."

"Why is that?" the detective asks.

"Because I hate him," I say, seeing no reason to lie. "I don't want anything that's his."

The detective shoots me a skeptical look. "And yet you're here?"

"He's still the only living parent I have and I want to know why a strange man visited his room before he went down."

"It was a heart attack," Isaac snaps. "His visitors are not your business."

"Not your ordinary visitor," Savage interjects.

"Who the fuck are you?" Isaac snaps.

"I'm the guy who will happily bust your chops," Savage replies, "and be equally fine when the detective arrests me for doing it. Though if he spends much more time with you, he might just cheer me on. And for your information, smart guy, if the detective here believed it was just a heart attack, he wouldn't be here."

I eye the detective. "Unless he chooses random rich heart attack victims to visit and make feel special? Perhaps with a donation in mind?"

The detective scowls at me. "I want to know what really happened to your father. Someone standing in this circle knows."

"And the doctor's opinion means absolutely nothing," Isaac replies. "Is that a new creative police protocol we should know about?"

"If you want to go with the doctor's word," the detective states, eyeing me "then what does the man who visited his room matter?"

"I never said anything about the doctor's opinion. That was brother dearest."

"Because," Harper states, as if I haven't answered, "if it was more than it seems, my mother could be a target."

"You've always been melodramatic, Harper," Isaac scoffs.

"Says the man who threw a fit and tossed boiling water on his brother's arm?" she charges.

I stiffen, not happy that she's doing this. It makes me look weak, not strong. "I'm sorry," she says, turning to me. "I know I'm not supposed to know, but he actually bragged about it at a party. He talked about taking down the big, bad SEAL who must not be big and bad at all. He's a monster that does things normal humans do not."

"You threw boiling water on him?" the detective asks, his attention hyperfused on Isaac.

"She's an exaggerator," Isaac states. "She wasn't even around when Eric and I lived together."

"And yet we're incestuous?" she challenges.

I grab her and turn her to face me. "Stop."

"He's capable of things I don't like to think any human being is capable of."

"Did he burn you?" the detective presses.

My jaw clenches and I rotate Harper, pulling her around to face the others, under my arm and by my side. "She's worried about her mother. Worry about the people who need saving. I'm not one of them." I eye Isaac. "I'm going to see our father."

"I'm not done asking questions," the detective states.

"You don't have the right to ask questions about a heart attack from natural causes. Let me know when you actually get serious about a real investigation." I pull Harper around the group and she and Savage enter the elevator with me.

Adrian stays behind.

The detective steps in front of the car. "I don't remember anyone saying the heart attack was from natural causes."

"Was it or wasn't it?" I ask.

"To be determined," he says. "But I'm not going anywhere until we know."

"Find that man who was in his room," Harper states. "Find him and you'll be the hero we all need and want right now."

He studies Harper for several long beats and then looks at me. "I'm waiting on a copy of his will. I'm thinking it's going to be an interesting read." He releases the doors and steps away.

The will is certainly not in my favor. Should Isaac die, I'd inherit, that is, if there isn't another living sibling, and my gut says there was but no longer is.

Based on present circumstances, I'd venture to say that Isaac would have gotten rid of anyone who could take his inheritance, but I'm not worried about me. I'm worried about Harper. I need to see the wording in the will on her trust fund. As it stands, it might well look as if she's the one who directly benefits from my father's death, outside of Isaac.

"Fucktard," Savage growls as we begin to move.

None of us look at each other or speak as we ride the short few floors to the ICU level, all of us aware of the cameras recording us, but there's more. There's silence riddled with a mix of anger and consternation. For me, there's a whole lot of fucking numbers.

The elevator dings and Savage breaks the silence. "Jesse is waiting for us on our floor. Obviously one of ours."

I give him a barely perceivable nod and we exit the car to meet Jesse, a tall man with dark, curly hair. The greeting is short and we move past the elevators, toward the waiting area. We've just passed a hallway when Harper tugs my hand and steps in front of me. "I'm sorry. I'm so sorry I told them about the water."

I eye Savage over her shoulder and he gets the message. He walks away.

My hands come down on her shoulders and I walk her backward into the vacant hallway we were about to pass and press her to the wall. "I know you were emotional."

"I was and protective and I screwed up. In my mind, I needed that detective to know that you're the good brother, not the bad one."

Protective.

She's protecting me. *Fuck.* It's hard to be angry when she frames it that way. She protects who she loves. Even staying with the Kingstons was about protecting both her mother and her father's legacy.

I'm just not sure who looks better in the scenario he painted. The crazy first born or the abused angry half-brother. I'm fairly certain I look like a damn good suspect right about now.

Chapter One Hundred Three

Eric

Harper and I approach the ICU nurse's station to be greeted by a new face, a woman I estimate to be around thirty, wearing scrubs, her brunette hair pulled to her nape. "Can I help you?" she asks.

"Kingston," I say. "How is he?"

"And you are?" she asks, her lips pursing prudishly.

"His son," Harper states as if she knows I can't stomach those necessary words. God, I fucking love this woman.

The nurse frowns. "I just met his son and—"

"I'm the other one," I say. "How is he?"

"You don't look like your brother."

"Thank the fuck for that," I murmur.

"They're half-brothers," Harper quickly chimes in. "Call someone if you need to. We need an update."

I offer her a deadpan stare and while she hesitates, she gives us the information. "He's improved this morning. We moved him to a private suite one floor up."

In a suite, where he will be easier to get to for me and everyone else, I think.

"Define improved?"

"We took him off life support."

"Is he speaking?"

"No, I'm sorry. He hasn't regained consciousness."

She offers us instructions and we rejoin Savage in the lobby. "A little update," Savage offers. "We caught the FBI consultant asshole on film. We followed the street cameras and know where he grabbed a cab. We're working to track him that way."

461

"What about the woman?" Harper asks.

"She disappeared. We never caught her on camera. I assume she used a wig and change of clothes to pull that off, which makes me surprised the guy didn't do the same."

"That's odd," Harper says. "Why wouldn't he?"

"Contemplate it upstairs in my father's suite," I say, impatient to get this over with.

"He's not there yet," Savage says. "I just got word that they're moving him in fifteen minutes. Whoever told you he was gone now, was confused."

I frown. "Or they wanted to talk to me alone, in my father's suite." I kiss Harper. "Stay with Savage. I'll be right back."

"Stay with Jesse," Savage rebuts and waves Jesse in our direction. He lifts a hand my direction. "I'm going with you."

"Stay with Harper," I say. "This could be a ploy to get me apart from her. I want her safe."

"And what about you?" Harper asks. "Who protects you?"

"Me," I say, eyeing Savage. "I could kick his big ass, if I had to and if he keeps telling those bad dad jokes I might."

Savage snorts. "Let's spar, man. Name the day and place."

"Not today," I say. "Stay with her, Savage. Bring her up in fifteen."

I don't give either a chance to argue. I cut away from them and make my way to the nearest stairwell. Once I'm inside, I start the walk up, only to reach the door one level higher as Isaac does the same coming from the other direction. I'd assume it to be a set-up if he didn't look so damn uncomfortable, his expression sour. I'm betting he knew I was headed to the room, compliments of the nurse he sweet-talked. He didn't know I was taking the stairs. "What the fuck are you even doing here?" he demands, predictably attacking when he feels trapped.

"More like what the fuck was our father doing here to see me in the first place, Isaac? What did he want?"

"He thought you were going to come at us because of Harper's attack. He thought he could convince you otherwise. Obviously, he was wrong or he wouldn't be in that bed right now."

I take a step toward him and to his credit, he doesn't back up. "We both know I didn't do that to him." I take another step. He sways slightly. He wants to bolt. "We both know you hired a hitman to kill him."

"You bastard." He swings at me.

I catch his wrist and shove him against the wall. "Do you really want to fight me, brother?" I ask. "Because I have a lot of turning the other cheek to make up for."

He laughs. "Hit me. Your violence will speak worlds to the police."

"Are you going to have them check your balls after I bust them? Because I'd like to stay and watch."

The color drains from his face. "I didn't hire a fucking hitman."

"You're in trouble," I say. "We both know it. That trouble has now landed on my doorstep and I want it off."

"I told you to leave back in Denver. I told you to get the fuck away."

"And yet Gigi not only wanted my help, she took off. She's in hiding instead of here, by her son's bed. What is she afraid of, Isaac? You or the mob, who I know you've fucked around with and pissed off."

"My business is not your business."

"You made it my business by going after Harper."

"I didn't go after Harper."

"How much do you owe them?"

He spits in my face. I don't so much as flinch. "Let's be clear, Isaac. I don't have to bust your balls. The mob will cut them off. And if you were counting on Dad dying and leaving you the money, you have a problem. He's going to make it and if you kill him now, you'll get attention you don't want and neither does the mob. They might just kill you to cut off the bleeding." I release him. "You need me. Get smart and ask for help before you take everyone down with you." I turn to the door and open it, leaving him in the stairwell. And yes, I wipe his disgusting spit away.

A few minutes and queries later, I'm standing in a suite with an empty bed and a sitting area. I enter the room expecting something, though I don't know what. I walk into the bathroom and attached to the mirror is an envelope that reads "Eric Mitchell" and it's not coded. This is not the same kind of message as before. I grab the envelope and right when I would open it, a tingling sensation slides up and down my spine. I slide the envelope into my pocket and exit the bathroom, my eyes searching the room. It's empty, but someone was here.

I walk to the door and look left and right down the hallway, but I find no one. It's a quiet floor and a quiet moment. I step back into the room and pull out the piece of paper from the envelope that reads:

Eric–

You can't just let Isaac do what he has to do, can you? You're pushing the wrong people. If you keep pushing, I'm going to make you king and then you'll owe me. You can pay me my fucking money or I can take Harper as payment. Your move, savant. And that move is to look the other direction, and then back away.

It's in that moment that Harper and Savage walk in. "Find my father, Savage. Stay with him and keep Harper with you and safe. I'm going after Isaac."

Harper's eyes go wide. "What's happening?"

"Baby, I need you to trust me and stay with Savage. Promise."

"Yes, but—"

I kiss her. "Later. Everything later."

I hand Savage the letter and take off out of the door. A letter that wasn't from Gigi. It was from the mob and the only way I become king of the Kingston Empire is if everyone but me is dead.

Chapter One Hundred Four

Eric

The past...

Christmas hell.

That's what this is. I sit across from Isaac at a chess board while my father stands above us, watching us play. I plan to do what I always do. Let Isaac fucking win. He needs the ego stroking. I do not. I just want the fucking game over with. He makes a move. I make a move. He makes a stupid move and that forces me to act like an idiot and ignore it. He makes another move. Another *stupid* move and actually thinks it's smart.

"Your move, savant."

I can almost feel our father pushing me to push back, to take his pride, to cripple him. I almost feel sorry for Isaac for the way the bastard uses me to taunt him. In that moment, I hate my father more than Isaac. I make a stupid move and endure Isaac's gloating as he takes my king.

As if he's the king. As if he's telling me I will never be king.

---◦◦◦◦---

Three months later...

A new kind of hell.

That's what being pitted against my brother in a mock trial is for me. I can't win because I can't lose and that will lead to complications outside this auditorium. I sit behind the defense table, my mock client accused of a laundry list of white-collar crimes. I listen as Isaac leaves me a hole to bury his case. And I *am* going to bury his case. This isn't about family. This is about my career.

He walks back to his table but slides by mine first, smirking as he loudly jabs me with his favorite taunt of, "Your move, savant."

He walks away and sits down. I stand up and proceed to steal his false sense of security. I destroy his case, and him, in all of three minutes.

Present day...

I'm out of the hospital room door, headed to find Isaac and manage to get all the way to the exit before I stop dead. Not only is my father being rolled in my direction, I have a sudden realization that I shouldn't have missed in the first place. The wording of that note comes back to me "Your move, savant." That fucker. Harper's right. I'm operating on emotion because I all but allowed myself to be played. Isaac wrote that note.

I rush back the opposite direction and realize my father is being rolled past me, surrounded by a medical crew. And fuck, I might not love the man, but seeing him with tubes everywhere and pale as death punches me in the chest in a mighty way.

I follow him toward his room and Harper and Savage are ordered into the hallway. Harper spies me almost instantly and rushes toward me.

"What just happened?" she asks again.

Just thinking about the evil that is my brother, and the threat he made against her has me pulling her close, and kissing her. "Isaac happened," I say, sliding her under my arm meeting Savage's stare. "Did you read the note?"

"Barely. They ran us out of there, but yeah, I read the damn thing."

"Isaac wrote it. His way of trying to force me to protect him and keep him alive." But what doesn't make sense to me is the fact that it also forces me to protect my father. In fact, it protects my father over Isaac and I have no doubt, he needs my father's money.

"Are you sure about that?" Savage asks. "It's typed, not handwritten."

"What note?" Harper asks, and I take it from Savage and hand it to her.

She scans it, her pale skin turning paler as she looks up at me. "How are you sure it's him?"

"Because he's stupid enough to use the words 'your move, savant' which he used to say to me all the time when my father pitted us against each other. The message here is clear. If he doesn't survive, I inherit and that means more than money. I inherit his problems which includes the mob. Which also means I have to fucking fix them for him. Then I'll deal with him once and for all."

Harper turns to face me. "How? It's the mob."

"He threatened you twice, baby. He's going to pay."

"*How?*" she repeats.

"I might just feed him to the fucking mob and let them handle him."

Isaac appears beside us and I release Harper, taking the note from her. "Go check on my father, sweetheart."

She nods but she drags her hand down my arm in the process, lingering a moment before she turns away, as if she doesn't want to go. I motion to Savage and he follows her, though I'm sure he'd rather watch the show.

"*Your move, savant,*" I say, repeating his now infamous jab. "I am a savant, Isaac, but it doesn't take that skill to figure this out." I hold up the note. "Did you really think I wouldn't know you left this?"

"I have no idea what you're talking about."

"You left the note. You're in trouble with the mob. I already knew that, but you're on your own. The only way that note would motivate me is if there wasn't a layer of protection between me and you, but he's alive. There's two of you. One or both of you can handle this on your own."

"You don't know who we're dealing with," he hisses, closing the space between us. "They'll come for you. They already told me to go to you."

"I know who you're dealing with. I do my homework. You fucked with the mob. Now they're going to fuck you up. Not my problem, but if you hurt Harper, I will personally punish you, make you suffer and then kill you. Now, I'm going to leave this godforsaken hospital, and spend time with my woman." I start to walk away from him, but I hesitate. "If you kill Dad, you might inherit, but then you have to deal with the mob by yourself. And if you think the mob will just take what you owe them and forgive and forget, you're wrong. You need Dad to deal with this." I walk around him.

"He thought we needed you. That's why he came here. I didn't do that to him. I didn't hurt him. They did."

I pause and consider that possibility. Maybe they did. Maybe they didn't. He's still trying to get me to protect him.

I take a step and this time I don't stop. I walk to the room, catch Harper's hand, and set her in motion toward the elevator, with Savage quickly joining us. "What happened?" Harper asks. "What are we doing?"

"We're going shopping," I say. "Then we're going to dinner. And then we're going to fuck all night." I glance at Savage. "You're not invited. We'll meet you downstairs."

He laughs but he isn't laughing when we arrive at the elevator and I stop him from entering. "I meant it. You're not invited. Give us a damn minute alone, already. We'll meet you downstairs. And you and your people need to find the guy who approached Harper the last time we were here. Now, not later." Harper steps into the elevator and then I block the doors from closing.

"Right. Find the guy who claimed to be an FBI consultant. Beat him. Make him talk. It's a good mission. I accept. Jesse will wait for you at the door. I'll be there when you're ready."

I want to tell them all to fuck off, but I have no idea what threats or promises the mob has made. I only know what Isaac has said and his word is nothing.

I nod, then step into the car and join Harper, pushing the down button, and pulling her close. The way Isaac threatened Harper is grinding through me, and it's all I can do not to hunt him down and beat his face in. Savage stands in the doorway watching us until we're sealed inside. He's on edge, worried about what I will do next, worried about my loose cannon brother, and I am too, or I wouldn't be holding onto Harper a little too hard right now. She senses it, I know she senses it, gripping my jacket and saying nothing.

A short elevator ride later, we exit the building to an SUV waiting on us, with Jesse leaning on the door. He's a big dude, dark hair, kind of broody and quiet which suits me right now. I actually do like Savage, but the fucker talks too much and I need him out of my head right now.

Jesse opens the door for us and Harper climbs inside. I follow. Jesse doesn't ask a question or speak a word. He shuts us inside and leaves us in silence. The instant we're alone, I shrug out of my coat, and turn Harper to face me and fold her close.

She presses on my chest and inches backward, her gaze probing. "Eric. This is all scaring me. Why aren't you talking to me? What—"

I kiss her. Hell, I might fuck her right here. I need her that much, and that doesn't make her a weakness. It makes her the reason my brother, and anyone coming at us, would be smart to back the fuck off.

Chapter One Hundred Five

Harper

E ric is all over me, kissing me, his big, hard body pressed to mine, his tongue drugging me with lick after lick, his hands all over my body, and while it's easy to be lost in him and us, I need to know what is going on in his head.

Somehow, I find the will to push him back, to force him to stop kissing me. "*What* is going on with you?"

"*You.* You're what's going on with me and that's what I want. Fuck this damn family."

"*Talk* to me. You're on edge. I can feel it, which is understandable, but this is next level."

"Because I want to punish them. I want to end this with all of them suffering, but since those things are not options, I need another outlet."

"Me?" I ask.

He slides his hand over my hair and presses his forehead to mine. "Yeah. You. I need fuck and think."

Thankful for his honesty, and all that he feels is expected, it really is, I curl my fingers on his jaw. "Then let's go fuck and think."

"Not now," he says, kissing my forehead and then leaning back. "Later we'll do both. I promised you shopping and we're going shopping but we both need to eat first. Anyplace you want to go?"

"We can eat at home."

"You have nothing but what some shopper you don't even know picked out for you. We need to do this. I want to do it. And the best thing Isaac and his hoodlums can see right now is us not giving two shits about what he has going on. We'll go eat first and, on the way, we'll check on your mother. After we shop, we're going to eat lunch. We're going to be you and me—*us*—and forget all of them."

"Of course that's what I want," I say, "but we need this to be over. We need—"

"A break."

"There's an assassin running around, Eric. We can't just take a break."

"I hope like hell Isaac's people come after us. I'll deal with him, and then he'll be gone, but my gut says that he's not coming after us. He came for my father."

"I was attacked, remember?"

"It was part of the agenda that failed and per that note, you staying alive is his leverage. If you're gone, if I'm gone, Isaac is on his own." He squeezes my leg. "I promise you we're fine. Let's go shopping, after we eat. I'm starving."

"Me, too. I'm in."

He strokes my cheek. "No one is going to hurt you. I promise. This will be over soon."

"What do you want to eat?"

We're doing this. We're taking a break, which isn't really a break since the world could implode around us at any moment, but the truth is, if that's going to happen, we need to enjoy every moment we have together. I'm going to enjoy this man. "Your favorite restaurant," I say. "Take me there."

"I have a lot of favorites," he says, "but how about my version of Denver's North Italia here in New York City?"

"Perfect," I say. "I'm all in."

"You better be, baby, because I am." Again, he doesn't give me the time to respond. He exits the vehicle and I assume makes arrangements with our security team. I'm actually looking forward to sitting down with him and having time to talk, to find out what's really in his head.

But time ticks onward and I start to get uptight. I open the door and step outside to find Savage talking to Eric, and the stiffness of Eric's spine tells me there's a problem. I step between them and glance up at Eric. "How's it going?"

Eric glances down at me. "He had another heart attack but he's fine."

"Was there foul play?"

"Too soon to know," Savage says. "We had eyes on him. No nurse or doctor had visited him from the time he settled in his room until the attack."

"Could he have been poisoned again on the way to his room?" I ask.

"There's too many medical hands on him to rule that out," Savage answers.

"His heart was strained from the initial attack," Eric adds. "No one is going to question another attack," but he asks Savage the same question that's in my mind. "Where's Isaac?"

"He wasn't in the room, if that's your question. Do you want to make a showing at the hospital?"

"No," Eric says. "If the police come looking for me, let me know. Otherwise, get a man on his room, not just nearby. I don't care who I have to pay to make it happen. I need out of here before Isaac and I run into each other again. I'll beat his ass and end up in jail." He motions me to the car. "Let's go have lunch."

I exchange a look with Savage, in which we both agree. He's right. He needs a break. "I'll catch up," Savage says.

Eric gives him a nod and urges me to the vehicle. I climb inside again and Eric follows. Jesse joins us and Eric gives him the destination. Once we're on the road, Eric scoots low, leans his head on the seat and closes his eyes, his jaw set hard. I lean in close and lay my head on his chest. To my relief, he settles his hand on the back of my head, and holds me there.

His heart thunders under my ear, but I swear it's the numbers punishing his mind that I hear the loudest. We should be going back to the apartment, but for reasons I don't understand, he's not ready. Maybe once he's there he's afraid the numbers will win. And the numbers represent the Kingston family.

Chapter One Hundred Six

Harper

The battle for peace and calm inside of Eric is palpable.

Thirty minutes later, we're sitting in a cozy booth in the back of a restaurant that is dimly lit with dangling lights shaped like lanterns, sipping wine. Eric's tense, an edge to him, but he's better than I expected, and seems to be shaking his reaction to his father's second heart attack. His father is an abuser who treats him horribly, but he's his father, nevertheless and I suspect all of this stirs memories of losing his mother. No matter how bad the parent, the idea of no longer having a living parent on this Earth guts you and carves a piece of you out. I know this, because after losing my father, there were times, when irrational fear for my mother ruled my thoughts. I'd say this to Eric, but I sense that it's something better explored when the storm has passed.

The waitress appears and places our food in front of us and Eric's mood lightens. The tension in his shoulders uncurls, relaxing, which pleases me immensely. Soon I'm staring at a plate of delicious smelling pasta topped with sauce and cheese that matches Eric's. As silly as it might seem, I love that we ordered the same thing. I love that we connect on everyday things, that he's a man, not just a savant, with favorite foods and a love of coffee, and a past history of pain, love, and success. I want to know that person. I want to know all of him.

He watches me eagerly while I sample the food, and the apt way he waits for my approval of his favorite place here in this city charms me. And when his eyes light as I offer my approval, he lights me up, too, inside and out. I love this man. I hate what this family has done to him but I make no mistake by seeing him as defeated. He isn't. He's battling over what to do about Isaac and that mob note he faked and as much as I want to bring it up, I don't dare. He needs a break and even as he tried to take one, I can see that he's battling with his demons.

We're almost done with the meal when Mia shoots me a text about a couple's breakfast next weekend, and Eric seems pleased with this. "As long as we can do it safely."

"Of course," I say, and this spurs us to talk about Bennett Enterprises and where I might fit into the picture.

When we finally have coffees in front of us, I feel Eric's readiness, and even need, to talk about the deeper subjects in the air, but before I can broach any topic he does it himself.

"Back at the hospital, you mentioned losing your uncles right before your father."

"Yes. I watched my father suffer, only to end up gone himself."

"Was he close to them?"

"One of them. The other was difficult but not like Isaac."

His broad chest expands on a breath that he slowly inhales. "My mother doesn't know how many times and ways she's saved that man."

"Isaac or your Dad?"

"Isaac. She wanted me to be a part of a family and the only way that was possible, was to take Isaac's shit."

"Like throwing boiling water on you?" I dare.

"That was over a woman. He wanted her. She wanted me. He saw her with me at a party and when I got home, we fought. He threw the hole fucking pot on me. The only thing that saved me was wearing a leather coat and a scarf. That and I covered my face and turned."

"So, you didn't get burned."

"Oh, I got burned. My right hand." He shows me a scar I've never noticed.

My hand catches his, studying the injury, shocked I haven't noticed the thicker raised skin before now. "Oh my God. What did your father say?"

"He told me Isaac was making me a man and I should thank him. I have no idea what he said to Isaac. Obviously not much, since he's still bragging about it."

"What was Isaac's mother like? I mean, how is he so different from you? It must be the mother that made the difference, right?"

"I don't know. I never asked. She died before I ever came into the picture, at least from the standpoint of the family knowing me.

I believe that's why my mother was willing to come forward. She wasn't around to be hurt."

A really crazy thought occurs to me. "How did she die?"

"A car accident. Why?"

This sits all kinds of wrong with me. "Everyone seems to have accidents in this family."

Eric picks up his coffee, his strong hand and long fingers, wrapping the heavy white ceramic mug. The colorful tattoos inking his forearms draw my attention, the letters and numbers telling a story of this man, that intrigues me more every day.

He sips his coffee and sets it back down. "You think Isaac's mother was murdered?"

"I think that if we're looking for a motive in all of this, and a tie to you, that it stretches back to your beginning." I pick up my cup.

"You think this is somehow connected to my mother."

"Both of your mothers," I say. "I mean, I'd say Isaac's mother had a motive to kill your mother if she wasn't dead before that."

Ignoring his cup on the table, he reaches for the one in my hand and takes a drink. "We've certainly seen that my father is willing to kill." His cellphone buzzes with a text where it lays on the table and he glances at his screen. "Fuck," he types a reply and then sips his coffee.

"What is it?" I ask anxiously.

"One of the investors in the NFL deal. I've neglected everything over this Kingston debacle. I have to deal with real life and this deal, which is too fucking good to lose. I'm going to set-up a few calls for tonight when we get home." His phone buzzes again and he punches in another text message.

I watch him, savoring the word "home" because he used it with the word "*we.*" Our home. Our home together. He sets his phone aside. "Let's talk about you. Me. Us. Movies. Anything but that family."

"How about my house?" I ask. "I have to deal with it soon."

"Do you have a mortgage?"

"Yes. I do."

"Why don't we pay it off and rent it out?"

He means *he'll* pay it off, and I don't like how that feels. He owns me in so many ways right now. I just—I feel nervous. We're still new. What if something goes wrong? "I can sell it for a profit."

"Why? We'll keep it as a real estate holding."

He says this so nonchalantly and it's logical, but it feels uncomfortable and there's an uneasy sensation in my belly. He's also spoken of us—we'll keep it—and this unity pleases me. I don't know why this topic and handling of the property is bothering me, but it is. Or maybe I do know, as Lord knows I paid a therapist a pretty penny to help me analyze myself after my father passed. It's a fear of abandonment. Eric's trying to take care of me, but the only person who's ever done that for me, is my father. And then he died, and I had to just figure it out alone.

My mother was never much help.

I shove aside my unease, unwilling to allow my baggage to destroy a good thing with Eric. "Yes," I say, offering my agreement on his suggestion. "It's a good plan."

His phone buzzes again and this time, when he glances at the message, he reports, "Finally, an update on your mother. Per Adam, she's asleep."

"Honestly, that doesn't break my heart," I say. "I'm having a hard time with her willingness to look the other way where your father is concerned. How can she know what he did to your mother and stay with him?" Guilt eats at me. "I'm sorry. I shouldn't have even brought that up today, after everything this morning. And for not telling you sooner."

"You didn't want to punish me with something I can't change. I know that I don't blame you. I blame him."

I fiddle with the napkin and twist it in my fingers. "I hate that my mother is okay with this."

He covers my hand, where I'm attempting to destroy the linen, clearly reading my fidgeting as emotion. I thought my mother was a decent enough mother. Instead, she's not even a decent human being. "She's desperate and afraid," he consoles, "and she could be afraid of him. He's powerful and she knows he basically killed my mother. That has to come with fear. He's a bad person."

"And you saved him. Do you think you would have called the ambulance had you known about what he did to your mother first?"

He stiffens and pulls his hand back. "That's the second time you've asked me that. What do you want to hear, Harper?"

My heart leaps. Oh God. "It was just a poorly phrased question," I offer quickly. "I should have asked how you feel about that."

"I guess you should have."

I suck in a breath, shocked at his sharp tone, and I recognize my misstep in bitter clarity now. Yes, he's spoken openly about wanting his father dead. We fought over it before he left, but I realize now the reality of seeing his father have a medical emergency has affected him on a deeper level than I thought. And I get it. It's scary to feel you might be on this Earth and neither of your parents are alive. I've lived that. I know the feeling well.

"A man needs to know his woman believes he will do the right thing," he adds. "I could have killed him many times over the years and I didn't do it."

Guilt is back and stabbing me like a pitchfork this time. I said the wrong thing. I'm on a roll now. First the boiling water and now this. "I know," I say quickly. "It's just the way you were talking before you went to see him and I can't blame you for wanting him to pay."

He studies me for several long beats. "I guess it's easy to assume I operate like the Kingston family. My father's blood runs through my veins. I can't blame you for that."

I feel those words like a slap, and maybe I deserve it. It really was a stupid question. I don't think Eric would just watch someone die. He spent years fighting for our country and putting his life on the line for others. "Eric," I plead.

The waiter appears and Eric hands him his card and then glances at his watch. "I made a reservation at the Chanel store."

"Oh no," I say. "I don't need that kind of extravagance. Thank you, but I just need a make-up counter and a basic department store."

"I want to take you," he says, but there's a coldness to his tone.

"I have plenty of nice things already. The purse you bought me is at least five thousand dollars. I feel bad you spent that on me."

"I want to take you," he repeats.

"I don't even have an established job yet. I can't live off you."

"You have a job."

"I have to prove myself. I have money in the bank. And I'm not going to abuse yours. Most women would and I don't want you to feel I'm like that."

"You're not most women. You're my woman. I have money. It's something you have to get used to, but it seems like it's just another thing you're not comfortable with about me."

I blanch. "Wait. What are you talking about?"

"You asked me that too many times today."

"Why are you so angry with me? And don't tell me it's about shopping. I know today has been hard—"

"Do you?"

I breathe out. "Okay, I think we should leave."

"Fine. We'll go to my apartment."

His apartment.

Not home.

Not *our* apartment. It feels intentional. It feels calculated and I'm officially angry now, too, for about five different reasons. I push to my feet and make sure he doesn't have the chance to help me with my jacket. I start for the door and he catches my hand before I exit.

"Do not go outside in front of me when we have this shit going on," he warns, low and tight.

His touch is fire and ice, and flames of anger. I exhale a heavy breath and nod. He opens the door, and Jesse steps in front, guiding us forward.

I start walking and Eric's still holding onto me, but there is nothing romantic about it, more like possessive and I don't know why at this point. I'm clearly easily demeaned and dismissed. We arrive at the SUV and Eric opens the rear door. I attempt to enter the vehicle, but he holds me steady, facing him, and just stares down at me. He doesn't speak and I don't know what he wants. Time ticks and the air crackles, until finally, he says, "We have a lot to talk about."

He releases me, expecting me to climb inside and that's the plan, but not before I say, "I don't think we do." Only then do I slide inside the vehicle and scoot to the opposite side of where I entered, my side, away from him.

He joins me and shuts the door. "We'll talk," he says. "At my apartment."

Again, he's said it and this time I blow. "*Your apartment?* Maybe we should go back to Denver and talk at *my* house." I rotate and face forward. Jesse settles in behind the wheel and thankfully that means for now, the conversation about what is his and not mine, is over.

The SUV starts to move, and I'm hyperaware of the fact that Eric and I are not touching. I don't want to touch him right now, either, He's shut me out. I don't know what is going on with him, but I know neither of us can take this right now. We have too much eroding our bond, our lives. We can't do this. *I* can't do this. My fingers curl on my legs, and I'm suddenly about to explode.

Everything I knew as my world is no longer my world. All I have is him and this life we were starting together. Now, it's all about *his* apartment. *His* decisions. This has to be about us.

Thank God the ride is only a few blocks. We stop in front of the building. The doors are opened on both sides of us and I'd normally get out with Eric, but I don't. I slide out the opposite direction and I can feel Eric's eyes on my back as I do so. I round the SUV and find Eric there talking to Jesse. I walk ahead toward the doors. I need to get to the apartment before I start showing emotions right here in front of witnesses. I'll meet Eric at *his* apartment door. He didn't even correct me on that topic.

I rush through the doors of the building and through the lobby, barely waving at the doorman. I reach the elevator and gasp as said doorman steps to my side. "May I help you, miss? Do you have an invitation into the building?"

An invitation. To my own apartment, that isn't my apartment at all. Eric joins us, his eyes meeting mine. "She's with me."

"Right," I say. "Do I need a visitor's badge or something?" I'm not looking at the guard. I'm looking at Eric. "Something that says *temporarily yours?*"

His eyes flash and he shocks me by dragging me to him. "Is that where you want to go with this?"

"We're not alone," I whisper.

He looks at the guard and that's all it takes. The guard walks away and it's game on for me and Eric. The explosion is about to happen.

Chapter One Hundred Seven

Harper

E ric's eyes glint hard and he pulls me into the elevator and punches in the code for his floor. I don't know that code. Another reason to feel like I'm a visitor. He turns me into the corner, his big body crowding mine as the elevator doors shut behind him. "Don't trap me against the wall," I whisper, shoving at the hard, unmoving wall of his chest. "Don't bully me."

"That's what you think I'm doing? Bullying you?"

"Just back off and stop being an asshole."

"I *am* an asshole, Harper. I might even be the devil himself, a man willing to watch his father die. It's the Kingston blood, remember?"

"I misspoke and it was stupid and for that, I'm truly sorry. I don't think that of you."

He leans on the wall, hand on the wooden surface, chin tucked, the pulse of emotions telling a story. The apology changes nothing. He's angry. I'm hurt.

The elevator dings, he pushes off the wall, and takes me with him as he exits, anger radiating off of him and slamming right into my own. I'm furious with him and the reasons are many, so many that I am bursting to proclaim them all. He doesn't have to drag me to the apartment. I'm keeping pace with him. I'm right there at the door as he unlocks it, he who has a key while I do not. He shoves the door open and I don't wait for a visitor's invitation. I enter and whirl around to face him.

He locks the door and stands there, his back to me, his spine stiff, seconds ticking by like the arm of a clock weighted with lead. I can't take it. I don't want to wait to say my piece, but he doesn't want to hear it. He doesn't want to deal with me. I'm here, in his space, in his place, and right now, I'm pretty sure he asked me to stay because it was the heat of the moment. Buyer's remorse has now kicked in. Why am I going to waste my energy telling him all the things I feel that don't matter? This family is trying to suck out any part of me that is human. *He's* trying to break every part of me. I always knew he would.

I rotate and all but run to the bedroom. I need to pack what I have to my name and leave. I walk into the bathroom and realize I have nothing really, plus where am I going to go? Where am I safe? I shut the door and lock it. I wait then, hoping Eric will follow me. Hoping he will make this all go away, but there is no knock on the door. There is just silence and without question, I'm in full abandonment mode. I slide down the wooden surface and squeeze my eyes shut, fighting a pinch that promises to become tears. I don't know what is happening between us. I just know that I have nothing stable to call my own, not even my mother. Certainly not my house, because it's in Denver, and it's not safe.

My cellphone rings and I pull it from my pocket to find a blocked number. I think of Gigi immediately and answer the call. "Hello?" I'm met with static and the line goes dead. *Damn it.* I wait and hope it will ring again but it doesn't. Seconds tick by and nothing. I tamp down on my emotions, presently zapping my brain cells and decide I should tell Eric. Okay no. I have nothing to say to Eric at present. *Blake*, I think. I can call Blake, but quickly discard the idea. No, not Blake. He's too sharp. He knows me and he'll read me like a large print book, way too easily. He'll ask questions and I'll melt down. I think I have Smith's number and I scan my phonebook for confirmation. *Yes.* Blake seems to have put about everyone he could think of in my phonebook, even Mia and Grayson. My stomach knots. Like I belong here.

I draw in a breath and try to focus. I dial Smith. He answers on the first ring. "Are you okay?"

"Yes. I just got a blocked call. It went dead when I answered. I thought you might want to track it."

"Right. We have your phone monitored. If it was traceable in any way, Blake will have it handled."

"Okay, great thanks." I start to hang up.

"Wait," Smith says. "You sure you're okay?"

Damn it, even Smith knows me already. "This is all just—a lot. You know?"

"Yes," he says without hesitation. "Do you want me to get an update on your mother?"

"No. I'm going to call her."

He's silent a moment. "Let me know what I can do."

"Actually," my eyes burn, "if I needed a safe place to stay that's not here—"

"You're safe with Eric. Stay there."

"Yes, but—"

"Stay there," he repeats. "You need to stay there."

"Okay," I whisper and hang up.

He calls me back almost instantly. I don't take the call. I dial my mother. She answers. "Harper?"

She sounds lucid. "How are you?"

"Numb. I can't believe he's in the ICU. I can't believe I'm on lockdown."

It hits me that she has yet to ask if I'm on lockdown or safe. "To protect you."

"I need to be with him. If he's gone—"

"He's not. He's a stubborn bastard who won't die," I say. "Mom, I need to know what's going on. Why would anyone do this?"

"I don't know!" she declares, her voice a shrill attack. "You think I know?"

"You know what he did to Eric's mother and kept it silent. So yes, I think you know things you don't share. Bad things."

"I don't. *I don't.* I'm not that person."

"You knew he denied Eric's mother treatment. How do you live with that?"

"It wasn't true. I told you that."

"But while you were drugged, you were worried Eric found out."

"That's not true. I didn't worry Eric found out. There's nothing to find out."

"What is going on, mother?" I stand up. "Tell me now."

"I don't know."

"Is it the unions and the mob?"

"No—I—no—"

"It is, isn't it?"

"I have no idea what you're talking about." She sobs. "My husband is dying and my daughter's attacking me. This is just priceless. I'm hanging up."

"Okay. And don't worry, mom. I'm safe. Just in case you wondered." I hang up. I know she knows what's going on. I have to go there. I have to make her talk. Walker can take me there and protect me, although I really don't have any money. Not enough to survive on and pay them. Maybe I just need to go back to Denver. That's what I'll do.

I open the bathroom door and jolt to find Eric standing there, his hands on either side of the doorframe. He's so damn big and I can smell that earthy, male scent of him. And those blue eyes. Those blue eyes look at me with piercing judgment I don't want to feel from this man. And right now, now, he's all cold and calculated, unemotional. "Eric," I breathe out.

"You asked for a safe place to stay? You want to fucking leave?"

He's not cold and calculated anymore. He's angry all over again.

"What did you expect? Because the minute I hit a nerve, you shut me out. You let me feel temporary, like a house guest. *You* did that to me."

"We had a fight. People fight."

"And you treated me like shit."

"You think because I have that family's blood running in my veins, I'll control you and manipulate you with my money. And I don't like it. You want to leave, leave." He pushes off the doorframe and starts walking. I hug myself, fighting tears, certain he'll walk out of the door. But right when he would, he grabs the doorframe and lowers his head.

I suck in a breath, waiting for what comes next. Eternal seconds tick by and when he rotates to face me, tall and broad and too good looking for his own good, his blue eyes are still the orange fire of his anger. But he says nothing, as if he doesn't even know where to begin, but I do. From my heart.

"I know you're hurting," I say. "I do. But I'm in this, too. I lost my father, who I loved like you did your mother. And now my mother is a horrible person. I can't go to the house. I don't have a job—"

"You have a job. I told you that."

"We can't work together and I'm not taking a pity job."

"Neither me nor Grayson hand out pity jobs."

"I'm going to Denver. I'm going home." My eyes burn with the word "home" and I turn away from him, intending to go pack.

He catches my arm and walks me around to him. "Is your home in Denver, Harper? Is that what you are saying and is that what you mean?"

"You made me feel like I was homeless with nobody in this world who cares about me."

"That's not true. It will never be true again."

"I need to just go back to Denver, Eric. It's just," my voice cracks, "it's the right thing for me to do."

"I will *not* let you go back there, not now. It's not safe."

"I'm not an obligation."

"*This* is your home. With me. We talked about this."

"*Your apartment.* You said that intentionally with purpose and don't tell me you didn't."

"I was angry. It was a really shitty thing for me to do."

"Yes. Yes, it was. Because that kind of cut is not only deep, it bleeds bright red and leaves a stain that never washes away. And just to be clear, it's not your bloodline that scares me, Eric. I lost my father, the only person who has ever really been there for me. I had to get past that and stand on my own, fight on my own. I'm terrified of leaning on you, losing you, and having to reteach myself that. I know you don't understand and—"

He scoops me to him, and cups my head, his mouth closing down on mine, and I try to resist, I try so hard to protect myself for the lure of this man, and the pain he will bring me, but I am weak. The instant that his tongue touches mine, I melt for him. He can destroy me, that is clear, and I'm helpless to stop it from happening.

Chapter One Hundred Eight

Harper

Kissing Eric leaves me weak in the knees and panting, his body a shelter I both crave and fear, because that shelter no longer feels stable and strong. "I'm sorry," he says, his voice roughened up by emotion, laced with regret. "I'm really fucking sorry. *Stay with me*, Harper,"

I hear the plea and torment in his voice, feel the burn for him in every part of me, inside and out, I do, and it matters to me, but I feel the same things I did before he kissed me. And I worry that we're now hurting each other. And neither of us need that.

"I can't do this like this, Eric. I can't. I'm not in the right headspace to be treated like a houseguest. I can't do it. I just can't." I try to pull away from him, and he holds me steady, and my fist balls on his chest, my head tilting down in utter frustration and defeat. He catches my face and drags my gaze back to his. "I'm not in a good place. You know that."

"When we start tearing each other down, we're not in the right place together."

"This wasn't me tearing you down."

"It sure as hell feels like it, Eric."

Tension ripples along his jawline and settles in his voice. "I'm coming out of my skin right now. My mind is going crazy."

"I get that and why, too, but we're standing on a ledge together, and you're pushing me off when you should be holding onto me. Fight with me, fuck me, but don't be cruel."

"And what if you can't handle how I would fuck right now?" he demands, and I don't miss the challenge deep in his voice, or the instant crackles in the air between us.

The words pierce my already wounded heart. "I'll assume I can't since you already do. I'm going back to Denver," I say and my voice is remarkably calm when I'm quaking inside. I try to pull away from him, but frustratingly he continues to hold on and his mixed messages are torture. "Stop holding me here. I'm giving you what we both know you want."

"I asked what *if,* Harper."

"Which was spoken with the same intent you said 'your apartment.' To hurt me."

"I don't want to hurt you. Damn it, woman. I would never—"

"You don't even want to fuck me. Apparently, I'm too vanilla. I'm going back to my home, which is Denver."

"Home is here, with me and you are not even close to too vanilla for me. The answer to 'what if you can't?' should have been 'what if I can?' What if I can handle it? Because I need you, Harper. I need you like I have never needed in my life." His words are a deep, guttural confession. He needs me. I need him, too.

I breath out a shaky breath. "Why are we doing this to each other?"

"I did it," he confesses. "I'm fucked in the head right now. I hate him but I don't want him to die. He would probably feel relief if I was gone."

"I don't think he would. And you can't go anywhere. You'd take me with you because I'd never survive it."

His hand slides up my back, fingers splaying between my shoulder blades, his breath warm on my cheek. "You can't be with me and not give me everything. When I get like this—"

"I know," I say, aware that we are talking about those darker desires he's alluded to in the past. "I'm not afraid of anything with you."

"I would never hurt you," he says, and then gives a bitter laugh. "I guess that's not true. I hurt you tonight."

"We hurt each other. We can't do that again."

"Agree. One hundred percent agreed. I need—"

"Me, too," I whisper.

He eases back, studies me, a wicked burn in the depths of his stare, as he drags his hand over my breast, down my waist, to cup my backside and pull me hard against his erection."

"Very certain," I assure him, sounding breathless even to myself.

He plants me against the wall, tugs my blouse out of my skirt, and yanks it open, little buttons popping everywhere.

I gasp, and he says, "Now you'll have to let me take you shopping."

"I liked that blouse."

He slides it down my shoulders and pulls me to him. "I'll buy you another and you'll let me, understand?"

I laugh. "We'll see."

"Now you just want to be punished. I won't let you down."

Punished.

It's not the first time he's used this word and I wait for it to scare me, but I don't feel fear with Eric. Just remnants of the pain we'd burned into each other, and I don't want to feel it, or remember it. I want to forget. He uses passion and pain to bury his demons and I want to bury mine, too. "Punish me how?" I ask, my chin lifting, my stare boldly meeting his.

His eyes light with approval—I have not rejected the idea of punishment all together. He knows this and he understands the invitation I've given him to take me there, whatever "there" means to him. He tangles the silk of my blouse around my wrists, securing them behind me, and just that easily, I am at his mercy, but then haven't I always been? Leaning in and pressing his lips to my neck, his teeth grope the delicate skin, goosebumps splattering about my skin here and there. I suck in a breath, every part of me on fire. My nipples, my sex, even my skin is tingling. "You're mine." He drags his gaze to mine, the gleam of possessiveness and white-hot lust in his stare. "Say it."

I've told him the idea of depending on him scares me and I see this for what it is, him pulling down that wall. Forcing me to tear it down, showing me there's no pleasure in fear. But this is not just about me. It's about him, his need for control, and inside of that demand is the question of trust. Do I trust him? He needs my submission and for someone who has battled for my independence for years now, and just felt so very alone, I'm surprised how much I need it, too. "Yes," I whisper. "I'm yours."

But it's not enough for him. He wants more, "I own you. Say it."

"Yes," I concur, but I dare to add, "Do I own you, Eric?"

He tilts my face to his and says, "You owned me the minute you showed up at that pool party braless in that black dress. And the only time I've ever regretted that was the six years we were apart, and tonight, when I thought you were going to leave me."

It's as raw and real as anything he has ever said to me, and I feel myself melt right here in this bedroom, against this wall. I know he has given me this confession, because of what he feels he took away by pushing so hard tonight. And I need to hear it. I needed it so very badly. This answer pleases me and when his lips brush mine,

I feel that wall slide away, feel myself allow the vulnerability that comes with absolute trust.

"I want to touch you," I plead, and he folds me snug against him, the hard lines of his body absorbing the softness of mine. "Not yet, baby. Not yet," and somehow, he manages to unhook my new silk bra the personal shopper bought me four sizes in, and one actually fit. It's black, lacy, sexy, but he pays it no mind. He drags it down my arms, tangles it at my wrist with my blouse, and ties me up with it.

His gaze rakes over my breasts, my puckered nipples, and when his eyes meet mine again, the hunger in his stare steals my breath. "You're beautiful, Harper. Every inch of you."

The way he says those words, rough, and laden with lust, has my sex clenching. I have never in my life felt alive in the way I feel right now, with any other man.

He reaches up and teases my nipples, gently at first, and then he's tugging, pinching, to the point of pain that is somehow pleasure. I gasp again and tilt my head back, my eyes squeezing shut. He catches my face in his hand and drags my gaze to his. "Look at me."

"You're making me crazy," I pant out.

"I haven't even gotten started," he says, and he pinches my nipple again. I curl my fingers into my palms with the new wave of pain and pleasure. "Why do you want to punish me?"

"I thought you could handle me?" he challenges.

"I'm not sure you want me to."

"Oh, I want you to, sweetheart. You have no idea how much I want you to." He kisses me again, and the instant I moan with how much I want him, he denies me his mouth, reaching behind me and unzipping my skirt. And then he's on his knee, his hands running over my hips, over the silk tights I wore to stave off the cold, but they do nothing to protect me from the wicked impact of his touch.

He unzips my boots and I have no idea why him removing them is so sexy, but oh my God, I'm dying here. I want to touch him, but he's ensured he's in full control. The world around him has stripped it away, his father, his brother—me—and he wants it back.

When my boots are gone, he yanks roughly at my skirt, and it's moments before it's at my ankles and he's lifting me, freeing me from its restraint, but I'm not free at all. I will never be free of this man and what he does to me. And I don't want to be.

He reaches over his head and tugs his T-shirt off, tossing it aside, the bright colored ink on his arms, so damn hot, symbolic of everything that makes him who he is—rebel, SEAL, savant, self-made billionaire. Friend to those he cares about. It all comes together on that sleeve and I never get over how sexy it is, how much it makes me want him. It's symbolic. His fingers catch the edge of the tights, and he rolls them back just enough to kiss the sensitive skin there. My teeth scrape my bottom lip.

He's never going to be inside me at this point, I think. But that's the idea. He wants to torment me. He rolls the tights down lower, feathering kisses on my belly. My fingers ball around my clothing holding me captive when they want to be in his hair. He drags my tights all the way down, wraps his arm around my lower back just above my backside and lifts me, working them off my feet and tossing them aside. When he sets me back down, he squeezes my backside and presses his lips to my belly again, his gaze lifting to mine.

His fingers slide into the wet heat between my legs and I arch into the touch, my lashes lowering.

"Look at me," he orders again, but his fingers slide inside me and I can't seem to do it.

My punishment is his hand disappearing and him pushing to his feet, and grabbing my face, and not gently. "You do what I say right now. That's part of handling me right now. You understand? Unless you can't anymore. Unless you want to stop and if you do—"

"I don't."

"Then you do what I say," he repeats. "Understand?"

"And if I don't?" It's the question I can feel he wanted me to ask.

"Then I punish you."

Punish me. I should be scared, I should just say no, but I'm ridiculously aroused. "How?"

He squeezes my back side and gives me a little smack. I yelp and he says, "That was a warning shot. I'll spank you."

His fingers twine in the silky strands of my hair, tilting my mouth to his, and he devours me with a kiss, claims me in a way no other kiss has ever claimed me.

I'm breathless when he pulls me off the wall and toward the bed, stands me facing it and yanks away the ties on my hands. "Hands and knees," he orders.

My heart leaps and now I feel vulnerable in a whole new way. "Eric," I whisper, and I can't stop the plea in my voice.

He hears it, and turns me in his arms, folding me to him. "Too much?" and there is tenderness in him now I do not expect.

"No," I say, curling my fingers on his chest. "I'm just—I'm nervous."

"Don't be nervous. It's all about the complete escape."

"Will it hurt?"

"It's pleasure."

"And pain?"

He reaches up and pinches my nipple and I gasp, little darts of pleasure shooting straight to my sex. "Like that, sweetheart. Just like that." He kisses me and just that easily, I've forgotten the nerves and the fear.

When his mouth rips from mine, he sets me away from him, long enough to pull off his boots, and take off his pants. In seconds, he's naked, his cock jutted forward, and my mouth is dry, my legs slick from how wet he's made me. He steps to me, and molds me close, his hands on my backside, and he squeezes harder this time, and then gives me a sharper smack.

I gasp, and his hand is on my breast, his lips on my neck. He does it again, a squeeze and smack. It stings, but for reasons I don't even understand I want him to do it again. "We're going to start slow," he says. "I'm going to spank you while I fuck you." He rotates me to face the bed. "Hands and knees."

This time I smash my nerves, and do as he says. He follows me on to the mattress, his hands on my hips, sliding over my backside, his finger pressing inside me. I arch my back and his cock slides along the slick heat of my sex. He's so very hard, and I pant as he enters me, driving deep. That's when he smacks my backside, and before I can even register the sting, he's driving into me again. Another palm, and each time the sting intensifies, and oh God it hurts and feels so good, when he pumps into me harder. I lose reality. There is just his hand and his cock, and pleasure.

I'm so on edge, and when he rolls me to my side, him behind me, his hand on my breast, I grab it and hold it to me. He thrusts again, and it's all over. I tumble over, shattering in a crazy, intense quaking of my body. He groans near my ear, and quakes right along with me.

When it's over, emotions turn my throat to cotton and my eyes burn. "You okay?" he asks.

"Yes," I whisper.

He kisses my neck and says, "I'll get you something."

He rolls away from me and that's when the emotions kick up another ten notches. I want to move and try to shake it off, but I can't. Not with the dampness between my legs and eyes that might spill over. I suck in a breath and will my tears under control. He'll think I can't handle anything but vanilla and that's not it. I liked it. I did. I don't why I'm like this.

He returns and lays in front of me, pressing a towel between my legs and then cupping my face and pulling my gaze to his. "You aren't okay, are you?"

"I am, I swear. I liked it. I'm just trembling and kind of emotional. And I know you held back. I know that was too like what we did in the hotel room."

"I was not holding back, but pushing you too hard is pushing you away, and I have no desire to do so, Harper. And it was not just like when we were in your hotel room. And as for how you feel, the emotions are created by the adrenaline," he says, grabbing a pillow and sliding it under my head and his. "It's why people like it. It takes you away from everything and then forces the stress away. It becomes addictive."

"I see."

"If you let me spank you, over my lap, *really* spank you, you'll probably meltdown after. At least the first time."

I gape. "Over your lap?"

He laughs, one of his deep, sexy laughs and says, "Yes. And don't look so shocked. I promise you, you will like it."

"And what do you get out of it?"

"It's a control thing. I don't know how to explain it. I can give you just enough pain to feel good, and there's something really sexy about that. But we don't have to—"

"No, I did like it. More than anything I liked the intimacy of it with you."

"The complete lack of barriers," he says. "That's what I want with you." He strokes my cheek. "I'm really sorry about earlier."

"Me, too. I do not think you are anything like them or I wouldn't be here."

"I know. I was just hyped up. In a bad place. And it's *our* apartment." His hand finds my hip and he folds me close. "I don't want you to leave. Ever."

"I don't want to leave."

"Then let's talk about money. I worked hard for this and I had no one to share it with until you. All it is to me is proof that I am better than a Kingston unless we make it more. Buy what you need and don't buy the cheap stuff. I want my woman to have anything she wants."

"I have to make my own money. I want to be a power couple. I want—"

He leans in and kisses me. "I love you."

"I love you."

"And we already are a power couple. I'm better with you. I know you don't know that yet, but I do. Now let's get dressed and go shopping."

I laugh. "Are you serious?"

"Hell yeah, sweetheart." He stands up and pulls me with him, his hands slide under my hair and cups my neck. "I'm going to spank you again. Think about it. I will be."

I smile, and kiss him. "I will be, too."

And as we part our bodies and dress, the mood is lighter, and when we look at each other, I can feel the growing bond between us. Yes, we fought, but on the other side of it, we are stronger. And I hope that means our enemies are weaker.

Chapter One Hundred Nine

Harper

Eric gives me a true *Pretty Woman*, Julia Roberts experience. He leads me into the Chanel store, hands over his credit card, and tells them we are going to spend tons of money. And then he proceeds to have me show him every outfit. This repeats at several other stores, and even get my stop at the makeup counter. Eric is so genuinely pleased with my purchases, that I don't feel awkward. I am truly feeling like a princess, when we finally head back to the apartment.

Through it all we receive random updates from Walker, and everything is as calm as can be under the circumstances. It's the most relaxed I've ever seen Eric. But on the ride home, the mood is somber. Our little escape is over and we both know it's time to get back to business.

Once we arrive at the apartment, Eric tips the doorman to bring our bags upstairs and then tugs me over to the security desk, and the very man we'd fought in front of earlier.

"What are you doing?" I whisper urgently.

"Jonathan," Eric greets. "This is Harper. She lives here now. Treat her as such and not an intruder."

I can feel my cheeks heating while Jonathan pales.

"I had no idea." Jonathan said. "So sorry, miss. If you have your ID, I can get you registered properly."

ID. Oh no. I turn to Eric. "My purse. My credit cards. I haven't even thought about cancelling them. I have to go do that now."

"We'll get it handled." He eyes Jonathan. "Make sure it's not a problem."

"Of course." Eric gives me his back and leans in close to Jonathan and I have no idea what he says, but Jonathan has now paled to ghostly.

"Yes, Mr. Mitchell."

Eric catches my hand and leads me to the elevator. "What did you say to him?"

"I made sure you'll be treated like the princess you are," he says and winks. "And Adam got your purse, and it will be here tomorrow. I forgot to tell you."

I sigh in relief. "Oh good."

We ride up in the elevator with his arm wrapped around me and once we're at the front door he pulls me in front of him. "1021 is the code, but I change it once a week. Try it."

My heart swells with how much he's trying to make up for earlier. I punch in the code and try the door. Sure enough, it's open. I rotate and wrap my arms around him. "Thank you."

"I was alone, too. You know that, right?"

"I do. Not anymore though."

"No," he says with a curve to his lips. "Not anymore."

Chapter One Hundred Ten

Harper

I sort through my purchases while Eric attends his conference call. I'm feeling a bit out of sorts, without a career, and eager to talk through my future. For now, I choose a sink and put away my toiletries. When I'm organized, I try on my clothes again to be sure they are all keepers, and just as I finish up, Eric appears in the closet door, his light brown hair rumpled, his jaw shadowed.

His eyes are warm as he says, "Take whatever part of the closet you want, Harper."

I laugh and point to my section. "I kind of took that liberty."

"Good," he says, and I can feel he means it.

"How was your meeting?"

"Not bad. Not great. I need to talk to Grayson but he's in a meeting. You hungry?"

"Shockingly after our big lunch, I am. Is there a gym in the building."

"We have a gym. You know you really should take time to go explore."

"I guess I should."

He catches my hand and leads me out of the closet. "That's my side of the sink."

"Is it now?"

"Yes." I glance up at him. "Is that okay?"

"I always hated that side of the sink. It's all yours."

I laugh, and we head downstairs, debating our dinner choices. We ultimately order takeout from a Mexican joint Eric loves, and the delivery is fast, and the food amazing. I approve of his choice and soon our bellies are full, and we curl into an oversized chair in front of a stunning city view, the sun long gone. The city lights twinkling and winking, almost as if they're celebrating this chance we have at peace. Some part of me knows that we have a world of evil waiting for us outside this apartment but the idea that this is our safe place together, our home together, fills me with warmth I can't wish away. I need this. Obviously, Eric needs this, too.

And so, we sit there, staring out at the city in a few minutes of comfortable, relaxed quiet, each of us sipping from our glasses, enjoying a delicious red blend wine. Eric and I have just set our glasses on a small round stone table that is to his right, when he drags my leg across his lap. "Can you learn to love this city, Harper?"

"I already do. You're here."

"Bennett has operations all over the world," he says. "If you end up hating this city, we'll move."

That offer speaks worlds to me. He's all in with me. We really are the team that I doubted just hours ago. I lean forward and press my hand to his. "We can go where we decide we want to be, but I love that this place is your life. I love that it can be my life."

"It's already your life," he says, cupping my hand and kissing my knuckles. "It's our life, Harper."

"And I love that, but being here with you lets me learn all about you. I want to know your favorite places. I want to know your friends. I want to see your brilliant mind work and—" I consider a moment, then continue, "I want to know what every tattoo on your body says and the story that goes with it." I point to a row of numbers. "This one. What does it mean?"

He laughs, low and rough, so damn sexy. "That one: mud puddles."

I frown. "What? What does that mean?"

"Family and no, not my fucked-up Kingston family." He doesn't wait for the obvious next question. He launches into the story. "I was on a mission during a particularly bad rainy season in Europe. Me and three other SEALs had to drag each other through mud puddles that felt like quicksand to complete a mission and survive."

"And you helped each other," I supply. "The way family is supposed to help family."

"Yes. Exactly."

"I'd pull you through mud puddles, or well, I'd probably just fall in it with you."

He laughs again, and it's so good to see him like this. "I'd stay in the mud puddles if you were with me."

I smile at his reply. "What happened to those SEALs?"

"We stay connected, but it's more—a pack. We live our lives separately, but we have a communication system. If we ever need each other, we're there for each other, no questions asked."

I'm in awe of this discovery. He has SEAL buddies—no, *brothers*—that would come to help him if needed, and while I wonder if he's considered that now, with the mob, I find myself resisting the idea of letting that hell into our evening. As it is, I expect the phone to ring at any moment and while I welcome answers, I really do want this time alone with Eric.

We spend almost two hours drinking wine and talking about everything *but* the Kingstons. He gravitates toward telling me funny stories about a few of his Navy pals, which I believe is because they are so far removed from this life, this world. He meant it when he said he needed an escape. In turn, I avoid the Kingstons and share stories of my frequent outings with my father, who I went to a Sunday movie with two times a month.

"Movies," Eric murmurs, stroking a strand of hair from my eyes. "I haven't been to the movies in years."

"Me either," I say. "Not since he died. I just—I can't."

"What if we went together? A way to bring your father to me, since I can't meet him."

If the man is trying to make me fall more in love with him, it's working. "I'd like that," I say, my eyes burning, emotions expanding in my chest. "Very much."

"Well then, it's Friday night. Why don't we make it a Saturday night date?"

"I'd like that very much," I repeat, hoping it can happen. "But Eric, we're living in hell right now. Don't we need to deal with that hell?"

"We do. We will. In fact, right now," he stands and pulls me to my feet, "I'm going to put you in a hot bath and do some thinking while you're relaxing."

A few minutes later, we're in the bathroom where a luxurious bubble bath has been created with floral-scented bubbles we purchased while shopping. "This tub has never been used," he says, as I settle into the sunken egg-shaped sensation filled with warm water and he sets my newly filled wine glass next to me.

"Join me," I suggest. "Come try out your own tub."

"*Our* tub, baby," he says, sitting on the edge next to me. "And you just enjoy the bath. My head is clear for the first time in twenty-four hours. I'm going to put that empty space to use."

"That space that is your head is never empty, but I get it. Go. Do. Be the savant. I hope you find answers."

"Me, too, baby. Me, too."

The "baby" endearment is back. He doesn't use it often, but I wonder if it's during the times when he's most relaxed. The idea pleases me as I don't think he's had many of those moments in life, moments I equate to peace, which I would very like to deliver to him.

He stands and walks toward the door, and I sink into the bubbles, relaxed and happy, but I'm aware of the problems we have hidden from, the way they lurk just beyond the present. Eric does, too. It's why he's not with me right now. I cut my bath short and dry off, pulling on a pink silk gown Eric picked out today, and a matching robe. With my feet in slippers, I walk into the dark bedroom and go still.

Even before I see him, I feel Eric in the room. My eyes reach to the corner of the room, where he sits in an oversized chair, and I am certain there's a Rubik's cube in his hand. He's back in the real world now, strategizing his next move, *our* next move, but I believe it's more than that. I believe the numbers torment him, and keep him up at night.

I cross the room and curl up next to him. "How often do you stay up all night?"

"Too often."

"Right here in this chair."

"Yes."

"Then I guess I'll be sleeping here often."

He sits there for several silent beats and then reaches behind him, grabs a blanket and pulls it over me. I smile. He likes that I'm with him. And I wouldn't want to be anywhere else.

Chapter One Hundred Eleven

Harper

The next morning, I wake to the buzzing of an alarm, immediately aware of Eric's hard body next to mine, of me still pressed to his side. He shifts and reaches for his phone and silences the noise. "Damn," he murmurs, sitting up straighter. "I fell asleep." He sounds befuddled by this information, but I am pleased. My brilliant, amazing, gifted man is too troubled, and I can only hope I allow him some calm in his mind. Because no one else will. His phone is already blowing up with text messages, which tells me his silent mode goes off with his alarm. "And, of course," he says, "I have about twenty text messages."

"I'll put on the coffee." I kiss him and when I would stand, he captures my hand and stills the action, running his fingers through my tousled hair, tenderness in the action that steals my breath.

"I don't know what you do to me," he murmurs softly.

It occurs to me that he might actually feel I disrupted his process of problem solving. "Is that a good or bad thing?"

"Life is better with you in it," he declares, his finger tracing my jawline.

Warmth spreads through me with those words, and for the first time in a very long time, I feel as if I'm where I belong. "Eric," I begin, but his phone begins to ring, and he grits his teeth. "I need to find out what is going on."

I nod, kiss him on the cheek, and then whisper in his ear, "I love you," before darting away, feeling as if sunshine is on my shoulder.

With my phone in hand, I hurry downstairs, get the coffee started, and then check my messages, only to note a missed call from yet another unknown caller. It has to be Gigi, but there is no voicemail. In other words, Walker will already be aware of the call, and there is nothing I can do at this point that matters aside from wait for the caller to try me again.

There's also a text from Mia, just checking on me, and we talk about and forth by text as I wait on the coffee to brew. It's actually nice to have someone to chat with and tell about my shopping trip yesterday and at least live the short fantasy that is perhaps what would be normalcy in this new life of mine. A chat with a friend and coffee with the man I love. It's a bittersweet symphony as I know the calls and messages Eric is juggling at this very moment, says my sunshine will soon be suffocated by heavily burdened storm clouds.

The beeping of the coffee pot tells me the brew is complete and I shake off my thoughts, and steel myself for whatever news Eric will deliver when I return upstairs. We must endure the turbulence to find steady air. I learned that on the flight over here. With two cups of coffee in hand, I travel to the bedroom and enter just as Eric is hanging up from a phone call. I hand him a cup. "Thanks, sweetheart."

Not baby. The gentler moments, lost in each other, have officially passed.

I wonder what that call was about and I sink onto the cushion next to him. "Any news?"

"My father remains stable. No news on the birth certificate. And Blake tracked the guy who poisoned my father. He left the city and disappeared, which only supports the theory that he was a professional."

My brows knit. "Oh. I'm not sure if that is good or bad."

"Not much has changed. We know these are professionals. I doubt that guy was even in the warehouse in Denver. Most likely none of these are the same people."

"Okay well, that's not overly comforting. How many hitmen are there in the world?"

"More than you might think," he says grimly. "But most normal people won't end up on a hitlist." He shifts the topic, probably with the intent of getting the last one out of my head. "A few other updates. Your mother's highly sedated."

"Probably for the best."

"Gigi is still missing."

"Which reminds me," I say, setting my cup down next to his. "Last night when we were fighting, I got a call from an unknown caller but it went dead. I had another missed one today. I did tell Smith."

"He told me last night."

"I swear I hung up with that man and he tattled like a kid."

He laughs. "I guess he did." He sets his cup on a table and takes mine and does the same. "Let's go shower. I have a conference call for the NFL deal today and I need to run by the hospital first. You can get a quiet Saturday look at the Bennett operation and then sit in on the call."

"All of the above make me nervous for different reasons, but the hospital tops the list. Every time we go by there something crazy happens."

"We won't stay long. We'll go eat on the way." He stands and lifts me with him. "My favorite diner is around the corner and I want you to try it.

The idea of Eric showing me something he calls his "favorite" sends a little thrill through me, these little hints of normalcy teasing me with glimpses of me and him without the Kingston family. But my thoughts are fleeting as Eric pulls me under the spray of the shower and shows me just how much better life is with *him*. Mornings are not to be dreaded, but rather welcomed if they start like this.

Two orgasms later for me, and one for him, we both dress in casual winter clothing, and I've completely suppressed the whole assassin thing, until Eric slides his weapon into the back of his pants. We can pretend life is roses, but his gun reminds me, they have thorns. But I don't say anything. Better he have the gun, than not.

Once we're downstairs, Eric helps me with my coat and catches my lapels. "Don't let the gun make you nervous. It's just a precaution. Savage and Adrian are with us today."

"I've told you, I carry. The gun doesn't freak me out. In fact, I'm wildly comforted by a Navy SEAL man, carrying a gun he knows how to use. I just want this over. Did you ever get Grayson out of town? I talked to Mia this morning and she mentioned nothing about it."

"I talked to Davis this morning. He's working on it."

"He needs to be faster."

"Agreed. I told him the same thing. It's also past due we get you a weapon."

I don't argue, not after that incident with the man in the hospital. I'm not sure if it's legal to carry in New York City, but I don't care or ask. I need a weapon, at least until this is all over.

break

The diner is so close, and we walk with Adrian and Smith, one at our front, the other our rear. It's brutally cold though and I'm relieved when we enter the diner. Adrian and Smith, claim a table nearby, and close to the door. Me and Eric end up in a cozy corner booth with floral-printed seats and a wooden table, with egg white omelets and coffee as our chosen meals, both of us talking about the city when Eric's cellphone buzzes. He grabs it, reads a message and while his expression is unchanged, there is a slight crackle in the air, a barely perceptible tension in the line of his jaw. He sets his phone down and says nothing and I can almost see the numbers churning in his mind. It's not that he doesn't intend to tell me what's going on. He's simply lost in where whatever he has learned has delivered him. "What just happened?" I prod gently.

"Isaac managed to slip past Blake's man. They don't know where he is." His mind might be racing, but he speaks the words far more nonchalantly than they merit and sips his coffee, as if downplaying his worry for me.

My eyes go wide. "What? When did this happen?"

"On our way over here. They're watching my father, Grayson, and Mia. And us."

"It doesn't seem like Isaac could get by a Walker guy. They're all pretty sharp."

"He started running and darting through traffic."

"That's not good. Why? What do you think he's trying to do?"

"Why don't you ask Isaac," Isaac says, sliding into the booth in front of us.

My eyes go wide and Eric's hand slides to my leg, warning me to stay calm, telling me that he's here, he's got this. He's in control. Isaac, on the other hand, doesn't look in control. His hair is rumpled, dark circles shadowing underneath his eyes, his lips dry and cracked. "Let's have a real talk, *brother.*"

Chapter One Hundred Twelve

Eric

Isaac's face is gaunt and ruddy and he looks strung out, and as agitated as he was the night he threw that boiling water meant for hot cocoa on me. There's a desperation to him and desperate people do desperate things. I slowly reach behind me and remove my gun, setting it on my lap. Harper tenses with this knowledge, but to her credit holds it together and doesn't react. Adrian appears beside us and leans on the booth above me. "He came in the back door and ran for you," he explains before he glances down at Isaac. "You want to get up, Isaac, or should I lift you by your ears?"

I lift a hand at Adrian and wave him off. "I don't know if he's armed."

"It doesn't matter," I say. "I am and I'm a hell of a lot faster on the draw than he is."

Adrian hesitates but caves. "I'll be close." I don't take my eyes off of Isaac, but I'm aware when Savage backs away.

"Coffee?" I offer, motioning to the waitress with a pot in her hand and turning over the cup on the saucer in front of him.

The waitress fills his cup. "Can I get you anything else, sir?" she asks.

Isaac waves her off without so much a glance in her direction, and the message is clear: she's beneath him. He forces everyone he can beneath him. That's his way. Lift himself up by pushing others down. It's what he tried to do to me from the day he met me. As if I could come in and claim his empire when I'm not even a full-blooded heir.

"You were right," Isaac states, sipping his coffee black because of course, cream and sugar wouldn't be manly. "We have trouble with the mob, but they didn't leave the note. I left you that note in Dad's room."

I add some extra cream to my coffee. I might even need to add more sugar to get through this bitter bullshit. Fuck Isaac and all his bullshit.

"Did you hear me?" he demands, his tone nothing shy of venomous. "I left the note."

"I didn't know there was a question," I comment, my tone wry at best.

"You mean the note where you threatened me again?" Harper demands. "When you used me against your *brother*?"

He scowls at her. "I'm not behind the attack on you."

"Then who was?" Harper demands. "Your father? The mob? Because we all know you were ready to set me up with them."

He grimaces and eyes me, dismissing her and her accusations. "Dad knew you'd think it was me. He came here to convince you that it was *not*. Because the last fucking thing we need right now is to have you coming at us, too."

The last time we talked he said Dad came to ask for my help. He's a liar, and liars always forget their lies. I smirk. "Come at you? Why would I do that? We're family. Right, Isaac?"

"We *are* family. Which means the mob will eventually come for you and Harper. They will find someone in this family to make our problems with them right. Deal with them now or deal with them later."

I laugh and sip my coffee. "Barking up the wrong tree, *brother*. I won't help. You won't use Harper as leverage. I'll fucking make you pay for that ten times over."

"You don't know who you're dealing with," Isaac hisses, leaning in closer and pokes at the table. "This is the mob. They will come for you."

"How'd you even get in bed with the mob, Isaac?" Harper interjects.

He glowers her direction. "I didn't get involved with the damn mob, Harper. I was dealing with the union."

"Everyone knows the mob and the unions have been in bed," I say. "I assume you borrowed money, and then couldn't pay it back."

"One of the higher-ups at the union offered us an influx of cash to grow the business. He wanted more jobs. I wanted more money. It was a match made to happen."

"Isn't it illegal to get into bed with the union?" she queries. "Or at least unethical?"

"Fuck your moral compass, Harper," Isaac snaps. "I was trying to do what was best for the company. We were falling behind, thanks to those recalls." He eyes the jaguar on my arm. "Our competition is thriving. We are not."

I think through what I know and make assumptions. "You cut corners. It caused the recalls. The recalls caused financial distress. You borrowed Harper's trust fund but it wasn't enough so you borrowed money from the mob."

"The union," he bites out, denying nothing I've stated.

"Which is the mob," I remind him. "Once you owe them money, they will find a way to get the money which is why you don't do it. Good luck to you, brother. You're going to need it." I flag the waitress. "Check, please."

Isaac leans in close again. "You're a part of this. Why do you think Dad's in that bed right now? Why do you think Harper was attacked?"

"So you *do* know details of my attack?" Harper challenges.

He ignores her, his agitated attention locked on me. "Those attacks were a message to you and me. Fix this or else our people will get hurt. I'm not making this shit up."

Which means he's making at least some of this shit up.

"Be smart," he says. "Aren't you a genius?"

"It doesn't take a genius to stay away from this," I say.

"Your woman and your father were both attacked," he snaps, his foot tapping under the table, a nervous tic he's favored all his life, at least since I've known him. "Ignoring that sounds pretty fucking stupid to me."

"How much do you owe?" Harper asks.

"Yes, how much do you owe, *brother?*"

"Five million."

Harper gasps. I laugh. "I'll make sure you get a really snazzy casket when the time comes."

"Give me a stock tip," Isaac orders, but the command is weakened by the desperate note in his tone. "I know you did that for Dad once. One that gets me the money to pay this debt off. Then it's not your money."

He says that statement with absolute disgust, as if that action I took has been rubbed in his face over and over. Without a doubt, it has, and I get it. Dad sucks that way. He used me to abuse him, but holy fuck, he deserves to be abused. "No," I say simply.

"You're a stockholder now," he reminds me. "You think they won't come for you?"

"I could offer my stock to the mob," I suggest sardonically. "Will that work for you?"

His fingers curled in his palms, fists ready to lash out. "This is not a fucking game."

I consider him a moment, his eyes all but bulging with anger, a muscle in his jaw ticking. A look he wears often. A look I know well. It's called busted. "You're lying," I say. "There's more to the story and until you tell me everything, you're on your own."

"You're a fool who's going to regret this," Isaac snaps. "Don't say I didn't warn you." And with that threat, he starts to get up.

"What was Dad going to tell me when you had him poisoned?" I ask. "What don't you want me to know?"

"If I was going to poison anyone, it would be you." There's a brutal quality to that confession and I believe him. Harper has spoken of hate often in our time together. That word was created for Isaac. He hates me.

"You'll never get that stock tip if I'm dead, brother."

His eyes glint and slowly shifts his attention to Harper, his eyes lingering on her a moment before he pierces me with a stare. "You're going to help me, Eric. You just don't know it yet." He gets up to leave.

I read the message loud and clear. I shove my gun in my waistband, stand and step in front of him. "Do not push me, Isaac," I warn, my voice low, lethal. "If anything happens to Harper, I will strip you down to your underwear financially and stick you in a corner with your thumb in your mouth. Now, I suggest you leave before I decide to act on my fantasies right now, and they aren't nearly as kinky as they are bloody." I step aside.

He smirks. "For a smart guy, you're just as fucking stupid as ever and I predict you'll agree with me sooner rather than later." He starts walking away and it's all I can do not to yank him back, take him to the bathroom and beat answers out of him. I contemplate the merit of such a plan, when Harper steps in front of me and wraps her arms around me.

"Whatever you want to do right now," she orders, "kiss me instead."

I might just do that, kiss her right here in the middle of the diner, drive away all the demons my brother represents with the sweet taste of her, but we're not alone. Savage steps behind her, a grim look on his face that says he has news. And it's not good.

Chapter One Hundred Thirteen

Eric

Harper senses Savage behind her and twists around to find him there. "Savage," she gasps, and I know why. He's sporting a black eye the size of Texas. "What happened to your eye?"

Savage's eyes light with amusement. "Worried about me? Or sending me to my room for being a bad boy?"

"Seriously," she says. "What happened?"

"Me and my best friend got in a fight over a Snickers bar. That's the truth and don't ask for details. They're too sordid." He eyes me over her head. "Let's sit so I can speak freely."

I nod and ease Harper over to the booth, helping her slide in again. By the time I've joined her, Savage is sitting directly across from me. "What happened to your eye, Savage?" Harper presses.

"Same story, Harper," he says. "I'm sticking with it."

I can see a man avoiding a dark alley he doesn't want to travel, and I help him redirect. "Did you find the guy that cornered Harper at the hospital?"

"Yes," Savage says, and I can feel the punch of his relief that we're moving on, mixed with the grimness of his answer, even before he finishes with, "in a hotel bed, with his throat cut."

Harper sucks in air. "Oh God. *Oh God.*" She casts a panicked look at me. "Eric."

I pull her hand to my lap and cover it with my own. "Easy, baby. It's going to be okay."

That earns me instant rejection. "It's not okay," she insists, tugging her hand free as if she cannot bear to be contained in any way. "Nothing about any of this is okay."

"We are," I say. "*We are*. And we're what matters when this is all over and done."

Savage rolls on in with backup adding, "And you're going to stay okay. Better than okay. You have Eric and you have me, as well as my badass team."

"Isaac got to us," she points out, pinning him in a sharp corner.

He flicks a look at me. "I sent you a text giving you the heads up about Isaac."

I set my phone in front of Harper, showing her the proof that Savage did indeed warn us about Isaac. I just missed the message.

This does not compel her comfort or security, "We need this over, Eric," she whispers. "We *need* it over."

"One thing I've learned in my life, in the SEALs more than anywhere, is that pushing harder doesn't lead to an end. When you push too hard, too fast, just to do something, you end up doing the wrong something." I lift my chin at Savage. "What about the woman who was with the man at the hospital?"

"We caught her on camera leaving the hotel. We've been working to ID her along with law enforcement, and so far, it's a no go on a name."

"Wait," Harper says, her hands flattening on the table. "Are you suggesting that the woman who was with him killed him?"

"That's what we believe," Savage confirms. "That's our working hypothesis."

"Go further with that," I urge, wanting to know where the Walker team is taking this. "Play along. Assume out loud. Tell me where your head is right now."

Savage's eyes light and he leans forward. "Assuming you're right, and the message our newly dead, fake FBI consultant, gave Harper was from Gigi, the man and the woman worked for Gigi."

"But you think the woman killed the man," Harper says, jumping in. "How does that make sense?"

Savage taps the table and points at her. "Exactly. Which means that Isaac found out about them, but the man couldn't be bought."

"So they ended him," Harper supplies, following his lead.

"Or," I suggest. "He knew too much, maybe even tried to use it against Gigi, and she had him dealt with."

"Gigi," Harper says, sitting up straighter. "I told your team about a call I think was from her. Did your team track it?"

"It came from a café in Italy," Savage relays. "And yes. We believe that has to be Gigi and we're homing in on her."

"She must be trying to warn us," Harper says. "She didn't have that man killed. Isaac did. This is all Isaac."

"No," I say, my fingers thrumming on the counter. "Gigi is not the good guy in this."

"That doesn't mean she wasn't warning you about Isaac," Savage interjects.

I follow where he leads. "She just wants me to share the same enemies. He wants me to get rid of his enemies."

"That doesn't make sense if we're talking about Isaac," Harper argues. "He's her grandson. She knows how much you hate him. She knows pitting you against him, with you in the know, doesn't end well for Isaac."

"Which means one of three things," I say. "One: she's not warning you at all. She's hoping to use you again in some way. Two: it's not Isaac that she wants to warn you about at all. Or Three: Isaac's desperate enough to convince the mob, to kill everyone who stands between him and the inheritance. We need to know what was in those messages. And where those birth certificates they pushed us toward lead us."

"But if your theory is correct," Harper says, "they may just be leading us down a rabbit hole that Gigi dug for us."

I toss money on the table. "I'll know when we get that information," I say, eyeing Savage. "When do we get that information?"

He lifts his hands. "That's in Blake's court."

"I need to talk to whoever Isaac is talking to in the mob. Get me a number."

"That's crazy," Harper says. "Why would you do that?"

"I have a plan," I assure her.

Savage scowls. "You're going to call a mob boss on the phone?"

"He's just a man. You know that, Savage. We've both seen war and we both know how war tears away the armor and gets down to the skin and bones."

"But he doesn't think he's in a war," Savage argues. "He thinks he's hunting prey in your family and starting a war with him would be like saying you were taking on the Taliban by yourself, with the Walker army and nothing more."

I consider that a moment. "I don't want a war with the mob. I want to help them fight the war they have with my brother. If it even exists." On that note, I stand and pull Harper across the seat to her feet, my hand settling on her hip. "We're skipping the hospital. Let's go buy an NFL team."

Savage unfolds that big body of his to join me. "This is all about to blow the fuck up. You know why? Because you're about to blow it the fuck up."

Harper's eyes go wide, and I grimace. Thank you, fucking Savage. I don't even bother to reply. I snag Harper's hand and lead her through the diner and away from Savage. We exit to the outdoors, and I quickly pull her to the side of the door, behind a big fake tree of some sort, where I press her to the wall. "This is about to be over," I vow.

"But what does that look like?"

"Us, baby." I lean in and kiss her, tasting the fear on her lips that I don't want to exist. "Us," I repeat. "Us living a new life together, which we're starting now. Us happily ever after."

"You aren't the happily ever after kind of guy."

"I'm an us guy and there is no place you and I go, but happily ever after. I won't let it be any other way. This doesn't end any other way. That's a promise."

"Don't make a promise you can't keep."

Savage steps around the tree to join us, clearing his throat as he does. "Speaking of blowing this thing up. It's happening now." He holds up his phone. "Don't send me to my room just yet. I have more news."

Chapter One Hundred Fourteen

Eric

Turns out, it's not Savage that has news at all. "Blake's meeting us at your office."

"About what?" I ask, releasing Harper to turn and face him, my hands sliding under my jacket to settle on my hips. "Don't walk around whatever it is Blake wants you to walk around. That's not your style."

"No," Savage says. "It's not." He offers nothing more.

I narrow my eyes on him. "Spit it out, Savage. I can't pull this shit into the middle of my NFL meetings. I a have call set-up and a contract change to review. I owe Grayson, and everyone involved counting on this to be life-changing, my focus."

"I can't tell you what I don't know."

Frustrated, I take Harper's hand. "This has to wait until I get out of my meeting. Tell Blake not to come to the office. I'll go to him." I eye my watch. "It's later than I thought. We need a ride to the office."

"Jesse is waiting right around the corner?"

I nod and catch Harper's hand and start walking. "I'll meet Blake," Harper offers, keeping pace with me. "This has to be important. We need to know what it's about, but you're right. You need to focus. Take care of what you need to do for Grayson."

"I need you in my meeting," I say as we round the corner and bring Jesse into view.

"Me? I know nothing about this."

"If you're going to play a role in the NFL operation, you need to understand it from the ground up," I say as Jesse opens the rear door. "And you need to know it's what you want." I motion her inside.

She pauses before entering. "You want me to handle the NFL?"

"Yes. I do. And Grayson agrees. I talked with him this morning. We need expanded staff to manage the new operation. You've got a strong management track record, and to top it off you've handled Isaac and my father. You can handle a bunch of arrogant rich people and athletes."

"That's intimidating but a little exciting." She climbs inside the vehicle.

I'm aware of Savage at our back, and after Isaac's visit I'm not complaining. Obviously, he tagged out Adrian, but I suspect Adrian will get to the offices before we do. I don't know Savage well, but I know he walks a line, he's willing to step onto the gray between good and bad. I get him. He gets me.

I also get my brother.

Too well.

He doesn't know how well, but he will soon.

"We need to walk this," Savage announces. "There's a traffic jam an hour long."

I curse, and give him a lift of my chin. "You with us?"

"Me and Adrian. He's walking toward us from the building."

I give a nod and we cross the street. We've just hit the opposite sidewalk when an uncomfortable awareness washes over me. Someone is watching us beyond Savage. I pull Harper closer, under my arm. I don't tell her what I feel. I don't want to scare her. We're only a half block from the building when my phone buzzes with a text. I slow our pace in case it's an alert to detour, nonchalantly reaching for my phone to read a message from Savage, who's literally right behind me: *I feel it, too.*

"Everything okay?" Harper asks, shivering and I don't think it's the cold winter day. She senses something too. She just doesn't have the training to know what it means.

It's another two blocks before we reach the building, and Adrian is at the door waiting on us, when I never saw him on the walk, but I assume he was there. Harper hurries inside, a little extra lift to her step. Oh yes. She feels the urgency in me. She feels that we're being watched. I wrap my arm around her and guide her to security where we obtain a long-term pass for her. "You're official now," I say, as we stop at the elevator bank and I punch the call button.

She smiles, a beautiful smile, all the nerves she'd been throwing from the sidewalk outside, fading away into happiness. She kisses my cheek. "You're going to—"

I give her a little tug, aligning our legs and when she's nice and snug against me, my palm flattens on her lower back. "Make you come on my desk, and then later on your new desk."

She blushes a pretty pink. "You could get me fired."

Mischief twinkles in my eyes. "I know the boss."

"Hmmm," she murmurs playfully. "Well, if you know the boss."

"Did someone say the boss? I'm right here."

Savage. "Fucking Savage," I growl, but it's not a sincere growl. I flick him a look over her head and he gives me a barely perceivable shake of his head. He didn't find those eyes that were on us and he's nervous. Me fucking, too, because the assassin being gone doesn't mean anything at all with a professional operation. It might even be a way to throw us off.

The elevator door opens and Harper enters first, with me following. Savage is next. Once the doors shut Harper offers Savage a keen inspection. "That eye looks painful."

"So is an empty stomach," he says, "but it's worth it to enjoy a good meal. Same with a black eye. Sometimes it's worth it just to get to punch the other guy."

Here, here, I think. "He's not wrong."

The elevator doors open and I find Grayson waiting on us in the hallway with Blake standing next to him, both men in jeans and collared shirts. Blake, who I told to just fucking wait.

With a flex of my fingers at her back, Harper steps forward and I join her, Savage immediately at my opposite side. "You have a minute for me?" Blake asks.

"After my meetings," I say.

"Mitch Carmichael is running a half hour late," Grayson interjects. "I can give Harper a rundown of the players and meet you in your office in fifteen minutes." He inclines his head left at Harper. "Mia's in my office. Let's head in that direction."

None of this please me, not one little bit, and I pin Blake in a critical stare. "Can this wait?"

"No," he says firmly. "And we need to talk now and alone. You and me. Just you and me."

Chapter One Hundred Fifteen

Eric

Blake's request to speak to me alone is unexpected.

Alone.

As in without Harper present.

Blake's point is crystal clear. He's sheltering her from something. I don't believe Harper needs to be sheltered. She has an inherent need to feel in control, and under the circumstances, it's expected and understood. Knowledge is security, and it lends to the trust that will allow her to settle with two solid feet inside this new life. That doesn't happen by shutting her out.

My hand settles possessively on her lower back. "Harper can hear anything you have to say. She's with me. We're relocating her here. She's moving in."

"*Alone*," is Blake's only reply before he seems to feel a need to clarify. "Alone means alone and I don't ask for things without a purpose."

"My mother—" Harper begins, worry etched in her delicate features.

"Is fine," he assures her. "No one is injured. No one is in imminent danger." His eyes fall on me, with a heavy beat. "Are we doing this or not?"

In other words, he's not talking to me with Harper present, which at this point is illogical, as she'll ask me about it later.

Harper steps in front of me, offering her back to Blake and Grayson. "I'm going with Grayson. You go with Blake." She gives me a tiny nod, silently telling me this is fine. She's fine. *We're* fine.

"I'll find you when we're done." With this, she rotates on her heels, and indicates her readiness to Grayson.

Grayson and I share a look filled with unspoken words. He's worried about what this is all about and where it leads, and so am I. He motions to Harper and the two of them walk away. I stand flat-footed right where I am, waiting until the glass doors to the lobby close with their departure before I level Blake in a hard stare. "I have a massive contract to negotiate today. Whatever this is—"

"Can't wait." He scrubs his jaw. "Look, man, I don't like to throw heavy shit on you before a big meeting. I get it. The NFL is big, but so is this and you need to know before you walk into a meeting and get sideswiped by bad press."

I go still. "What bad press?"

"Can we get a room or something?"

I grimace and motion him toward the lobby doors and a minute later we're in a small conference room, sitting across from each other at a small round table. I don't sit down, my arms folding in front of me. "You have my undivided attention."

"Harper's mother is having a meltdown," he says.

"When is she not having a meltdown?"

"She wants to call the police and the press to tell them that you attacked your father because he denied your mother cancer treatments. She says she has proof you know about it."

"That's an amusing and now tiresome premise," I say dryly. "But she's not going to the damn press. That would fuck up her perfect world."

"You sure about that?"

"Yes, I'm sure. And as for my father denying my mother treatment, I know about it, yes, because she told Harper, and Harper told me *after* my father was already in the hospital."

"She says one of the nurses from the hospital in Germany where the treatment was denied will confirm you went there, and you met with them."

Irritation tics in my jaw. "I did. What else?"

"You did?"

"You want to know why," I say, my finger steepling in front of me, elbows on the arms of the chair.

"Yes, I need to know why. I'm part of your defense."

That tic in my jaw intensifies. "It was years later, after I turned eighteen. I battled with why my mother killed herself. Some part of me needed to hear she probably would have died anyway. And you know what? If her mother wants to come at me. Let her come. I didn't put him in the hospital. What else, Blake?" I press, sensing there's more.

"Your father met with the new head of the mob a few weeks ago, and Harper's mother was with him. Does that mean that she's involved in all of this? No, but I don't see how she's blind as a bat either. You have to see where that leads."

"Speak frankly, Blake. I enjoy a puzzle, but I have a meeting to attend. Where are you going with this?"

"Harper—"

"Did not know about the mob. She's not involved. And you're about to piss me the fuck off."

"Her mother is all she has," he counters, still pushing. "How far would she go to protect her?"

He's doing his job, which, unfortunately, would make me punching him inappropriate. But then, Isaac has a way of making me want to punch someone I never get to fucking punch. I change the subject. "What about the birth certificates?"

"We found Isaac's and it looks fine, but I did some digging. There was an amendment to it filed several years back and I can't get to the original. All versions were destroyed. The other birth certificate is a man named Ryan Kensey. Does he sound familiar to you?"

"Not at all. I need an address. I want to go see him. Now. Tonight. I'll charter a plane."

"Impossible. He died a few years ago. We're looking for a connection between him and the family. More soon."

"How did he die?"

"A car accident."

Alarms go off in my head. "Find out the details on that accident. Compare them to the accident Isaac's mother had years back."

His inspection turns probing. "You think Isaac killed his mother and Kensey?"

"Look closer. Answer that question with facts."

"All right then, back to Harper's mother. I can't hold her prisoner. That's kidnapping. If she wants to use her phone, I have to let her use her phone."

I pull out my cellphone and dial Grayson. "Is Harper standing there with you?"

"We're taking a tour."

"I need her. Now. Lobby conference room."

"You got it. We're right around the corner." I disconnect and slide my phone into my pocket.

"What's the plan here?" Blake asks.

There's a knock on the door and Grayson opens it. "Now?"

"Now," I say, and he backs up, allowing Harper to enter.

She appears, and I swear just seeing her, punches me with awareness no other woman has ever made me feel. It's not like I didn't just see her minutes ago. "What's happening?" she asks and Blake steps around to allow her to join us at the table.

"Your mother is threatening to call the police and the press and tell them that I knew my father denied my mother medical care, therefore I tried to kill him."

"You didn't even know when your father fell ill," she argues. "I didn't tell you until afterward, when she called and confessed knowing about it to me."

"I went to the facility in Germany. I was trying to find peace in her suicide. I did ask why she was denied, but they gave me the standard—not enough spots—reply."

She studies me for several beats. "I know how you reacted when I told you. You didn't know." She looks at Blake. I'll swear my life on that." She reaches into the small purse hanging at her hip and pulls out her phone. I don't ask what she's doing. I know.

She punches in a number and a minute later I hear her say, "Mom, don't talk. Listen. If you come at Eric, you're coming at me. I'm moving in with him. We're together. And we both know he didn't attack his father. You know why he was attacked."

Her mother is silent so long that Harper adds, "The smartest thing you can do is to tell me everything, but since you won't, let me make this crystal clear. Those men are men Eric hired to protect you because there's an assassin on the move. Gigi fled the country, we assume to save herself. I'm going to have Eric pull all of those men. You're on your own. I hope you don't die but if you do, I love you." She hangs up and slides her phone back into her purse. "Pull your men, Blake. If you don't, she won't feel the effects of what I just said." Her gaze slides to me. "It's time for your call."

I stare at her, this beautiful, strong woman, and I feel things that I can't even name. She stood by me. There was no hesitation, and I can't say that it was a conscious test, but if it were, she'd pass with flying colors. I look at Blake. "Pull your men from direct contact, but keep them close. I'll call you for an update when I get out of the meeting."

"Understood," Blake says, walking toward the door.

Harper's cellphone starts ringing. She surveys the number and disconnects. "It's her. I know her. She needs to squirm."

In that moment, I decide she's more than a princess. She's a queen. One who I think rules me and I don't even give a fuck.

"My father and your mother attended a meeting with the mob boss."

"Not Isaac?"

"All I know is there was a meeting that involved your mother and my father."

"Well, if you expected a shocked reaction, I'm beyond that with my mother. Let's go make NFL magic.

Yes, I think. Queen indeed.

A few seconds later, with Harper by my side, we walk down the halls of Bennett Enterprises on our way to a meeting worth billions. And I don't think it will be the last time we do this together. I didn't know I needed Harper in my life, but I do now. And every second she's here, I grow more willing to do whatever it takes to keep her by my side. I will do anything to protect her.

Chapter One Hundred Sixteen

Harper

We meet Grayson and Mia in a private conference room next to his office. "Davis tells me I have a chopper scheduled for tomorrow to the Hamptons. I'm supposed to meet with Jon Moore." He glances at me and offers a quick explanation which I really appreciate. "He's the CEO of a consortium with deep pockets." He returns to his point. "He's supposedly fueling a competing consortium trying to bid against us on the team. I'm meeting him because he called and asked to see me." He pins Eric in a potent stare. "You wouldn't have anything to do with that, now would you?"

Eric's expression never changes. "I wasn't aware Jon was involved."

"That's why you have me," Davis says, from the doorway, also dressed in casual clothing—jeans and a company logo shirt. "To find these things out." He doesn't look at Eric, and with good reasons. This has to be the ploy to get Grayson out of town, Eric's alluded to on several occasions, and I already know Grayson is sharp as a whip, and will pick up on any clue he's given. I don't even know these people and no doubt, Davis asked Jon to play a game for him.

Davis eyes his phone and then says. "The call is ready for us. And they don't know about Moore. I think we should keep it that way."

"We'll talk about Moore when we're done in here," Grayson says, his gaze meeting Eric's. "Don't you agree?"

"I'm never very agreeable," I reply. "Which is why you like me so damn much." With that, Eric's hand slides to my back and urges me to sit.

Our call starts, and when I'm introduced, I slide into shmooze mode, pleased when I get the three men on the line laughing. They actually tell Grayson I'm charming and the look of approval in Grayson's eyes pleases me.

Eventually we get to talking about the contract, and even knowing very little about these negotiations, I feel we end on a good note with positive moves to a final agreement. When the meeting concludes, we exit the room and Grayson motions between Eric and Davis. "My office, you two." While Davis and Eric never look at each other their energy reads—*we're screwed.*

Eric stands his ground and presents his case. "What if Jon really is plotting against us and you blow him off? You're the one who knows him the best out of all of us and he's close to you. And he's a good friend to have on our side. Just make sure he is."

"My office," Grayson repeats and this time, he starts walking, which clearly equates to—nice try.

Eric's jaw clenches and he glances down at me. "This may take a while." With that, he and Davis, follow Grayson toward his office, where the three friends will butt heads in a brutal struggle over who gets to protect who. Considering the reason for the war ahead, I think there are worse battles to suffer.

I think he's right. He kisses me and walks away. "How about some coffee?" Mia asks. "We never really finished our last cup."

We head toward the breakroom and I glance at my phone to find ten messages from my mother. I punch the last one, which will be her at her most agitated. *He's guarding me because he's hiding from his own secrets, that I know. You're guarding him because you're brainwashed. I'll handle him. You'll thank me one day.*

My stomach churns. How is this person my mother?

And what exactly is she going to do to "handle" Eric?

Chapter One Hundred Seventeen

Harper

I don't dare discount my mother's threat toward Eric, when she seems to be all about tsunami-style reactions to everything these days. "I have a little problem, Mia," I announce. "I need to go to the conference room. I'm sorry."

"Can I help?"

"No, thank you. It's my mother being difficult."

"Ah," she says, understanding registering. "Well go. Handle it. I'll be here if you need me."

I believe her and I appreciate it, but this thing with my mother is embarrassing. I hurry back to the conference room where we met Blake and shut the door before punching in his number. "Thank God," I breathe out when he answers. "My mother is just insane."

"She's a character," he replies, which I translate to he concurs. "I heard the message," he adds. "What's your take?"

"I don't know this version of my mother to answer that question."

"You know more than you think. Go with your gut."

"She won't do anything to hurt her reputation or that of the company. I don't think she'll go after Eric publicly."

"But you think she'll go after him?"

"If she gets a chance," I confirm, and I hate how easily I answer.

"Then we don't let her get the chance," he concludes.

"You make that sound easy."

"I've contained military geniuses," he assures me. "I can handle your mother."

"Has she called anyone?"

"No one. I'll keep monitoring. You just stick by Eric's side and keep doing what you're doing."

We disconnect and the door opens. Eric joins me and I don't get up. I think he'll want to sit to hear about my mother. "Well?" I ask.

He claims the seat next to me. "He's going to the Hamptons."

"Oh good. Considering his mood, I'm not sure how you managed that, but I'm glad you did."

"He didn't fall for the David ploy, but I made him think about Mia's safety." Concern slides over his face. "What's going on? Why are you in here?"

I sigh. "I already talked to Blake."

His hand flattens on the table, as if he's ready to launch himself into action. "That doesn't sound good."

"It's just my mother again."

"And?"

I replay my mother's message and the ending really grinds through me. *I'll handle him. You'll thank me one day.*

When it's over, Eric says, "It's more of the same. Why are you worried? Where's your head on this?"

"I've never heard her speak a vicious word in her life until recently and it's really making me think bad things. I'm just worried and Blake said to go with my gut. That means there's a reason to worry." I draw a breath and dare to ask what I've barely let myself think. "Did she hire the assassin?"

"They came after you. Surely you can't think your mother would try to have you killed?"

"Guess who gets my trust if I die?"

"No," he says. "I don't believe she'll go after you. And we now know she's involved enough that she knows that trust money is locked down by the mob." He stands and pulls me to my feet. "Get this out of your head. Your mother did not try to kill you."

"She inherits everything. What if she never intended to kill me. She was just going after me to distract the police when she had you and your father killed?"

"No," he says. "Sorry, sweetheart, but she's just not that smart."

He's not wrong.

She's not.

But then again, she's showed a new side of herself and appears to be nothing she seems.

Chapter One Hundred Eighteen

Harper

A sea of sharks.

A sea of emotions with shark fins, and sharper teeth.

That's what I feel like we're living right now.

When Eric and I arrive home, we end up naked and in bed, and while it's a grand distraction, filled with lots of hot and tender moments, when it's over, I'm back in that sea, with my mother back on my mind.

"Could my mother do something like that?" I ask, scooting to the edge of the bed, my back to Eric. It's appalling to think that she might actually go after the man I love and try to kill him.

Eric seems to know actions work more than words at this point. In other words, it doesn't take Eric long to get me dressed and a drink in my hand. Or for me to shove a Rubik's cube into his hand before telling him to figure this all out. "No pressure," he says teasingly, but I'm sure he feels those words on a very real level.

We're at the kitchen island at this point. "Can you pull up the will? We need to look at her part more closely. And I need to change mine."

"You already know she inherits." He slides his Mac in front of him. "But I do need to read the entire document in more detail. I'm sending it to you, too."

"I don't have a computer."

He pulls out his phone. "I'll fix that. Your purse and computer are at security compliments of Adam"

"Oh good," I breathe out. "I can go get the package."

He's already on the phone. Ten minutes later there's a knock on the door, and the front desk has delivered my things.

Now we're both locked and loaded on the will, and I decide I need coffee, not a drink, and put a pot on. Once we both have steaming cups in front of us, I consider my mother again. "Has anyone looked into her finances?"

"I'm sure Blake has, but she wasn't on the radar at all before now. I doubt he's looked closely."

"But she is now," I say, my throat suddenly tight.

His hand comes down on my leg. "Maybe she really thinks I'm the one who poisoned my father. They hate me, Harper. I assure you, she's heard nothing but another form of poison where I'm concerned. Don't assume the worst."

"How can you be this kind about her? You know what she did."

"She hid what he did to my mother. She didn't do it."

"It's not much better. Back to the will. Who inherits if you die?"

"I'm not in the will. She inherits if the eldest son dies. That's Isaac."

Thirty-five minutes later, we know nothing else. "It just feels off," I murmur. "Like we're missing something. And why does it say eldest son, and not Isaac by name?"

"I have no idea but the birth certificate the first message alerted us to has been found. He's dead. We just don't know how he connects to the family. But the interesting part is how he died."

"Car accident," she supplies, her tone grim.

"Yes, and what I didn't tell you was the guy who worked for my father and helped ink the deal for my guardianship, also died. And you want to guess how?"

She gapes. "Oh my God. A car accident?'

"Yes. On the money."

"This is all starting to add up. I bet you had a sibling and Isaac got rid of him. Gigi would have likely known. It really makes sense that she had those notes delivered to us."

He picks up the cube, and stares down at it. "We're close, but I can almost feel the sands of time, slipping through the glass. If we don't figure this out, and end it, this whole situation is going to blow. And it's going to blow big."

A chill runs down my spine.

He's right. I feel it, too. Something is coming.

Chapter One Hundred
Nineteen

Harper

Eric sets me up in an office at Bennett and we eat lunch in my new, quite luxurious work spot that comes complete with a city view. We spend some time going over the NFL contract and Eric leaves me a while to study it while he catches up on a few work projects. And it feels good to have a purpose, and some idea where this drastic career change is leading me. When Eric finishes up his work, we head to the hospital. Isaac and the detective never show up nor does trouble of any sort. Another one of those bittersweet victories.

For the rest of the afternoon, we hang out at the hospital, and while some might say it's for show, I know it's more. Eric's father is just that—his father—and no one can wipe away the invisible bond of parent and child. It defies hate. It is simply nature.

Later that evening, we eat pizza in bed, and laugh over *Friends* reruns, and it's good, really good, but as we lay down to sleep, with Eric's mind calm enough for him to actually do so in the bed, unease roughs up my belly, a sense of foreboding, a vise on my chest. Somehow though, with Eric's arms wrapped around me, the shadow of slumber overtakes me.

I wake with a jolt to sunlight and sit straight up to find Eric standing at the window, fully dressed, staring out at the new day, a cup of coffee in his hand. "What time is it?"

He rotates to face me, sunshine lighting his blue eyes with a hint of gold, the stretch of his black T-shirt over his perfect chest, awakening all the parts of me that hadn't yet caught up until now.

"Early."

"Oh God. Why? What happened? Did Isaac do something? And your father? Is he okay?"

He laughs low and rough. "That was a lot of panic in thirty seconds," he says, crossing to sit down next to me. "Everything is fine. I just woke up so I got up."

I reach up and stroke my fingers down the damp tendrils of hair curling at his temples. "I wish you would have woken me up."

"I kissed you and told you I was getting up, but you never even moved. Obviously, you needed rest." He presses his cup into my hand. "Now you need caffeine."

I accept the cup, the intimacy of sharing his cup, a dash of sweetness I clearly need this morning. I've barely had a sip when my mind jolts again. "My mother—"

"Chartered a late flight into New York. Blake texted me right after you fell asleep. She's in a hotel room sleeping. She didn't get in until a few hours ago. Her flight was delayed."

I scowl with this news. "That can't be good."

"We have everyone in one place now," he says. "I don't think that's a bad thing. When people play in the same pond they start fighting and we'll be here to see."

"Okay. I guess. What about other news?"

"None." He covers my hand where it rests on the cup and sips, his eyes holding mine. "Just you, sharing my bed, and my coffee, the way it should be. So relax, baby, and enjoy the ride while we can."

His voice is velvet that soothes my frazzled nerves, the endearment of "baby" a splash of happiness. It tells me he's in a good place this morning and he doesn't want to be there alone. This lights me up and I smile, before I sip the coffee. "It's delicious," I say, savoring the chocolatey flavor like I'm savoring this moment with this man. "What is that?"

"Coconut creamer."

"Okay, no wonder. That's sinful."

He laughs, his lips curving into a smile, and God he has beautiful lips. He doesn't smile often and it's another thing that pleases me. I decide right then to see that smile often. It's a mission and one I will embrace for the rest of my life. "Finish that cup," he says. "I'll grab another." He stands up and heads toward the kitchen, a hero who gives away his coffee for his woman. What more could a girl want?

More of him.

I want more of him.

Exactly why I stand up and follow him, remotely aware of the fact that my hair must be standing on end, and my make-up smudged everywhere, but I don't care. I feel that comfortable with Eric. It's hard to believe we fought over the apartment and me feeling like I didn't belong. It was like a bleep on the screen, an emotional day that wasn't about us at all. Because the truth is, I feel that at home here, and so very easily, and that's a bit surreal. Everyone wants that kind of comfort with another human being, but how often do they find it?

Eric makes a beeline for the coffee pot and reaches above it to a cabinet to remove another cup. I stop at the island behind him. Obviously aware that I'm here, he eyes me over his shoulder. "You should explore the apartment. Find out what's here. We can go shopping." He fills his cup and turns to me.

I laugh. "You are shopping." I set my cup down. "I love everything here, especially you." I sober, thinking about my mother. We're going to run into her. Of course, we will. "Nothing my mother says matters to me. You know that, right?"

He puts away the creamer and steps to the island across from me. "I *know*, baby. I *know*."

"Then why am I not at her hotel right now, confronting her, getting what we need, and just ending this? Then we can enjoy that ride you mentioned every day, not just for little fleeting moments."

"We need to watch her. We need to see who she meets. What she does."

"The feeling we had last night, about something coming. We can't wait. No, I don't want to wait. I'll make her talk. I'm going to shower and then I need to just go see her, Eric." I sip the coffee. "Decision made."

"Harper, we need—"

"We need—"

"Each other," I say leaning on the counter.

His eyes warm. "Yes. We do. Don't forget that but you know that's not my point."

"You're trying to protect me. Thank you, but I got this." I turn and head for the bedroom, snatching my phone from the coffee table on the way.

I half expect Eric to follow, but his cellphone rings, and I fight the urge to turn and find out who's calling. I need a shower. I need to be dressed. I need some semblance of control and that feels like it comes from my mother. This idea quickens my pace and it's not long before I'm under the spray of warm water, suds in my hair, and try as I might, I can't stop thinking about Eric downstairs, about the call that had to be some kind of news I don't know.

I finish up and once I'm out of the shower, there's still no Eric. It feels off. It feels like I need to get downstairs. I hurry into the closet, pull on a pair of dark jeans, a lacy pink blouse, and boots. I hurry through my make-up routine and then start drying my hair. That part isn't fast and it's driving me nuts. Finally, it's dry, flat ironed, and I'm about to head downstairs when my cellphone rings. I glance at the caller ID, and the international number sets my heart racing. I grab the phone and quickly answer. "Gigi?"

"Yes. Listen quickly. They've found me. I need to tell you before I can't."

"Tell me what?"

"I need to," the line cuts out, "and then," more static. "Isaac is," more static. "And your mother knows the truth about Eric. She knows, Harper. I'm sorry, but—" There's a pounding sound. "Oh God. Oh God. They're here. It's over for me." She sobs. The line goes dead.

"Oh my God," I whisper, and quickly dial Blake.

He answers on the first ring. "Blake, Gigi just called me. I couldn't make out half of what she said but someone was there for her. She was scared."

"I picked up the call," he says. "We're tracing it. More soon." He hangs up. Obviously, this is time sensitive. I grab the sink. *The truth about Eric.* What does that even mean? Well, I know it's not good. I know that already but what is it that Gigi seems to be warning me of? I don't understand any of this. I push off the counter and turn to exit the bathroom when Eric appears in the doorway, his hands on either side of the archway. His expression is taut, jaw hard, eyes haunted.

"What happened?"

"He's dead."

I jolt with the words. "Your father?"

"Yes. My father."

Shock radiates through me. He's lost his father and the fact that he hated him only makes this more confusing to him, painful in ways that torment and cut. And perhaps more devastating. He's lost the final link to his mother. I close the space between us and wrap my arms around him, holding him, but he doesn't touch me.

He doesn't move, but I can feel his body humming. I can feel the savant in him, battling to take control and if that part of him wins, I know the numbers will cripple him. And I know this is the part of him that he dreaded me ever seeing.

Chapter One Hundred Twenty

Harper

Lies.

We can hide from the truth, but we can't hide from death. It finds us all, often sooner than we expect. Eric's father's death has shaken him. I know this. He still hasn't moved, hasn't touched me. "Touch me," I order, tilting my chin up to look at him. "Let me help."

"I'm fine," he says, his eyes steely, the lines of his face all dark shadows and torment.

I reject this answer. I reject his withdrawal, his refusal to let me inside the pain I know that he feels. "You're not fine and you're not alone. You don't do this alone. You don't feel this without me. I'm here. I'm with you. I'm—"

His hands come down on my shoulders, his forehead settling against mine. "I'm okay."

"No." My hands press to his face. "You're not okay, but you're not alone either." He needs to hear that again. I feel it. I know it. I press on his chest, inch back to let him see the truth in my eyes, to let him feel my presence. "I understand every conflicted feeling you have right now. I understand that you need to melt down and you can do that with me. You don't have to hold back. You don't have to fear how I'll react. I love you so much, Eric."

"I love you, too, so fucking much." He tilts my gaze to his. "I fell in love with you the moment I met you. You're why I'm still standing right now."

Tears pool in my eyes and his mouth closes down on mine, his tongue stroking deep, his kiss hungry, edgy, desperate, but when

I would sink into him, when I would pull him deeper into our connection, the doorbell rings. "That's Savage," he breathes out, tearing his mouth from mine, the torment of that effort radiating through him into me. "He's taking you to see your mother. You need to tell her about my father. I told the detective you'd handle it."

"No." I wrap my arms around him again. "No. I can't leave you. Not now. Not yet. You didn't even want to touch me seconds ago. You're still trying to get a handle on this. You're not okay."

"I'm fine. I promise."

He keeps saying that for a reason. He's not fine at all. "Eric," I whisper.

He inhales and walks me backward, pressing me to the vanity, his hands on either side of me. "She's your mother, Harper. She needs you."

"Does she? I'm not sure I know her anymore. Maybe this is what she wants."

"Assume it's not."

"What if it is?"

"You'll know. You'll feel it when you tell her, which is why you need to tell her before someone else does. As cold as this sounds, if there was ever a time that your mother would tell you everything she knows, it's after she finds out my father is dead. But the whole idea here is to make sure no one else ends up dead."

"You're right. You're right. I have to go see her. I have to go now, I just—"

He kisses me, long fingers splayed tenderly on my jaw. "I promise you, I'm okay."

"Your body is vibrating," I argue, "I can almost see it. I can feel it."

"It's something that happens when the numbers are flying at me too fast."

"I've never seen this before. It scares me."

He gives my cheek a quick brush of fingers. "The numbers in my head will keep me sane until you can save me later when we're alone." He pushes off the counter and laces the fingers of one of his hands with mine, setting us in motion.

I snatch my purse as we walk, following him willingly, but my eyes pinch and burn. I didn't like his father, and neither did Eric. But he was still *his father*. He's also dead now. That's hard to process. That's hard to get my mind and emotions around, but I have to be strong for Eric.

We start down the stairs and my mind is on my mother. Oh how a week changes things, even a few days. There was a time when I would have been crushed for my mother, fearful for her even, but now I don't feel those things, and that's painful in an entirely different way. I've lost her and it happened a long time ago. I just wasn't willing to admit it.

Eric releases me by the couch and heads toward the door. I hug myself and watch as he opens the door and Savage enters the apartment. Savage who is bigger today than normal, which is a silly statement. He's not bigger. He just feels really big and broad and towering, perhaps because all of this feels big right now.

He gives Eric a once over. "You okay?"

"I hated him," Eric replies, almost as if he's reminding himself of this fact, using that detail to shove aside grief.

"Like I said," Savage repeats. "You okay?"

"Pretty fucking shitty," Eric replies, shocking me with his honesty.

"Of course you are," Savage says, his hand catching Eric's shoulder. "Grayson's on his way over here."

Eric rejects Grayson instantly. "He needs to step back from this until we know more."

"I thought, I assumed, he had a massive heart attack?" I question, hurrying to join them, looking between both men. "Is there a question about how he died?"

"The police are involved," Savage says. "But under the circumstances, that's expected."

"They have no proof of murder," I argue. "Right?"

"Nothing has changed," Savage states. "There was no one in the room with him when he died. There was no evidence of foul play at this time. All that points to a problem is that hotel footage of the man we found entering his room under the guise of being an employee."

"Who we know to be an assassin," I remind him.

"There's no proof of murder," Savage replies. "Maybe your mother can offer insight into exactly what happened the day he collapsed." His phone buzzes with a text. "Grayson's on his way. He left Mia behind. He thought you'd want to talk one on one."

"I need to stay close to Harper," Eric states. "I've changed my mind. I'm going with her. I want to be at the hotel in case she needs me."

"And what if Isaac shows up?" I challenge. "You'll both be on edge, years of history between you. You'll both end up in jail." I step in front of him and plant my hand on his chest. "Stay here. Savage and I will go and come right back. Please. I beg of you."

"She's right, man," Savage says. "And Blake's on his way over here anyway. He wants to talk about what comes next."

"We bury him," Eric replies dryly. "That's what comes next."

I swear his body vibrates beneath my touch with those words. "Eric," I whisper softly.

"I'm coming with you," he says. "I'll stay out of sight, but I need to be there if you need me." He eyes Savage. "Have Blake meet me at the hotel."

Savage studies him with hard eyes, and a harder set to his jaw, before he gives into the inevitability of his employer's order and inclines his chin. "Understood," he says, pulling his phone from his pocket and shooting off a text.

"What about Grayson?" I ask.

"We'll turn him back around," Savage replies, "but I suggest you call him, Eric. He won't take the dismissal easily."

Eric nods and walks to the hallway table, sticking his gun in his waistband and then opening the drawer to remove what I suspect is yet another weapon. I'm going to tell my mother that her husband is dead, and yet, I feel as if we're headed to war. Are we? Is this where we reach our conclusion? Is this where the truth explodes and destroys anyone it can in its path?

Chapter One Hundred
Twenty-One

Harper

A few minutes later, the three of us are loading into an SUV.
Savage is in the passenger seat, while Smith takes the wheel. "I
thought you were with Grayson," Eric says, eyeing Smith as he and
I get settled in the back.

"I was already in the SUV to take Grayson to see you," Smith
says. "It made sense to drop him off and pick you up. We have men
with Grayson and Mia."

Eric nods and settles into his seat, his hand finding my hand, but
he doesn't look at me. He just holds me. He holds me like he doesn't
want to let go, like he feels like he'll never touch me again once he
does. He's lost everyone and I know he feels like he'll lose me, too,
and yet, he's put it all on the line with me. He's decided I'm worth
the risk.

Savage's phone rings and I'm jolted with the memory of the call
from Gigi. I consider telling Eric about it, but I quickly nix that
idea. I see no good in telling him that his grandmother was being
attacked, or so it seemed. He might hate her, but he just lost his
father. He's about to let me walk into a situation he feels is volatile.
Now is not the time to tell him. I can't risk being a trigger that
brings him to his knees.

We pull to the side alleyway by the hotel and me, Savage, and Eric
get out of the SUV. "What are we doing?" I ask Savage.

"We're having you wear a wire." he holds up the device and Eric
snaps it away from him, stepping between me and Savage, blocking
me from his view.

"We need to put it between your breasts," Eric explains. "That's
the best spot to pick up the conversation and remain unseen."

I nod and he helps me place the microphone and wires, his deft fingers working with the ease of experience, and while the intimacy of the touch lifts goosebumps on my skin, nerves work a number in my belly. "Whatever happens," he instructs, "whatever she says, keep her talking. Find out everything you can so that we can do just what you said: end this."

"Okay. Yes. I'm in for that strategy."

"I'll be close. I'll be listening in. Let's test the sound."

We do that with the aid of Savage and Smith. Once we're done, Eric motions for them to leave us alone. Eric then removes a small handgun from his waistband. "Just in case."

My hand flies up in rejection. "This is my mother," I remind him.

"I get that," he assures me. "But as you pointed out, what if Isaac shows up?"

I inhale and let it out, nodding my understanding. He walks me through how the weapon functions and I slide it into my purse.

"You need to walk around the front and enter the lobby. If you need me—"

"I always need you," I say, pressing to my toes and kissing him.

He cups my head and gives me a long, drugging kiss. "Then hurry up and come back to me," he says, turning me to face in the direction I need to walk.

And so, I do. I walk away from him, and my gut twists with the idea feeling that I'm leaving him behind, not just headed to a meeting with my mother. I round the corner and enter the hotel, and for no good reason, I feel like I'm never going to be the same. Like we're never going to be the same.

Chapter One Hundred Twenty-Two

Eric

The numbers in my head count down and fling sequences at me in a random rotation that might mean something if I slowed them down. I don't even try. They haven't stolen my control. At this point, they pulse and spin, they fill my mind, but they don't own it. I meant what I said to Harper. They're cold comfort right now, the distraction that won't let me chase ideas and emotions. They allow me to hyper-focus on this moment, to narrow my thoughts. To walk down the alleyway in pursuit of Harper, with Savage by my side, in controlled agitation. "You didn't call Grayson," he reminds me. "He's texting me and you."

I don't look at him. "He'll understand. He'd be just like I am right now if this was Mia walking into a minefield."

"You really think her mother's that volatile?"

"She does," I say, as we round the corner to the hotel entrance. "She knows her mother and the very fact that she's worried about her agenda speaks volumes to where we're at right now. Her mother is a problem."

"Agreed, but she wouldn't hurt her daughter."

I eye Savage. "If I thought she would, Harper wouldn't be going up to the room alone." We pause at the entrance of the hotel. "We stand out together. You take the lobby. I'm going to the bar where Blake can meet me." I don't wait for his approval or agreement. I enter the hotel, a fancy number with a big price tag befitting the Kingston standard. I walk through dual seating areas hugging my path, eyeing the registration desk to my left, where Harper is now turning away from the counter. She hurries to the right, and then walks into the bar, not toward the elevators.

I pass the desk and turn left to a sitting area that is a bar occupied with couches and chairs in burgundy and brown, with oversized pillows meant to irritate people, or at least me. Harper motions me forward, and screw it, I'm here. If there's someone watching, they might as well know, because then they also know I'm trouble they don't want. I close the space between her and me and sit down. "She's not answering in her room. They won't let me up." She pulls out her phone. "I'm trying to call her." She listens a minute and it clearly goes to voicemail. "Mom. Mom, I'm here at your hotel. I need you to call down and let me come up." She disconnects. "I'm worried. What if she found out he's dead and is melting down? I think I should ask the manager to walk me up, or just to go check on her."

"Yes. Do it. I'm not going with you. I don't want him telling her that I'm by your side, and her using that as a reason not to see you."

Harper shoves her phone back inside her purse and hurries away. I move to the other side of the table to be able to watch her. The waitress approaches me and I order a whiskey. Blake slides in across from me. "Make that two."

The waitress hurries away and Blake wastes no time getting to the point. "There are things you need to know before Harper heads upstairs to see her mother."

"Speak quickly."

"I know what Gigi meant when she called Harper."

I stiffen. "Gigi called Harper?"

"You don't know?"

"No, I don't fucking know. When?"

"Right when you were finding out about your father, man. I'm sure that's why she called me and didn't tell you. Gigi thought she was being attacked. It was my man trying to get to her but that worked in our favor. She called Harper and ran her mouth."

She didn't fucking tell me. I don't like that. I don't like it one fucking bit. "Did she now? What'd she say?"

"That her mother knows the truth. That Isaac knows that you're not a bastard. Harper didn't catch that part of the conversation. The call was choppy but we cleaned the recorded version up. She said, that you're not a bastard."

"What the hell are you talking about, Blake? Stop speaking in code because I'm focused on Harper right now. Not a game and a puzzle."

"Read this." He slides a folder in front of me and I stare down at the contents, reading a summary that has me sucking in air.

It's then that Harper pokes her head into the bar. "They're taking me upstairs. I'm going up now." She dashes away toward the elevator and I want to run after her. I have to stop her because I know what her mother is going to tell her. I know what Harper might think. I know what I would think if I was her. This might be the end of us. I stand up and start walking, but Blake catches my arm.

"Let her go."

My scowl is instant. "You think I did this? You think I killed him?"

"No, man." He stands and faces me. "But I think Harper's about to find out who did. Let her. End this."

"She's going to tell Harper everything in that file I just read."

"Yes. She will. And Harper will either believe in you or she won't. Don't you want to know which it is?"

I inhale and sit back down. Blake sits down across from me this time. We both turn on our headsets and we listen as Harper chats with the hotel employee leading her to her mother's door. "She flew in late," Harper says. "She's tired, I'm sure, but—well, as I said, her husband died and I'm terrified she found out and had a medical crisis."

"Of course," the other woman says. "I have our team on standby to get medical help for her quickly. Here we are," she adds.

I can tell they've stopped walking. There's knocking on the door. "Mrs. Kingston?" calls out the other woman.

"Mom?!" Harper shouts out.

This continues for a good five minutes. "When do we open the door?" Harper asks.

It's right then that I hear the door open. "Harper. Jesus. How did you even find my hotel?"

"Oh my," the hotel employee says. "I'm sorry. I didn't mean—she was worried and—I can escort her back downstairs."

"No," Harper's mother states. "She can come in."

"Thank you," Harper says, I assume to the attendant. "Thank you for your help. She did nothing wrong, mother. There's something I need to tell you."

There's movement and the sound of the door opening and shutting before Harper's mother says, "You won't talk me out of going to the police. He tried to kill my husband. He tried to kill your *step-father*. Eric did this."

"Eric didn't do this."

"You think he came back for you? He came back because he wants the empire. He came back to claim the empire. I know. You should know, too."

"He doesn't want the empire. I don't know where this is coming from, but that isn't important right now. Mom. Mom—your husband has died. He had a massive heart attack and he died."

"What?"

"He died. He's gone. I'm sorry—"

She sobs, and then screams, a blood-curdling scream. "Eric did this!" she shouts. "He caused all of this. He's the end of us all."

Chapter One Hundred Twenty-Three

Harper

My adrenaline is pumping so hard that my hands are shaking. My mother hugs herself, tears streaming down her face, and only now do I realize that she's fully dressed in jeans and a T-shirt. Her computer is open on the coffee table of the living room hotel suite, a pot of coffee next to it. She wasn't asleep when I was calling her. What was she trying to prove?

Anger surges through me. She's playing games. She's not who I think she is and I don't know what that means. And yet she sobs, "He did this," blaming Eric. "Eric's the reason this happened. The minute he came into this world, into this family, he changed the future. He changed everything."

"He was here before we were here," I remind her. "What are you even talking about, mother?"

She turns away from me and runs right into the coffee table, yelping, and starting to tumble. I catch her arm and turn her to face me. "I need to know what you're talking about."

"You don't. You don't need to know. He's gone now. It's too late. He's gone!" She shouts out that last statement, shaking with the words, and on another sob, she falls to her knees. I go down on my knees in front of her, scared now with the intensity of her reaction. "Mom. Mom, are you okay? Do I need to call for help?"

She sucks in a breath and grabs my arm. "Xanax, by my computer. I need a Xanax."

I glance at the bottle and back at her. "How many have you taken?"

"None. None today, but give me the whole damn bottle. I can't take this pain." She reaches for it and I grab it.

"No," I say. "One. Just one until you see a doctor."

"I loved him. I really loved him. Now he's gone and I can't fix it. I'm alone. So very alone."

I don't feel the sympathy for her that I should and I don't know why. This is my mother. She's hurting. I just—this isn't the person I know. I read the label on the bottle and stand up, opening the bottle to count pills while she crawls to the couch and sits down. Satisfied that I'm not helping her overdose, I offer her a pill. She downs it in between sobs and sips of coffee.

"I can't believe he's gone. I did this. I did."

"What does that mean, mother?" I demand, sitting on the table in front of her. "What does that mean?"

She buries her hands in her face and sobs some more.

"Mother." I grab her hands. "I need to know what happened."

"We thought it was Eric he was after, not your father."

"He's not my father," I say, feeling a pinch of guilt for saying that right after he died. It's just—he wasn't my father. "And what do you mean, coming for Eric? And who is we? What is this about? Eric?"

"Yes. Eric. Isaac's mother had an affair. He's not the real heir. He's not even a Kingston. Eric is the heir."

I blanch, stunned by this news. "How can that be?"

"She fucked around, Harper. How do you think it can be? And her lover, Isaac's father, is dead. It was a car accident, they say, but I don't buy it. Why do you think he ended up dead right after Eric was introduced to the family? Isaac knew he wasn't the heir. He didn't want anyone to find out."

I blanch. "Isaac knows?"

"His mother told him," she says. "And he killed her, too."

"Why would he kill her? Wasn't she on his side?"

"I have no clue, but Gigi is certain that he did."

I blanch. "Gigi knew about it?"

"Yes. She's why all this came out. She hated Isaac's mother. She was looking for something to control her with and found more than she bargained for. Everyone knew but his father."

"Gigi didn't tell him?"

"Isaac was the grandson she'd helped raise. She didn't want him disinherited and treated like an outcast. Then Eric showed up. That's when Isaac's father died, by the way. Someone wanted him gone. You can guess who that was."

"Isaac or Gigi?"

"She says it was Isaac. I don't know. Maybe Gigi killed them both to protect Isaac."

I can barely catch my breath. I swallow bile and force my voice to stay steady. "How do you know all of this? How can you be sure it's even true?"

"Gigi told me. She panicked when Isaac got the mob involved with the family. She thought he was going to get us all killed, which he might just do before this is over. She told me everything then."

"But you didn't tell your husband?"

"She was sure Eric would take the company if he knew he was the heir, so she needed you to be his damsel in distress, to appeal to Mr. Navy SEAL to save the day."

"She gave him stock."

"She controlled what he got. That was her plan."

"You helped her? You knew she sent me to get him?"

"No. Of course not. I told her no. I told her that Eric knows his father basically killed his mother. No good could come out of giving him a key to revenge."

Her eyes are now remarkably dry. Because of the Xanax? Or is there more to her motives? "Why did Gigi run?"

"For her life. She told Isaac that his father was coming here to offer Eric part of Isaac's stock to get out of this mess. The next thing we all know, the wrong man is in the hospital."

I stand up in shock. "The wrong man? What does that mean?"

"We thought Isaac would go after Eric. Obviously, he decided he just wanted to inherit. That's why Gigi ran. Isaac doesn't know I know any of this, but he knows she knows. She could ruin him."

"You believed Isaac had killed not once, but twice, and you were okay with him going after Eric?"

"Not to kill him. You think I wanted him dead? Eric can handle himself for God's sake. He was a SEAL."

"What if Isaac had come for me? He had me attacked at the warehouse. Eric saved me."

"You were attacked?"

"Yes. And I can't prove it, but I'm almost certain that Isaac set it up. He had a bank account in my name. He was setting me up to look like I was stealing from the mob. Eric wiped out the proof. Eric saved me in that warehouse or I'd be dead, the fall guy for the mob." A bad thought hits me. "I assume since you took my trust, my life insurance would have gone to the family, too. My death would have paid off the mob."

"No. No, Harper. I didn't—I had no idea—and—"

"And you let Isaac come after Eric. What did you think he would do to Eric, mother? He was going to lose everything."

"There's no proof that he killed anyone! I didn't believe it. And he didn't kill Eric. He killed his father!"

"Their father had a heart attack. Just like Isaac's mother and father had a car accident. He won't go down for this, but you think he won't find out what you know? You think he won't come for you? I suggest you go to Gigi and go quickly."

"Eric killed his father. I'm going to tell the police. You need to stay away from him."

I lean on the table facing her. "You think that lie will save you from Isaac? I don't." I push off the table and walk toward the door.

"Harper! Harper, come back here!"

I don't stop. I don't even think about stopping, but with every step, blades cut me. I'm bleeding inside and it's like her voice is acid being poured in freshly cut wounds. I open the door and find Eric standing there. We stare at each other as my mother screams and tears prick my eyes.

Desperate to escape her screams, I step into the hallway and shut the door.

"I don't want the money," he says, his voice low, rough. "I didn't know and it wouldn't have mattered if I had. I don't care about anything but you."

"I know that," I whisper. "I know."

I don't know who moves then. Me. Him. Both of us, but we collide and hold onto each other, just hold each other. Neither of us wanting to let go.

Chapter One Hundred Twenty-Four

Harper

"**I** don't know what to do, Eric," I whisper, hugging myself with the impact of the bitter truth I cannot deny. "She's my mother, but she—she's not a good person."

The door opens behind me and my mother gasps. "You," she hisses at Eric.

"Yes," Eric says, his tone hard, a blade of steel. "Me. I'm still alive." I rotate to stand next to him, keeping my hand at his back. He doubted me. He doubted us. No. He feared I'd believe the worst of him and that's exactly why my hand settles firmly on his back. "And so is Harper," he adds. "I'm keeping her that way and since that means dealing with Isaac, that means you, too, but for now, I suggest you leave. Stay hidden until this is over."

"I have a husband who needs to be buried."

"He wanted to be cremated. Have a service later, not now. Get on a plane and go to Europe with Gigi. Don't come back until this is over."

He's protecting her and despite all my anger at her, all the pain of today's revelations, this calms me. This allows me to breathe. He's the reason I can breathe. Savage steps to Eric's side. "We can escort her to make arrangements and then set-up her travel."

"Who are you?" my mother demands.

"One of the men keeping you alive, even if you don't deserve us," Savage snaps, clearly aware of what's occurred. He was listening in. God, Eric was listening in. He heard every brutal moment I just shared with my mother.

"Do what they say, mother." I keep calling her mother. I normally call her mom, but she's different to me now. I can't change that reality. I wish I could. "You'll live. You'll survive. You and Gigi might just want to stay in Europe indefinitely. Have the funeral there. You two loved Italy. It'll give all your rich friends an excuse to go to Italy. I can't believe I just said that." I press my hand to my stomach. "I need to leave." I twist out of Eric's arms and start walking.

Blake steps to the end of the hallway, waiting on me.

"Harper!" my mother calls out. "Harper."

But I don't stop. I keep walking the eternal hallway that eventually leads me to Blake. "You okay?" he asks.

"Not really. I just—I need out of here. I want this over."

"I don't blame you. We'll help get you all the way to the other side of this."

Eric steps behind me, his hands on my shoulders, and I twist around to face him. "I want to go home."

"Then let's go home." He takes my hand, kisses my knuckles, and then folds me under his arm, and in silence, we head to the elevator. I ride down with him on one side of me and Blake on the other. Savage must have stayed with my mother and I think that's a good thing. He's strong. He can handle her. He'll keep her alive and keep her from getting anyone else killed.

Once we're back in the SUV with Smith behind the wheel, I rest my head on Eric's chest. We don't speak. We just hold each other, bleeding together, the salve to each other's wounds. A sanctuary in our bond, a place above hell where we can't fall when we're together. He's lost a father. I've lost a mother, but we have each other. I feel that now. He feels that now.

Smith and Blake, who rides shotgun next to Smith, seem to understand our need for each other and privacy, if you can call this privacy. Or maybe we're all in shock at the magnitude of evil that this family proved capable of. Maybe we all need this timeout.

In a short ride, we arrive at the apartment and Blake joins us at the elevator. "I need to debrief with you both. I'll make it quick."

I'm torn by this request. I both crave information and crave the sanctuary that is Eric's apartment that is our new home together. Eric looks down at me. "Are you up to this?"

"I want this all over, so yes. If it helps us get to 'the end,' please."

And so, we all load into the elevator and head to our floor. Eric opens our door and we enter the foyer and I swear, it's home. *I'm home.* My house in Denver was the only place I felt I belonged because I never fit inside the family circle or the company circle.

How was that ever a life I wanted? Here, it's Eric's hand on my back, his earthy scent in the air, his presence even when he isn't touching me that soothes, arouses, and excites. With him is where I belong.

The three of us head to the kitchen, but Eric detours to the bar, and returns with three glasses and a bottle of honey-flavored whiskey. He fills my glass first. "You need this."

"Yes," I say. "I do." I down the amber liquid, letting it warm my throat, while Eric fills his and Blake's glass, then refills mine.

Blake downs his drink. "I think we all needed that. We found Gigi, Harper. The man she thought was attacking her was our man just trying to make contact. She's safe. She's being protected."

"And what does she have to say about all of this mess?" I ask.

"She confirmed everything your mother said without much more detail, and the same kind of speculation and talking in circles."

"What about the messages?" I ask. "Did she have them sent to us?"

"Yes," he confirms. "She confirmed that she sent the messages. She was afraid to go to you directly. She wasn't sure Isaac wouldn't find out. She's old and wasn't sure how to prevent being recorded and hacked. She was afraid of Isaac finding out and lashing out. She also didn't think Eric would believe any information that came from her. She didn't know the man who delivered one of the messages was dead, but she believes Isaac killed your father. She also thinks he killed Richard, one of the men that helped intimidate your mother. She offered that information so randomly that my gut is she had something to do with his death. Interesting tidbit. He died in a car crash like Isaac's mother and father."

"So did Isaac or Gigi kill them all?" I ask incredulously.

"We may never know," Blake says. "I believe they were all professional hits and I'm not sure it changes anything. Isaac's fate is in your hands, Eric. We'll move forward as you see fit and Gigi is exiled, in hiding for the rest of her short life. She has no intention of returning anytime soon. She's too afraid. She's going to wait and see what happens between Eric and Isaac."

"Of course she is," Eric says dryly, sipping his drink, savoring the amber liquid while Blake and I have gulped. "I have a plan to deal with Isaac forming in my mind. I need the night to sleep on it."

"You could easily take his inheritance," Blake states. "You could simply ask for a DNA test."

"I don't need the money." Now Eric downs his whiskey. "I don't want that mob-infested empire."

"He'll always be threatened by you," I say, this new fear hitting me hard and fast. "He'll always be gunning for you. And Gigi. You know he's hunting Gigi."

"I couldn't give a shit about Gigi," Eric replies. "Fuck Gigi, but Harper's mother is going to be with her, so we'll have to protect her."

"My mother basically sent Isaac to kill you," I remind him.

"She's your mother, sweetheart. I'm not going to have her blood on my hands. She'll inherit. She'll be fine. And I told you, I have a plan forming to deal with Isaac." He strokes my hair and eyes Blake. "What else do I need to know?"

"The police aren't likely to question you any further. Not unless that report comes back with poison, which we both know it won't. That's a non-issue that lets Isaac, and Gigi if she's a part of the murder, walk. The mob, on the other hand, isn't going away like the police."

"The mob and Isaac will wait until tomorrow. What else?"

"Grayson is losing his mind wanting to talk to you."

"I'll call him."

"Then I'll leave," Blake concludes, eyeing me. "You were brave, Harper. That was a lot of shit to get unloaded on you. And you stood by your man. Respect. You have my respect." He turns and leaves, and Eric and I watch him as he exits the apartment.

Once the door shuts, we turn to face each other and then it's just us, me and this man who has changed my life. This man that I love. "You're not the bastard anymore," I whisper.

He pulls me to him. "I'll always be that family's bastard. And you'll always be my princess." His mouth closes down on mine, and in that moment, in this place and time, I know that the bastard and the princess coming together has changed lives. Changed me. Forever.

He has changed me forever.

Chapter One Hundred Twenty-Five

Eric

Everything that has happened in the past week explodes inside me and for once, this doesn't drive me to near insanity. I'm not consumed by the numbers that I would be at any other time. I'm consumed with Harper. I'm consumed with need and I can't undress her fast enough. We can't undress each other fast enough. We're both shirtless, and she's braless, her breasts high and full, her nipples puckering beneath my fingers when I pick her up and carry her to an oversized chair, laying her down, dragging away her shoes and pants. Wasting no time undressing.

I'm thick and hard and she's naked and waiting on me. I have a moment when I think about a condom, when I think about how much I don't want my child to be a Kingston, but then I look at Harper. I sit down next to her and I pull her into my lap, straddling me, and I know, I know something is different. I know that I'm not a Kingston. I'm a Mitchell. I will always be a Mitchell, and one day, when I know she's ready, Harper will be, too. And God willing, if she gets pregnant again, we'll have a baby that will be as she once declared: a Mitchell.

I lift her, pressing into her, the wet tight heat of her body taking me, pulling me close.

"Use me," she whispers, wrapping her arms around my neck. "Use me to deal with all that this day made you feel. I can handle anything."

My hand settles between her shoulder blades. "I know you can. You've proven that over and over, but all I need right now is to make love to the woman who has become my everything." I roll her over, lay us side by side, the ottoman under our feet. Her leg is over my hip, and I stroke her face, even as my cock presses deep inside her. And then I do just what I said. I make love to her. I revel in the sweetness that is this woman and what I share with her, and there are no numbers attacking my mind. There's just us. There's just the sanctuary of this woman. I don't rush. I don't want to rush because right here, like this, intimately buried inside her, no one can touch us. No one can take her away.

When we both collapse, melting into each other and the cushion, we lay there staring at each other for long minutes until I whisper, "We'll make our own family."

"I thought you didn't want a family?"

"I thought I didn't want a lot of things until you."

"Good, because we've been having a lot of sex without a condom. Not that I think I can get pregnant, but if I did—"

"We'll be parents this time. If you don't, we'll get a dog."

She laughs. "A dog?"

"Yes. I've actually never had a dog."

"Me neither. Maybe we should get a dog."

"A dog it is," I say, kissing her temple. "Hang tight. I'll get you a robe." I pull out of her and walk to the bedroom, pull on pajama bottoms and grab a towel and her silk robe.

A few minutes later, we sit on the couch, wine glasses in our hands in place of the whiskey. "We should start looking for a dog, right after we get you fully moved. What do you think?"

"Funny how I don't want to go back there, back to Denver. I don't want anything I left there. Of course, that means I have to spend money. I guess I'll get my trust fund now. I can feel like I contribute then. Or will that just make Isaac want to kill me?"

I lean in and slide silky strands of her hair behind her ear. "Isaac will be dealt with. And so we're clear, my money is your money now. We're going to the bank and—"

"No, Eric. I can't—"

I kiss her. "You can. We're together now. Sharing my life means *sharing my life*, baby."

"I need to earn my own way."

"You have a job with double the salary you were earning at Kingston."

"I was making a pretty decent salary."

"And now you'll make more. That has nothing to do with me. That's the way Grayson operates. He pays well and expects loyalty. He knows you'll make the investment worthwhile."

"This is what you do for everyone you hire?"

"I promise you, Harper, I wouldn't lie to you. I've had too many lies in my life and so have you."

She covers my hand with hers. "I won't let you regret hiring me. I won't let Grayson regret hiring me either. And we both know I got this job because of you."

"You got this job because of your experience at Kingston."

"With your help, but I really am going to make you happy you believed in me. I want to prove myself. I think maybe Mia can help me carve out my little place outside of your success."

"She seems eager to do that and more."

"I like her." My eyes go wide. "Oh God. You need to call Grayson."

"Right. You're right." I stand up and hunt down my phone to find about ten text messages from Grayson and three calls. I dial him.

"Holy hell, I've been worried," he answers. "How are you? What can I do?"

I walk to the window and stare out at the dark city without really seeing it, replaying the past week in my mind as I update Grayson. "My God. You're the heir."

"Yes, but I don't want the money or the mob connections that come with it."

"You have to take down Isaac or he'll keep coming."

"I will. I am. That's next. After tonight."

"You have a plan, don't you?"

"Always," I say. "You know I always have a plan. I'll update you soon. Right now—"

"You need your woman. Understood. Tell Harper Mia and I are here if she needs us."

"She knows that already," I assure him before we say our goodbyes.

I turn to find Harper curled in a corner of the couch, her glass in her hand. "All is well?" she asks.

"Yes. He's eager to lend his support to you and me. Mia, too."

She straightens and I sit down next to her again. "How are you feeling about your father?" she asks, as if her mind has been solely on me.

I consider that for a moment and I have no real answer. "I don't know. I'm not sure him being gone has really hit me. How are you feeling about your mother?"

"Hurt. I feel hurt like I never even knew her. I feel like I've been alone for a very long time, and pretending I wasn't. I knew. Some part of me knew."

"You're not alone now."

"Neither are you."

"You belong here, Harper," I say, repeating what I once told her. "You belong with me."

"Yes," she says, repeating what she once told me. "I belong with you, and you, Eric Mitchell, belong with me."

I kiss her, a deep, passionate claiming, and it's there in our kiss, our need for one another, our fear of losing each other. Our promises not to let that happen. Our promises to hold on forever.

Chapter One Hundred Twenty-Six

Eric

I wake the next morning before Harper and pull on pajama bottoms before heading downstairs and making coffee. While it brews, I stand by the window and look out at the city without really seeing it, a cube in my hand, wondering what my mother would think if she knew what I know now. I'm about to walk away from the very empire he one day wanted me to rule.

There are only three ways to do that and protect Harper. Kill Isaac or send him to jail are high on the list, but they leave me with the company and the mob, both of which I don't want. The other option is to imprison him in his own hell and his own creation.

I walk to the kitchen, refill my cup and start making calls. Interestingly enough, when I contact my father's attorney, I find Isaac has already talked to him. He's pushed for the reading of the will, which will take place Wednesday, at rocket speed. Of course, I haven't heard a peep of it from Isaac, but the timeline works for me. It's a chess match and he too often forgets he might be a champion, but he's not a bastard with everything to prove by winning.

I make a few more calls, including one to the mob boss, Nicolas Marshall, which is quite lengthy but productive. Once that's done, I pour a cup of coffee for Harper, doctor it with the peanut butter cup creamer she loves, and head to the bedroom. I find her in her robe, at the window, talking on the phone.

I join her and offer her the cup of coffee. She kisses me and eagerly accepts, sipping the beverage before she says, "When do you get to Europe, mother?" her eyes meeting mine, letting me know she has details to share.

We both sit down in the chairs by the window and share the coffee while the conversation with her mother drags on. Finally, Harper disconnects and sighs. "Thank you for the coffee."

"Everything okay?"

"She's handling your father's arrangements today and leaving tomorrow. Did you hear the will reading is Wednesday? She and Gigi are calling in remotely. Blake's team is scrambling their connection so they can't be found."

"Isaac pressed for an immediate reading, no doubt to payoff the mob."

"Hopefully he does and quickly, but how are you handling your stock? How does that complicate things?"

"It doesn't. Because I have a plan, remember?"

"Yes. The plan you haven't told me about. Can I hear now?"

"Why yes, you can, because you're a part of it and it's going to play out right before the reading of the will."

"Tell me," she urges.

"I know you didn't want to go to Denver, but we need to. After this, though, we don't ever have to go back if you don't want to."

She nods, looking earnest. "I'm listening."

We arrive in Denver Tuesday night and go straight to a hotel. For reasons Harper can't explain, she doesn't want to be at her house, but I get it. There are triggers to pain and I've spent a lifetime learning how to avoid my triggers. She has the right to her own and they seem to include most of the city. She doesn't want to hit a favorite restaurant. She wants room service, so we order, then I dial Isaac.

"Were you planning on speaking to me after he died or just ignoring me?" I ask.

"What is there to say?" he replies. "He's dead. I didn't want to hear you tell me how damn happy you are about it."

"I'm the happy one? Interesting, considering you're the one who rushed to read the will. We need to meet."

"Not happening."

"If you want to inherit, you need to meet me before the reading. Tomorrow morning. Ten AM at the Kingston offices. If you no-show, you won't like the surprise you'll get at the reading." I disconnect. He doesn't call back.

Harper fills my glass with whiskey. "Drink some for me, too," she says. "I can't handle the hard stuff and function even if I wish I could right about now."

I pull her onto the couch beneath me. "I'll take your mind off of tomorrow."

There's a knock at the door. "What about the food?"

"Eat first for energy. Then I'll have you for dessert."

Wednesday morning doesn't come soon enough for me. It's the day Harper and I finally claim our freedom from this damn family and start our life together. She's prepped. She knows exactly what's going to happen. We arrive at the Kingston offices early and exit the Jaguar I've rented to meet Adam at the door. "Good thing I was still in town," he says, joining us, no doubt packing a gun or three under the leather jacket he's wearing.

"Lucky us," I say dryly.

"Thanks for being here, Adam," Harper chimes in. "I'm nervous." Right then, the source of her nerves arrives. A black 911 Porsche pulls up next to my car. "That's him," Harper murmurs. "Now I'm really nervous."

The mob boss himself, Nicholas Marshall, is a valid reason to feel a bit uptight. He comes from a long line of mob bosses and prides himself on his business savvy. He's Italian, but his grandfather wasn't, thus the last name. That lack of representation of his heritage often creates a need for him to feel he must overcompensate and prove he's mob boss worthy. In other words, no one fucks with him and lives.

He exits his vehicle, towering over the roof, and scanning until he eyes my lifted hand. He waves back, his dark hairy curly and his shiny suit, gray but those details don't matter. What does is the fact that he's a bastard like me with a complicated back story that I knew would work in my favor, the details of which include: we're the same age, he inherited because of his mother, and he has a brother he hates.

His bodyguard is now outside of the car, a giant of a man, who wears an equally expensive suit that looks like it was made for his smaller brother. That really cannot be comfortable. They walk our direction, and the bodyguard lingers behind a bit while Nicholas joins us, his eyes falling on Harper, and I know why. Not only does she look stunning in an emerald green dress and boots, she's my weakness. He wants me to know he knows. He eyes her and then me. "She's lovely. What now?" He's not a man of many words. Good. I don't have any desire to talk to him either nor do I want Harper to know he just threatened her.

"We go inside and wait for Isaac," I say, opening the door and motioning to Harper to enter first, a part of our plan. This tells Nicholas it's safe inside and it ensures no one but me is at her back.

With some careful maneuvering, we walk Nicholas, his bodyguard who doesn't speak, and ourselves to the downstairs conference room. I take the end cap on one side of the table with Harper by my side. Nicholas takes the other with his guard by his side. Adam stays at the front door to escort Isaac to join us. "Contracts?" Nicholas asks.

I shove the folder in front of me across the table lightning quick, and it stops in front of him. He opens it, glances at the documents and then nods. "Acceptable. No turning back now."

"That's the point," I say, aware of Harper's nervous energy beside me, which is why my hand settles on her knee.

Footsteps sound and Isaac opens the glass doors and enters the room. "What is this?"

"Have a seat," Nicholas orders.

Isaac looks as if he's seen the grim reaper.

"Don't look at him," Nicholas snaps. "He's not the one who matters in this room. I am." He literally points at a chair. "Sit."

Isaac inhales and tugs at the jacket of his blue suit, a tell-tale sign of nerves I learned about him years ago. He sits down. I speak. "We both know I'm the true heir to the corporation and the inheritance of my father. We all know you killed to keep that secret, but we've also agreed that jail is too good for you."

"What the fuck are you talking about?" Isaac bites out.

"I took a DNA test and thanks to the right people in the right place, took one from Dad before he was cremated this morning. The results will go to Nicholas. Why? Because I've not only signed over my stock to him, should you hurt me, Harper, her mother, or Gigi, I've signed over the fortune I'll inherit from the estate as the true heir. Harper is keeping her trust. You may inherit under the false pretense of being the eldest son to the Kingston empire, knowing that test will prove you have no rights to any of the fortune."

"You have to have my DNA to prove I'm not the heir, dipshit," Isaac snaps, eyeing Harper. "You are nothing but a pain in my ass. You brought all of this on. You should have died in that warehouse back in Denver."

"You hired the men who attacked her?" I demand.

Isaac fixes me in a hateful look. "Damn straight. You both should have gone down that night. I won't go down now. I'm not giving up my DNA."

"I do believe I can find a way to get that DNA from you, Isaac," Nicholas interjects, speaking to his bodyguard in what I know to be Italian. The bodyguard smiles, giving a nod. Isaac pales.

"And about the rights to the fortune," Nicholas states. "I own the rights because I own you now, Isaac the fake heir. I will always own you." His lips quirk evilly. He's enjoying this. I'm not. This is never where I wanted to land with Isaac. This is not how my mother wanted my story to end with the Kingstons, but it ends as nobly as it can, and in her honor.

Isaac actually looks a bit green now, like he might upchuck. His gaze rockets to mine. "You can't do this. We need to talk."

"He already did," Nicholas says, holding up the envelope and then eyeing me. "Take your pretty lady out of here. Go collect her money and be gone."

I stand and help Harper to her feet, my gaze landing on Isaac. "He'll control you, and someone needs to," I say before I lead Harper to the doors and out of the conference room. We exit the Kingston facility and I speak to Adam. "It's done." I shake his hand and then Harper and I start walking, the fingers of one of our hands locked until I open the passenger door of the Jaguar for her.

She rotates to face me. "I almost feel sorry for him."

"Don't. He killed people. He would have killed us. It's done now."

"It's done," she repeats, a sense of disbelief in her words.

I cup her face. "Now we begin our new life."

Epilogue

Harper

Two months later...

I exit the conference room in the Bennett corporate office with Dan Miller, the soon-to-retire head of Miller Enterprises, next to me, adrenaline coursing through me. The meeting was good, so very good. We pause in the hallway and shake hands, with him giving me a little wink as well. "You know how to make a grandpa happy there, ma'am. A second life after retirement. I'm excited."

"As are we," I assure him, thankful I'd bonded with him when he was supplying parts to Kingston in mass volume. "As are we."

I hand him off to my assistant, Meika Reynolds, who looks about twelve and manages everything like she has a hundred years of experience. She's amazing and a sweetheart to boot.

Once she and Dan depart, I dash toward Grayson's office and his assistant is nowhere in sight, but I don't even knock. I know the whole clan is inside waiting on me. I burst into the office and find Grayson, Mia, Davis, and Eric waiting on me. Eric is the one I'm focused on, though, and God, he's gorgeous in a blue pin-striped suit, his blue eyes piercing as he anticipates my update. Everyone is staring at me and I explode with the news. "We did it!"

Clapping ensues and Eric and I rush toward each other, colliding in a huge hug. "You did it?" he confirms, kissing my neck and leaning back to look at me.

"*We* did it. He wired the final two hundred and fifty million we needed for the NFL buyout while he was here. It's done."

Shouts of joy explode all over in the room and they are loud and plentiful. When we all come down enough to speak, I breathe out, "Now I've earned my keep."

Mia laughs and rushes around the desk to hug me. "Honey, you earned your keep the minute you walked in the door." She's become a good friend, the kind I didn't make time for in Denver. The kind I needed and didn't even realize how much.

"You earned more than your keep," Grayson offers, while Mia releases me, and Eric settles his arm around my shoulders. "One percent of the profits," he adds. "Your one percent. Not Eric's. He already gets his share."

I'm stunned, unable to fathom how much money that might be, when I shouldn't be. I've seen who Grayson is up close these past couple of months. "You're generous as always. Thank you, Grayson."

"Very generous," Eric says. "It's a lot of money, but it's not about the money, now is it." He glances down at me. "It's about your freedom."

I instantly know what he means. It's a part of the many things we lay awake and talk about often well into the wee hours. I've always had dreams and aspirations that I do not want to be swallowed by Eric's money and power, any more than I want him to believe I'm with him for those things. As I've told him, if he knows I could walk away at any moment, he knows I choose to stay.

"Go celebrate with your man," Grayson orders.

Thirty minutes later, Eric and I lounge on the leather couch in the corner of his office. We have glasses of champagne in hand and I swear the Manhattan skyline is dancing in celebration for me.

"It's hard to believe we're here now, after all the challenges we have faced. We're like a television soap opera that got cancelled," I joke.

Eric laughs. "Yes, I suppose we are." He sets his glass down. "Speaking of, and I hate to bring this up now, but I heard from your mother."

I can't help but feel a little twist in my belly at this news. In the two months since she went to Europe, I've spoken to her once, and it was not pleasant. "What did she say?"

"Now that the drug test came back clear and the heart attack ruling was filed officially, she's holding a service in Italy, where she plans to live with Gigi."

"When?"

"Next week, but we're not invited. Obviously, neither is Isaac. She just wanted to be sure, when we heard the buzz about invitations, we didn't decide to come anyway."

"Of course she did. Any news on Isaac and whatever might be going on with him?"

"Coincidentally I talked to Blake today, but I wasn't going to tell you until after the deal closed. Isaac inherited and moved into the Kingston mansion. Nicholas invested money in the company. All is well for him, aside from the part where he's ruled by the iron hand of the mob."

"It's better than he deserves," I say, tilting my head to study him. "How do you feel about not being invited to the service?"

"I didn't want to go in the first place. I will never mourn a man who denied my mother medical care."

And he hasn't. Not beyond a few days of battling through a few confusing emotions, he's been at peace. I believe he really doesn't want to go to Italy, not for the service.

Together we celebrate our win today. Together we heal. Together we are better. Together we are forever.

Two months later...

The NFL deal is complete and Eric and I stand at the top of the Rockefeller Center in the center of a swanky party filled with investors and guests in celebration. I'm in a teal gown to match the team colors as is Mia, while Eric, Grayson, and Davis wear teal-colored ties. The evening is spectacular and as the night tracks on, Eric takes my hand and sneaks me out of the party.

"Where are we going?"

"It's a beautiful night and I need you to myself for a few minutes."

I smile with this declaration, and we head downstairs, exiting to a cool beautiful evening with the stars twinkling above. I think we're stopping at the ice rink, but he guides me toward a limo. "We're leaving? In a limo?"

"Yes. We are."

A driver opens the door for me and I give Eric a curious look. "What are you up to?"

"Wait and see."

I laugh, and filled with joy that only this man gives me, I slide inside the car. A few minutes later, we pull up to a little wine bar we adore. "Isn't it closed?"

"Not for us."

I'm incredibly charmed that he's created our own private celebration. Arm in arm, we walk toward the door and the owner, Max, who we have gotten to know, holds the door for us. We share a greeting with him and then enter the dimly lit bar, which is lined with quaint bookshelves and rows of wine bottles, with dangling lights above us.

We settle into our favorite little private nook with a red couch and a table made of a tree trunk, a bottle of champagne waiting on us. "This is amazing," I say, and I can feel myself glowing.

Eric settles onto the couch next to me. "You're amazing." He takes my hand. "You've changed my life, Harper."

"*You've* changed *my* life, Eric. That's an understatement. You—you're my best friend."

"Then marry me."

I blink, my breath lodging in my throat for just a moment. "What?"

He goes down on one knee and presents me with a velvet box. "Marry me, Harper." He opens the lid and inside is a stunning heart-shaped diamond with a delicate etched design around it. I cover my mouth, my eyes burning. "It's stunning. It's so amazing."

"Harper—"

"Yes. Yes, I'll marry you." I wrap my arms around his neck and hug him. "Is this a good time to tell you I missed my period?"

He pulls back. "Wait. What? You did?"

"Yes, but it might not mean anything and—"

He kisses me, a deep, passionate kiss that says it all. He wants everything. I want everything. Together, we *are* everything.

THE END

Don't miss the other Scandalous Billionaires!

https://www.lisareneejones.com/scandalous-billionaires.html

Want another KindleUnlimited read from me? Check out my Inside Out series! Grab the first few chapters plus exclusive bonus scenes here: https://bookhip.com/DHFRRLM

How It All Started...

One day I was a high school teacher on summer break, leading a relatively uneventful but happy life. Or so I told myself. Later, I'd question that, as I would question pretty much everything I knew about me, my relationships, and my desires. It all began when my neighbor thrust a key to a storage unit at me. She'd bought it to make extra money after watching some storage auction show. Now she was on her way to the airport to elope with a man she barely knew, and she needed me to clear out the unit before the lease expired.

Soon, I was standing inside a small room that held the intimate details of another woman's life, feeling uncomfortable, as if I was invading her privacy. Why had she let these items so neatly packed, possessions that she clearly cared about deeply, be lost at an auction? Driven to find out by some unnamed force, I began to dig, to discover this woman's life, and yes, read her journals—dark, erotic journals that I had no business reading. Once I started, I couldn't stop. I read on obsessively, living out fantasies through her words that I'd never dare experience on my own, compelled by the three men in her life, none of whom had names. I read onward until the last terrifying dark entry left me certain that something had happened to this woman. I had to find her and be sure she was okay.

Before long, I was taking her job for the summer at the art gallery, living her life, and she was nowhere to be found. I was becoming someone I didn't know. I was becoming her.

The dark, passion it becomes...

Now, I am working at a prestigious gallery, where I have always dreamed of being, and I've been delivered to the doorstep of several men, all of which I envision as one I've read about in the journal. But there is one man that will call to me, that will awaken me in ways I never believed possible. That man is the ruggedly sexy artist, Chris Merit, who wants to paint me. He is rich and famous, and dark in ways I shouldn't find intriguing, but I do. I so do. I don't understand why his dark side appeals to me, but the attraction between us is rich with velvety promises of satisfaction. Chris is dark, and so are his desires, but I cannot turn away. He is damaged beneath his confident good looks and need for control, and in some way, I feel he needs me. I need him.

All I know for certain is that he knows me like I don't even know me, and he says I know him. Still, I keep asking myself — do I know him? Did he know her, the journal writer, and where is she? And why doesn't it seem to matter anymore? There is just him and me, and the burn for more.

Grab the first few chapters plus exclusive bonus scenes here:
https://bookhip.com/DHFRRLM

Also By Lisa Renee Jones

Surrender

WHITE LIES

Provocative
Shameless

TALL, DARK & DEADLY / WALKER SECURITY

Hot Secrets
Dangerous Secrets
Beneath the Secrets
Deep Under
Pulled Under
Falling Under
Savage Hunger
Savage Burn
Savage Love
Savage Ending
When He's Dirty
When He's Bad
When He's Wild
Luke's Sin
Luke's Touch
Luke's Revenge

LILAH LOVE

Murder Notes
Murder Girl
Love Me Dead
Love Kills
Bloody Vows
Bloody Love
Happy Death Day
The Party Is Over
The Ghost Assassin
Agent vs. Assassin

DIRTY RICH

Dirty Rich One Night Stand
Dirty Rich One Night Stand: Two Years Later
Dirty Rich Cinderella Story
Dirty Rich Cinderella Story: Ever After
Dirty Rich Obsession
Dirty Rich Obsession: All Mine
Dirty Rich Betrayal
Dirty Rich Betrayal: Love Me Forever
Dirty Rich Secrets
His Demand
Her Submission

THE FILTHY TRILOGY

The Bastard
The Princess
The Empire

THE NAKED TRILOGY

One Man
One Woman
Two Together

THE BRILLIANCE TRILOGY

A Reckless Note
A Wicked Song
A Sinful Encore

NECKLACE TRILOGY

What If I Never

Because I Can
When I Say Yes

THE TYLER & BELLA TRILOGY

Bastard Boss
Sweet Sinner
Dirty Little Vow

WALL STREET EMPIRE

Protégé King
Scorned Queen
Burned Dynasty

STANDALONE THRILLERS

You Look Beautiful Tonight (L.R. Jones)
A Perfect Lie
The Poet
The Wedding Party (L.R. Jones)

*eBook only

About the Author

New York Times and *USA Today* bestselling author Lisa Renee Jones writes dark, edgy fiction including the highly acclaimed *Inside Out* series and the crime thriller *The Poet.* Suzanne Todd (producer of Alice in Wonderland and Bad Moms) on the *Inside Out* series: *Lisa has created a beautiful, complicated, and sensual world that is filled with intrigue and suspense.*

Prior to publishing, Lisa owned a multi-state staffing agency that was recognized many times by The Austin Business Journal and also praised by the Dallas Women's Magazine. In 1998 Lisa was listed as the #7 growing women-owned business in Entrepreneur Magazine. She lives in Colorado with her husband, a cat that talks too much, and a Golden Retriever who is afraid of trash bags.

Made in the USA
Columbia, SC
18 March 2024

33255923R00345